For Madis

When the Tamarind Tree Blooms

I hope you enjoy.

Elaine Russell

My Best,

Elaine Russell

Belle Histoires
2743 14ᵗʰ Street
Sacramento, California 95818
www.elainerussell.info

Publisher's Note: This is a work of fiction. Names and characters, places, and incidents are a product of the author's imagination. Locales and public names are sometimes used for atmospheric purposes. Any resemblance to actual people, living or dead, or to businesses, companies, events, institutions, or locales is completely coincidental.

Cover Design: David Provolo
Cover Art: Jackie Pope and Photograph: Walter Humphreys

When the Tamarind Tree Blooms — 1st ed.

ISBN 978-1-7324994-9-2

We must let go of the life we have planned,
so as to accept the one that is waiting for us.

Marguerite Duras

Chapter 1

Vientiane, Laos—May 14, 1931

On a Thursday in mid-May, I balanced on a bough of the ancient tamarind tree, gazing over the wall of the home for orphaned girls. The surrounding streets were empty, except for an oxcart rolling down the lane, its wooden wheels creaking over the rutted dirt. Young novices at the Buddhist temple across the way napped on the covered porch of their quarters, occasionally swatting at flies or wiping sweat from their brows. Most sensible people retreated inside at this hour, but I refused to be sensible. The indolent afternoon awaited relief, the heat bearing down, shimmering off dusty lanes, holding the air suspended with hardly a trace of oxygen. Even the warblers and larks had ceased to trill. With the onset of the monsoons, dark clouds converged on the horizon over Siam across the Mekong River, tantalizingly close, inching toward town to unleash the miracle of a cooling downpour.

Once more foolish hopes filled my heart. This year my mother would return. Only a distant, hazy memory remained of fourteen years before—my mother clutching me and sobbing as a French woman tore me from her arms. "I'll come for you when the tamarind tree blooms again," Mother had called after me. Every May the blood orange orchid-like petals burst into flower, holding the promise of Mother's words. And every May I waited, searching for her in the streets below. Blooms faded, petals drifted to the ground, yet here I remained. Unclaimed. The same questions crowded my heart. Why had she abandoned me? Where was she now? In two days, I would turn eighteen and leave this unhappy place. I must find my mother and discover a way back to my beginning.

A crown of dense fern-like leaves, the color of fresh cilantro, brushed my face, shielding me from the fiery sun. My fingertips grazed the swirling grain of the gnarled bark, the indentations and unexplained bumps, discolorations and bare spots, testimony to years of weathering, woodpeckers, and voracious insects, each imperfection as familiar to me as the contours of my face. The tree's strength and survival skills inspired me. For years this tamarind tree—*mak kham*, as the Lao gardener called it—had grown straight and tall, expanding its lush canopy. The regal giant had thrived long before the French proclaimed their right to rule Laos almost forty years ago, and long before the orphanage trapped the tree's sturdy trunk within the courtyard. Like it had trapped me. Half the massive branches spilled over the wall, as if uncertain where they belonged, attempting to escape.

I sympathized with the tree's dilemma. I, too, questioned where I belonged: half and half, half French, half Lao, neither one nor the other. The French word for our kind—*métis*, or *métisses* for girls—was rife with negative connotations. Many terms had been coined for our unseemly blend of races: half-breed, half-caste, impure, *sale* (dirty) *métis*. Those of us at the orphanage were *déraciné*, uprooted—ripped from our families and native Lao culture, everything familiar, to be raised as French citizens. The Lao described us as having "a touch of French blood," sometimes spoken in a derogatory manner, but other times simply as a statement of fact. We were the inevitable consequence of French men living in a faraway colony where few French women had followed. Many men took a Lao mistress, a *phu sao,* or young maiden. In the early years, French officials chose to look the other way, until the *métis* became too numerous to ignore.

"Vivi, are you there?" my dear friend Bridgette called from below. "Director Bernard wants to talk to you."

"Coming." What did he want now? Probably to harangue me anew for my many faults and insolence. But on this day, at last, I could finally ask about my past, the story of my parents, and how I had come to live at the orphanage. For years he'd told me he couldn't share this information until I turned eighteen. The moment had arrived.

From my perch, I spotted Bridgette, my savior, the person who had kept me sane through all the tumultuous years. She was standing in front of the large concrete-and-plaster house, with its small brass sign to the left of the front door: *Société d'assistance aux Métis, Maison Pour Filles Abandonnée*. Bridgette and I hated the building's faded mustard-yellow walls and black trim that made it appear as if in mourning for all the young charges who had lost their parents or been forced into the care of the French. Negotiating my way down the tree, I dangled from the bottom branch and dropped onto the bench beneath it, causing my pleated skirt to fly up.

Bridgette giggled. "*Oh là là*! What would Maîtresse Durand say if she saw that trick?"

I struck a pose, hands on hips, head titled to one side, lips pursed, mimicking the models in the French fashion magazines our teacher Mademoiselle Courbet sometimes brought us. "Two more days, and I won't have to worry about the director or Maîtresse."

Bridgette's sweet face, normally full of smiles, transformed into a pout. "How can you leave me?"

"I'll only be fifteen minutes away, silly. When you turn eighteen in August and are free, we'll begin our new lives together." I crossed the courtyard and slipped my arm through hers.

Sunlight reflected golden streaks in her auburn hair, which flowered into waves down her back. Slender and graceful, she stood four inches taller than my five feet. We had spent hours examining our faces in the mirror, guessing which parent we resembled most in the melding of our French and Lao blood. Bridgette could possibly pass for French, taking after her father with her long, straight nose and light creamy skin. Only her slightly narrower eyes and fuller lips gave a nod to her Lao heritage. I had tawnier skin, straight ebony hair, a broader face and flatter nose, leaning more Lao than French. Wherever our features had originated, most people usually recognized our blended backgrounds.

We entered the dark foyer where the shutters had been drawn tight against the unrelenting heat. The house seemed eerily quiet. The older girls had gone to their rooms or the library to study for final exams the next day, while the little ones played in the backyard by the dormitory. A loose plank in the floorboards creaked as we tiptoed past the office of Maîtresse Durand, our guardian and the enforcer of Director Bernard's endless rules. She had taken the position fifteen years before when her husband, a government administrator, had died of cholera six months after arriving in Laos. For unknown reasons she had chosen to stay on, awarded the position of headmistress at the orphanage. She oversaw the daily feeding, clothing, and care of up to thirty girls, aged three to eighteen years old.

"Mademoiselles, what were you doing out front?" A stern, disembodied voice drifted from her office. Bridgette and I made faces at each other, struggling to stifle our laughter.

"I wanted to pick some tamarind blooms, Maîtresse." I stuck my head around her doorway to show her the sprig of flowers I'd placed in my braid. "They look so pretty."

"Don't let me catch you out there again," Maîtresse answered, shaking her head. "Go see Director Bernard immediately, Geneviève."

Bridgette grabbed my arm. "This is your chance to ask about your parents, so be nice and don't make him angry." She gave me a quick hug. "Good luck."

"I'll be good." Goosebumps crept down my arms in anticipation. I'd waited so long to hear the truth. Who were my parents? Were they still alive?

Bridgette smiled. "Come to the salon when you finish; Mademoiselle Courbet promised to play her new records from France."

I smoothed the dark-blue skirt and white sailor blouse of our hated school uniform, which made us look like escapees from the French navy, and rapped on the director's door.

"Enter," a voice barked.

Director Bernard perched behind his mahogany Louis XV

escritoire, with its elegant, curved legs and ormolu bronze fittings. He'd had the desk and a matching chair shipped from his family's estate in France, a fact he never failed to mention to orphanage visitors. Narrow seams of light seeped through the shutters, penetrating a thick cloud of cigar smoke to paint the room with narrow stripes like prison bars. The director, a short, spare man in his middle years with a balding pate and unremarkable features, was neither attractive nor ugly, simply ordinary. It was his personality that made him repulsive. No matter the temperature, he dressed in tailored white or tan linen suits with carefully knotted blue ties. Life appeared to hold little pleasure for him, other than his ability to torment the girls at the home with his rules and "the necessity for order and discipline."

"Mademoiselle Dubois, you know I don't appreciate being kept waiting," he said, his words clipped. "Your manners are unacceptable, right to the end."

He laced his hands together and rested them on top of the desk, staring at me over gold-rimmed glasses, his lips forming a tight line. The occasional shrieks of children playing out back drifted in as the glass-domed clock on the bookshelf ticked seconds into minutes. The director remained silent, as if expecting an apology.

I stared back without a word, burning with a familiar anger for this man who had turned my childhood into a string of battles and unjust punishments. When I had first arrived as a young child, I'd no intention of causing trouble, but I soon found his restrictions untenable, his desperate need for control impossible to accept. He imposed hundreds of rules as we marched through our days on an endless schedule of sleeping, rising, dressing, eating, school, study, and chores—five minutes in the bathroom, ten minutes for breakfast—no exceptions, no questions, no choices. Why did I have to sit in the library doing homework, unable to leave until every girl had finished? Why wasn't I allowed to talk to the Lao cook and housekeepers to learn Lao words or hear about their lives? Why was I forced to go to Catholic Mass every Sunday, when I didn't believe anything the priest had to say?

The director would pounce on my smallest infraction: I hadn't spoken to him with enough respect; I'd encouraged other girls to misbehave; I was three minutes late to dinner. We were mired in a constant test of wills, like two actors endlessly rehearsing the same scene from a badly written play. Perhaps, at times, I provoked his anger out of sheer frustration, aggravating the situation with my tart responses. Bridgette always tried to calm me, begging me to hold my tongue. Punishments were swift. I was sent to my room without dinner, denied special outings, forced to scrub toilets or bathe the smaller children. When Director Bernard's temper boiled over into a roaring fire, he would slap me across the face and lock me in the downstairs hall closet overnight. I never let him see me cry.

Maîtresse was never as harsh and unbending, and she could even be understanding. But when the director lost all reason, she stood on the sidelines, watching the chaos unfold; her forehead might wrinkle as she bit her lip, yet she never came to my defense, the fear of losing her job overtaking her instincts. Only once did she step in to spare me serious harm, when the director reprimanded me for slurping my soup, leading to a heated debate and a stream of insults. Unable to stand his assault any longer, I threw my bowl on the dining room floor, breaking it into a dozen pieces. The director became so enraged he began punching me about the head and shoulders with his fists, until Maîtresse pulled him away, crying out.

Now, the director cleared his throat and placed several sheets before me. "I've prepared your emancipation papers. You must sign these copies, acknowledging your discharge from the orphanage on Saturday."

I studied the thick papers bearing his signature and a red ink seal, thinking how desperately I had awaited the moment when I could walk out of the orphanage to a new life free of this despicable man. But a sudden flood of unease washed over me on seeing the official documents, and my heart stumbled. An uncharted future loomed as blank as the pages in the leather-covered journal that Bridgette had given me to celebrate my coming of age. Everything I knew about the world and life I'd learned in school, from the books in our small library, or from French magazines. How would I handle the challenges that might confront me outside the home's walls? My hand shook as I signed my name with extra curlicues and flourishes, trying to exhibit a level of confidence that failed me.

My immediate situation was settled. I'd been offered a teaching assistant position at the French public elementary school, and Mademoiselle Courbet, a teacher at the *lycée*, had agreed to rent me a room in her home until August, when Bridgette would be free. My friend and I planned to work and save money for as long as necessary to make our dreams a reality. The most pressing goal for me was to discover what had happened to my family and sort out what that meant. But eventually Bridgette and I wanted to go to a university in Paris. From an early age, I'd understood that if I hoped to have a future of my own choosing, I must earn top grades and continue my education. We longed to travel through France and all of Europe, perhaps to America. Marriage, children—all that could come later.

The director smiled. "On Saturday you celebrate your eighteenth birthday and become an independent adult. Henceforth, you may make your own decisions. The Assistance Society has provided you with a fine education and appreciation of the culture of our French homeland."

Did he expect a thank you? I offered none. True, I'd been provided with an adequate education given the limited public and private schools available to French students in Vientiane, for which I was grateful. Lao students had no options beyond middle school in Laos, having to travel to Hanoi, Saigon, or even Paris to attend a *lycée* and go on to a university. Only the privileged few could afford it. But how did the "culture of our French homeland" have any relationship to a French/Lao *métisse* born in a country half a world away from France?

"You can thank your good grades and my recommendation for your new position at the elementary school," the director continued.

"Madame Moreau is impressed with your excellent command of French and your strong mathematical skills."

Madame Moreau directed the only public primary school, reserved for French children and a handful of wealthy, elite Lao, Chinese, and Annamese students. Since the French government had declared the *métis* to be French citizens some years back, the orphanage girls had attended this school. Instruction was entirely in French, while Lao, our native language, was forbidden, as if it was tainted, inferior. I carried painful memories of French classmates who shunned and taunted the orphanage girls, the *sale métisses*. Once more I'd be sequestered in the rarefied world of "French Laos," as the French *colons* referred to their privileged lives, separate from the *indigènes*, or native people. This teaching job, with its adequate salary, was far from my dream, but it was preferable to the other options offered—Monsieur Martel's tailoring shop or the Chinese laundry. Friends at the orphanage thought me lucky.

Director Bernard straightened a pile of papers on his desk. "Of course, I don't need to remind you how important your final exams are tomorrow. Despite your difficult behavior, you've always been an excellent student. I'm disappointed you haven't applied for a scholarship to the Université de Indochine in Hanoi, or an institution in France," he said. "I'd be pleased to write a recommendation and feel confident you'd be awarded a scholarship."

"I hope to do that next year, but I have other priorities right now."

Director Bernard gave me a thin, parsimonious smile. "You've grown into a proper young French woman."

"And a proper young Lao woman," I countered, although I had virtually no idea what it meant to be Lao. My native country remained as mysterious to me as the far-off metropole of France. Growing up in the confines of the orphanage, I'd only glimpsed life on the streets of Vientiane while walking to and from school or marching to Mass on Sundays. The Lao vendors, who sold produce in the markets or ran small shops, gazed at the orphanage's *métisses* with equal parts curiosity and discomfort. We were strange specimens kept in a cage, rarely allowed out for others to view.

Oblivious to the sensibilities of the *indigène* and *métis* students attending the French schools, our French teachers had often expressed their disdain for Lao and other native races, calling them inferior, with savage beliefs, repellant customs, and childlike behavior. Anger filled my heart as the non-French students, myself included, sat with eyes lowered, humiliated. The French government's *mission civilisatrice*, their justification for creating the Indochine colonies, was intended to raise the native population's standard of living and cultural practices to meet French ideals of civilization. But it was clear that the Lao and others would always be lesser beings in the eyes of the French. As would the *métis*. The orphanage's role was to fashion us into good French citizens, loyal to a country most would never visit and to the benevolent French colonial rule of our native land. And for this, our keepers expected gratitude.

The director tapped his fingers on the desk. "Really, Geneviève, we've had this discussion before. Assuredly you have both French and Lao blood, but you are extremely fortunate to be recognized as a French citizen, with all the privileges that entitles you to. Whatever you choose to make of your life is up to you."

I handed him my signed emancipation papers. He added them to the pile and closed the cover of the folder, where *Geneviève Dubois* was neatly printed across the front. I'd never seen it before, but of course there had to be records of my time at the orphanage, my birth, my parents. The answers to all my questions must be inside.

The moment had arrived. My heart jumped like a sleeping dog startled by a loud noise. My mouth turned dry as I struggled to keep my voice even and conciliatory. "Now that I'm turning eighteen, you can tell me about my mother and father—my background."

"I'm afraid you arrived here without any information about your past." He kept his eyes focused on my folder. "Besides, the Assistance Society policies don't allow us to reveal these details."

I blinked several times, trying to comprehend. "How is that possible? You always told me when I turned eighteen—"

"We're often not told of the circumstances that bring our wards to the home, whether the parents have died or if they wish to remain anonymous," he interrupted. Fine beads of sweat formed on his forehead as he continued to avert his eyes.

"I didn't appear out of nowhere." I felt sure he was lying, keeping the information from me as one last act of punishment. "My mother brought me here. I remember her kneeling down next to me by the tamarind tree, promising to return. You must have something."

He flipped through the pages inside my folder and his mouth twitched. Why wouldn't he look at me? "You were released to authorities in Luang Prabang, then transferred here. I can offer nothing more." He ran a hand over the few remaining strands of graying hair combed across the top of his head.

"I came from Luang Prabang?" I asked. "I don't remember that." How could I have a vivid image of my mother in the courtyard next to the tamarind tree? Now he claimed that she had given me to officials in Luang Prabang.

"It's not surprising you've forgotten. You were barely four at the time." He finally raised his eyes to meet mine. "Pursuing the past will only bring unhappiness, Geneviève. Focus on your future."

He picked up my folder, heading to the cabinet along the side wall, pulling a small brass key from his pocket.

I held out my hand. "I'd like to see my file, please."

His body stiffened as he clutched the folder to his chest. "I can't allow that. This is confidential information. Only Maîtresse and I are allowed to view it."

"How can it be confidential? It's *my* file. *My* information." My voice grew shrill. "Why can't I see it? You're hiding something from me."

"Those are the Assistance Society's rules." He quickly unlocked the bottom drawer and the folder disappeared, slipping in among a mass of papers out of my reach. He locked the drawer and placed the key on the desk beneath the lamp. "When you leave on Saturday, I'll provide you with your emancipation documents."

He slithered around front and sat on the edge of his desk, clamping a damp hand on my shoulder, like a venomous snake dropping from a tree. "If you need advice or help, Geneviève, you can always call on me." His voice was suddenly kind, as if he'd been a dear friend rather than my tormentor these many years. "I'd be happy to meet you for dinner occasionally and hear of your progress."

Wary of this uncharacteristic friendliness, I jumped up and opened the door, stepping into the hallway. "You must have an address for the Assistance Society in Luang Prabang where I can write?"

His face darkened. "There is no point in contacting them. They won't provide any additional information."

"The least you can do is give me the address," I said, struggling to keep myself from screaming at him. For my entire childhood, he'd dangled the promise of revealing my past before me, but it had always been a lie. I felt an overwhelming desire to wrap my fingers around his neck and squeeze the air from his lungs. What pleasure it would give me to see him squirm in fear, after all the ways he'd found to make me cower. My only consolation was that in two days, he would no longer have any power over me.

He shrugged. "I'll attach the address to your papers. There is nothing more I can do for you at this point but wish you well in life."

Chapter 2

I stumbled down the hall, finding refuge in the shadows of the foyer, as tears of disbelief and anger filled my eyes. How could the director mislead me all these years, only to dismiss my desire to learn about my parents with such indifference, more so impatience, as if my past was of little consequence? There was no reason to refuse showing me my file unless he was hiding something. I would not let him stop me from uncovering my story.

Wiping tears on my shirt sleeve, I followed the sound of music drifting from the salon. I found Bridgette and our friends, Madeleine and Lucienne, kicking up their heels, mimicking Mademoiselle Courbet as she did a two-step to a lively recording of piano and saxophone on the Victrola. Mademoiselle waved for me to join them. She dipped forward, her finger-waved hair falling in a white-blonde curtain across her face, then twirled around as her skirt lifted, revealing her shapely legs.

We all adored Mademoiselle Courbet, with her striking beauty and chic sense of fashion. She taught French literature and grammar at our private French *lycée,* while the orphanage engaged her as a tutor and instructor of comportment. She was the only adult we knew who liked to laugh and have fun, who treated us with respect and listened to our worries. She had saved me from the ire of the director and Maîtresse on more than one occasion.

Bridgette raced over and grabbed my hand, pulling me next to her. "Come. It's the latest thing."

I attempted to follow the quick movements, similar to the Charleston, which everyone adored. Soon giggles overcame me, easing the profound disappointment weighing on my heart.

When the song ended, Mademoiselle Courbet stepped over to the Victrola to lift up the needle. "How do you like it, girls?" she called over her shoulder.

"Wonderful," Madeleine cried out.

"It's called the 'Black Bottom Stomp.'" Mademoiselle chuckled. "By Jelly Roll Morton and the Red Hot Peppers. Imagine these names. The Americans are very droll, don't you find?"

Lucienne clapped her hands. "Let's do it again."

Mademoiselle replaced the needle, and we began our enthusiastic gyrations once more. This time I fell into the rhythm effortlessly, lifting my skirt above my knees, kicking up my legs, releasing my anger.

The salon door burst open. Maîtresse Durand stood in the entrance glaring at us, her broad shoulders pulled back straighter than ever. Everything about Maîtresse was drab, from her limp hair streaked with gray and pulled into a tight bun, to her pasty skin and dark circles under her eyes. She appeared permanently unhappy, as if sentenced to a life of mediocrity and disappointment.

Mademoiselle Courbet raced to stop the music.

"What is the meaning of this?" Maîtresse demanded in a high, reedy voice.

Mademoiselle laughed and waved a hand through the air. "We're only having a bit of fun. I'm teaching the girls the latest rage from America. This crazy dance traveled all the way across the oceans to the edge of civilization here in Laos." She winked at us.

Maîtresse Durand's face flushed a deep red. "We are not running a Paris dance hall, mademoiselle. Have you forgotten they have final exams tomorrow?" Her gaze fell on us. "Girls, go upstairs at once and study." She turned on her heel and left, slamming the door behind her.

Mademoiselle sighed. "I'm so sorry, *mes chéries*. She's right, you must study and get excellent scores on your exams. We'll try another day."

Bridgette and I retreated to our bedroom, which we had occupied since turning fifteen. Two single cots, a nightstand, and a small dresser packed the tiny space, leaving barely enough room to move about.

Our few clothes and a single towel each hung from hooks along the walls. The only decorations were a wooden crucifix and a faded print of Botticelli's *Madonna and Baby.* Yet for Bridgette and me, the room represented the ultimate luxury, our own private retreat, after years of sleeping on bunkbeds in the dormitory that sheltered up to twenty other young girls.

"Unfortunately, we must study, or we'll never get scholarships to a university next year," I said. In truth, however, I was not worried for myself as learning came easily, and I always earned high marks. My sixth-year teacher, Monsieur Macron, said I absorbed knowledge the way the earth sucks up rain and sunshine. But Bridgette struggled, and it was only with my help that she managed to pass. "We can review biology together."

"Okay," she reluctantly agreed. "But first, tell me about your meeting with Director Bernard. What did he say about your parents?"

I plopped down on the bed with a loud sigh, repeating my conversation with the director and his denial of having any information. The anger formed a knot at the top of my neck. "I know he's lying, because he has a folder with my name on it that's filled with papers. When I asked to see it, he refused, claiming it's confidential. How can *my* information be confidential?"

"That's insane."

"Then he acted all friendly and said I could call on him if ever I needed anything. As if I would."

"He's so disgusting," she said.

"He can't possibly understand what it's like to not know about your past, to not have any roots."

"Sometimes I think it would be better if I didn't know." Bridgette's voice fell to a whisper. "Then I could imagine a kinder father who loved me."

Bridgette's story was not unlike many of the girls in the orphanage. She had arrived at the home the year we both turned eight. Her French father had drifted in and out of her mother's life, as his post in the military took him back and forth between Vientiane and remote stations in the provinces. She remembered two versions of this man from her early years—the one who arrived for a visit full of smiles and affection, sometimes a small gift; and the one who drank excessively, becoming angry and abusive, screaming at her mother and sometimes little Bridgette. Her mother's prominent Lao family had disowned them, ashamed of the affair and a *métisse* child born out of wedlock. They'd had to exist on the wages her mother earned cleaning houses, along with occasional contributions from her father.

Shortly after Bridgette turned seven, her father returned to France, promising to send money and come back to them, but they never heard another word. Her mother died of typhoid fever the following year, and an aunt she had never met before deposited Bridgette at the orphanage. It was a tragic story, but a lucky outcome for me. We had become inseparable.

I often wondered if my father had been the same, mistreating and abandoning my mother and me. I had vague recollections and faint images of my mother, like a dream you struggle to recall when awakened from a deep sleep. I could picture her sewing late into the night by a kerosene lamp or wrapping her arms around me as we slept on a mat on the floor. I didn't have the slightest memory of my father.

"Even if my past is unhappy, I must know," I said at last. "I can't feel complete until I do."

"We must"—Bridgette hesitated—"we must retrieve your file from the director's office tonight. It's right there for the taking."

My mouth dropped open. "Break into his office and steal it?" I could barely utter the words. My friend, who always followed the rules, had never suggested anything so bold in her life.

"You can read the file and put it back without him ever finding out. He has no right to keep it from you, Vivi."

I blinked several times as my mind embraced the idea. "What if we get caught?"

"What can he do to you when you're leaving on Saturday?"

"But you'll still be here. I should go alone."

"Let me keep a lookout for Maîtresse, at least." She shrugged. "You'd do the same for me."

———

The clock in the entry hall downstairs struck eleven. An hour earlier, Maîtresse Durand had come upstairs for bed. We waited.

Bridgette toyed with the ruffle on her nightgown sleeve. "Take a look."

Trying to ignore the fear tunneling down my middle, I peeked into the hall. Maîtresse had extinguished her lights, and everything was quiet. Bridgette and I tiptoed along the hall and felt our way down the dark stairwell, clinging to the railing. If anyone caught us, we'd plead hunger and a trip to the kitchen. While it was strictly forbidden to take food in between meals, it was a lesser offense than what we planned. The floor planks in the entry groaned under our weight, as if urging us to turn back. To my surprise, the door of Director Bernard's office was open.

"Stay here and watch for Maîtresse," I whispered.

Bridgette's eyes grew wide. "I'm afraid."

"Come, then." I groped my way to the desk and turned on the small lamp, my trembling fingers barely able to grasp the switch. I searched for the file cabinet key, but it was no longer there.

I knelt by the cabinet drawer and pulled a hairpin from my pocket, working the lock with one side of the metal, twisting and turning until it gave way with a small click.

Bridgette let out a whoosh of air. "Bravo."

When I slid the drawer open, the smell of musty air and wood shavings fanned over our faces. The alphabetical files were stuffed with crackling, yellowed papers. I lifted the one marked *Geneviève Dubois* and started as a wood beetle scurried from the pages onto the floor and disappeared under the cabinet. Placing the file on the desk under the light, I opened the cover as Bridgette peered over my shoulder. The inside page read:

Geneviève Dubois (Lao given name Sakuna)—born May 16, 1913, in Luang Prabang. Arrived at Société d'assistance aux Métis, Maison Pour Filles Abandonnée, Vientiane, May 18, 1917.

"Sakuna—what a pretty name," Bridgette murmured.

Miscellaneous papers recorded health checkups with my height, weight, and illnesses across the years, as well as school grades and annual evaluations. I scanned several progress reports and comments from teachers, Maîtresse Durand, and Director Bernard:

February 20, 1920—Geneviève is a bright and able child but often challenges authority. She must learn to focus her energy on her studies and accept her place in life. She still yearns for her mother and often cries herself to sleep.

March 19, 1924—Geneviève is a difficult child, asking endless questions, particularly about the orphanage and her past. It becomes quite exhausting. She must ground herself in the present.

September 4, 1928—While a diligent student with top marks, Geneviève is proving to be a troublesome young woman who leads other girls astray, fomenting open rebellion against school and orphanage rules. She must conduct herself in a proper manner.

Bridgette giggled. "Naughty Vivi. I should add my own comment: the most loyal friend and dearest person. They know nothing of you."

I smiled. "None of it matters." I thumbed through to the last page and found an official intake form stapled on the back cover.

French father—Henri Dubois, worked in Luang Prabang 1910–1915. Returned to France.

Lao mother—Laya of Luang Prabang (last name unknown).

Twin brother—Antoine Dubois (Lao given name Vinya)—delivered to the Société d'assistance aux Métis in Pakse in May 1917.

The final line sent me reeling back, clutching at Bridgette's arm. I slowly shook my head. "Impossible. How could I forget a twin brother?" I remembered living in a tiny wooden house with my mother, listening to the deafening roar of rain pounding on the tin roof, cooking on a fire outside, and Mother's tears in the night. There was no trace of a brother.

"I knew he lied." My voice shook. "He looked me in the eyes and lied about everything."

Floorboards creaked above us. I stood rooted to the floor, numb, my mind racing.

Bridgette grabbed a scrap of paper and a pen from the desk drawer and copied down the information. "We have to get back to our room." She stuffed the paper up her nightgown sleeve.

I recovered enough to straighten the file and place it back in the cabinet. My hands shook so violently that I couldn't get the drawer to lock.

"Leave it," Bridgette said, grabbing my arm and pulling me up.

Steps pounded down the hall and the door flew open. Maîtresse Durand shined a flashlight on us. "This time you've gone too far, mademoiselles."

Chapter 3

I had underestimated Director Bernard's vindictiveness, the depth of his fury. When he arrived at the orphanage at eight o'clock the next morning, Maîtresse Durand immediately reported our nocturnal transgressions. Having been confined to our room, Bridgette and I heard nothing of the encounter, but later Lucienne described the turmoil overheard outside the director's door—raised voices, pleading, a fist pounding the desk, drawers slamming. The house buzzed with whispers as the girls speculated on what had happened and the possible penalties.

Bridgette and I had dressed for school, unsure if we needed permission to leave or if we should simply go. We couldn't be late for exams. Surely the director wouldn't keep us from taking them, but nothing was beyond him, and a widening canyon of distress made it impossible to sit still. Bridgette kept running to the bathroom, the only place we were allowed outside our room.

Maîtresse appeared at our door not long after reporting to Bernard. Her normally rigid shoulders had collapsed like a deflated soufflé, and her face spoke of a betrayal too great to express. "Leave for school immediately," she said, "before Director Bernard changes his mind again. I barely convinced him to let you go, but he agreed, and you'll meet with him this afternoon. In the meantime, try to do your best in the exams and complete your baccalauréats."

All through the previous night I'd been too keyed up to sleep. As I lay awake, I wondered if Director Bernard and the Assistance Society had managed to hide my location from my mother, just as they had hidden the existence of my brother from me. What if all these years she had been trying to find me and my brother without success?

Bridgette and I had also fantasized about running away after exams. But how could we hide in a town as small as Vientiane? And where would we go? We toyed with the idea of escaping into the countryside but given that I spoke only six words of Lao, and Bridgette had the mostly forgotten vocabulary of an eight-year-old, it seemed unrealistic. Our features would immediately give us away, whether we hid among the French or the Lao. I tried to reassure Bridgette, and myself, that the director would calm down, that it couldn't be as terrible as we feared.

I was wrong.

Exams offered a temporary reprieve, although we were exhausted and it was difficult to concentrate, knowing what awaited us on our return. Despite my red-rimmed eyes and fuzzy brain, the fear of failing sent a surge of adrenaline through me. I had no regrets for what I'd done and wouldn't allow it to ruin my future.

Late in the afternoon, Maîtresse led us toward Director Bernard's office. Placing a hand on my arm, she said, "*Do not* provoke him any further, Geneviève."

"Can you come with us? Please," I begged. "You know how he is."

She paused. "I'll try."

Maîtresse walked in and settled on a chair off to one side, while we sat in front of the director's desk.

Bernard looked over at her. "Why are you here? I didn't invite you."

She leaned forward. "I believe it's best to have a neutral party present, given how high emotions are running at the moment."

"What are you implying?" he sputtered. "Oh, fine, but don't interfere."

I clung to Bridgette's hand. Sunshine and a light breeze poured through open windows, belying the gloom within. A slight flush filled the director's cheeks, and his jaw was clenched so tight that the muscles in his cheeks rippled.

"It was my idea," I blurted out. "Bridgette only—"

"Silence," he thundered, holding up a hand. "I'm not interested in your excuses, Geneviève. I thought by now you would have learned that you can't simply do whatever you please without consequences."

He turned his gaze on Bridgette. "As for you, mademoiselle, except for meals and attending Sunday Mass with Maîtresse Durand, you will remain in your room until your emancipation in August." A cry escaped from Bridgette's lips. "You'll meet with Mademoiselle Courbet three days a week in the library so she can tutor you for the mathematics course you need to repeat for your baccalauréat. Maîtresse will make sure that you receive no privileges or treats." His eyes landed on me. "And certainly no visits from Geneviève."

"But you can't do that!" I cried.

"I can."

His glacial voice sent a chill down my spine. Maîtresse folded her hands in her lap, staring at the floor. Her lips quivered ever so slightly.

Bridgette squeezed my hand. "It's okay, Vivi." She squared her shoulders. "I'm not in the least sorry, Director Bernard. You are a terrible person for not telling Vivi about her family. She has a right to know."

Maîtresse glanced up, shaking her head. I'd never heard Bridgette talk back to the director in all our years at the orphanage. I wanted to stop her, but I was proud of her courage.

The director drew a deep breath as his face turned a shade of purple. "Bridgette, go to your room. Now!" he roared. "You will never speak to me like that again."

I nodded to Bridgette and whispered my apologies. Guilt weighed on me for how she would suffer without any freedom or outings, but most of all for the withdrawal of the cook's bonbons and cakes that she adored. She strode from the room with her head held high, slamming the door shut.

"How could you look me in the eyes and lie like that?" I exploded. "To let me go through life, not knowing I have a twin brother. It's monstrous." I glanced at Maîtresse, hoping for support, but she was hunched over, her eyes on the floor once more.

"The Assistance Society doesn't allow us to give out private information. We find it better for our charges to move forward, rather than pursuing an unhappy past. It's not your place to question what I do."

"It's *my* life, *my* past, not yours."

"You've always been a willful, stubborn child. Now you'll pay the price." His threat hung in the air.

My breathing grew shallow, waiting to hear what diabolical way he'd found to punish me. His parting gift.

"I paid a visit to Madame Moreau this morning and informed her of your reprehensible behavior," he began. His lips curled into a satisfied smile. "Her offer for the teaching assistant position has been withdrawn. She cannot allow someone of such low moral character to work with her young students."

Maîtresse started and looked up, her eyes wide. Clearly she had not been privy to this decision. "Is that really necessary?" she said in a low murmur, but the director ignored her.

I swallowed hard, trying not to give him the pleasure of seeing my shock. What in the world would I do without a job, an income? How would I get by?

"Against my advice, Mademoiselle Courbet is still willing to have you live temporarily with her. But you will have to find employment on your own. Don't bother asking me or Maîtresse Durand for a recommendation." He sat back in his chair, taking off his glasses and rubbing his temples. "I'm deeply disappointed, Geneviève. For someone with such potential, you've continually chosen the wrong path and done nothing but cause trouble at the orphanage. Be ready to leave first thing tomorrow morning."

There was no room for discussion. But I wanted nothing more than to leave, to walk out and start anew.

It was nearly mid-morning when I woke to finish packing my belongings. I'd spent half the night awake again, tossing and turning, trying to quell my panic. Whatever would I do? I had less than two piastres saved from our meager allowance, and no idea how to find a job. What if Mademoiselle Courbet told me I had only a few days to find other lodgings? Where would I go? I only knew a handful of other teachers, none of whom would help, particularly if Director Bernard had his way. How far would he spread stories about me to ruin my chances for other job offers? I wouldn't put anything past him.

The larger French community remained an unknown to me. Twice a year, on Christmas Day and Bastille Day, the Resident Superior of Laos invited the hundred or so French residents living in Vientiane and surrounding provinces to his home for celebrations. Director Bernard and Maîtresse Durand would march the orphanage girls—freshly scrubbed, ribbons tied in our hair, and wearing our best outfits—to the festivities and line us up like a regiment of the French army ready for inspection. With pasted-on smiles, guests patted the little ones on the head and murmured how adorable they looked, then nodded indifferently at the older girls, as if we were mentally deficient or physically deformed. As long as I'd lived in the home, only one young girl had been adopted by a French couple. We were inconvenient reminders of the illicit affairs no one wanted to acknowledge. The guests soon turned back to their cocktails, chatting with friends, their duty completed, while we were served lunch at a table in the garden, separate from the other attendees. Gifts were distributed at Christmas—toys and games for those under twelve and notebooks, pens, or jewelry for older girls, along with bags of used clothing. I always thought I heard a communal sigh of relief as we left the parties and returned to our cloistered world.

Reclining on her bed, Bridgette sniffled into her handkerchief as I placed the last of my belongings in the small wicker valise Maîtresse had brought me. Besides the navy skirt and white linen blouse I was wearing, my remaining wardrobe consisted of a second chemise and pair of bloomers, a nightgown, a faded cotton dress, a skirt I'd made myself, a tan cardigan sweater, and a blue voile dress. The last item, a used dress donated to the orphanage at the Christmas party a few years before, was my only good outfit. I saved it for Sunday Mass and special occasions. Lucienne would keep the sailor blouse of my school uniform. I wore my one pair of brown leather pumps, scuffed and well-worn at the heels.

"I'm sorry about your party last night," Bridgette said for the third time. "I know everyone wanted to say goodbye." Maîtresse had canceled the dinner planned to celebrate my birthday and emancipation.

"It's not important. All I can think about is what I'll do next. Hopefully Mademoiselle Courbet will help me."

"Don't worry, she won't be mad, not like the director."

"I hope not." I sank onto my bed. "I'd feel so much better if you were coming, too. We can face anything together."

"It's less than three months until my birthday, although right now that feels like forever. If only you could visit me." She looked up with the pleading eyes of a puppy begging for food. "Promise to come to Mass on Sundays. Maybe we'll even get to speak."

"I promise, but once you're free, I won't go back to Sacred Heart. You know how I feel." The church was yet another force dominating our lives with rules and threats of punishment—sins had to be confessed and countered with acts of penance to avoid the ultimate penalty of going to hell. "If there is a God, Bridgette, he must be a kinder being than we've been taught."

Bridgette's mouth bunched up in disapproval. It was the one thing we disagreed on, as she was devoted to the church. We had agreed it was best not to discuss our views and simply to support each other in our choices.

Bridgette refolded her handkerchief. "Who will comfort me when I have a bad dream?"

It pained me to think of my friend waking in the middle of the night from nightmares, terrified and crying out, reliving her father's rages and frequent abandonment. "Pretend I'm here and telling you to breathe deeply then think of something happy. Imagine us in Paris at university or traveling to Florence. We have our whole lives ahead of us."

She crossed over to the dresser. "Don't forget this." She picked up the black-and-white photograph of the two of us standing arm in arm by the tamarind tree in the courtyard, trying to look glamorous. Mademoiselle Courbet had snapped the picture last October and given us each a framed copy for Christmas. Bridgette handed it to me with a dramatic sweep of her arm. "So you remember what I look like."

I couldn't help laughing. "As if I could forget." I wrapped the frame in my nightgown and placed it in my bag next to the black velvet jewelry box, which contained a pair of brass earrings shaped like the Eiffel Tower and a delicate silver bracelet—more gifts from donors at Christmas parties.

"I wonder if your brother looks like you," Bridgette said, brightening. "Maybe we'll fall in love and marry. Then you and I will be family forever."

I chuckled. "That would be perfect, but first I have to find him. I'll write immediately to the orphanage in Pakse and to the Assistance Society in Luang Prabang, although I'm not hopeful they'll tell me anything. Perhaps if I plead my case properly."

"Once we save enough money, I'll go with you to search for them." Bridgette patted my arm. "Don't worry, we'll find a way."

"Last night I thought of looking for Sylvie Bisset," I said. "She might know of jobs and have advice on places we can rent once you're free." Sylvie had left the orphanage two years before.

"It's odd she never came to visit us," Bridgette said. "And she never goes to Mass."

"I can't blame her for wanting to forget this place. I plan to do the same. Maybe she feels the same about going to church as I do."

Bridgette flipped her hair over her shoulder. "Remember the day we ran into her on the way to school? She hardly spoke to us."

I shrugged. "I'll ask Maîtresse if she knows where she lives."

Reaching into the dresser drawer, I pulled out my most prized possessions. They were the only things that had come with me to the orphanage fourteen years before. Giselle was a foot-tall French doll with a painted porcelain face framed by coffee-colored hair tied back in a frayed green ribbon. She wore a yellow eyelet dress with a green sash around the waist. A tag attached to the right arm read, *Geneviève, Ma belle petite, Avec tout mon amour, Papa,* in faded ink. For many years, Maîtresse had restricted my play time with Giselle to an hour or two on special occasions, and only under her supervision, using it as a bribe to get me to behave. It angered me at the time, but now I was grateful. She had kept me from ruining this priceless gift, the only thing I owned from a father I couldn't remember.

I kept Giselle wrapped in the silk scarf my mother had left me. It was a long, narrow rectangle woven with silk threads of blue, the color of an early morning sky, and deep turquoise. A pattern of silver strands decorated the ends. Once when no one was around, one of the housekeepers had shown me how to hang my *pha biang*, as she called it, over one shoulder, around my back, and over my front again. She called the design a traditional *naga* pattern, after the mythical serpent spirit that protected the Mekong River. She'd promised the *naga* would protect me as well, and she felt sure this was my mother's intent.

I placed my doll in the valise and attached the leather straps as Madeleine and Lucienne rapped on the door. "Maîtresse wants to speak with you before you leave," Lucienne said.

Madeleine insisted on carrying my case, while Lucienne took my bookbag.

I gazed around the room that had been my home for the past three years. Every trace of my existence was now erased, except for the dent in the wall where I'd once thrown my bookbag in a fit of pique with Director Bernard. I wished there were more happy memories to carry with me besides those of my friends.

"I can't even walk out with you," Bridgette moaned, a fresh flood of tears dribbling down her cheeks. "I'll send you letters through Mademoiselle Courbet."

I hugged her, struggling to hold back my emotions. "I'll do the same. And we'll wave at Sunday Mass. Even the priest can't stop us from doing that."

She pulled back, smiling. "But we'll have to confess to such a grave sin."

"The months will go quickly. You'll see."

It was like having my arm torn from my body, to let go of her hand and leave her there totally forlorn.

Maîtresse was waiting for me in her office.

"It's been a difficult set of days, Geneviève," she said in a weary voice. "I'm sorry things had to end on this note." She handed me a manila envelope. "Here are your emancipation papers." She patted my hand as I took the package. "You are a bright and capable young woman, and I know you'll find success."

I nodded, reflecting on our many clashes over the years and her stern responses. While she had never yelled or physically hurt me, I couldn't forgive her for the times she stood by silently, ignoring Director Bernard's abuse. Yet, there had been moments of compassion. In my first years at the orphanage, she had held me in her lap and hugged me tight as I sobbed day after day for my mother. Once, I had adopted a baby swift that fell from its nest and tried to nourish it back to health. When the poor little thing slipped from this world, Maîtresse gave me a shoebox for a coffin and helped me dig a grave in the far corner of the backyard.

"Thank you, for everything," I said after a moment. She blinked hard, as if surprised by these words. Her expression softened, and her lips turned up in the closest thing to a smile she could manage.

I started to leave, then stopped. "Do you happen to know where Sylvie Bisset lives? I want to visit her."

She shook her head. "Stay clear of that girl! She's taken the wrong path since leaving the home, one I certainly hope you'll never stoop to. Guard your reputation, Geneviève; it's all you have. People will judge your behavior and who you associate with, and remember rumors and gossip run rampant in this town." Her words puzzled me. Whatever did she think I would do wrong?

She surprised me by coming around the desk and grabbing my shoulders in a brief hug. "Take care of yourself. I wish you luck," she said, her voice tight.

Lucienne and Madeleine walked me to the front courtyard. There were tears and hugs and promises to meet up in the future. I stopped to touch the trunk of my old friend, the tamarind tree, remembering all the years I'd spent among its protective folds, watching for a mother who would never come. But I was grateful for those brief hours filled with possibilities.

My heart felt unbearably heavy as I left the only home I'd ever known and the few people who cared for me, who in some way resembled a family. With all the courage I could muster, I gathered my valise and book bag and stepped through the gate into the dusty street outside. This was my birthday present from the orphanage.

Freedom.

Chapter 4

All the way to Mademoiselle Courbet's house, step by step, I struggled to comprehend that I was truly on my own, a realization that filled me with alarm and drained the air from my lungs until my legs grew weak and I had to pause to take several deep breaths. Nothing of my current situation matched the rosy future Bridgette and I had imagined all these years; Director Bernard had ruined it all.

Mademoiselle's two-story French colonial home was located on a lane leading to the river in the French section of town. Eight streets from the orphanage, no more than fifteen minutes' walking, but a lifetime away. Few people stirred here. Leafy trees sprinkled dappled shade across gardens bursting with colorful flowers, providing a peaceful buffer between neighbors. I'd never dreamed of living anywhere so grand.

Mademoiselle was waiting on the front veranda. Her hair framed her face and set off her remarkable lapis-blue eyes, like deep pools of water. I was, as always, in awe of her beauty, with skin as clear and smooth as Giselle's porcelain face. At the orphanage we felt sure she couldn't be much older than us, as she acted more like a student at our *lycée* than one of the stuffy old teachers.

She looked up as I opened the garden gate and flashed a bright smile, rushing down the path to greet me. "*Chérie*, I'm so happy you're here." She kissed me on both cheeks.

I burst into tears, overwhelmed by her warm welcome. "Oh, mademoiselle, I'm so grateful to you after what's happened. If only you can forgive me…"

"Hush, hush, poor dear, it will be fine," she said, patting me on the back. "First, let's get you settled in your room, then we'll have a nice chat."

An older Lao woman with graying hair emerged through the front screen door. She bowed her head in a *nop*, palms together facing up under her chin. "*Sabaidee*," she murmured, the traditional Lao greeting, meaning "be well and happy."

"This is Mali, my housekeeper," Mademoiselle Courbet said. "Tell her if you need anything."

I smiled and nodded. Mali insisted on taking my valise as we stepped into the airy entry hall. A vase filled with purple and white orchids infused the space with their sweet scent as we continued up the staircase and down the hall to the back corner of the house.

Mademoiselle Courbet opened a door, and we entered a bedroom at least four times the size of the cubbyhole I had shared with Bridgette. Sunshine streamed through half-open shutters, framed by organdy curtains. The rosewood furnishings included a four-poster double bed covered with a blue, flowered quilt, nightstands on each side, a large double armoire, a dressing table with a mirror and small bench, and a caned rocking chair with a blue cushion.

"Mademoiselle, it's so beautiful," I managed at last.

"First of all, no more 'Mademoiselle.' Please call me Catherine."

My eyes widened. "If you wish. It may be hard at first."

She laughed and put an arm around my shoulders. "I'm no longer your teacher, and it makes me feel very ancient to be addressed so formally." She paused. "May I call you Vivi, as your friends do?"

"That would be nice."

"The toilet and bath are across the hall, and Mali left towels on the bed. After you unpack, join me on the veranda."

"It won't take me long."

She turned to Mali. "Would you please make us fresh coffee?"

I waited until they left to open my valise, embarrassed by the tattered state of my wardrobe—a small hole in the hem of my good blue dress, a stain on my sweater sleeve, and everything worn and faded from a hundred washings, until the fabrics looked like the slightest tug might tear them in half. I hung the dresses, skirt, and nightgown in the armoire and placed my underthings, jewelry box, and Mother's scarf in the dresser drawers. After seating my doll on the rocking chair cushion, I knelt down to stroke her hair. "We will never be shut away again, Giselle. I promise you."

I stood at the window a moment, admiring the view of the back garden, a peaceful refuge. Koi fish swam in a small pond below an arched bridge, and lotus plants floated on the water's surface, the large white-and-pink blossoms unfolding like a sacred offering. I breathed deeply as a sense of relief and well-being filled me.

Mali brought a lacquered tray with fresh cups of *café au lait* and biscuits on a delicate china plate painted with pink roses.

"Your home is wonderful, Mademoi—I mean, Catherine." It felt strange to call my teacher by her given name. *Former* teacher, I reminded myself.

Catherine stirred sugar into her cup as wisps of steam curled into the air. "My parents built this home in 1916, after we moved to Vientiane."

I had wondered how she could afford such a large, lovely place by herself. "I thought you came to Laos from France, after you finished university."

"I was born in Paris, but my family moved to Indochine in 1913 when Father was appointed assistant to the Resident Superior of Tonkin. I was seven and my brother five at the time. We moved to Laos three years later, and I grew up here, except for several summers in France when Father had leave. Then I went back to Paris to attend university."

I sipped my coffee, calculating Catherine's age at twenty-five, only seven years my senior.

Catherine gave a soft laugh. "I'm giving away my age, but I have no secrets. When Father transferred to Vientiane, Mother wanted to design a home of her own. And *voilà*. Our family loved Laos, with its warm climate and relaxed pace of life. People are so kind and easygoing. When Father's commission with the government ended, he took a job with Bonnet's Imports." She shook her head. "Some of the French do nothing but complain and can't wait to complete their assignment and return to France. I don't understand it."

"Are your parents here now?" It had never occurred to me she might not live alone.

"They returned to France last June after Father retired. He has health problems, and Mother insisted they go back to France for better medical treatment. It's a little lonely in this big house, which is one of many reasons I decided to offer you a room."

"I can't thank you enough." She was asking only fifteen piastres per month for the room, with meals—a small sum, considering that a croissant cost twenty cents, or one-fifth of a piastre. But finding a job was urgent if I hoped to pay my rent. The back of my throat grew tight as tears threatened again. "I'm grateful you are still willing to have me. I promise to find a job right away and give you the rent. If you'll let me explain what happened…" I desperately needed to make her understand my predicament.

"Please don't worry, Vivi, we'll work this out." Catherine lit a cigarette and took a long draw. "I'm not upset with you. Maîtresse said you broke into the director's office to look at your file. Why don't you tell me what happened? Take your time."

I drew in a deep breath and began with what I remembered of my childhood, my few memories of my mother, and the day the Assistance Society took me from her arms. It was like a great spool of thread rolling across the floor and gathering speed; the more I spoke, the faster my story unfolded. "Director Bernard always refused to answer questions about my family, promising to tell me more when I turned eighteen. I waited all these years. Can you understand my anger when he denied having any information about my past, when he refused to show me my file? He looked me in the eyes and lied." I gripped the edges of my chair, and my voice shook. "How could he not tell me I have a twin brother in Pakse?"

Catherine gasped softly. "I had no idea. How unbearably cruel of the Assistance Society not to inform you and to keep you from your own brother. Whatever is their reasoning?" She sat forward in her chair. "I would have done the same."

"I don't regret it. At least I know my parents' names, that I have a brother, and that we came from Luang Prabang." I heaved a great sigh. "But now the director has had my teaching assistant job annulled. I don't know what I'll do."

Catherine patted my arm. "I tried to convince Director Bernard to reconsider and told him his punishment was too harsh, but he became terribly angry. He would never admit to being wrong, I fear. And I can't afford to lose my work at the orphanage. The director holds a great deal of sway among French *colons* in this town. It's best we find you another job as soon as possible, and you must stay clear of him. In the meantime, don't worry about the rent. You can pay me later, when you have an income."

"Thank you. Do you have any ideas where I might look for work? I don't know anyone. I don't even speak Lao."

Catherine pushed her hair back. "We'll make a plan. My dear friend Marguerite is secretary to the Resident Superior of Laos. She has endless connections and hears the latest news and gossip. I'm sure she'll have some leads. Perhaps there are openings in the telegraph service or the customs office. Also, a group of friends is coming for drinks tonight before we have dinner at the Cercle—do you know the French club on the river? I'll introduce you to a couple who may need an au pair. Would you be willing to do that temporarily, until you find something better?"

"Yes, I'll do anything."

"Good. As for the language, Mali and I can teach you Lao, although my pronunciation is atrocious. But Mali will work with you." She sighed. "It's so shortsighted, not teaching you girls to speak your native tongue. I'll never understand."

"I want to send letters right away to Luang Prabang about my parents, and another to the orphanage in Pakse to reach my brother. Can you...help me?" I asked, beginning to cry. Exhaustion and the tumultuous emotions of the past few days overcame me.

"Of course I'll help." She handed me a lacy handkerchief. "Have a good cry, dear, and you'll feel better. This is an enormous transition for you, but as my mother always says, everything will work out in the end, and you'll wonder why you ever worried so much. It's quite exciting, really. You have a brother to meet and your whole life ahead of you."

I nodded, comforted by her words.

"I almost forgot to tell you," Catherine went on, "my brother, Julian, is headed back to Vientiane as we speak and will arrive in a couple of weeks. He's been in France the last four years attending the Sorbonne and finished his degree last month. He plans to start an import/export business." She smiled. "He's a bit of a dreamer, but I can't wait to have him home. You'll get along famously, I'm sure."

She stood up. "Come. We'll walk around the grounds before lunch. Mother devoted a great deal of time to developing her gardens. They're an excellent place to contemplate life and work through your troubles."

Chapter 5

I spent the early afternoon in the back garden, sitting on a bench under the broad canopy of a banyan tree, marveling at the dozens of twisted roots that dripped down from the heavy branches, boring into the earth to provide support. As Catherine had suggested, the garden was a wonderful place to contemplate my future. The heady scent of jasmine engulfed my senses, and the mysterious names and vibrant colors of ruby heliconia, magenta amaranth, indigo jacaranda, and wild scarlet ginger seduced me, calming my nerves. An expanse of purple bougainvillea cascaded over a stone wall, encroaching on a nearby mango tree. I longed to be as tenacious and unfettered as this vine, with hidden thorns to protect me. I imagined my future uncoiling like the tightly furled fronds of pale green ferns, pushing up from the damp soil, seeking traces of daylight.

How fortunate I was to have Catherine's aid. I didn't have to worry about finding another place to live, as I'd feared, but I still desperately needed a job. Who would hire a girl of eighteen with no experience or skills?

I tried drafting a letter to the Assistance Society in Luang Prabang, asking them to release information on my past. But it proved more difficult than I'd imagined; I struggled to express my desperate need to find the people who had brought me into this world. How could I reach these misguided bureaucrats with their incomprehensible rules and make them understand? Perhaps sending a polite request devoid of emotions would be most effective. If only they would give me my mother's full name, it might be enough to find her or her family. I jotted down ideas and phrases, yet nothing fit together into a coherent appeal.

When the heat became too oppressive, I returned to the house. Catherine met me in the hallway. "Why don't you enjoy a nice bath to refresh you for this evening? My guests arrive at six."

I ducked my head, wondering if I smelled. At the orphanage, we were allotted a ten-minute bath once a week. I could never relax and enjoy the time, knowing the next person was waiting impatiently outside the door.

Mali showed me how to turn on the water heater and run a bath, adding the sweet scent of frangipani oil. I reveled in the luxury of slowly washing my hair and soaking in the hot water until my fingers began to wrinkle.

I stood by the back window in my room, combing my freshly washed hair until it fell smooth and shiny down my back. My only choice for the party was my blue dress, a shapeless drape of voile that fell to the middle of my shins. I slipped on my silver bracelet and studied myself in the mirror. It was the best I could do.

At a quarter to six Catherine knocked on my door. "Are you dressed?" she called.

"Come in."

Wearing a mid-length lavender crêpe tea dress, she looked as if she'd stepped out of one of her Paris *Modes et Travaux* magazines. The skirt clung to her slender body, wrapping around the front with a gathered piece that fell in folds down one side, while narrow straps crisscrossed her bare back, holding up the bodice. She'd pinned her hair back with a silver comb on one side and wore pearl drop earrings and a matching necklace.

She studied me for a moment. "You look lovely. I know Maîtresse always strictly forbade makeup at the orphanage, but I don't think a touch of lipstick will taint you now that you're eighteen."

I clasped my hands together. "Oh, thank you."

We crossed the hall to her room, which was even larger than mine. It was painted a pale blue and had an enormous canopy bed, with a silk cover woven in a Lao pattern of indigo blue and emerald green.

Catherine sat me on the bench in front of her vanity. I stared in awe at the collection of jars—creams, powders, rouges, and lipsticks—along with a silver hairbrush, comb, and mirror set, and four crystal perfume atomizers.

Catherine opened a tube of dark pink lipstick. "Put a little on the end of your finger and dab it on your lips."

I gingerly touched my lips, turning my head to observe the color from different angles in the mirror.

She laughed. "Okay, go like this." She showed me how to rub my lips together to even out the color. "Perfect! Now we must get downstairs before the guests arrive."

In the salon two settees covered in faded rose-colored silk, and a collection of wooden and rattan armchairs with flowered print cushions, gave the room an elegant but slightly worn appearance. Everything was ready: the low tables stocked with silver cigarette boxes and lighters next to crystal ashtrays; bottles of champagne, decanters of liquor, an ice bucket, and seltzer water arranged on a teak drink trolley; feathery ferns sprawled over giant Chinese pots in the front corners of the room; and an extravagant arrangement of orange canna and red hibiscus filled a vase next to the Victrola on the sideboard. Dozens of candles and the electric wall sconces filled the room with soft light, as two punkah fans, hanging from the high ceiling, waved back and forth like palm fronds to create the impression of a breeze.

Catherine poured a half glass of champagne and handed it to me. "Have you had champagne before?"

"Last New Year's Eve, Director Bernard allowed the oldest girls a taste."

"Sip it slowly. We can't have you tipsy." Catherine hesitated a moment. "I hate to sound like a prudish maiden aunt, but I must offer a bit of advice before anyone arrives. You're a beautiful young woman, Vivi, and men will find you appealing and exotic, given your mixed heritage. You can expect a great deal of uninvited attention."

I stared at the bubbles rising up the sides of my champagne glass, wondering what could have prompted such a statement. No one, besides Bridgette, had ever told me I was pretty. I shifted from one foot to the other, unable to meet Catherine's eyes.

"I don't mean to embarrass you," she continued. "Just be cautious, as your life at the orphanage was extremely sheltered. Gossip is a favorite pastime in this town, and you don't want to be the target of malicious rumors. If any of the male guests make you ill at ease or say anything inappropriate, please tell me."

I thought of Maîtresse Durand's warning that morning about guarding my reputation. True, I had little experience, having rarely spoken to the boys in school beyond discussing homework or exams.

Catherine glanced at her watch. "My friends should be here any minute."

"I'm a little nervous."

"They're lovely people, mostly, although they can get a bit unruly after a few drinks. You'll be fine." Catherine lit a cigarette. "Marguerite is bringing her new beau, an officer who arrived recently in Vientiane. She's very taken with him, which isn't at all like her."

Mali answered a knock at the front door, and a tall, slim woman made her entrance. She wore a Chinese Mandarin gown, like I'd seen in the window of Wong's Mercantile. Pink and yellow peonies embroidered the peacock-blue silk dress, with its high collar and frog clasps that ran diagonally down the front. Slits ran up the sides to the middle of her thighs, and the fabric clung to her curves. She'd pinned a gardenia over her left ear. She crossed the room, teetering on three-inch gold lamé heels.

A robust older gentleman, wearing a full-dress military uniform with medals dripping down the front, followed behind her. He pulled aside her luxurious long tresses, nearly as bright red as her lipstick, to whisper in her ear. Marguerite laughed and batted at his hand.

Catherine gave her friend a quick embrace. "Mademoiselle Marguerite Vanier and Captain Charles Martell, let me present Mademoiselle Geneviève Dubois."

Marguerite startled me by rushing over, grabbing my shoulders, and kissing me on both cheeks. She smelled of alcohol, cigarettes, and gardenias. Green eyes, the color of fresh mint, drew attention away from her slightly hooked nose. "I've heard so much about you, dear girl." She tossed her beaded evening bag on a side table and proceeded to inspect me as I shrank from her gaze. "Aren't you gorgeous! Charles, isn't she lovely?" Charles grinned and nodded. "I guarantee you'll turn a few heads tonight. The wives will be wild with jealousy."

"Marguerite, really, you say the most inappropriate things," Catherine chastised. "She's already nervous."

"But it's true." Marguerite snickered. "You're every French wife's worst nightmare." I didn't know how to react to such a disconcerting claim, except to blush.

A dozen more guests arrived, filling the salon with the sound of voices, laughter, and ice clinking in glasses. Despite the pressing heat, men wore dinner jackets and ties or dress uniforms dripping with ribbons and medals, reeking of sandalwood and other spicy scents to cover the underlying odor of sweat. Women shimmered in silk, satin, and chiffon gowns in a rainbow of shades, their flowery perfumes competing with the increasingly thick cloud of cigarette smoke. I felt like a spectator at a sophisticated play, watching as people floated past, flirting and teasing one another, sipping their drinks, issuing up witty remarks that met with clever retorts or a coy tilt of the head. Marguerite held a couple captive with a story about the Resident Superior, her husky laugh reverberating around the room. Someone put a record on the Victrola, and Josephine Baker sang "I've Found a New Baby," as Mali wandered in and out with plates of hors d'oeuvres.

Catherine put an arm through mine and escorted me around the salon to meet her friends, who congregated in small groups. Wearing her brightest smile, she introduced me as her former student, assuring everyone I was a bright and capable young woman, someone she greatly admired. After a short pause she would add that, if anyone knew of a job opening, please let me know. The men responded with polite nods and platitudes—*best of luck; something will develop, I'm sure; I'll keep you in mind*—while their wives studied me with appraising eyes, issuing unreadable smiles, murmuring greetings empty of warmth. It felt exactly like the indifferent attitudes I'd been subjected to every year at the Resident Superior's Christmas and Bastille Day parties. No one asked questions or offered advice, nothing that might prolong the conversation. It was as if we were speaking across a great distance, and they were afraid I might come closer. Each guest would quickly find an excuse to leave—one person needed to refresh his drink, another headed to the toilet, while several guests spotted friends they urgently wanted to greet.

Catherine, tireless in her efforts, started to introduce me to a heavyset older matron. "Madame Herbert, let me introduce—"

But the woman interrupted. "Really, the nerve. I already know about this thieving little *métisse*. What can you expect from half-breeds?" She pivoted and stormed away.

Catherine blanched. "Oh, Vivi, I'm so sorry. There's no excuse for such behavior, but her husband left her last week for his Lao mistress. She's falling apart."

I felt sorry for the woman, but why would she detest me simply because I was born half Lao? I hung my head, wanting to fade into the walls, hoping no one else had heard her comments.

"Come this way," Catherine said, "and meet my friends who are thinking of hiring an au pair." She led me to a couple I'd noticed arrive earlier. The husband, tall and lanky with dark hair and eyes and a neatly trimmed mustache, reminded me of the movie star Charles Boyer. His mouth curled into an enigmatic smile, making it unclear if he was amused or bored.

"I want you to meet Madame and Monsieur Fontaine," Catherine said. "This is Geneviève Dubois, my former student."

Madame Fontaine, short and slightly round with strawberry-blonde curls, could not have been more unlike her husband. She exuded nervous energy, waving her hands in the air as she spoke, speaking in bursts.

"Catherine mentioned you're available to help...with our children. We have four boys under the age of seven...I simply can't keep up with them." A trill of laughter trailed her words. She tilted her head to one side, studying me, then glanced at her husband, as if gauging his reaction.

I smiled. "It must be a great deal of work. I'd be happy to help."

"I can always count on Mademoiselle Courbet to assist," Madame Fontaine said, with an edge to her voice. "I'll call you if I decide to hire someone." With that, she disappeared.

Monsieur Fontaine shrugged his shoulders. "You'll have to excuse my wife. She's a little scattered at times, but I can assure you she is greatly in need of assistance. Our children are wild animals." He glanced at Catherine and sighed. "Excuse me." He stepped away to greet another couple.

"It's not ideal, Vivi, but it might suffice to start," Catherine whispered. "Jeanette is quite hopeless at managing their household, even with two full-time servants. Marcel gets very impatient with her."

"I hope she calls." In truth, I dreaded the thought of taking care of privileged French children, but anything that brought in money would do for the moment.

A young officer stepped forward, raising an eyebrow. "And who is your lovely young guest, Mademoiselle Courbet?"

Catherine hesitated. "Lieutenant Toussaint, this is Mademoiselle Dubois."

He bent over and kissed my hand. "Delighted." His eyes slowly grazed the length of my body, and I found myself inching back from him. "I don't believe we've met before, as certainly I'd remember."

Like a good soldier, he stood at attention; I thought he might even click his heals together and salute. His thick dark hair, slicked back with an abundance of pomade, gave the illusion of a helmet framing his face. Powerfully built, he grinned at me with his over-generous mouth, demanding my attention. I wouldn't have called him handsome, but he had a rugged appeal that some women might find attractive.

Catherine pulled on my arm. "Please excuse us, lieutenant, I want mademoiselle to meet some friends who just arrived." She led me away, whispering in my ear, "Don't go near him. He's notorious for chasing every skirt in town, then bragging about his conquests."

Before leaving to check on her guests, Catherine presented me to Collette Martin, who was standing alone by the front window. Collette had a surprisingly youthful face despite her white hair pinned in a bun at the nape of her neck. Her pale green chiffon dress clung to her shapely figure, and silver Buddha earrings dangled from her ears. Her eyes studied me a moment. "Well, aren't you a pretty little thing." She patted my arm in a familiar way. "Catherine has only good things to say about you."

"She's very kind."

"Yes, isn't she." Collette took a sip of her drink, swaying like a stalk of bamboo in a breeze. "You're looking for work, I hear."

"I'll take anything."

"Don't hope for much from this crowd, except maybe a job caring for their children." She burst out laughing. "But no wife will want you in her home. You'd be much too tempting for her husband." A surge of heat rose up my face.

"Oh, I've embarrassed you." Her drink sloshed in her glass as she stumbled to one side, and I had to grab her elbow to keep her from falling.

She ran her fingers over the sleeve of my dress then turned me around to examine the back. "This used to belong to my friend Annette. She donated it to the orphanage, I believe." I nodded. She giggled like a schoolgirl. "The fabric is rather worn, but I assure you, it looks much nicer on you than it ever did on Annette. And this blue is perfect for your darker complexion." She pointed to the hem. "Ask Catherine's housekeeper—Mali, isn't it?—to fix that tear."

I was at a loss for words. The next thing I knew, she was waving to someone across the room and tottering off, leaving me alone in the corner. Her seemingly innocent comments, laced with barbs, left me further deflated. Was this her intention or simply the alcohol obliterating any sensitivity to my feelings? I edged my way toward the door, hoping to slip upstairs to the safety of my room. I didn't belong at this party. Surely most of Catherine's guests thought I should be next to Mali, serving drinks and hors d'oeuvres. Maybe they were right.

Lieutenant Toussaint appeared at my side, exhaling gin fumes in my face. "Mademoiselle, I hope you're coming to the club for dinner."

I stepped aside. "I can't this evening."

His hand gripped my shoulder, and he pushed me against the wall. "Oh, you must. I want to dance with you."

"Some other time." I was trapped, unsure how to politely escape. The thought of his forceful arms around me made me shudder.

"In that case, I'll call you to set a date for dinner next week."

"Thank you, but I'll be busy searching for a job."

He stood back, his shoulders squaring once more. "Surely you can find time for an evening with me." He sounded incredulous over my refusal. "A young *métisse* like you should appreciate offers of friendship."

Catherine swooped in. "Excuse me, lieutenant, but I must borrow mademoiselle once more." She led me to the back of the room. "That man is so annoying. Stay here while I check in with Mali. We'll be leaving soon."

I watched the guests from my isolated corner, wondering why they couldn't take an interest in me instead of treating me like an embarrassing nuisance to avoid. I had expected more. It seemed my only safe alternative was to join Mali in the kitchen.

As I passed through the entry hall, I heard whispering: "Marcel, not here." Muffled giggles drifted from the shadows beneath the stairway. I could barely make out Catherine, leaning against the wall, and Monsieur Fontaine with his arms wrapped tightly around her waist, his body pressed against hers. I gasped as he bent down and kissed her with an intensity that made my face burn.

Chapter 6

I hurried through the dining room into the kitchen, my face flushed to the tips of my ears. Hopefully Catherine had not seen me, or I would never be able to face her again.

Mali looked up. "Mademoiselle Vivi, please sit." She indicated the wooden table by the back door. "I'll serve your dinner once the guests leave." And she disappeared.

I sank into the chair where she had laid a place setting, grateful for the momentary solitude, feeling the muscles in my shoulders slowly relax. I tried to reconcile the scene I'd witnessed with the person I idolized. How could Catherine be embracing someone else's husband? Was it nothing more than a brief lark, a playful joke on Monsieur Fontaine's part? Or was this the "uninvited attention" Catherine had warned me about earlier? But she'd seemed a willing participant, returning his ardent kiss. This strange turn of events baffled me.

Catherine popped her head through the kitchen door, giving me a start. "We're off to the club. I'll see you in the morning, probably rather late." She darted off, like a hummingbird come and gone in a fraction of a second.

Mali returned and placed a tray of dirty glasses on the counter, then took a bowl of beef bourguignon from the oven and set it in front of me. "*Bon appétit.*"

"Will you eat with me?"

"I already had my meal." She set to washing plates and cocktail glasses.

Had I made her uncomfortable? Perhaps she would not consider eating with me, any more than the cooks at the orphanage would have joined the girls at the dining table. Yet I was only a boarder, half Lao, eating at the kitchen table. Where was my proper place in Catherine's household?

"Have you worked here long?" I asked to bridge the silence.

"Fifteen years. Mademoiselle Catherine's mother hired me when they first moved to Vientiane and the children were little," she said, her voice wistful.

Mali's life had been spent in the service of others. I didn't want this to be my fate. "Do you have a family?"

Mali smiled. "My husband and five children live in a village outside of town. I go home every other Sunday and Monday. And I see my husband when he comes to town once a week to sell our vegetables."

How could these few days off be adequate? I wondered if the cooks and cleaning women at the orphanage had families, and how often they saw them. The director and Maîtresse never allowed the girls to talk with them, to ask about their Lao lives, ones that might be similar to my mother's. Now I had an opportunity to get to know Mali and ask about her family, their customs and beliefs. I desperately longed for a connection to the other half of me that remained a mystery, foreign and distant from my current reality, someone who could fill in the empty spaces.

As I finished my meal, Mali picked up a tray with leftover hors d'oeuvres, a ball of sticky rice, a banana, a mango, and two little cups of coconut water. "I'm taking these to the spirit house," she announced. "I'll be right back."

"Is that the little house on a pole in the front garden?" I'd noticed many similar structures by homes and businesses around town. "What is it for?"

She smiled. "Come, if you like, and I'll explain."

I placed my empty dishes in the sink and followed Mali outside. It was dark now, but candles glowed along the pathway. The spirit house was about two feet tall and a foot wide, made of wood, with a steeply pitched roof of bamboo.

Mali cleaned the platform of spent incense sticks and remnants of old food. "This is a shrine for the protective spirits, or *phi,* who keep Mademoiselle Catherine's home safe. We provide them a place to dwell and eat, and they prevent harmful spirits from entering the house and causing trouble."

"Are there many harmful spirits?" I asked, unfamiliar with the idea.

"Oh yes. Sometimes it's the souls of people who died nearby and can't let go of this life, or spirits from nature who hold a grudge and wish to do mischief." She placed the food and drinks on the shrine.

This intrigued me, even though the concept offered as much logic as the saints, angels, and demons of Catholicism. Had my mother and her family carried out a similar tradition? Despite my doubts, I wanted to help Mali maintain the spirit house, to be sure to keep us all safe.

When we finished, I said good night and retreated to my room, completely drained and overwhelmed by the past few days. It was only eight thirty, but I put on my nightgown and climbed into bed beneath the mosquito net, sinking into the soft feather mattress and pillows, the ultimate extravagance after the thin, hard pad on my cot at the orphanage.

I wished Bridgette was here to help me puzzle out the evening. Catherine's guests had greeted me as an unpleasant interruption, someone to avoid, as if I had an incurable, contagious disease. I'd been an easy target for insults—half-breed, thief. My parents' unpardonable sin of giving birth to a *métisse* was clearly an embarrassment to French *colons.* The thought of Lieutenant Toussaint, arrogant and aggressive, frightened me even more, with his attentions and false familiarity, treating me like a servant he could order to accompany him to dinner.

If this was the reception I received from Catherine's friends, people I might expect to be sympathetic and kind, then how would total strangers react to me? I had to prepare myself for much worse.

My brain slowly shut down, my eyes no longer able to stay open.

The first light of day eased its way across the room to my bed as bursts of birdsong drifted from the garden, rousing me from slumber. I popped up with a start, unsure of my surroundings, until I remembered the move to Catherine's and the party the previous evening. The clock on the nightstand read six fifteen, and the house remained silent. Mali had told me she would leave before dawn for her village, while Catherine would sleep long into the morning.

I dressed and slipped out the front door, eager to explore the streets of Vientiane, excited to wander alone wherever I wanted, something the orphanage had never allowed. At last I could observe the town and local people up close to better understand this unknown part of myself. The early morning air felt cool and inviting, like a soft breeze after a rainstorm that caresses your skin.

A short walk brought me to Rue Maréchal Joffre and the intersection with the town's main thoroughfare, recently renamed from Avenue Resident Superior to Avenue Lang Xang. The colonial government had decided to honor the powerful former kingdom of Lang Xang, which had ruled Laos for three hundred and fifty years until the early 1700s. Constant wars with neighboring kingdoms had slowly torn it apart until Siam imposed its will on the Lao people. Now the French controlled Laos, painting themselves as saviors, protecting Laos from its greedy neighbors. I wondered how shifting from a Siamese master to a French one had given Laos greater sovereignty. Ironically, Avenue Lang Xang was lined with French colonial government offices and businesses.

Several blocks on I reached Rue Tafforin and the bustling covered market with its long halls of half-walls and thatched roofs. Bridgette and I had begged Maîtresse to take us there many times, but she refused, claiming the local people and the things they sold were dirty and unfit for young French girls. We might catch any number of diseases.

I strolled among the bamboo stands, captivated by the items for sale—hand-woven fabrics, silver and gold jewelry, metal tools and knives, cooking pots, wooden bowls, wicker baskets, dishes. Local people glanced up at me as if surprised by my appearance, not quite Lao, not quite French, an aberration that still seemed to make them uncomfortable, even after all these years of French colonial rule.

Lengths of silk in vibrant colors, as alluring as the flowers in Catherine's garden, drew me in. I stopped at a stall, and the woman lifted her hands into a *nop*, bowing and murmuring, "*Sabaidee.*" Feeling awkward, I returned the greeting, garnering a broad smile. She held up a length of green silk with a gold pattern woven along one side and spoke rapidly, demonstrating how to wrap it around the waist and fold it over to make a *sinh*. I shook my head, not understanding her Lao. "Color perfect…for pretty girl," she said, switching to halting French. I promised to return soon and purchase some fabric.

In the next hall were stands of fruits, vegetables, butchered meats, along with cages holding live chickens, ducks, small birds, and frogs.

Behind the covered market, a group of stands offered meals and snacks—soups, grilled sausages, cured beef strips, sticks of sugar cane, dried mango, and other mysterious dishes. My stomach growled with hunger. I felt in my pocket for the small reserve of coins I had saved from my allowance. Once girls turned fifteen, the orphanage gave them fifty cents, or half a piastre, a month. A young woman about my age stirred a pot of simmering liquid that smelled delicious and made my mouth water. I pointed to a wooden bowl, and she filled it with hot soup, while I held out my palm with half a dozen coins worth five, ten, or twenty cents. She nodded and took five cents. "*Khop jai,*" I said, thanking her in Lao, one of the few phrases I knew.

I sat on a three-legged stool at a tiny table under a leafy fig tree. Pieces of chicken, onion, lemongrass, red pepper, ginger, and rice noodles floated in the rich broth topped by a slice of lime. The spicy flavors burned my tongue.

Reveling in my newfound freedom, I relaxed in the shade, observing locals as they strolled past. Groups of Lao and Annamese women ambled by with their purchases, laughing and chatting. Families stopped for a snack, the children jumping up and down with excitement as they agonized over what to choose. Everyone appeared happy and no one seemed in a hurry, as if they didn't have a worry in life. I tried to imagine my mother years ago, shopping in a market like this, bringing my brother and me with her, possibly even with my father, a loving family out together.

The shock of seeing Catherine and Monsieur Fontaine kissing the night before kept niggling at me, however, like a loose tooth demanding my attention. My idol was flawed. Was she truly having an affair with him, or were they simply flirting, playing games with one another? The heated passion of their kiss made it hard for me to believe the relationship hadn't gone further. How long had it been going on? Did Catherine think about his wife and four children when she was in his arms? I knew nothing of life or love, the reasons people made such choices, but no one would learn of her transgressions from me, not even Bridgette.

Four teenage boys wandered into the eating area, teasing and pushing one another, speaking too loudly. Like a pack of dogs on the prowl, they circled two young girls selling dried fruits. Egging each other on, they spoke words I couldn't understand, but the intent was clear. The girls tried to ignore them at first, then waved them away, which only prompted more outbursts. One of the boys grabbed a slice of dried mango and stuffed it in his mouth. An older woman, who was selling sausages at the next stand, rushed over, yelling at the boys and slapping their arms until they moved on.

To my dismay, they angled in my direction, staring at me, whispering in one another's ears and snickering. One boy, with long hair hanging over his eyes, boldly stepped near, prompting the others to hoot and shove him. "Girl, come for good time," he said in heavily accented French. I froze, unsure how to escape their attention. The older woman reappeared, shouting and hitting the boys with the handle of the fork she used to turn her sausages. The culprits ran off laughing.

I stood and bowed in a *nop*. "*Merci, khop jai.*"

"Bad boys. Be careful," she said, returning to her grill.

My pleasant morning disrupted, I headed in the opposite direction from the young men. While French classmates at my *lycée* had often teased and taunted, I'd never expected anything like this from locals in a public place. Shaken and on alert, I retraced my steps. The rising temperature of the day drew me toward the peaceful flow of the river, away from the bustle of the main streets and into a quiet lane. As I walked, I glanced over my shoulder every few minutes, jumping at the sound of a twig breaking or an animal scurrying under a bush until I reached the riverfront.

Along the Quai Francis Garnier, longboats and fishing skiffs bobbed in the water, their lines tethered to the muddy banks. Farmers lined the shore, squatting on their haunches, selling produce from rattan mats spread on the ground. Where the makeshift market ended, a café served food and drinks to patrons sitting at crudely built tables and chairs. A group of older men sipped tea and filled the air with a stream of cigarette smoke. On the far end, two young Frenchmen huddled with a Lao woman, sipping bottles of beer. One man had his arm about the girl's shoulders, whispering in her ear, causing her to giggle and lift her hand to cover her mouth. The other man glanced up with a bored expression and caught sight of me. A slow smiled crept onto his lips, and he held up a hand.

"Mademoiselle," he called out, "come join us on this fine morning." Turning from his gaze, I quickened my pace. He jumped up from his seat and started toward me, weaving an irregular path. "Mademoiselle, come. I won't bite." He laughed and came closer.

I sprinted as fast as I could down the road and up the next lane before daring to look back, relieved to find no sign of the Frenchman. Panting, I headed to Catherine's home, trying to understand why these men felt they had the right to approach me in such a rude manner when I had done nothing to attract their attention or encourage them. How could I avoid these situations? My long-awaited freedom, the ability to go out into the world alone and do whatever I wanted, was not what I'd expected. Would it always be so difficult?

When I entered the hall, the grandfather clock chimed ten thirty. I'd lost track of time and it was too late now to make the ten o'clock Mass. I hated to disappoint Bridgette, but the thought of going out again was too daunting.

Catherine sailed down the staircase dressed in a light khaki skirt and lavender blouse.

"There you are. Have you been out exploring?"

I nodded.

"I'm spending the afternoon on the river with a friend and probably won't be back until late," she said. "Help yourself to anything. Mali left us lots of food." She stopped a moment. "Will you be all right?"

"Of course." This was not the time to tell her of my morning. "I have to write my letters to Luang Prabang and Pakse and one to Bridgette, of course."

Catherine adjusted her straw hat in the mirror. "Oh, by the way, I'm sorry to say, but Madame Fontaine decided not to hire you as their au pair. Frankly, I think it's because you're so young and pretty, and she's jealous. It's probably for the best."

"She called you?"

"No, I spoke to Marcel," she answered casually.

"That's fine." I thought how uncomfortable and slightly complicit I might feel if I'd had to work for Madame Fontaine when her husband was betraying her with Catherine. Perhaps Catherine was meeting *him* this afternoon. Nothing would surprise me.

"I must run, but I invited Marguerite for dinner tomorrow. She's going to check at her office for job openings, and we'll come up with some ideas." She waved over her shoulder, skipping out the front door, carrying a quilt and picnic basket.

Alone, frightened, and unsure of my new life, I recalled the events of the party the night before and my morning out in Vientiane being harassed by young men. During fourteen years of living at the orphanage, I'd rarely had a moment alone, unless I counted the hours watching for my mother from the branches of the tamarind tree. Or the nights Director Bernard had locked me in the front closet. At times I'd longed for a private space to retreat to, but now the silence of the big empty house confounded me. Whatever would I do for the rest of the day? I missed Bridgette beyond reason.

Chapter 7

Marguerite arrived for dinner on Monday evening and flopped down on the settee in the salon with a loud huff. "I learned today the Resident Superior is leaving, and yet another short-term appointee will begin next week. Why can't the government find a permanent candidate instead of this string of temporary posts? Every time a new boss arrives, I'm afraid he'll replace me."

"Who would dare try?" Catherine said. "You've been secretary to the resident superiors for eight years. You run the place." She handed me a glass of soda water with lime and Marguerite a gin and tonic.

"They hardly acknowledge me." Marguerite took several gulps of her drink. "But enough of my complaints." She lifted several pages from her purse and handed one to me. "Here are the addresses and names of those in charge at the Assistance Society in Luang Prabang and the orphanage in Pakse."

"Thank you." I stared at the neatly written addresses. "I'll add them and post my letters tomorrow." I had spent Sunday afternoon struggling through multiple drafts of my appeals, revising them again that morning to incorporate Catherine's suggestions. "How long does the mail take to get there?" I asked Marguerite.

She waved her hand through the air. "Delivery is always a gamble in these parts, depending on weather, river conditions, and mechanical problems with the boats, which happen all too frequently. A letter traveling on the mail motorboat might be in Luang Prabang within a week, but it's as likely to take two weeks. Going south, the regular ferry service from Vientiane to Pakse is only four days, but the ferry only leaves once a week. A friend of mine recently received a letter from Champasak that had been mailed two months ago. Heaven only knows what happened. The unpredictability of the mail is the reason the wire service network is so extensive. It's essential for people to communicate quickly."

"I'm sure you're anxious to hear back, but be patient," Catherine added. "If too much time passes, you may have to send a second inquiry."

After finally finding leads to my family, I wanted answers now, yet after fourteen years of waiting, a few more weeks would have to be tolerated.

Marguerite handed me another sheet. "These are the current government job listings designated for French widows and orphans, including the *métis,* of deceased civil servants. To qualify, you'd need to provide a letter verifying that your French father claimed you as his child and is now deceased."

"I don't know anything about my father, except that he went back to France in 1915. He may still be living," I said. "Only the orphanage could provide that information, and Director Bernard would never help me."

"I was afraid of that," Marguerite said. "There are only two openings at the moment, anyway. With the world economy collapsing, budgets have been slashed, and many vacant posts are left unfilled."

I glanced down at the two listings: *dames-lingères.* One was at the French guesthouse and the other at Mahasot Hospital. "Laundresses?" I asked, unable to hide the disappointment in my voice.

Marguerite took a sip of her drink. "It's a broad category. At the guesthouse you'd be supervising the Lao women who do the laundry and cleaning. The opening at the hospital involves overseeing the cooking and distribution of meals."

"I don't even know how to cook," I murmured.

"The advantage is, government salaries are higher paying and more secure." Marguerite lit a cigarette and blew a thick stream of smoke into the air above her head. "But I can't see you in these damn jobs. You'd do better applying to local businesses."

"Aren't there openings at the telephone exchange or wire service?" Catherine asked. "Vivi could apply on her own as a French woman."

"Hah!" Marguerite scoffed. "They only hire French woman when forced to by the government. They prefer Annamese workers, who accept a quarter of the salary they pay French employees."

"Is that true for Lao employees as well?" I asked.

Marguerite crossed her long legs, bobbing her foot back and forth. "They rarely hire any Lao. The government has brought hundreds of Annamese from Tonkin, Anam, and Cochinchina to fill administrative positions. Unlike in Laos, the *indigène* children in those colonies get a good education. French officials claim the Annamese are better trained and work harder." She shrugged. "Maybe it's true. The Lao are very relaxed about life."

I stared at her with dismay. "But why is the pay so low?"

"Because they can get away with it," Catherine said. "The government and private businesses exploit the *indigènes*. French women get higher salaries to accommodate their higher standard of living. It's terribly unfair."

"Where does that leave me? Would a private business consider me French or Lao?"

"You must rightfully present yourself as a French citizen and demand a proper salary," Marguerite said emphatically.

"Do you sew, Vivi?" Catherine asked.

"I'm hopeless with a needle."

"Can you type?" Marguerite tried. I shook my head. "What about bookkeeping?"

"I had high scores in mathematics." I perked up, relieved to identify something I excelled in. "But I haven't any training in accounting."

"Of course not, you only finished school last week." Catherine sat forward and patted my arm. "An office job would be best. Certainly you can file papers. Or you could be a clerk at a dry goods store, maybe a dress shop. A French business, of course, since you don't

speak Lao yet. I'll make a list of places for you to try tomorrow—
Bonnet's Imports, where my father worked, and a number of others."

"I searched the advertisements in the *Vientiane Times* today," I
said, "and found a listing for a clerk at a Chinese grocery store and
another at a print shop."

Marguerite snuffed out her cigarette. "Don't bother. They won't
pay you anything."

"Marguerite and I will ask our acquaintances again for leads,"
Catherine added.

The telephone rang in the entry hall, and we heard Mali
answer. After a moment she appeared in the doorway. "It's a call for
Mademoiselle Vivi from a Lieutenant Toussaint."

"Oh heavens," Catherine said. "Vivi, shall I deal with him for
you? He's not the kind of man you want to go out with."

"Good God, no," Marguerite agreed.

"I told him at the party Saturday I couldn't go to dinner, but he
didn't believe me. He thought I should be grateful for his offer."

"He'll try to bully you into accepting if you talk to him." Catherine
headed toward the hall. "I'll take care of it."

Marguerite and I listened as Catherine, her tone light and airy,
explained it was impossible at the moment for me to go out with him.
"You're right, she's a lovely young girl, and how kind of you to want
to help, but she needs time to settle in and find a job, get her footing.
I'm sure you understand." Catherine laughed at his response then said
au revoir.

"Thank you," I said when she returned. "I've never been asked out
before, and he made me very uncomfortable."

I paused a moment, pressing my fingers along the edge of my
hem. "I need to tell you about what happened yesterday." I explained
about the local boys at the covered market and the Frenchman along
the river who had harassed me. "They scared me, and I didn't know
what to do. How can I avoid these situations?"

"Oh dear," Catherine said, "this is exactly what I warned you about the other night—men being attracted and acting inappropri-ately. You must be careful to avoid these situations."

"But I did nothing," I protested.

"Of course you didn't," Marguerite said. "Men are idiots, whatever their age. As annoying as these incidents may be, you'll be perfectly safe in the daytime about town—not that I'd want you wandering down a deserted alley. But if men harass you, pretend you don't hear them and walk away with confidence, head held high, shoulders back. If they persist, be noisy and draw the attention of other people, to embarrass them."

Catherine got up to mix fresh drinks. "If you go on a job search alone tomorrow, don't wander into bad neighborhoods, and only go into respectable-looking establishments."

"She's eighteen, not five, Catherine," Marguerite chided.

"Still, be selective. If you wait until Wednesday afternoon, I could come with you."

"No, no. I don't want to waste your time. I'll be fine," I said, try-ing to sound confident even though the prospect of crisscrossing town hunting for a job terrified me. "I'm not sure what areas I should avoid."

Catherine nodded. "I'll mark a map for you."

Marguerite took her drink from Catherine. "I'll check for open-ings at companies the government does business with, where I have long-time acquaintances."

Catherine smiled reassuringly. "I'm sure you'll find something soon."

"I'll do my best."

My letters to the Assistance Society and the Pakse orphanage lay on my dresser, written in my best penmanship, carrying my dreams of the past fourteen years with pleas for help and understanding. On Catherine's recommendation, I'd kept them formal and to the point, devoid of anger or emotion.

As much as I had struggled with the letter asking for information on my parents, a separate letter to my brother in Pakse had flowed from the core of my heart, reaching out to a stranger—yet someone who was my own flesh and blood, who had shared my mother's womb with me and come into the world at my side.

Geneviève Dubois
14 Rue des Fleurs
Vientiane, Laos

May 18, 1931
Cher Antoine Dubois,
My name is Geneviève Dubois. In 1917, when I turned four, I came to live at the Société d'assistance aux Métis, Maison Pour Filles Abandonnée in Vientiane. Last Saturday, a few days before my eighteenth birthday and emancipation from the orphanage, I gained access to my file and learned that I have a twin brother—you, Antoine Dubois—sent to the orphanage in Pakse.

The Assistance Society had not planned on telling me about you, and I assume you were not informed of my existence. The file stated the names our French father as Henri Dubois and our Lao mother as Laya (no last name listed), who lived in Luang Prabang where we were born. Our father returned to France in 1915. There was no explanation as to why we were turned over to the orphanage system.

Naturally, this news came as a great shock, as I'm sure it will for you. I am overjoyed to find I have family, and it fills me with great hope for the future. With luck, you will safely receive this letter.

Please write to me at the address above—I'm staying with my former teacher. I long to meet you whenever possible.
With affection,
Your sister Geneviève

Chapter 8

Wearing my blue dress, which Mali had washed and mended when she arrived back from her village the evening before, I set out on Tuesday morning to find a job. I had knotted my hair in a bun at the nape of my neck, with the hope it would make me appear older, and had practiced in front of the mirror detailing my limited qualifications while downplaying my lack of experience, trying not to stumble over my words. Catherine had marked a map of Vientiane with the locations of Bonnet's Imports, the Customs Bureau, two French clothing shops, and one of my favorite stores, Bourdain's Stationery and Books. My highest hopes rested on this last option with its genial young owner, Monsieur Simon. Catherine also drew circles around several neighborhoods to avoid.

A blanket of steamy heat wrapped around me as I stepped out of the house, dampening my skin, like the early morning dew that often hovered over the Mekong River. After mailing my precious letters at the post office, I marched to my first destination, imagining myself an explorer in unknown territory.

At Catherine's urging, I called first on Bonnet's Imports, her father's former employer. I presented the letter of recommendation she had written to Monsieur Roy and waited in the reception for over an hour. At last, a heavyset man with white hair and a beard, looking like a dour *Père Noël*, escorted me to his office. He posed one question on my education and another on my previous work.

"I'm sorry, Mademoiselle Dubois, but given your lack of experience, I can't envision a position you would be capable of filling. I wish you the best of luck." The interview ended in less than five minutes.

My next stops proved equally unsuccessful. Marguerite's contact at the Customs Bureau sounded terribly annoyed at being bothered, assuring me there were no openings. Catherine's friend, Madame Dupont, at the À La Mode Fine Apparel, greeted me kindly but said business was slower than ever and she couldn't possibly hire anyone.

The sun had not yet reached its peak and my first three attempts had failed. The day stretched endlessly before me. My dress was soaked with sweat, and a fine layer of dust had turned my shoes from dark brown to gray, making me look like a tattered rag doll dragged through the mud.

Half a block away I reached Chez Josephine, the more expensive of the two French clothing establishments. It was located next to Estelle's Patisserie, with its enticing smells of butter, sugar, and chocolate. Telling myself to be brave and confident, I stepped into the tiny shop, relieved to find there were no customers at the moment. Racks of dresses, skirts, slacks, and blouses hung along the walls, while tables down the middle held light wraps and lingerie. A painting of the Eiffel Tower hung on the wall above a glass case displaying jewelry, gloves, and sparkly hair ornaments. Everything was spotless and neatly arranged, giving the impression of another place and time—somewhere in France, I assumed.

A pencil thin, middle-aged woman was arranging nightgowns on a table. She wore a stylish, narrow black skirt and white silk blouse with a pleated collar. Her dark, chin-length hair was curled in Marcel waves. She looked up, seeming startled by my presence, and assessed my appearance.

"May I help you?" Her question sounded more like a warning.

I cleared my throat. "Madame Trembley, my name is Geneviève Dubois. I'm seeking employment and wondered if you might need help in your pretty shop."

"Where are you from? I've never seen you before."

"I'm staying with Mademoiselle Courbet, who suggested I speak to you." My voice shook slightly.

"I've heard about you—the *métisse* orphan."

"I completed my baccalauréat last week, excelling in mathematics."

"But not fashion, I see." Her lips curled in disgust at my damp, rumpled dress and scuffed shoes. She waved her hand around the empty shop. "Does it look like I need help?"

"Perhaps something part-time," I offered. "I can clean or do anything you want."

"Mademoiselle, my clients are primarily French women who come here looking for high fashion and the familiarity of home. They prefer to be around their own kind." She brushed past me, as if ridding herself of a piece of lint clinging to her skirt.

I stood there breathless, hands clenched. "There is no need to be so rude, madame. You may think I'm not 'one of your kind,' but I am half French and a French citizen. Meeting you makes me ashamed to acknowledge that." I spun around and stomped out, slamming the door behind me.

I immediately regretted letting my temper get the better of me, but how could I be expected to accept such cruel treatment, being dismissed as unworthy of even being considered for a job? Had Madame Trembley spoken to me in this manner due to my age and inexperience, or simply because I was *métisse*?

I longed to run home and hide in my room, but I didn't have the luxury of being so easily defeated. I continued on to the one store where I could happily picture myself working: Bourdain's Stationery and Books.

Twice a year at the end of the school term, Maîtresse Durand had escorted the four girls with the highest grades, which always included me, to the store. It was such a treat to lose myself among the books, enjoying the musical crackle of crisp pages, plunging into stories set in far-off places. I'd never had enough money to buy anything more than a pencil box, but Maîtresse allowed each girl to select one book, which she purchased for the orphanage library.

The young store owner, Monsieur Simon, had inherited the business from his father, who had died suddenly of yellow fever the year before. The other girls and I found him handsome, in a bookish manner, with his unruly, wavy hair, round tortoiseshell glasses, and colorful bow ties. He always had a candy for us and a joke to tell. It amused us to see Maîtresse suddenly transformed into a blushing schoolgirl by his teasing and flattery. *Oh, Monsieur Simon, you are too kind,* she would gush.

I took a deep breath and approached the counter, where he was crossing items off a list. "Bonjour, Monsieur Simon, I'm Geneviève Dubois. I've been here with Maîtresse Durand a number of times."

He looked up and a smile illuminated his face. "Mademoiselle, of course I remember you. How may I help?"

I explained that I'd graduated from school and left the orphanage a few days earlier. "I adore your store and would love to work here."

"I remember how you enjoyed browsing through the bookshelves. So, what would you propose to do?"

"I excelled at mathematics, so perhaps I could help with the accounting. Or work at the counter." I paused. "Really, I could do anything you have a need for. I'm very flexible."

He bit his lower lip and checked his watch. "Hmm. I've not had lunch yet. If you have time, come with me, and we can talk further." I nodded enthusiastically.

He informed his assistant, then led me down the street away from the center, taking a narrow lane toward the river, chatting the whole time about a recent shipment from France with a half dozen new novels that might interest me. He named authors and titles while his hands sailed through the air, as if he were conducting an orchestra. "I bet you like romantic novels," he said with a wink. His gray eyes, flashing with excitement beneath dark lashes, mesmerized me, and I thought he would be a far more suitable match for Catherine than Monsieur Fontaine. If I got the job, I might find a way to bring them together.

After passing a row of modest French colonial homes, he turned up the path of a pale-yellow cottage. I stopped midway, unsure where we were going. He pulled out a ring of keys and unlocked the door, turning to me. "I live so close to the store, I always come home for lunch. My housekeeper prepares my meals. Do you mind?"

I hesitated a moment. "No. No, of course not." I followed him into the silent house and a tiny kitchen off the entry hall. "Is your housekeeper here?"

"She comes for a few hours in the late afternoon to tidy up and cook meals, but she left some vichyssoise with bread and cheese." He grinned. "We won't go hungry." He pulled out a tureen of soup and several packages from the icebox, then retrieved two bowls and a platter off the shelf above the sink. "Would you mind unwrapping the cheese?"

I stepped up to the counter and pulled a wedge of brie and some type of hard cheese from their paper wrappings, placing them on the platter.

"So, tell me about your background, mademoiselle. How long did you live at the orphanage?"

His relaxed, friendly manner set me at ease, and I recited a brief history of my time at the home. "I always had top scores at school. I'm sure I could be of help to you."

"Impressive." He moved closer, grabbing spoons and knives from a basket on the counter, causing his arm to briefly brush against my breasts. "Do you know anything about your parents?" he asked, without missing a beat.

Flustered, I stumbled through an explanation of my recent discovery of my parents' names and the existence of a twin brother. "I've sent letters to inquire about them. I desperately want to find my family."

He placed an arm about my shoulders. "How terribly sad to be kept from them all these years."

"Thank you for your concern." The heat of his body burned through my dress, and alarms rang in my head. I tried to break free without being too obvious, but his grip grew stronger, holding me close.

Then he stepped back as if nothing had happened. "If you'd like to wash up, the water closet and bathroom are down the hall," he said.

"Thank you." I hurried off to find the toilet, my cheeks flushed and my heart racing. Perhaps I had misinterpreted his moves, and his concern was sincere. I passed a bedroom on the way with an unmade bed and clothes scattered everywhere.

When I finished washing my hands and emerged from the bathroom, Monsieur Simon was standing outside the bedroom. "There you are. We'll eat in a moment, but let me show you a collection of my favorite books. Some are quite valuable. Perhaps you've read many of them, but you're welcome to borrow any you want." He put his hand on my elbow and led me into the bedroom to a beautiful teak wood cabinet. He pulled open the glass doors with great fanfare, as if displaying rare pieces of art.

Wary and ill at ease, I stepped away. "Why don't we eat? You must need to get back to the store."

He moved closer and placed his arm around me once more. "Don't be shy. I want to be your friend and help you." He bent down and kissed my neck, then my ear.

Shock surged through my body like I'd been bitten by a deadly spider. My body coiled into a tight spring. I shoved him away and backed up to the doorway. "Please stop. I only wanted to work at your store."

He crossed his arms with a sardonic smile. "A pretty young *métisse* like you needs a protector, someone to keep you safe. As it happens, I'm good friends with Director Bernard, and he tells me you're rather naughty."

My breath caught in my throat. I had been right to fear that Director Bernard would spread rumors about me in the French community, ruining my chances for a job, turning me into a pariah.

Monsieur Simon stepped forward, reaching for my arm. "No one has to know if we're close."

I spun around and flew down the hall and out the front door, sprinting down the lane as his mocking laughter echoed after me. I ran toward the river, the closest direction where I might find other people. Reaching Quai Francis Garnier, I collapsed against a bread-fruit tree with trembling legs barely able to support me. How could I have been so foolish to trust him and enter his house? He'd seemed so nice, like he was truly interested in me. I'd never dreamed that asking for a job could be misconstrued as an invitation to seduce me. Were there women who submitted to this kind of abuse out of desperation? Catherine and Maîtresse would learn of Monsieur Simon's betrayal, even if he would likely deny any wrongdoing.

Chapter 9

I walked along the river, hoping the flow of water and gentle rocking of the boats would calm my pounding heart and erase the images of Monsieur Simon with his arm around me, kissing my neck. Down the road, a boisterous crowd of French *colons* filled the tables on the stone terrace of Pierre's Bar & Café.

"Mademoiselle," a voice called out. I glanced over as Lieutenant Toussaint rose from a table where he was sitting with two other officers and waved to me. "Wait." I braced myself as he ran across the road, wearing the hungry grin of a tiger ready to pounce on its prey. "Join me for a drink."

I stood with my mouth open, not able to bear another intrusion by some boorish, senseless man. "No. Mademoiselle Courbet is expecting me," I said, my voice sharp and angry.

"Oh come, she won't mind if you stop for a drink." His insistent words enraged me. He grabbed my wrist and started dragging me toward the bar.

In the middle of the street, I pulled back with all my force. "Let go! I said no." I was nearly hysterical, feeling trapped and helpless.

His grip only tightened. "Don't be like this. People are watching."

"Toussaint, what the devil do you think you're doing?" Marcel Fontaine appeared out of nowhere. He pulled the lieutenant's hand from my arm. "She said *no*. Leave her alone."

Toussaint's face puckered into a violent storm as he glanced from Monsieur Fontaine to me and back again. Several bicycles heading down the road had to swerve around us. "Fine," he said at last and marched off.

My savior guided me back to the riverside path. "What an ass.

I'm sorry he bothered you."

"Thank you. I didn't know how to get away."

"Catherine told me he's been after you, and he doesn't give up easily." He turned briefly as a man at the bar across the way stood up, waving his drink in the air and calling to him. "Should I accompany you to Catherine's?" he asked.

"No, I'm fine. Go back to your friend." I nodded a goodbye and hurried away, turning down the next lane before breaking into a run. Monsieur Fontaine's concern and kindness had surprised me, and once more I wondered about the nature of his relationship with Catherine.

When I finally reached the safety of home, I collapsed on the chair next to the entry hall table. The day had leeched every ounce of energy from my body and crushed my spirit. I felt like a beetle someone had stepped on and mashed into the ground.

Mali came to greet me. "Mademoiselle Catherine should be back—" She stopped midsentence. "What's happened?"

"Oh, Mali, it was terrible...these men..." I dissolved into sobs.

Mali put her arms around my shoulders and patted my back, murmuring, "There, there." I thought this must be what it is like to have a mother who loves and consoles you. "Poor dear. Go take a cool bath, and I'll fix you a treat. Come back with your dress and underthings so I can wash them. Then we can talk if you feel like it."

A half-hour later I drifted back downstairs, my mood improved after a lukewarm bath laced with frangipani oil. I was determined to push all thoughts of Monsieur Simon and Lieutenant Toussaint from my consciousness. A glass of lemonade and a piece of coconut cake waited on the kitchen table for me, like a big comforting embrace. I took a bite of cake, imagining it must be the taste of manna from heaven.

"It's so wonderful. Will you teach me how to make it? I've never cooked anything and need to learn before Bridgette and I live on our own."

Mali smiled. "I'll show you, but perhaps you should start with some basics, like baking a chicken and steaming vegetables."

"You're right. Bridgette and I would eat only sweets if we could."

We sat for a moment in silence, then she asked, "Do you want to tell me what happened?"

In halting spurts, I recounted my terrifying experience with Monsieur Simon. "I was so shocked and frightened. How could he try to take advantage of me like that?" I gulped some lemonade, as tears dribbled down my face. "Then, coming home, I ran into Lieutenant Toussaint." I described his alarming attempt to force me to join him and how Monsieur Fontaine had come to my rescue.

She clucked her tongue several times. "These men will face their evil ways one day, if not now, then in the next life. Don't let them take away your happiness; focus on the good in your life."

I stared down at my empty plate. "I'll try."

She patted my arm. "Take some quiet time to reflect and find your inner peace once more. If you want to come to my temple with me, it is a very good place for this. Maybe tomorrow."

We heard the front door, and Catherine strode into the kitchen. "Vivi, have you been crying?"

My unhappy story poured out once more as I chastised myself for being so naïve. "I was stupid to trust Monsieur Simon, but I never imagined his intentions."

Catherine sank onto the chair across from me. "You did nothing wrong, but it's yet another example of why you must be careful. Men are incorrigible!" She shook her head. "That despicable, ridiculous man with his silly bow ties and pretentious airs, thinking he is charming and irresistible. Marguerite and I will think of a way to deal with Monsieur Simon."

"Can you tell Maîtresse, since she sometimes takes the girls there?"

"Of course. She must be informed."

"No one I visited would even consider hiring me." I winced slightly. "I'm embarrassed to say, I got rather angry with Madame Trembley for the way she spoke to me." I let out a long sigh. "And then I ran into Lieutenant Toussaint."

Catherine listened with growing concern, tossing her head and swearing under her breath. "Thank heavens Marcel was there. You've had a terrible day, my dear. Stay home tomorrow and rest," Catherine said. "I'll be free in the afternoon, and we can do something together." She pulled two letters from her handbag. "These should cheer you up."

Once in my room, I plopped on my bed and tore open the first envelope with my name scrawled in Bridgette's slightly messy handwriting.

Chère Vivi,

Mademoiselle Courbet (how strange that you call her Catherine now) brought your letter yesterday. I missed you at Sunday Mass but can understand how you lost track of time—how exciting to be free to wander about town on your own!

I can't begin to tell you how much I miss you. It feels like years since you left, instead of three days. Saturday night I hardly slept without the sound of your soft breathing across the room. Strange shadows floated on the walls and ceiling, until I had to hide under the covers.

Maîtresse lets Lucienne and Madeleine spend evenings with me (once the devil goes home), and last night Lucienne shared one of the chocolates she received for her birthday. Heavenly! On Sunday, Cook made passion fruit tarts and sent a secret package to me via Madeleine. So, I'm not suffering.

Something surprising—it turns out Lucienne knows where Sylvie moved two years ago, as they wrote to each other once or twice. I hadn't realized they were friends. She lives at the Lambert Boarding House on Rue Augustine. Hopefully she is still there.

I've been sketching some of the flowers growing in the back garden, at least the ones I can see out the window. They're not particularly good, but I enjoy it immensely. Maybe I can get a job drawing. Are there jobs like that?

Nothing more to report, as I don't go anywhere or do anything.

Fingers crossed that you receive answers to your letters right away. And please, please come to Mass on Sunday!
Hugs and kisses,
Bridgette

Innocent Bridgette, how much she had to learn about the outside world—the kinds of pitfalls and dangers that had confronted me in the space of only a few days. But I would not tell her of my difficulties and disillusion her before she even had a chance to enjoy a new life free of the orphanage. Let her remain hopeful in anticipating the future. She would learn the truth soon enough.

I hurriedly opened the second envelope, wondering who else could be writing me from the orphanage.

Chère Geneviève,
Enclosed you will find fifty piastres, an amount the Assistance Society provides to each girl turning eighteen and leaving the orphanage, a gift to help you transition to your new life. I regret to say Director Bernard tried to keep me from giving you the money, but upon reflection, I do not believe it is his decision to make. Withholding the money would be stealing and goes against all my principles and those of the Assistance Society to aid you girls in building a happy future.
I hope you will do well and succeed at whatever you attempt.
My best wishes,
Maîtresse Durand

Relief washed over me at being granted this reprieve. I didn't have to panic about finding a job—at least not yet. Maîtresse had proved herself a worthy person, acting in my best interest, and for that I was eternally grateful. The first thing I did was pay Catherine the rent, which she accepted reluctantly, saying I should wait until I found employment. But I was an adult on my own now. I must meet my responsibilities.

Chapter 10

The next morning I longed to pull the covers over my head and hide, like a mud turtle burrowing into the soggy banks of the Mekong River. I felt woefully inadequate to the task of finding employment, as if I'd been told I must catch a fish in order to eat, but I didn't own a fishing pole or net and had no idea where to find fish. Yet I wouldn't capitulate and stay home, as Catherine had suggested. I must continue the search. Even if the salary might be lower than elsewhere, I decided to try the Chinese grocery. Perhaps, not being French, they would be more welcoming of a *métisse*.

Huang's Groceries was located on a street lined with brick and cement shophouses, where proprietors lived above their businesses. Red silk banners hung down building fronts with store names written in French and Chinese characters: Wong's Furniture; Chang's Fine China; Best Silk Fabrics; Zhou's Herbs and Cures. Halfway down the block I found the grocery.

Long and narrow, the store was packed with goods that reeked of musky, pungent odors—rice noodles, sauces, preserved fruits, dried mushrooms, herbs, and other unusual-looking items, while huge hemp bags of rice were stacked nearly to the ceiling in one corner. Two shelves on the left wall featured wines, tins of liver pâté, and other specialties imported from France. Two Chinese woman wandered up and down the aisles, while a Frenchman searched the wine selections.

A middle-aged Chinese man, wearing wire-rimmed spectacles, his thick black hair sticking straight up as if he had suffered a fright, manned the cash register.

I smiled. "*Bonjour*, I'm Geneviève Dubois. I'm applying for the opening you posted in the newspaper." I held out the advertisement.

"What you can do?" he asked in broken French.

"Whatever you need: unpack boxes, stock the shelves, work at the cash register…" I searched for something more. "Take inventory."

He grinned and shook his head, as if I'd told him a good joke. "You too young and little. How you lift boxes?"

My mouth felt parched. "I have a baccalauréat, and I…I'm very good with numbers."

As I waited for his response, a beaded curtain at the back of the store rustled, and a tiny woman emerged, hurrying to the front. "Who you? What you want?"

The couple, presumably husband and wife, spoke rapidly back and forth in Chinese while she waved her hands at me. "No job. You go," she said, turning to me.

"If you'd give me a chance for a week," I pleaded. "Then if you're not happy—"

"We know your kind. No good," she interrupted, grabbing my arm and pulling me to the exit, pushing me out the door. "Go!"

With that I found myself on the street, trying to comprehend what had happened, hoping no one had noticed me being thrown out of the store like a petty thief. The woman's reaction made no sense. What had she meant by "your kind"? Did she view a *métisse* as unacceptable in her world?

I made a hasty retreat back to Avenue Lang Xang and plodded down the street, deciding what to do next, unsure how much more humiliation I could withstand. Would every business, whether French or Lao or Chinese, reject me based only on the fact that I was a *métisse*? The possibility filled me with despair, and I longed to return home and spend the afternoon with Catherine.

I reached Wat Sisaket, the Buddhist temple on the corner, which I had passed many times and wondered about. The simple life of the monks at the small *wat* across from the orphanage had intrigued me, listening to them chant prayers and beat gongs. Mali's suggestion that

I take a quiet moment to step back and reflect, to restore my inner harmony, came to mind. It seemed a tall order at the moment, but I ventured through the temple gate and found a peaceful haven, empty except for two young monks with shorn heads and saffron robes, who were sweeping the dirt-packed grounds. One of them glanced up and nodded.

I strolled around the covered walkway that circled the courtyard, in awe of the hundreds of small arched niches carved into the walls, each holding a tiny Buddha. Below, dozens of larger Buddhas rested along a low shelf and on the ground. The statues' other-worldly, serene expressions eased my discomfort. My breathing slowed and the unhappy lump inside my stomach began to dissolve. I wanted to be like these Buddhas, unperturbed and above the fray of life.

In the center of the courtyard, the roof of the *wat* swept down in multiple tiers, like whimsical slides, curving up at the corners. Elaborate carvings of fantastical creatures, painted and gilded, decorated the portals and eaves, while dragons guarded the stairway balustrades. I longed to venture inside but was unsure if strangers were welcomed.

Two elderly women emerged from the *wat,* slipped on their sandals, and left through the gate. A moment later, a young Lao man emerged. His shiny dark hair, cut short along the sides and back but with bangs that nearly covered his eyebrows, gave him the air of a schoolboy. He wore Western-style pants and a traditional cream-colored Lao shirt with a Mandarin collar. He glanced at me as he put on his shoes, and I turned away, embarrassed to be caught staring.

He walked over and bowed in a *nop*. "*Sabaidee.*"

I gave a small nod, ready to flee. He said something in Lao, but when I seemed confused, he switched to nearly perfect French. "Have you been to Wat Sisaket before?"

I shook my head, not wanting to engage any further with him. Surely he thought me as dense as a water buffalo, but how could I trust any man at this point? It struck me as terribly bold of him to speak to a strange woman in the middle of a Buddhist temple, yet his manner was not aggressive or threatening, and he lacked the bravado of others who had harassed me. Perhaps he wanted money.

"Excuse my forwardness. I'm Bounmy Savang." He bowed slightly. "You appear a bit lost." His voice was low and soft.

"Geneviève Dubois," I offered at last. He was tall compared to most Lao men, standing a good head above me. From his refined features and clothes and manicured nails, it was clear that he was not a laborer or farmer, but a person of some means.

He waved a hand toward the temple. "The École Française d'Extrème Orient is currently renovating the interior murals. I came to observe the progress."

"Do you work at the temple?"

"No, but I study Buddhist art. This is the oldest original temple in Vientiane, built over a hundred years ago, unique in that the architectural style is Siamese rather than Lao. Sadly, all the other ancient *wats* here were destroyed in wars with Siam or other kingdoms. Perhaps you know this history."

"A little, but I've never visited the temples."

"Are you here from France?" he asked, studying me as if trying to decipher my origins.

"I grew up in Vientiane."

He appeared perplexed. "I'd be happy to show you inside and explain about the art."

I hesitated, on alert, but decided nothing dire could happen at a Buddhist temple tended by two young monks in the middle of the day. On the porch we removed our shoes and stepped inside the cool, dimly lit *wat*. An altar held a huge gold Buddha surrounded by offerings: lotus flowers, fresh fruits, and lighted candles and incense.

He touched the carved and lacquered screen in front of the altar. "This is decorated with the *naga* design, the dragon-like spirit that protects the rivers and oceans," he said.

"I have a scarf with a *naga* woven into the fabric that my mother gave me."

"Ah, she wants to protect you," he said with assurance. I appreciated that he interpreted the meaning of the scarf in the same way I had—a sign of her love and caring.

His long, graceful fingers pointed to the faded murals on the temple walls. "These are scenes from a story about one of Buddha's former lives. You can see where the original art has been restored. It's a slow process requiring great skill and patience."

"Are you an artist, Monsieur Savang?"

He put his head back, chuckling, revealing dimples in his cheeks. "Most definitely not, but I appreciate fine work."

"I see." I studied his face, finding him attractive in an imperfect way, with ears that stuck out a bit and a wide crooked smile, offset by high cheekbones and a narrow nose. There was something elegant about his unassuming manner and quiet way of speaking.

"What is the meaning of the Buddhas on the small shelves?" I asked.

"Worshipers offer the figures to earn merit—that is, to bring blessings to their family and ancestors in this life and the next. It's part of the Buddhist philosophy."

"I'd like to learn more about Buddhism. I was raised Catholic."

"The *phasong,* the monks, offer lessons at some of the temples." He stepped aside as a woman entered and knelt before the altar to pray. "Perhaps we should leave," he whispered.

Outside, I turned to him. "Thank you for showing me the temple, but I must go."

"May I walk with you?"

My distrust returned tenfold. "To the next corner," I allowed.

He kept a respectable distance between us, walking with his hands clasped behind his back, as if understanding my wariness.

"Do you work nearby?" I asked, curious to know what he did in life.

"Yes, for the government. I'm attempting to develop foreign trade." He pointed down Avenue Lang Xang. "My office is that gray building over there."

"Are you not working today?"

"Yes, but I like to spend my lunchtimes exploring local *wats*, as I only moved to Vientiane last month."

"Where did you live before?"

"I was raised in Luang Prabang, but I've recently returned from school in Paris."

"Oh, I'd love to go to Paris," I said, my voice filling with wonder. "What was it like?"

He smiled. "Everything you can imagine—beautiful, exciting. I was sad to come home."

We walked in silence for a moment. "Do you live nearby?" he asked.

"Not far. I turned eighteen a few days ago and left the French orphanage. I'm staying with my former teacher."

"You're lucky. It's not easy to find a comfortable place to live for a young woman alone."

"My teacher is very kind, but I must find a job to earn my keep."

"That's not simple, either." He paused a moment. "My cousin Kham Savang owns the shipping company River Transport. He's always in need of someone who speaks French well."

I glanced at him, uncertain if this was a genuine offer or a way to lure me into a compromising position. I wouldn't risk finding out. "I may have a job caring for the children of a French family," I lied.

He pulled a silver case from his pocket and handed me his business card. "If that doesn't work out, please call me, and I'll introduce you to my cousin."

I stopped at the corner. "Thank you, Monsieur Savang. I enjoyed the tour of the temple."

He smiled and gave a slight bow. "Mademoiselle Dubois, the pleasure was all mine. I hope we cross paths again soon."

Halfway down the lane I turned to look back. He was standing in the same place, watching me. I waved and continued on, intrigued by this new acquaintance, hoping he might be different from the others, interested in me as a person and not as a possible conquest. My instincts told me he wasn't anything like Monsieur Simon or Lieutenant Toussaint. There had to be decent and trustworthy men somewhere.

"Bounmy Savang," I said out loud, enjoying the way "Bounmy" rolled off my tongue.

Chapter 11

Catherine and I sat on the veranda on that Friday morning, eating pastries and sipping coffee. Since I'd moved in two weeks before, we'd settled into an amiable routine, sharing breakfast and sometimes dinner if she was at home. She told amusing anecdotes about some French children she was tutoring over the summer and filled me in on the latest from Bridgette and the orphanage, while I lamented my fruitless search for employment and the endless wait for answers to my letters about my family. At times, we were equally comfortable sitting in silence, and I grew more at ease with her, feeling less of an intruder in her home.

Several evenings each week Catherine went out with friends for dinner—perhaps that meant Monsieur Fontaine. I had seen them out my bedroom window one afternoon embracing in the back garden under the banyan tree. What was the nature of their relationship? Were they in love?

On days when Catherine ate out, I joined Mali in the kitchen, reassured by her even-tempered presence. After much cajoling, I'd convinced her to eat meals with me and share stories of her childhood and family, explaining I wanted to learn about the Lao way of life. She had grown up in a small village where multiple generations lived together under one roof. Half the other households were relatives—aunts and uncles and cousins who toiled together in the fields, caring for one another's children and elderly, each pitching in to do their part. I came to appreciate the deep sense of connection and loyalty she felt for extended family and neighbors, the meaning of community. As I listened, I imagined this could have been the story of my mother and her family.

Mali answered my endless questions, recounting how she and her husband had met when she was only sixteen and he was eighteen at a festival of a neighboring Buddhist temple. "He stole my heart without ever speaking a word, so handsome with his shy glances," she said, her face folding into a gentle smile. "His family came a week later to negotiate our marriage, and we wed the following month." The more I learned of Mali's past, the more I wondered why my mother had not married a Lao man. What had led her to my French father?

"My husband is the *naiban*, village chief, and we've been blessed with five children and two grandchildren already." Mali described each child's personality and funny antics. Her second oldest boy, nineteen, was courting a young woman in a nearby village, and planned to marry soon. She promised to invite me to the wedding so I could experience the marriage ceremony and meet all her family.

I envied her children having a mother who clearly adored them, even if she was gone much of the time working at Catherine's. She had made the sacrifice so her children could continue their schooling and choose their future. Had my mother loved me and my brother this much? If so, why had she abandoned us?

When it came to teaching me Lao, Mali was relentless, drilling me over and over again. I knew how to count to ten and say the names of different foods in Lao, but I felt slow and dull-witted, struggling to master the pronunciation of the six Lao tones. A word could mean different things depending on which tone was used. I had never struggled this way as a student, and it wounded my pride. But how lucky I was that Mali was willing to share her life and introduce me to my Lao heritage.

Catherine spoke, interrupting my thoughts. "Marguerite and I are attending a special ceremony this afternoon at Wat Pha That Luang. The École Française d'Extrême Orient is funding a major restoration of the *wat's* stupa, and the temple monks invited the Resident Superior and other guests for a blessing. Prince Phetsarath Rattanavongsa had a hand in the planning. Have you heard of him?" I shook my head. "He's a cousin of Sisavang Vong, the King of

Luang Prabang, as well as the highest-ranking Lao official in the colonial government. He's a much-respected scholarly man who promotes Lao Buddhism and culture."

I immediately thought of Monsieur Savang and wondered whether he might come to the ceremony given his interest in the temples. Each time I passed by Wat Sisaket or his office on Avenue Lang Xang, I found myself watching for him, but to no avail.

"Come with us," Catherine said. "It will be interesting."

"I'd love to." I placed my coffee cup on the table. "When will you go?"

"We should leave here by three. Why they scheduled it at the hottest time of the day is beyond me, but I promised to accompany Marguerite. Charles left yesterday for an assignment in Luang Prabang and isn't sure how long he'll be gone, so I'm trying to cheer her up. I've never seen her so smitten with anyone."

"This morning I'm planning to visit a friend who left the orphanage a few years ago," I said. "I thought she might have advice on looking for a job." I had repeatedly put off searching for Sylvie, troubled by Maîtresse's warning that I should stay away from her. Yet I had promised Bridgette to try to find her.

"I'll be tutoring Bridgette." Catherine ran her fingers through her unbrushed hair. "Let's meet back here for lunch."

I sighed. "Poor Bridgette. I wish she could come."

"I can't fathom Director Bernard's motives in locking her away. He is a vindictive, small-minded man."

I slumped in my chair, filled with regret. "He's punishing Bridgette to upset me. He has a terrible temper—spanking the girls with a wooden paddle and slapping the older girls, primarily me, across the face." Anger swirled in my chest as I thought of the constant confrontations with the director, and I saw no reason to hold back. "He often locked me in the hall closet overnight, or confined me to my room without meals. Once he took my doll, the only thing I have from my father, and threatened to throw it away."

Catherine's frown deepened. "I didn't know he was that bad. Although, his wife left him last year and returned to France amid rumors that he abused her." She paused a moment. "But this is outrageous. I'll write to my mother immediately. She's good friends with the former orphanage director, who's still on the board of the Assistance Society." She shook her head slowly. "Knowing this will make it even harder for me to be civil to that man. I already try to avoid him as much as possible."

Catherine glanced at her watch and jumped up. "I must get dressed and go."

I found Sylvie's boarding house on the map of Vientiane, located in the same neighborhood as Monsieur Simon's house. A fifteen-minute walk brought me to a large two-story building of wood and plaster, which looked a great deal like the orphanage, only painted white with dark blue trim. Two young Frenchwomen, not much older than me, sat on the front veranda, drinking coffee and chatting. They stared at me warily as I started up the path.

"If you're inquiring about a room, there aren't any available," one girl said, as if challenging me to come closer.

I stood at the bottom of the steps. "I don't need lodging. I'm looking for a friend who lives here, Sylvie Bisset."

"Oh, that one," the other girl scoffed. "She moved out last fall."

"Do you know where I can find her?"

The first girl shrugged. "Last I heard, she was living in the alley behind Wong's Laundry, where all the Chinese shops are." She looked me up and down in my simple white blouse and navy skirt, still looking like a schoolgirl. "I'd think twice about going there."

The other girl gave a short laugh. "Someone told me she painted her front door red. How perfect."

Disconcerted by the warning, I thanked them and retraced my

steps to the main road, then continued on to the street lined with Chinese shophouses. What had prompted Sylvie to move to this neighborhood? Wong's Laundry was on the corner of a smaller, seedier street. Halfway down it intersected with a narrow alley filled with crudely built shacks, the roofs fashioned of tin and bamboo strips. They reminded me of the huts that farmers built in the middle of rice fields to provide shelter from the sun and rain, except these unsightly hovels were crowded together, appearing to hold one another up. I'd never come upon an area as poor and dreary as this.

The stench of human waste drifted from privies out back of the structures. A Lao woman dressed in a cotton *sinh* and a loosely slung *pha biang* that barely concealed her breasts stepped outside her door and poured a pail of dirty water onto the ground. Her body sagged with the burden of her life. She quickly disappeared.

A sinister pall hung in the air, a presentiment of danger as I caught sight of a red door two places down. I walked closer and studied the cracked and peeling door with its garish red paint, trying to find the courage to knock. I was about to abandon my visit when the door swung open and a middle-aged Frenchman with a large, protruding stomach stumbled out of the shack, reeking of liquor. He shielded his bloodshot eyes against the sun's glare. His shirt was untucked and askew from being buttoned in the wrong holes, leaving one shirttail longer than the other. What was he doing in this disheveled state at eleven in the morning?

A woman in nothing but a flowered cotton robe rested against the door frame. She pushed aside her tangled hair. Black makeup was smeared beneath her eyes, and a dark bruise covered the right side of her face. "Come back tonight," she said. The Frenchman stole off down the alley without a response.

I stared in disbelief. "Sy-Sylvie?" Her eyes opened as wide as the full moon. "It's me, Geneviève."

"What are you doing here?" she asked, pulling the robe tighter. Her face had become harsh and angular, and her body was nothing more than a collection of sticks. "How did you find me?"

"Lucienne had your address at the boarding house, and a girl there told me where you'd moved."

"Well, you found me. What do you want?" Her voice was angry and defiant.

"I left the orphanage two weeks ago, and Bridgette will be free in August. We wondered how you were doing and wanted to see you. I'm searching for a job." I didn't bother asking if she had ideas about where to look, as clearly her life had taken a disastrous turn.

"That bastard Bernard didn't find you work? He stuck me at the Chinese laundry over there, but that didn't last long." Her lip curled into a sneer as she nodded toward the hovel behind her. "That's why I'm living this glamorous life."

"Was that...your boyfriend?" I asked, desperately hoping there might be an explanation other than the man being a paying customer.

She let out a harsh laugh. "One of several."

A shudder rippled through me, and my stomach filled with acid. What had led her down this degrading path?

"What are you staring at?" she spat out. "You're shocked? Don't be so naïve. I'm not the only *métisse* to end up earning her living on her back."

"I'm sorry," I whispered.

"Don't be." She took a cigarette from her pocket and lit it, blowing smoke above her head. "It pays well enough, and I don't need your pity." And with that, she stepped back into her hut and slammed the door.

I fled down the alley, desperate to get away from Sylvie's hopeless situation. Girls who arrived at the orphanage recounted many tragic stories—parents who abandoned them, fathers who drank or smoked opium or abused their mothers—but I'd never known anyone who had ended up selling their body to make a living. Why hadn't Maîtresse helped her?

Wandering aimlessly, I kept visualizing Sylvie's bruised face and emaciated body. How did a young woman, especially a *métisse,* manage to survive on her own? Whatever would I do if no one hired me? Only then did I fully appreciate the loss of the teaching position that Director Bernard had stolen from me. Even being an au pair sounded appealing at this point, but that was out of reach as well. I might be reduced to washing laundry or cleaning houses, but I vowed I would never end up like Sylvie. Never!

At one of the Lao cafés along the riverbank I spotted Monsieur Fontaine seated by himself, a collection of beer bottles lined up on the table. He was slumped over, his head in his hands. I picked up my pace, hoping to avoid his attention, but he sat up to take a swig of beer and caught sight of me.

"Mademoiselle, wait," he called, standing up and staggering toward me. "Please, I need your help." He stopped and stood, weaving slightly, as if buffeted by a strong wind. His clothes were rumpled and dirty. "I didn't do it. I never... You have to tell Catherine. I was drunk and passed out on the porch. That's all." His disjointed words spilled out in a rush.

I stepped back, confused. "I, I don't know what you're talking about." Our last meeting had been the day he'd saved me from Lieutenant Toussaint. I owed him the courtesy of listening, but he made no sense.

"My wife won't listen. Tell Catherine it's a misunderstanding." His voice grew frantic. "I'd never do that. You have to believe me."

"I must go, but I promise to tell her." I knew this was the only response that would allow me to leave. He remained planted there, near tears, as I walked away. Something dire had happened, but I didn't want to get involved.

It was a little after one o'clock when I reached the house. I checked the silver platter on the entry hall table where Mali placed the mail, hoping for a response from Luang Prabang or Pakse, knowing it was unlikely this soon. Nothing.

Mali motioned to me from the dining room. "Come." She closed the kitchen door once we were inside. "A friend called Mademoiselle Catherine and told her something terrible," she whispered, "but she wouldn't say anything to me. She's in her room crying. Mademoiselle Marguerite arrived ten minutes ago and is with her."

I knew immediately—Monsieur Fontaine. "I'll go up and see if I can help."

The door to Catherine's room was half open, and Marguerite was sitting beside her on the bed, rubbing her back. I paused, unsure what to do.

"You always said he was only a bit of fun, that you didn't take him seriously," Marguerite said.

"I knew...he couldn't...be trusted," Catherine sputtered between sobs. "But the servant...I can't believe Marcel would take advantage of that poor young girl."

"He's a despicable bastard." Marguerite lit a cigarette and handed it to Catherine, then lit another for herself. "Adèle Chancy told me Jeanette's in a rage and is determined to leave as soon as possible for Saigon and a ship back to France."

"I feel sorry for Jeanette," Catherine said softly, wiping her cheeks and nose with a handkerchief. "And terribly guilty. I betrayed her. How could I have been such a fool, telling myself our affair was harmless?"

"Men are pigs!" Marguerite erupted. "I can only hope that Charles will behave while he's in Luang Prabang. You can't trust any of them."

I didn't want to intrude and embarrass Catherine, but perhaps she needed to hear Monsieur Fontaine's explanation. I rapped on the door, startling them both.

"Oh, Vivi, did you overhear us talking?" Catherine asked. Her face crumpled with despair. "Did you already know about Marcel and me?"

I shifted from one foot to the other. "I saw you together at your party." My eyes met hers. "But I didn't think badly of you," I lied.

"It's over, and we don't need to mention him again," Marguerite said.

"I saw Monsieur Fontaine as I was coming home." And I told them what had passed, how he'd sworn he was innocent.

"Of course he'd say that," Marguerite snapped. "He's a good liar."

"I didn't understand what he was talking about…but he seemed to be telling the truth. He was desperately upset."

Marguerite gave a dismissive wave of her hand. "You're too innocent to know the difference."

"Perhaps he's been falsely accused." Catherine let out a dispirited sigh. "But it doesn't matter. This had to end. I'm sorry, Vivi, that you've seen me making such a fool of myself with a married man."

"It doesn't matter. I'm sorry for everyone." I hesitated, at a loss for what to say. "Will we still go to the ceremony?"

"Yes," Marguerite insisted, although Catherine looked doubtful. "We'll knock on your door when we're ready to leave."

I retreated across the hall to my room, shut the door, and threw myself across the bed, surprised by the tears that sprang from my eyes hot and fast—tears for Sylvie and all the women betrayed by selfish, heartless men. Monsieur Fontaine had used his good looks and charm to manipulate his wife and Catherine, and possibly the servant. Had he truly forced himself on a powerless young girl, assured that if she accused him of violating her, no one would believe her? The servant most likely needed the job to support her family and would not have been able to say no. I didn't want to believe it, but the accusation remained, a cloud of doubt soiling Monsieur Fontaine's name. I had no idea how to determine the truth.

I remembered Marie, who had arrived at the orphanage when barely fourteen. Maîtresse soon discovered she was pregnant, and the director had transferred her to a private home. During her short stay, she shared her story with some of the older girls, and we learned how babies are made. Her French father had lived with her mother for fifteen years, siring Marie and a younger sister, until one day he left without explanation for France. Her mother sent Marie to work for an older Frenchman, a friend of her father's, who soon demanded she come to his bed each night. Her mother appeared complicit in the arrangement, perhaps hoping the man would marry her daughter. When the French administration learned of her situation, they insisted the mother give her up to the orphanage.

All these stories circled back to my mother. Had my French father used her in this same, shameful way? I needed to discover the truth, even if I feared what I might learn.

Chapter 12

Catherine rapped on my door a few minutes before three. "Vivi, are you ready?" Her eyes were red and puffy, but she looked lovely in a simple dress of pale blue chiffon, her face powdered and her lips a ruby red.

"We should leave for the temple. And I'm treating you and Marguerite to dinner at the Cercle after the ceremony." She glanced at my rumpled skirt and blouse. "Why don't you put on your blue dress? We'll wait for you on the front porch."

I changed into my tired blue dress, the only outfit suitable for such an occasion, grateful to Mali for keeping it clean, mended, and pressed. I desperately needed something new, but I hesitated to spend any of the money from the Assistance Society before finding a job.

"Don't you look nice," Catherine said when I joined her and Marguerite. I forced a cheerful smile.

Marguerite crushed a cigarette in the ashtray and stood up. She wore a print dress of bright red roses with a skirt that swirled around her legs. I tried not to stare at the ruffled neckline, which plunged into a deep V, revealing a great deal of cleavage. It seemed inappropriate for visiting a Buddhist temple, but who was I to judge?

"Three single ladies out on the town." Marguerite raised an eyebrow. "Let's see what kind of trouble we can get into."

Catherine gave a harsh laugh. "I, for one, don't need any more trouble, thank you. And I think Charles might object to that plan."

Marguerite slid her arm through mine, steering me to the front gate. "Well, at least we can have fun."

Catherine flagged a horse-drawn carriage for the ride to the temple. As we turned down Avenue Lang Xang, the sun beat down from between scattered clouds, shrouding the afternoon in suffocating heat. The humidity clung to my skin, and sweat trickled down my back. Marguerite lifted her long locks off her neck and pinned them on top of her head.

"Have you ever been to Phra That Luang?" Catherine asked. I shook my head. "It's one of the most important temples in Laos, built over four hundred years ago, on the site of an early Hindu stupa."

"But it was destroyed by invading armies," Marguerite added, "and the colonial government tried to restore it in 1900, or thereabouts. The architect ruined the design, though, and the work was shoddy. Now the stupa is falling apart." She laughed. "Undaunted, the French government is going to try again."

The carriage turned into the *wat*'s main gate. The vast scale of the stupa was different from anything I'd seen before, with three progressively smaller tiers, like a wedding cake, which formed a bell-shaped top porting a needle-thin pinnacle. Up close, the temple was tired and worn with sagging parts, crumbling walls, and broken or missing adornments.

We joined a crowd of French and Lao guests gathered before an open-sided building adjacent to the stupa, where an altar held a large golden Buddha. Although we were standing in the stupa's shadow, the heat was overpowering, and many of the women waved fans back and forth. I recognized a few people from Catherine's party and smiled at them. But their eyes slid past me, as if I didn't exist. My breath caught in my throat as I caught sight of Madame Trembley of Chez Josephine and Monsieur Simon from the bookstore chatting only a few feet in front of me. I lowered my head, hoping they wouldn't notice me.

Marguerite nodded toward the three men standing next to the altar. "That's the new Resident Superior, Monsieur Chatêl, next to Prince Phetsarath and the head monk of the temple." A young monk came forward and lit candles and incense on the altar.

Near the front, a man turned and scanned the crowd. Bounmy Savang. His eyes landed on me, and he gave a muted smile with an almost imperceptible nod, before turning his attention to the front. My heart beat so fast that I felt faint in the steamy heat. Had he watched for me these past weeks, as I had searched for him?

The portly Resident Superior, wearing a white uniform covered with colorful ribbons and shiny medals, made a short speech lauding the generosity of the French government and the École Française d'Extrème Orient for restoring and preserving ancient Lao art and culture. He mopped his red face with a handkerchief, panting in the heat as he promised that the stupa would be rebuilt to its original glory, omitting any mention of the failed first attempt by the French. The audience applauded enthusiastically.

The next speaker, Prince Phetsarath, wore a silk cream-colored Mandarin jacket, white stockings, and a bright orange *salong*—a long piece of cloth wrapped around and through the legs, resembling knee-length baggy pants. In flawless French, he emphasized the profound importance of the Buddhist temple and stupa both historically and culturally to the Lao people and expressed his gratitude for the French contribution.

The head monk, wrapped in his saffron robe, bowed to the Resident Superior and Prince Phetsarath, then knelt before the altar and began chanting a blessing. He continued for some time as people fanned themselves and rocked from one foot to the other. The monk finally stood and lifted a silver bowl and a brush made of bamboo. He dipped the brush in the bowl and sprinkled water on the Resident Superior and Prince Phetsarath, then stepped down the stairs and anointed the gathered crowd, all the while chanting.

Marguerite whispered, "He's blessing everyone with sacred water."

When the formalities were over, Monsieur Chatêl and Prince Phetsarath mingled with the crowd, greeting guests. Catherine and Marguerite chatted with friends. No one spoke to me or acknowledged my presence.

Madame Trembley nodded her head toward me, speaking to the woman next to her in a voice loud enough for many of her words to reach me. "A *métisse*, naturally…doesn't belong…terribly rude… disgusting." I backed away, thankful that at least Monsieur Simon was no longer there.

Director Bernard appeared out of nowhere, marching toward me. I'd seen him at Mass the Sunday before, guarding the orphanage girls to make sure I could do nothing more than wave to Bridgette and the others. Now, he brushed past me, purposely knocking into my shoulder, before stopping. "I've heard stories, Geneviève. You're already making quite a reputation for yourself," he murmured. "Not surprising given your character." He continued on and shook hands with a man, exchanging pleasantries in his unctuous manner. I clenched my hands, consumed with anger.

Up front, Monsieur Savang was speaking with another Lao man who bore a close resemblance to him. Like Prince Phetsarath, the two were dressed in silk jackets and brightly colored *salongs*, reminding me of drawings in a picture book, like fairytale characters come to life. Monsieur Savang excused himself and came to my side.

"Mademoiselle Dubois, I was hoping to see you here. It's a very special occasion."

"I, I'm glad to see you…as well." I stumbled over my words, mortified that my dress was soaked in sweat and sticking to my body.

He nodded toward Catherine. "Is that the teacher you're living with?"

"Yes, Catherine… I mean, Mademoiselle Courbet. She invited me to attend."

"I hope you enjoy your day." He nodded. "Please excuse me, but duty calls." He left me feeling like an abandoned child, once more conspicuously alone.

A few minutes later, Marguerite and Catherine collected me, and we headed for our carriage.

"Let's go to Pierre's for a drink," Marguerite suggested. "It's too early for the Cercle."

"Excellent idea," Catherine agreed.

"Should I come?" I asked.

"Of course," Marguerite said. "You must try a Singapore Sling, one of life's great pleasures in the tropics."

"I've never been out at night before," I confessed. "Or had dinner in a nice restaurant."

"You poor dear, so sheltered and innocent," Marguerite said. "We'll introduce you to Vientiane's exciting nightlife."

I stole a last glance at Monsieur Savang as he conversed with the Resident Superior. His presence at the ceremony with Prince Phetsarath surely meant he was well connected. Our brief exchange had disappointed me, but it was ridiculous to expect he'd be interested in someone like me. I sighed and turned my thoughts to the evening ahead.

The carriage dropped us at Pierre's Bar and Café, and we settled inside, under one of the big fans swaying overhead. I hoped the faint breeze would help dry my damp dress. Marguerite waved to friends at another table.

"That's the owner, Pierre Lemont." Catherine nodded toward a burly man with a scruffy beard and thinning gray hair. "He came to Laos five years ago searching for gold, like so many men drawn by newspaper stories claiming treasures were available for the taking. The reality turns out to be quite different, of course. When Monsieur Lemont failed to find riches, he opened the bar."

"A very happy ending for the French community," Marguerite added.

Pierre appeared beside us, and his face lit up. "Mademoiselles, what a treat to see you. And who is your lovely young friend?"

"This is Mademoiselle Dubois. She's staying with me for the moment," Catherine said. "Vivi, Monsieur Lemont."

He bowed. "It's an honor. Please call me Pierre, my *chérie*, as everyone does."

"We'll have three Singapore Slings," Catherine said, "only light on the alcohol for our friend. She's not accustomed to drinking."

Marguerite scoffed, "I'm sure she can handle one drink."

After the drinks arrived, Marguerite held up her glass. "*Santé!* May we all find a decent man one day. With twice as many French men as women living here, how can it be so difficult?" Catherine smiled sadly as we clinked our glasses.

A first sip revealed sweet fruit flavors, a touch of sour, and a bitter aftertaste that lingered on the back of my tongue. The cool potion slid easily down my throat. "It's so good. What's in it?"

"Besides a lot of gin, there is pineapple juice, grenadine, cherry liquor, and I can't remember the rest." Marguerite smiled. "Pierre boasts he adds a secret ingredient that makes his the best anywhere."

"Be careful, Vivi, it's very potent." Catherine rested her chin on her hand, looking gloomy. "What a shame alcohol leads people to do such terrible things."

"Have you heard from your brother?" Marguerite asked Catherine. "A wire arrived yesterday at work from an officer headed to Vientiane. His ship docked in Singapore Wednesday, and I wondered if Julian might be on the same boat."

Catherine's expression brightened. "I expect to hear from him any moment. What a relief it will be to have him safely home again. Maybe Julian can protect me from bad influences."

Marguerite smirked. "Not likely."

I glanced outside to the patio, and the air fled from my lungs. Monsieur Fontaine veered toward us across the terrace. His normally slicked-back hair hung down over his forehead, and his clothes looked even worse than they had that morning. He tripped over a chair, nearly falling, but the man at the next table caught him.

Marguerite turned toward the commotion. "Oh, good God. It's the bastard himself."

Monsieur Fontaine lunged in our direction. "Catherine, the woooman of my dreams."

The bar grew quiet as others watched the unfolding drama.

Catherine turned deathly pale, her eyes fixed on his approach. "Marguerite, do something!"

Stopping in front of our table, his gaze fell on me. He struggled to stand up straight, weaving back and forth. "Did your little orphan tell you I'm innocent?"

Marguerite signaled to Pierre. "Marcel, go away," she hissed. "Catherine doesn't want to talk to you."

"I didn't do anything, Catherine. You have to believe me," he pleaded.

Catherine stood. "Get out of here. You're nothing but a liar and a drunk."

Pierre and the friend who had caught his fall dragged him away.

"I love you, Catherine, more than anything," he called over his shoulder. The friend led him down the street.

Catherine sank into her chair, putting her head in her hands. "I'm mortified."

"No one cares," Marguerite insisted. "They all know what an ass he is." The other patrons resumed their conversations as if nothing had happened. "And they can all go to hell anyway," she added.

"Vivi, I'm sorry to drag you into this," Catherine said, looking up at me with tears in her eyes. I stared at her, unsure what to say to comfort her.

"Well, now he's done something inexcusable. It's over," Marguerite said.

"I've been such a fool." Catherine grabbed a cigarette and lit it. "Some role model."

We sat quietly, sipping the last of our drinks until Marguerite waved to Pierre and ordered another round.

"Only pineapple juice for Mademoiselle Dubois," Catherine said.

The alcohol had made me woozy, and everything around us appeared like a blurry photograph. I wanted to let my mind drift far from the unhappiness of the day. Was this what people hoped to accomplish by drinking? To disappear from reality?

Marguerite cocked her head to one side with an inquisitive look. "Who was that young Lao man you spoke with at the ceremony?"

I ran my finger over the beads of condensation on my glass, surprised she had noticed. "His name is Bounmy Savang. I met him at Wat Sisaket one afternoon." I looked up. "He works with Prince Phetsarath."

"Have you seen him since?" Catherine asked, sounding worried.

"No," I said quickly. "But he gave me his card and said to call if I was still looking for employment. He offered to introduce me to his cousin, Kham Savang, who owns River Transport and might have a job opening."

"*Prince* Kham Savang," Marguerite said, "which means Bounmy Savang is a prince as well, part of the royal family of Luang Prabang."

My droopy eyes popped open.

"The royal family is quite large because the men have multiple wives and concubines, which means lots of children. King Sisavong Vong has at least a dozen wives." Marguerite winked at me. "That must keep him busy at night."

"Marguerite! Don't embarrass poor Vivi," Catherine chided.

"She's a big girl." Marguerite lit a cigarette. "Anyway, the royal court is a complicated place. The king, his wives, and their children make up the Main Palace. Then there's the Front Palace, with the king's siblings and cousins, who run the kingdom in cooperation with the French colonial government. The lesser royalty and aristocrats, scholars and such, are called the Back Palace." She shrugged. "No telling where your acquaintance fits into the giant family tree. Anyway, the government uses River Transport all the time, so perhaps you should contact your friend."

"Is that really wise?" Catherine asked. "You wouldn't want him to get the wrong impression."

"You worry too much." Marguerite clucked her tongue. "River Transport would be an acceptable place to work."

"Make it clear from the start that you're only interested in a job," Catherine insisted.

Excitement rushed through me at the thought of calling Bounmy. "I'll contact him next week."

Catherine finished the last of her second drink and pushed the glass away. "Perhaps we should take a walk before going to the club. If I have another drink, someone will have to carry me home." She stood and smoothed her dress as Marguerite left money for the bill.

"My head's a little foggy," I admitted.

Catherine put her arm through mine. "No more drinks for you tonight. We are corrupting you, and that simply won't do."

"Better to teach her to recognize her limits," Marguerite said, pulling the pins out of her hair and letting her red waves cascade down her back. "Although I suppose we should set a good example. But that's no fun."

Despite a half-hour stroll along the riverfront, we were one of the first parties seated in the dining room at the Cercle. Housed in a buff-colored building near the river, the club provided French *colons* and other Occidentals a place to gather, play tennis, or relax in the lounge with French newspapers, magazines, and games of chess or cards. They drank at the bar and ate French meals in the restaurant upstairs, with its dance floor and tables set with white linens, fine china, crystal glasses, and a bevy of waiters attending to their every need. The moment we crossed through the lounge, curious eyes turned on me—a half-breed tagging along with two of their own.

By the time our entrées arrived, the dining room was nearly full of men and women dressed in evening wear, as if eating in an exclusive restaurant in Paris. But the thrill of coming to this sacred haven quickly dissipated for me. I felt completely out of place, unsure how to act or what to say in such a rarefied setting, trapped among

French patrons looking down their noses at me.

We nibbled our meals, pretending to enjoy them, but a somber haze of despair cloaked our table. Catherine's spirits seemed to sink lower with each passing minute, while Marguerite struggled to keep up a conversation, offering tidbits of gossip from her office.

"Oh look," she said, "there's the new Resident Superior with Prince Phetsarath and his young brother Prince Souvanna."

I turned my gaze to the table, hoping Bounmy might be among the party, but he was nowhere to be seen.

"Everyone is talking about Prince Souvanna," Marguerite said, lowering her voice. "Apparently, he refused to marry the Lao princess the king selected for him because he wants to marry for love. He's currently courting a *métisse* named Aline Allard. Word is, the prince and Aline are very much in love, but the king forbids royal family members from marrying anyone French, which includes the *métis*, since you're half French."

"What a romantic story," I said, thinking it sounded like something in a Jane Austen novel.

Marguerite shrugged her shoulders. "It's not clear if there will be a happy ending or not."

"Are there ever any happy endings?" Catherine asked, pushing her hair back from her face. "I'm sorry to be so glum, ladies." Yet another sad sigh escaped her lips. "And I was supposed to be cheering *you* up, Marguerite."

"We understand." Marguerite patted Catherine's arm.

"I want to go home." Catherine's eyes brimmed with tears. "I can't stand being around these people another minute. They all know what's happened and that I'm part of the story."

Our big night out ended at a quarter to eight, before the dancing had even begun, but I was relieved to escape and return home where I could breathe freely once more. The day had overwhelmed me: the discovery of Sylvie's hopeless situation, the allegations against Monsieur Fontaine and Catherine's heartbreak, and my disappointing exchange with Monsieur Savang. In the past two weeks, a constant stream of unsettling situations had confronted me, things I'd never imagined possible when Bridgette and I had daydreamed of an exciting, rosy future outside the orphanage.

I climbed into bed with pen and paper ready to create an alternative story for Bridgette, one that would spare her the sadness enveloping me. My letters to her omitted all my troubles and reported only happy news and funny anecdotes. As long as she remained in the orphanage, I would shield her from the reality.

Chapter 13

"How are you feeling today?" I asked Catherine as we ate breakfast the next morning. She'd been very quiet, hardly touching her pastry while drinking cup after cup of coffee and smoking nonstop. Her swollen, red-rimmed eyes told of a night of tears and little sleep.

She gazed out into the garden. "Depressed, angry—mostly at myself. I still can't believe Marcel would do something so awful. He may drink too much, but he's not like that." She gave a sad half-smile. "I'll recover eventually."

"I wish I could help."

"I'd prefer not to talk about it anymore."

I bit my lower lip, wondering how to broach the subject of Sylvie, which weighed on my mind. "Did you know Sylvie Bisset? She left the orphanage two years ago," I said at last.

"I met her briefly when I started working there."

"She's the friend I went to see yesterday." I detailed what I'd discovered of Sylvie's dismal circumstances working as a prostitute.

She frowned. "I'd heard rumors."

"How could this happen?"

Catherine sipped her coffee, considering her response. "Perhaps she started dating a man and became his mistress, then he abandoned her." Her voice was strained. "Men take advantage of young girls, particularly *métisses*, who are struggling on their own without family, trapped by society's prejudices. Unfortunately, she's not the only one to end up like this. It makes me terribly angry."

"But why didn't Maîtresse help? How could she let this happen?" Filled with indignation, I searched for someone to blame.

"I know she tried, as she truly cares for you girls, despite her stern manner." Catherine sighed. "This is why I offered to rent you a room. You are such a dear person, and I couldn't bear to see you subjected to the difficulties faced by Sylvie and others like her."

"I don't understand how she could lower herself to this point."

"It's hard to know what one might do when truly desperate, Vivi."

I sat back in my chair. "I suggested she could live with Bridgette and me when we get a place, but she acted as if she was fine, said she's making good money. She told me to leave her alone, that she doesn't need my pity."

"I'm sure she was humiliated to have you find her like that."

"I want to help." I looked up, full of anguish. "What can I do?"

"Allow her some time. Maybe when Bridgette is free, the two of you could talk with her again and convince her to try a different path."

"This will devastate Bridgette. I won't tell her now." A puff of air escaped my lips. "Now I understand why Maîtresse told me to stay away from Sylvie." Guilt crept in as I realized once more how fortunate I was to have Catherine's support and guidance to ease my transition to a life on my own.

Catherine reached over and touched my arm. "Life is terribly unfair, chèrie. I'm sorry I don't have any easy solutions."

"Isn't there anyone to stand up for these girls? It's bad enough we're taken from our mothers, often by force, and raised in an orphanage."

"I agree, the lack of assistance and concern is appalling."

My mind searched for ways to do something, but what influence or skills did I have to right these situations? Then it struck me, and I sat up, thrilled by the thought. "When I go to university in a year or two, I could study law and become an advocate to fight this unjust system. I could represent mothers trying to keep their métis children and aid those coming out of the orphanages."

"Oh, Vivi," Catherine said, a smile lighting up her face. "What an excellent ambition. You'd be perfect. I must warn you, women still face a great deal of discrimination, both getting into law school and practicing after. But I have faith in your abilities."

A young Lao boy appeared at the gate and surprised us by scurrying up the garden path. He bowed deeply in a *nop*, then handed an envelope to Catherine, saying something in Lao I couldn't catch.

Catherine handed it to me. "It's for you. He was told to wait for your answer."

Mademoiselle Dubois was written in beautiful, fine strokes of black ink on thick, cream-colored linen paper. Even so, the thought crossed my mind that it might be an error. Surely the message was intended for someone else, someone grander than me. My heart skipped a beat—perhaps it was an answer to one of my inquiries about my family? But those would come by mail.

Catherine insisted the boy sit on the steps out of the sun to await my response, and Mali brought him a glass of water.

I broke the wax seal and lifted out the note.

Chère Mademoiselle Dubois,

How nice to see you at Wat Pha That Luang yesterday. I apologize for not being able to speak with you longer, but I had official duties to fulfill. I have thought of you often since we met at Wat Sisaket, but I didn't know how to reach you. Yesterday a French acquaintance was able to give me Mademoiselle Courbet's address.

I hope you will not find me too forward, but I would enjoy seeing you again and hearing how your search for work is progressing. Did you take the job as an au pair? Would you meet me tomorrow in the afternoon for a walk and tea? Please invite Mademoiselle Courbet to accompany us if you would feel more comfortable.

I know this is rather short notice, so advise me if there is a more convenient date and time, perhaps the following week. Please return your response with the boy.

With best regards,
Bounmy Savang

I met Catherine's curious gaze and read the note aloud to her. "Would you like to see him?"

"Yes. He's very nice. And he might be helpful in finding a job."

She paused a moment, her expression dubious. "I suppose it would be acceptable if we invited him here for tea tomorrow. That way I can be present, but also give you some time with him."

"Are you sure?" I asked, unable to hide my excitement.

"I'll ask Marguerite to join us." She chuckled. "She keeps the conversation lively and is excellent at prying information out of people."

"Oh, thank you."

Catherine directed me to the top drawer of the escritoire in the library for paper and pen. The boy received my carefully composed invitation with more bows and disappeared out the front gate, taking with him my blossoming hopes.

I turned to Catherine. "I want to use a little of the Assistance Society money to buy a new dress. Everything I own is worn and ugly. Would you help?"

"Of course. You desperately need a new outfit." She gave me a sly smile. "How perfect for your tea with Monsieur Savang."

"I want to look my best." I shrugged with pleasure. "And I need something nice for job interviews."

She thought for a moment. "Chez Josephine is out of the question."

"That's the last place I will spend my money," I agreed.

"Let's start at À La Mode, as Madame Dupont carries some modestly priced items. If that fails, there's always Wong's Mercantile. When you have more time, I know a wonderful Lao seamstress who charges practically nothing and can make anything you want."

"It would be heaven to have a new skirt and blouse."

"Once you find employment, you'll feel more comfortable spending your savings."

She placed her coffee cup back on the tray and paused. "Vivi, I want to say a word about Monsieur Savang. You hardly know him, of course, but do be careful. If he is a royal prince, you should not expect too much."

"What do you mean?"

"Depending on his family's position in the royal court, he may not have a great deal of choice about his future and the women he sees."

I found her words puzzling. "Are you thinking of the story Marguerite told about Prince Souvanna last night?"

"Exactly. You're too young to be thinking of marriage—you've never even been on a date, for heaven's sake—but keep in mind that it's unlikely there would be any future with the prince." She picked at the crimson polish on her nails. "And you must be careful being seen in public with him. People always assume the worst and love to gossip."

"Whatever would they think?"

Catherine cleared her throat. "They might assume Monsieur Savang has taken you as his mistress."

I sat up, shocked at the notion. "But why?"

"As we talked about earlier, many *métisses* without someone to guide them get involved in inappropriate relationships with men. You can see where it led Sylvie." She crossed her legs. "I'm sorry to always sound so negative, but it's not a fair world, particularly for the *métis*."

I simply nodded, hoping Catherine didn't believe I could ever fall so low. "I'll be careful."

Catherine and I both bought dresses at À La Mode under the attentive care of Madame Dupont. We posed in front of the mirrors and giggled as we tried on numerous styles and colors. It made me happy to see Catherine's mood lighten, momentarily distracted from her troubles.

My new dress was the loveliest thing I'd ever owned, made of a soft crêpe in the brilliant green of a newly sprouted rice field. A cream-colored sash encircled the waist above a skirt that flared out into gentle folds. The bodice was cut in a modest boatneck with cap sleeves. When I twirled before the mirror, it sounded like a breeze rustling the fronds of a palm tree. It would be my talisman, a harbinger of good luck.

After our purchases, Catherine treated me to tea and chocolate éclairs at Estelle's Patisserie. We chatted about fashions and what jewelry would go well with our new purchases. This was what I had always imagined of an older sister, a friend and confidante to guide me through life's maze.

When we returned home, a disappointed sigh escaped my lips: once again there was nothing for me in the mail tray. I could hardly stand the wait.

I joined Mali in the kitchen, where she welcomed me with a big smile and asked if I'd help make prawns with coconut milk for dinner. I'd begun assisting her whenever possible, asking questions and writing down instructions. She'd taught me how to chop vegetables, select seasonings, and steam rice, while making me repeat the Lao words for different ingredients.

My enthusiasm bubbled over as I told her about our shopping excursion and described my new dress. "I'll model it for you later."

"It's nice to see you so happy, Mademoiselle Vivi. And I'm sure it cheered up Mademoiselle Catherine." We would never have betrayed Catherine's trust by discussing her situation, but I knew Mali was well aware of what had gone on with Monsieur Fontaine. She had told me that most Lao servants who worked for the French were connected through family or friends, and they all gossiped and shared stories. There were no secrets.

I glanced over at Mali. "Did Catherine tell you we have a guest coming for tea tomorrow?"

"Oh yes." She raised an eyebrow. "I understand a special young man is calling on you. I promise you a nice tea."

"If only my friend Bridgette could be with us," I said, thinking of her continued incarceration. But it was only temporary and held no comparison to Sylvie's terrible existence, reduced to the basest form of living.

"Bridgette will be with you soon," Mali said.

"It's not that." I couldn't help myself from sharing Sylvie's story. "I feel so awful for her and all the *métisses* who end up this way. If only I could help."

Mali remained silent for some time. "There may be little you can do, especially if she doesn't want to change." She glanced over at me. "This may be Sylvie's destiny, her karma for actions in a previous life. You can only hope she reaches a higher level of understanding that alters her future, if not now, then in the next life."

"I tried to tell her she doesn't have to do this," I said. "But she got angry and slammed her door in my face."

"I know you mean well, but she must reach this awareness on her own."

I was grateful for Mali's calm and easy presence, her willingness to listen without judging and to offer wise advice. If she experienced hardships from being away from her family or had other problems, she never complained. I wanted to be like her, unruffled and at peace with whatever unfolded.

Mali patted my arm. "Why don't you come with me to the temple tonight? We'll pray for Sylvie to be enlightened and see a better path."

"Is it allowed?" I asked, surprised. "Will my prayers be heard, even though I was raised Catholic?"

"Of course. If your heart is pure, all things are possible."

After dinner, we walked three blocks to the temple where the monks chanted their evening prayers. "They're reciting part of the Pali Canon, the teachings of Buddha, to assist in their meditation," Mali explained.

When the monks had finished and retired to their living quarters, we took off our shoes and entered the *wat*. We lit incense sticks and placed them in the sand-filled brass urn. I followed Mali's lead, kneeling down and sitting back on my legs, putting my hands together before my chest and bowing my head. Three times we leaned forward to touch the ground then sat back again. The peace and quiet of the temple soothed me as I stared at the benign face of Buddha, silently praying that Sylvie would find the strength and will to change her life, to purify her thoughts and actions. Then I prayed that the truth about my family would soon be revealed. I was uncertain if a greater power was truly listening to me, but the possibility eased my troubled heart.

Chapter 14

Marguerite showed up fifteen minutes early for the tea, wearing an uncharacteristically staid navy skirt and white blouse. She administered her usual kisses before spinning me around to examine my new dress. "Don't you look glamorous!"

"It suits her perfectly," Catherine said. "Not too dressy for day-time, but it will work for evenings with the right jewelry."

Marguerite chucked me under the chin. "How could any young man resist this ravishing beauty?"

"Don't get carried away," Catherine said firmly. "She's too young to get involved with anyone."

"But not too young to have admirers and a bit of fun," Marguerite protested.

Marguerite chuckled as I continually jumped up to peer out the front window at the slightest sound. "The Lao have a more relaxed sense of time, Vivi," she said at last. "They are often quite late to appointments. It drove the last Resident Superior wild, as he was a very punctual man."

Bounmy knocked on the door at five minutes past four, and I thought his relative promptness a good beginning. He wore a European suit of gray linen, a starched white shirt, and a sky-blue silk tie, appearing cool despite the afternoon heat. When he removed his straw boater, his thick dark hair was parted on one side and neatly combed in place with hair cream.

I introduced Catherine and Marguerite in a voice that sounded unnaturally high to my ears. He smiled, revealing his endearing dimples, and shook hands, murmuring in formal, slightly stilted French how delighted he was to meet them. We settled in the front salon as the fans whirled overhead.

Bounmy studied the room. "Your home is beautiful," he remarked, perched on the edge of the settee, his back rigid, as if ready to bolt at any moment.

"Thank you," Catherine said. "My parents built it when my father was first posted here with the government."

Mali wheeled in the trolley with the best china teapot and cups, filled with platters of finger sandwiches and sliced mango, as well as small cakes and lemon tarts from Estelle's Patisserie.

"Mademoiselle Dubois says you recently moved to Vientiane, Monsieur Savang," Catherine said. "How do you like it here?"

"I'm enjoying exploring the area and local temples," he answered, crossing his legs and resting his clasped hands on his knee. "I was only here once before, as a young child."

"You work in the government administration, I understand," Marguerite said.

"Yes, with Prince Phetsarath. I'm trying to develop opportunities for foreign trade." He smiled ruefully. "Not an easy task given the state of the world economy at the moment."

Mali passed cups of tea around. I noticed Bounmy's cup rattle in the saucer as he set it down. Was he as nervous as I was?

Marguerite sat forward, plucking a lemon tart from the platter. "I first met Prince Phetsarath while he was collaborating with the Resident Superior on creating the School of Law and Administration for Lao students."

"The prince is anxious to see more Lao trained for civil service positions, reducing the need to bring additional Annamese workers here," Bounmy said, wearing a neutral expression, but I detected a touch of bitterness in his voice. "The latest census revealed there are more Annamese than Lao living in Vientiane at present." He paused a moment. "It seems unfortunate."

I remembered what Marguerite had told me about the government importing hundreds of Annamese to fill jobs because Lao workers were not well educated and lacked the same work ethic. I admired Bounmy for speaking out, especially given Marguerite's position with the Resident Superior.

Marguerite pushed her hair behind one ear. "Understandably, it has caused concern among the Lao."

Catherine offered sandwiches to Bounmy. "As a teacher, I believe it's essential the colonial government provide better educational opportunities for the Lao. It's been sorely lacking, particularly for girls."

Bounmy nodded slowly. "There should be at least *one* public *lycée* in Laos. Otherwise, how will the Lao ever progress?"

Anger welled inside me again for this injustice inflicted by the French. The colonial government always arranged things to suit their needs rather than those of the Lao people.

"Monsieur Savang returned recently from school in Paris," I said after an awkward silence.

Catherine smiled. "How long were you there?"

Bounmy's voice became more animated. "I spent a year at the Lycée Montaigne, finishing my baccalauréat and improving my French, then attended the École Coloniale for three years, earning an administrative certificate." He paused. "My father studied in Paris as a young man and was keen for me to do the same."

"What does your father do?" Marguerite asked.

I winced. Surely Bounmy found their endless questions intrusive, like an interrogation of a suspected criminal.

"My father is Minister of the Treasury for the Kingdom of Luang Prabang," he responded, as casually as if saying his father was a farmer in a small village.

Catherine's head jerked up. "Then we should be addressing you as Prince Savang."

He waved a hand in a dismissive gesture. "I prefer to leave my title for official business and court ceremonies."

My heart sank. Bounmy was truly a prince, his father a key advisor to the king, part of the Front Palace that Marguerite had described. Our worlds could not be any farther removed from each other. Why would he take an interest in me?

"And how did you find Paris?" Catherine asked, sipping her tea.

His serious, intent face transformed into a dreamy expression, a smile playing at the corner of his lips. "Such a beautiful city. I had trouble concentrating on my studies with all the wonderful things to see and do. I'm afraid Laos feels rather small to me now."

Marguerite shrugged. "Laos has its charms."

We nibbled sandwiches and sweets, politely commenting on the ceremony at Wat Pha That Luang and the lack of respite from the hot weather and heavy rainstorms. As if on command, a crack of thunder permeated the room and a short deluge drenched the house and terrain outside, making us giggle at the coincidence.

When the conversation lagged again, Bounmy turned to me. "Did you take that position with the French family looking after the children?"

"No, I'm still searching for work." I was too embarrassed to admit how humiliating my job hunt had proven.

Marguerite stood up unexpectedly. "I sorry to be so abrupt, but would you please excuse us, Monsieur Savang? I have something urgent to discuss with Mademoiselle Courbet."

Catherine's mouth gaped open. "But surely it can wait."

Marguerite turned to me. "The garden will be lovely and cool after the shower. Why don't you take your guest for a stroll?"

Catherine gave in reluctantly. "We'll be in the library if you need us."

Bounmy jumped up to shake hands with Marguerite and Catherine, appearing perplexed by their sudden departure. "Thank you for the nice afternoon. It's a great pleasure to meet you both."

I led Bounmy to the French doors at the end of the hallway leading into the lush garden. It amazed me how the extravagant plants and flowers flourished despite the extreme heat, with only unpredictable rains to replenish them. We strolled across the bridge, stopping at the top for a moment to watch the koi fish dart back and forth from shade to sunlight, their brilliant orange and red scales shimmering underwater. I searched for a way to describe my recent job interviews without sounding pathetic but came up short. No one at the orphanage had ever called me quiet or shy, yet somehow this man rendered me nearly mute.

"I hope I didn't say something to offend Mademoiselles Vanier and Courbet," Bounmy said at last, sticking his hands in his trouser pockets.

"Not at all. I believe Marguerite wanted to give us some time alone to talk." We continued across the bridge to the bench under the banyan tree where I wiped away the rain.

"Tell me of the jobs you've applied for, Mademoiselle Dubois."

I straightened my shoulders. "I've interviewed at a number of different businesses, but no one wants to hire someone so young and inexperienced." I didn't add *and métis*. "I'm good with numbers and earned top scores in mathematics at school, but it doesn't seem to be enough."

"Those are important skills. What about trying the elementary schools? There's a great need for well-educated teachers."

I sighed. "I was promised a teaching assistant position, but…it's a long story."

He turned his head to one side. "Please tell me."

"Where should I start?" I described growing up in the orphanage, wondering where I had come from, who my parents were. My words tumbled out, steeped in the unhappiness of my confusing childhood. "I want to know the truth." I hesitated, staring at my hands resting in my lap.

He leaned in, as if needing to better hear me. "Continue."

I told him everything: about Director Bernard hiding the truth about my twin in Pakse; how he made sure the offer for the teaching assistant position was withdrawn; how I would be lost if it were not for Catherine. As I spoke, I looked into his dark, attentive eyes, noticing tiny gold specks in his left eye for the first time. And, although I strained to hold tears back, they escaped down my cheeks, a small sob erupting.

Bounmy started. "How could anyone be so cruel?" He handed me his handkerchief. "I'm so sorry." His tender gaze made me want to lay my head on his shoulder to take comfort. "Your story is very disturbing," he continued, "but I doubt the government will intervene. Let me talk with Prince Phetsarath about this. He carries a great deal of weight in this town."

"I don't want to trouble you." I dabbed at my tears. "I wrote my brother in Pakse right away and the Assistance Society in Luang Prabang about my parents. I hope to hear back soon."

"I'm not sure how to help, but if there is anything…please ask." A large blue butterfly hovered near us before changing course and landing on a purple bloom. "The least I can do is assist you in finding employment. This evening I'll call my cousin Kham Savang, who I mentioned before. I feel sure he can find a position for you."

"Thank you." I drew in a ragged breath. "You must find me pitiful."

"Not in the least. You've been treated very unfairly," he said.

I managed a small smile. "Tell me more about Paris. My friend Bridgette and I hope to go to university there one day."

"You would love it." His gaze drifted out over the garden, and his face relaxed, as if he were recalling a pleasant dream. "I shared an apartment with four cousins. The youngest didn't take his studies seriously and was sent home after failing half his courses, so the rest of us learned from his mistake and worked very hard. The professors opened my eyes to the many wonders of the world—miraculous places and events I'd never heard of before. I studied in cafés, drinking endless cups of coffee, or sometimes in the parks. My cousins and I wandered in search of inexpensive restaurants, trying different kinds of food, or we went to the cinema and musical concerts. On my one free day each week I wandered through museums, studying art." He smiled. "You can imagine how difficult it was to stay focused on lessons."

"What was your favorite place?"

He pursed his lips for a moment. "Hmm, impossible to choose. The Louvre is a remarkable museum with paintings and sculptures that amaze and inspire. And I loved sitting in the Luxembourg Gardens—right across the street from the École Coloniale—watching the world go by as I studied."

"And the Parisians, were they nice?"

He chuckled softly. "They regarded us as a novelty, rather like a strange species escaped from the zoo. Many stared at us without the least hesitation." His expression turned somber. "Some people were friendly, but many made impolite remarks about the color of our skin or our oriental features. They were incredulous upon discovering we spoke French and understood their comments." He smoothed the top of his hair, which had begun to break free of the hair cream and fall over his brow. "Once a little girl asked me how I could see anything when my eyes were such tiny slits."

"How awful. What did you do?"

"I found it best to ignore these things." He gave a wry smile. "It was a humbling experience after growing up in the royal court, spoiled, and being told that I'm superior to others. It's a shame— most people in France have never heard of Laos and have no idea where it is."

"That's so sad…and unfair."

"Have you heard about the International Colonial Exposition that opened this week in Paris?" he asked. I shook my head. "It's meant to inform the public about colonies around the world, not only those of France but other European nations and the United States. I was sorry to miss it and not see how the Indochine colonies are portrayed. Prince Phetsarath helped organize displays on Laos."

"It strikes me as terribly wrong that the people and cultures of these colonies are being turned into entertainment, exhibits in a museum."

"I agree. But at least the Occidentals will know we exist and hopefully better appreciate our people."

"Would you go back to Paris?" I asked.

"I'd like to one day." His sparkling eyes met mine. "If I have the proper traveling companion."

Chapter 15

I stood in front of Catherine and Mali for inspection on Monday morning, once more in my tired blue dress. Mali told me she had prayed at the temple earlier to bring me good luck at my job interview.

Bounmy had sent a note the evening before, saying he would come to escort me to meet his cousin at eleven o'clock.

"Are you sure I shouldn't wear my new dress?" I asked for the second time.

Catherine tucked a stray wisp of hair behind my ear. "I think it's too much for this type of business. You look lovely and professional in this."

"I'm so nervous."

"You are a special person, Mademoiselle Vivi," Mali said. "They would be wise to hire you."

Catherine pulled a piece of lint from my sleeve, appearing as unsettled about the interview as I was. "You are fortunate to have a friend like Prince Savang, but be careful about the circumstances of the job."

I wasn't sure exactly what she meant, but before I could ask, I caught sight of Bounmy coming up the path. "Wish me luck."

Catherine gave me a quick hug. "We'll have a grand celebration tonight with Julian." A wire from her brother had arrived late Sunday, informing her he should reach Vientiane the next day by early afternoon. She and Mali had risen at dawn to clean house, arrange his room, and plan a special meal.

Bounmy bowed and greeted Catherine, then turned to me. "Shall we go?" A *pousse-pousse*, a two-wheeled rickshaw, waited outside. "It's not far, but I didn't want you to get too warm or dusty."

"How thoughtful," I said. "Thank you."

We squeezed into the seat, barely large enough for two people. The Lao porter, slightly built and little more than skin and bones, strained to drag our weight down the street. As we bounced along, I couldn't avoid sliding into Bounmy, no matter how hard I tried to lean away. He smelled of sandalwood and coconut, and the warmth of his taut muscles touching my arms and legs set my heart galloping. I'd never been in such close proximity to a man before, and I had to concentrate to keep my breathing even.

Sleep had come in short fits the night before, as I woke numerous times and relived the afternoon with Bounmy and every word he had spoken. His kind eyes and concern for my problems had eased any doubts about his intentions. I wasn't sure why he'd taken such an interest in me, but my instincts told me he could be trusted, even if Catherine remained more circumspect.

Bounmy smiled. "Don't be nervous. Let me tell you a little about River Transport. My cousin Kham took over the business when his father died last year and is still learning how things work. He could benefit from someone giving him a fresh perspective on the operations. The office is such a mess, I don't know how they can function."

Hopefully his cousin would give me a chance despite my age and inexperience. "How many people work for him?"

"There are two accountants and a warehouse supervisor, and they hire day laborers to load and unload shipments. It's the biggest transport company along the Mekong, as almost all foreign goods flow into Laos through Bangkok to Vientiane, then up or down the river. He has smaller offices in Luang Prabang, Savannakhet, and Pakse as well."

This piqued my interest. Perhaps the job would provide a way for me to travel in search of my family—assuming, of course, I received information on my brother's whereabouts and answers about my parents from the Assistance Society. I planned to send a second set of letters, if nothing arrived soon.

"It's so kind of you to arrange this and bring me today."

He shook his head. "It's no trouble."

We reached Quai Francis Garnier and turned left, passing a tiny woman in a cone-shaped bamboo hat, who carried huge baskets of daikon hanging from a pole balanced across her frail shoulders. A bicycle raced past in a death-defying balancing act, loaded with three huge bags of rice tied across the back fender. I still marveled at the hard labor performed by Lao workers each day, the constant effort of families to sustain their tenuous lives. Perhaps I appeared privileged to them, dressed in nice clothes and riding in a *pousse-pousse* with an aristocratic man. But my existence felt as precarious as theirs in many ways. I shivered to think how quickly my fortunes could turn.

When we arrived at River Transport, there were two longboats towing a large raft, which had moored along the riverbank. The vessels sat low in the water, piled with wooden crates and hemp sacks. An army of scrawny men, wearing nothing more than loose pants, hauled bundles nearly twice their size up the steep bamboo ramp and into the warehouse.

Bounmy led me into a cramped two-room office connected to the warehouse. Two men sat at their desks, which were covered with stacks of paper, poring over ledgers. Piles of documents and folders covered the furniture and floor. Upon seeing Bounmy, the men jumped up with a *nop*. "*Sabaidee, sabaidee*," they murmured.

A man emerged from the second room, and Bounmy introduced me to his cousin Prince Kham Savang. Kham's eyes traveled up and down my body until I wanted to sink into the floorboards.

There was little family resemblance between the cousins. While Bounmy was tall and thin, with well-proportioned, refined features, Kham was squat and brawny, with a broad forehead, an oversized jaw that jutted out, and thick lips. He wore Western pants and a loose cotton shirt with a Mandarin collar common among Vientiane merchants.

Bounmy turned to me. "I'm sorry, but I must get back to work. We have an important meeting with trade officials from Burma this afternoon. When you finish, the *pousse-pousse* will be waiting for you outside to take you wherever you need to go."

"Thank you for everything. Good luck with your meeting." I felt terribly alone and uncertain as he opened the door to leave.

Bounmy pivoted in the doorway and spoke to Kham in Lao, his voice cool but firm. I caught only a word here and there, unable to comprehend what he'd said.

"Yes, yes, don't worry," his cousin answered in French.

Kham led me into his office and cleared a pile of papers from the extra chair next to his desk. "Please, Mademoiselle Dubois, sit down." He spoke French with a pronounced Lao accent. He took a sip of tea from a tin mug and sighed. "I'm not sure how you know Bounmy, but he says you have an urgent need for work"—he gave a half-laugh, as if telling a joke—"and that you have a talent for numbers."

The tone of his voice made my acquaintance with Bounmy sound suspect. My voice wavered as I described the top scores I'd earned in mathematics at school. "I don't have experience in accounting, but I'm quick to learn. I know I could do the work."

Kham shrugged with indifference. "The men in the next room have worked here for many years keeping detailed accounts and know every aspect of this business better than I do. I don't need another accountant, but perhaps there are other tasks you could fulfill."

The tiny shred of confidence I'd brought to the interview quickly disappeared as I searched desperately for an opening, something I might offer. Then I remembered Bounmy's comment about the office's disorder. "It does seem you need someone to clean and organize the office and records. The business would run more efficiently and save you money."

Kham scowled for a moment, then burst out laughing. "You are most observant, mademoiselle." His fingertips tapped the desk several times. "Let's see what you can do over the next month. I'll pay you twenty piastres a week?"

My mouth dropped open. I could hardly believe such a generous salary, more than twice what I would have earned with the teaching assistant position I'd been denied. "That...that would be fine," I sputtered.

"You can start tomorrow. The office is open from eight to six Monday through Friday, and Saturdays until noon." He paused. "No woman has ever worked here, so the men may resist your efforts, especially the accountants. You'll have to prove yourself to them and me." Not bothering with niceties, he stood and pointed the way out.

"I'll do my best," I assured him. "Thank you." I made a *nop* and left.

My heart overflowed with gratitude for Bounmy's thoughtfulness in leading me to his cousin. Thanks to him, a job with an extremely generous salary brightened my future. Kham had been abrupt, even rude, but I would work hard and impress him with my efforts. I couldn't wait to write Bridgette about my good luck and send Bounmy a thank-you note.

Chapter 16

I took the waiting *pousse-pousse* to Madame Ketthavong's, the Lao seamstress Catherine had recommended. My new salary would allow me to order a skirt and blouse. Her shop was located in a house on a narrow lane a short ride from the center of town. The homes of wood and bamboo with thatch roofs rested on poles five feet off the ground. Chickens roamed up and down the dirt road, pecking at tufts of weeds, while the smell of wood fires and steaming fish and vegetables filled the air. The porter dropped me off in front of a home with a neatly printed sign—*Madame Ketthavong, Seamstress*. I tried to pay him, but he assured me that the monsieur had already covered the fare.

I hesitated outside the building, not seeing anyone about. Next door an old Lao woman, nothing more than weathered skin covering protruding bones, perched on a stool by the entrance to her home. A cotton *sinh* and white blouse hung loosely over her withered body, and a network of deep lines etched her sun-stained face as she glanced at me with cloudy, red-rimmed eyes. She was washing long beans and watching over a chubby toddler, who sat on the ground scraping dirt into small mounds. All at once her face lit up, and a smile revealed her toothless gums. She began to rattle on in Lao, but I could not decipher anything she said. I shrugged my shoulders and apologized in French, saying I did not speak Lao. With considerable effort, the old granny stood up on shaky legs and strained her head to look at my face, hampered by a pronounced hump in her back. She spoke louder, as if this would help me understand.

A nicely dressed middle-aged woman stepped out of the seamstress shop and introduced herself as Madame Ketthavong. "Can I help you, mademoiselle?"

"Mademoiselle Courbet recommended you. I'd like to order a skirt and blouse." The old woman edged closer, continuing to speak and waving her arms.

"Don't pay attention to Granny," the seamstress said. "She's not right in the head anymore."

"What is she saying?" I asked.

"It's nothing. She thinks she recognizes your face."

I shook my head at the ancient woman and turned away, trying to ignore her. But her insistent, urgent tone drew me back.

"Could you ask her how she knows me?"

Madame Ketthavong gave a *tsk*. "You shouldn't encourage her. She is very old, and her mind plays tricks."

"Please."

Madame Ketthavong spoke back and forth with the old woman. "She says you both worked for a French family. You helped her when she got in trouble with the mistress."

I puzzled over this for a moment. It made no sense. The grandmother gently touched my cheek with her gnarled fingers. She wore an expression of tenderness, speaking a single word over and over. Laya.

"She thinks your name is Laya," Madame Ketthavong said.

"That was my mother's name," I whispered. An eerie feeling crept over me.

"It's a common enough name, mademoiselle," Madame Ketthavong said softly. "Why don't we go inside?"

"Yes, of course." I patted the old woman on the arm, feeling sad to leave her, and climbed the steps into Madame Ketthavong's shop.

A large worktable was piled with half-finished projects—a basted bodice with only one arm, a collar covered with lace, and a green linen skirt, the pleats pinned in place, waiting to be sewn. The seamstress owned a lovely old French Hurtu sewing machine with its lyrical, arching design and inlaid mother-of-pearl decorations, which made it look more like a work of art than a utilitarian machine. Maîtresse Durand had ordered a similar one from France, in an attempt to teach the girls at the orphanage to sew. The shelves behind the worktable held bolts of cotton, linen, crêpe, voile, satin, and silk in a rainbow of colors.

Still distracted by the old woman's words, I told Madame Ketthavong that I needed clothes for work. "I'm starting a job tomorrow at River Transport," I announced proudly.

Madame smiled and offered me a chair next to a low table covered with French and English pattern books and fashion magazines. "Look through these and show me the styles you prefer, mademoiselle. Then we'll pick fabrics."

I forced myself to concentrate on the task at hand, leafing through magazines and pattern books. The clothes must be appropriate for work, but versatile enough for other occasions. I wished Catherine had come with me or, even better, Bridgette.

I showed Madame Ketthavong pictures of a flared skirt and two patterns for simple blouses with short sleeves. She took my measurements and suggested a tan linen for the skirt, a pale blue cotton for one blouse, and perhaps a deep rose color if I desired a second top. After I learned how reasonable the cost would be, I ordered the skirt, two blouses, and a navy-blue polka-dot shirtwaist with a white Chelsea-style collar. The price for all four items was less than I'd paid for my new green dress.

"I'll have them for you on Sunday," Madame Ketthavong promised. "Come early in the morning before the sun is too warm." She bowed and thanked me.

Stepping out of the shop, I blinked against the blinding afternoon sunlight. The grandmother and toddler had disappeared, leaving me both relieved and disappointed. The exchange with the old grandmother, and her insistence that she recognized me, left me desiring to know more. The sound of her murmuring "Laya" over and over haunted me. Was it possible there could be a link?

I strolled home along the river road, stopping at a stand to buy a cup of coconut water then sitting in the shade to sip the refreshing drink. A warm tingling filled my body as I remembered the sensation of Bounmy's limbs pressed against mine in the *pousse-pousse*. I felt an urgent need to be near him, to hear his voice and see his gentle smile. Should I call him that afternoon to tell him I would be starting work the next day and thank him? Perhaps that was too forward, the kind of behavior Catherine discouraged. It was better to send a thank-you note. The more I thought about Kham's attitude—the way he had stared at me, his remarks insinuating something unsavory about my relationship with Bounmy, his seeming indifference to hiring me— the stronger my misgivings. But I needed the job.

A team of twenty young men rowed past in a racing longboat, practicing graceful, measured strokes that propelled them forward at great speed, gliding over the water. If only I could slide through life as effortlessly. Every day taught me how little I understood of the world and dangers lurking in unexpected places.

I crossed Catherine in the entry hall getting ready to leave. "How did it go?" she asked.

"I have a job. At least, he's giving me a month to see how it works out."

"Wonderful!" She turned toward the mirror to arrange her straw hat. "I'm on my way to fetch Julian, but I want to hear all about it later." She whirled around and gave me a quick hug, her high spirits floating around us. "Oh, there's a letter for you from Pakse. I hope it's good news." Grabbing her clutch bag off the table, she disappeared out the front door.

I snatched the letter from the silver platter.

May 23, 1931
Société d'assistance aux Métis
19 Rue du Marché
Pakse, Laos

Chère Mademoiselle Dubois,

I received your letter today with its surprising news regarding Antoine Dubois. I'm afraid Antoine left the orphanage when he turned eleven. He was a very intelligent and well-behaved child, who I greatly enjoyed, and I was able to obtain a full scholarship for him to study at the prestigious College Chasseloup-Laubat in Saigon. He continued on there after it became a lycée. *I am writing to the school today, asking if they know his current whereabouts. I hope to hear back within a few weeks and will forward any information to you as soon as possible.*

I was unaware Antoine had a twin sister. I can't understand why this information was not provided to the home when he arrived here fourteen years ago. The Société d'assistance aux Métis has adopted policies they believe in the best interest of the children under their care; however, I do not always agree with certain choices. In this case, I find it terribly wrong to keep siblings, twins no less, from finding each other.

I will assist you as best I am able. Please be patient.

With deepest regards,

Christophe Augustin, Director

I sank onto the chair next to the hall table, rereading the words once, then twice. His response was encouraging, but the news left me in limbo once again, disappointed yet hopeful. The orphanage director was clearly a kind soul who cared about my brother and wanted to aid him in reuniting with his sister, a completely opposite response from Director Bernard. I had no choice but to wait and hope the school in Saigon knew where Antoine was living. I would write Monsieur Augustine immediately to thank him for his efforts and emphasize how urgent it was for me to find Antoine. Waiting. Still waiting.

Mali emerged from the kitchen. "Does the letter bring good news, Mademoiselle Vivi?" she asked hesitantly.

"I think so." I explained about the orphanage director's search for my brother.

"He will find him," she assured me. I wished I could be as certain.

She patted my shoulder. "Come have lunch."

I sat at the kitchen table and slurped down chicken noodle soup as I shared the details of my interview with Kham. Then I described my encounter with the old woman next to the seamstress's shop. "It seems impossible, but I can't help thinking there's a connection. How could she know my mother's name?"

Mali gave a small shrug. "My mother is like this. Her mind slips in and out of the present, but events long ago remain very vivid for her. Perhaps you should try talking with her again to see if she remembers something more."

"I'm going back to pick up my new clothes early Sunday morning, so I'll try to see her. But she only speaks Lao."

Mali glanced up. "I'll come with you and translate."

"Would you? Won't it interfere with your weekend at home?"

She picked up our dishes and carried them to the sink. "I can leave for my village a little later."

"Are these for the spirit house?" I asked, noticing a tray with rice, bananas, cups of tea, and incense sticks. "May I take them out?"

Mali smiled. "Of course."

I took the tray, happy to be useful, and replaced the food and incense, saying a brief prayer to protect the house and the people living in it. A deep contentment filled me on taking these first steps to discovering my Lao soul.

Afterwards I retreated to my bedroom, stripping down to my cotton chemise and bloomers and curling up on my bed. I'd hardly slept the last two nights, too excited about the tea with Bounmy then my job interview. My eyes grew unbearably heavy.

Chapter 17

A loud bang sent me bolt upright in bed, struggling out of the haze of a frightening dream, soaked in sweat. Director Bernard had been hovering over me, yelling angry, unintelligible words in my face. He'd held my shoulders down and raised a hand to slap me. I'd been desperate to escape, but I had to find Bridgette first. Now, I shook my head, trying to erase the image, thankful to find myself at Catherine's house.

After a moment, I realized the noise had come from the hallway. Someone must be hauling Julian's luggage upstairs and into the room next to mine. I lay back against the pillows, sapped of energy by the late afternoon heat, dozing on and off.

It was after five o'clock when I fully woke. The upstairs was quiet, so I slipped across the hall to take a cool bath and wash my hair, brushing it dry in the last of the sunshine streaming through my bedroom window. After some consideration I slipped back into my blue dress, wanting to make a good impression on Julian. I sighed, examining my shabby appearance in the same tired outfit and worn, scuffed shoes. My next purchase would have to be a new pair of pumps.

Feeling shy and uncertain about meeting Catherine's treasured brother, I paused near the bottom of the stairs to gather my courage, as their voices drifted from the salon.

"How does a gin and tonic sound?" Catherine asked.

"Perfect." Julian cleared his throat. "I know you've always had a soft spot for stray mutts, Cat, but whatever made you decide to take in this *métisse* orphan?" His words came out terse and unhappy.

"The orphanage director is a vile man who treated her unfairly. I couldn't leave her to the wolves."

"You could have warned me that I'd be sharing the house with a total stranger."

"Really, Julian, try to be more compassionate. So many of these poor girls leave the orphanage and end up destitute. Before long, they're some man's mistress, or worse."

He let out a weary sigh. "Sorry. I'm exhausted emotionally and physically. I have little tolerance for unpleasant surprises."

"I know you're going through a terribly difficult period, but Vivi's a lovely girl and will only be here a few months. She won't get in your way."

"I'm sure it will be fine," he said, but his voice still rang with irritation.

I stood frozen on the stairs, my body sagging, wounded and confused. It had never occurred to me that Julian might think of me as an unwanted nuisance. The thought of facing him all evening and trying to be pleasant made me wilt. I considered running back upstairs to hide. Was he upset over living with a stranger or was it the fact that I was a *métisse*? Why hadn't Catherine told him about me?

"I'm going to find Vivi," Catherine said. She rounded the doorway and started as she spotted me on the stairs, briefly frowning. "There you are. Don't you look nice?"

I forced a bright smile, not wanting her to know I'd overheard the conversation. "Sorry to be late. I fell asleep this afternoon."

"Come meet the prodigal brother, returned home at last."

I followed Catherine into the salon, my head spinning with misgivings, both embarrassed and angry that he could so easily dismiss me as unworthy of sharing his house. I didn't want to be a burden, but he could at least meet me before passing judgement.

Julian rose, slowly unfolding his long frame. A flicker of surprise flashed across his face, as if someone other than whom he'd expected stood before him. He quickly stepped up and offered me a hand as Catherine made the introductions.

"Mademoiselle Dubois, delighted," he said.

I searched his expression, seeking the disdain and frustration of his earlier comments. He had Catherine's white-gold hair and brilliant blue eyes. A strong jaw and slightly crooked, longer nose gave him a more masculine version of her pretty face. No doubt he'd spent his privileged life pampered and spoiled, with little regard for others. Yet Catherine had as well, and she was kindness itself.

"Monsieur Courbet," I said quietly, pulling my trembling hand from his grasp.

"Call me Julian. We'll be living under the same roof, after all," he said, still sounding annoyed. "May I address you as Vivi?" I nodded. He stepped aside, motioning for me to sit down.

My back stiff, I perched at the other end of the settee, feeling unwelcome and trying to avoid his intense regard.

"I made you a gin and tonic. See how you like it," Catherine said, handing me a drink. She turned to Julian. "Tell us about your stop-off in Singapore."

"Always an interesting experience when I'm with André," Julian said. "He's a friend I grew up with here who also went to Paris for university," he explained to me. "He finished a degree in engineering and mining and has plans to put his training to use in this lost corner of the world, determined to find treasure where others have failed."

"Like Pierre Lemont," I said.

"Old Pierre? Exactly." Julian lit a cigarette and blew smoke rings into the air. "But Pierre didn't have the slightest idea what he was doing, while André comes armed with the latest sighting and excavation equipment. I may give him a hand now and again."

"And how was the ship? Did you save any pretty young damsels in distress?" Catherine quipped.

Julian chuckled. "The youngest woman we met had to be at least forty. André and I got stuck dining with two colorful old geezers from England, who drank themselves silly every night—not that André behaved any better—and recounted endless tales of their exploits in Singapore and Penang. They're engaged in some sort of murky import business; we never really figured out what. When we docked in Port Said and Djibouti, they insisted on taking us to the most unsavory places. I could tell stories, but they're unfit for you ladies to hear. I had to keep an eye on André as he was usually too drunk to make rational decisions."

Catherine shook her head. "Mother should never have let you and André go off on your own."

"I am a grown man." He grinned. "Mostly. Need I remind you, you're only two years older than me. And what about you, Cat, have you been seeing anyone?"

Catherine concentrated on arranging the folds of her skirt. "No one special. There are few choices in these parts." I could see her pain was still too fresh and feared she was close to tears.

"Too bad." He sat back with an air of confidence, resting an arm along the top of the settee, one leg casually across the other, at ease with himself. He clearly enjoyed being the center of attention, the hero of his own stories. The word that came to my mind was arrogant. But perhaps his earlier comments about me had tainted my impressions.

Mali came into the salon and gazed lovingly at Julian, clearly thrilled by his return. "Dinner is ready. I prepared all your favorite Lao dishes, Monsieur Julian."

"How I've missed your cooking, Mali." He jumped up and threw an arm around her shoulders. "There was nothing in Paris that could come close." She blushed and swatted at his arm, obviously pleased.

The dining table was set with the best china, silver, and linens, and candlelight filled the room with a soft glow. Julian held my chair, then ran around to seat Catherine.

Mali delivered a collection of steaming bowls and platters to the table, a rainbow of scents and colors, beaming at Julian as he exclaimed over each addition. In the past, she had served a few of these Lao dishes, but normally she prepared simple French fare.

I was excited to learn more about Lao food and see if any of the flavors brought back memories of when I was a young child living with my mother. Were these the dishes my mother had cooked? Mali placed a plate of fresh lettuce leaves, mint, and cilantro, along with slices of lime and bright red peppers, in the center of the table.

"How do I eat these?" I asked.

"They are for the *laab moo*, this one here with pork, and the *laab kai* with chicken." Mali pointed to the bowls filled with finely chopped meats and vegetables. "You wrap the *laab* in the lettuce leaves and add whatever you like." She named other dishes: "Here is *mok pa*, steamed fish in banana leaves, and *tam mak hoong*, papaya salad. Be careful of the *cheow bong* sauce. It's very spicy." She hurried back into the kitchen once more. It seemed sad and unfair that she wouldn't sit down and eat with us when she'd been part of this family for fifteen years, but it was not the order of things.

I placed a tiny bit of *cheow bong* on my plate. "How hot is it?" I asked.

"Not that bad," Julian said, but a playful smile gave him away.

"Don't listen to him," Catherine scoffed. "It will make your tongue burn for hours. Try a tiny speck first. If anything is too spicy for you, eat some sticky rice to cool your mouth down."

"Didn't they serve Lao food at the orphanage?" Julian asked.

I shook my head. "Only French food."

"Oh, Vivi, I forgot to ask about the letter from Pakse," Catherine said.

I reported the news from the orphanage director in Pakse on my brother and that he had written to the *lycée* in Saigon to learn of Antoine's current whereabouts. Julian listened with a puzzled expression.

Catherine explained to him how I had discovered my parents' names and the existence of a twin brother in my orphanage file. "The director here had no intention of sharing any of it. Vivi is trying to find her brother now."

Julian's jaw hung down, and he took a deep breath. "How diabolical. Can that even be legal?"

The unexpected sympathy in his voice surprised me, given his earlier displeasure over my presence. "I'm sure I'll find my brother soon, and hopefully I'll be able to learn more about my parents." I swallowed hard, fighting the tightness in my throat that threatened tears.

"And how was the interview at River Transport today?" Catherine said, as if sensing my precarious emotions.

I described my brief meeting with Kham and his offer to hire me on a trial basis for a month. "I'm not sure exactly what I'll be doing, but the office is a terrible mess, so I'll start by cleaning and organizing things."

"I hope it works out," Julian said, taking a sip of wine. "Kham and several of his cousins attended the *lycée* in Hanoi while I was there. Kham was a year ahead of me, but I remember he was a bit rough-mannered and not much of a student."

"Did you know his cousin, Prince Bounmy Savang?" Catherine asked. "He introduced Vivi to Kham."

"We were in the same class." Julian chuckled. "We had a rivalry going for top scores in almost every subject. It didn't make us the best of friends."

"Well, now he's a pleasant young man who recently returned from Paris and works with Prince Phetsarath on foreign trade." Catherine paused. "We had him for tea on Sunday."

"Really? I'd like to renew my acquaintance with both the princes. They could be helpful with my import/export business."

The thought of Julian using my friendship with Bounmy or my job with Kham for his benefit made me bristle. But Vientiane was a small town, and he would undoubtedly find a way to meet with them one way or another.

Julian was pleasant enough the rest of the evening, inquiring about my life in the orphanage and my schooling with what seemed like genuine interest, or at least curiosity. Knowing his misgivings about having me in the house, I resolved to stay out of his way as best I could. Undoubtedly my life was of little consequence to him one way or the other.

Chapter 18

At two minutes before eight o'clock on Tuesday morning, I stood before River Transport, finding the office and warehouse tightly locked. Minutes ticked by, and I began to wonder if I'd misunderstood the work hours or the day Kham expected me to start. The warehouse supervisor, Monsieur Phoummathep, finally showed up thirty-five minutes later. He looked me up and down, a line knitting his forehead. I gave a *nop* and introduced myself, explaining it was my first day. He grunted and spat on the ground before unlocking the office door.

I stood in the dim light, considering what to do. The front room was jammed with two desks, a filing cabinet, a rectangular table, three chairs, and a bookshelf, which ran along the side wall, leaving little space to move about. The air smelled smokey and moldy with neglect. Everything was dirty and disorganized: desktops covered with papers and tea stains, ashtrays overflowing with cigarette butts, and loose sheets littering the floor. After clearing a stack of papers from the spare chair next to one of the desks, I dragged it to the table, the only place left for me to work.

The accountants arrived at nine. I bowed in a *nop* and introduced myself. They reluctantly gave me their names. Monsieur Chan was an older Chinese man with sparse, white hair and papery skin that showed the dark blue veins in his hands. His coworker, Monsieur Nguyen, was a younger Annamese man with thick glasses and dense black hair. Both spoke passable French. They sat down at their desks, ignoring me and burying their noses in ledgers with finely lined pages covered in rows of numbers.

Monsieur Chan looked up after a moment to where I was sitting. "That's my chair."

"May I use it, please? There's nowhere else to sit."

His eyes narrowed. "Where are the papers I had on it?" I nodded toward the stack on the bookshelf. "You can't rearrange things. I have a special filing system that you wouldn't understand."

"I'm sorry. I'll check with you on everything first," I promised.

He clucked his tongue several times and went back to his accounts.

I inspected a stack of documents on the table, relieved to find correspondence and invoices were written in both French and Lao. A half-hour later, embarrassed, I inquired where the toilet was located and if there was running water. Monsieur Nguyen sighed and led me outside, pointing to a ramshackle outhouse set among the trees by the riverbank. "There's a sink in the warehouse." He left me to find my way.

The outhouse was a filthy box of drooping, decaying wood, filled with cobwebs and geckos that seemed to close in on me when I shut the door. There was nothing more than a gaping hole in the battered floor emitting horrible smells that made me gag. I would use it only when in dire need.

I found a tiny metal sink and a barrel of water in the warehouse. I washed my hands, without soap or towel, and discovered the water drained out of the sink into a bucket underneath the pipe. Next to the sink was a table with a kerosene burner and kettle, as well as a green pottery teapot, tin mugs, and a jar of tea leaves lining the shelf above it. The teapot had dark stains, and rancid water filled the bottoms of several cups. There were no cleaning materials. As I considered the conundrum of what to do, Kham appeared at my side.

"What in the world are you doing out here?" he asked, obviously annoyed. "They didn't tell you this area is for the warehouse workers?" I shook my head. "We have a boy who delivers tea twice a day to the office from a stand up the road."

I felt foolish and angry with the accountants.

"Come." Kham led me back in the office and called the warehouse supervisor to join us. Speaking French, he informed the three men of my "trial" position, which made me worry he already planned to let me go after a month. He introduced the three men, describing their roles in the business.

"I realize there has never been a woman in the office before, but even in Laos the world is changing. Please work with mademoiselle," he said. "Explain how the business runs and answer her questions. She will be looking for ways to help you with your work and free up your time." His introduction was far from an enthusiastic endorsement of my presence, but at least he had laid out some parameters.

Kham announced that, after consulting with them, I was authorized to suggest new record and filing systems to improve operations. When Kham finished speaking, the men bowed, their faces remaining impassive, and they offered lukewarm assurances that they would cooperate.

Clearly it would take time to gain the trust and acceptance of the others. To these men I had little value, being only a young woman, a *métisse* at that. I was an invader in their domain, a threat to their routines and ways of doing business that had remained unchallenged for decades. I would have to tread carefully.

I asked Kham for a key to the office so I could arrive early when no one else was there. He scrunched his face up for a moment, as if uncertain he could trust me, but then he handed me a key. "Be sure not to lose it."

By Friday my hopes for making any progress in reorganizing the office or gaining the confidence of my coworkers had been stifled, lost among the stacks of papers piled around the room.

Mali had accompanied me early on Wednesday to the covered market to purchase a broom, pail, mop, soap, and rags. Over the next few days, in the early hours before the others drifted into work, I scrubbed desks, shelves, walls, and the floor, careful to return papers and files to the same places as before. No one acknowledged my efforts, but the cleanliness boosted my optimism.

I had hoped to build some kind of comradery and common purpose with the accountants and the warehouse manager, but the men largely ignored me as I pored through stacks of invoices, bills of lading, and receipts, trying to make sense of them. There didn't seem to be any discernable system for tracing an order from start to finish. I asked lots of questions. The men simply glared at me defiantly and answered over and over: *This is the way we have always done things.* I became a pesky fly, buzzing about the room, refusing to go away.

No one had the authority to oversee the business except Kham, and he was too busy meeting with clients and negotiating fees with boat operators to focus on office procedures. Most days he vanished shortly after arriving and did not reappear until late afternoon, never telling us where he was going or when he would return. If clients came by the office, they would only speak to the accountants, acting as if I didn't exist.

Kham left me to my work, offering an occasional nod as he came and went. Several times I glanced over to find him staring at me from his office with an odd smile on his lips that left me ill at ease. Whatever was he thinking? But it was his treatment of the two accountants that concerned me most: speaking to them with impatience, never happy with their answers. One afternoon he yelled at Monsieur Chan and pounded on his desk before storming out of the office and slamming the door. Another day he called Monsieur Nguyen into his office and thrust some papers under his nose, screaming at him for an error, then throwing the papers in the poor man's face. I made a concerted effort to keep out of Kham's way.

I drafted a chart of the steps in the shipping, billing, and accounting processes to show the flow of paperwork as best I could determine. Then I listed improvements to increase efficiency. The changes made perfect sense to me, like solving a complicated algebraic equation. Before I could approach Kham, I wanted to meet with the other employees again to get their reactions and support. The prospect left me quivering.

That afternoon, Bounmy stopped by the office. My heart bumped against my ribs, and my cheeks grew hot when I saw him come through the door.

Messieurs Chan and Nguyen jumped up and bowed, looking surprised to see him. After greeting the men, Bounmy turned to me. "I wanted to see how you're faring."

"I'm very happy," I said hastily, knowing my coworkers were listening. Surely they found it curious that Bounmy had befriended someone like me. I was grateful Kham was out of the office.

"Why don't we step outside," I suggested, leading the way.

"I hope I haven't embarrassed you by coming, but I've been thinking about you all week. Thank you for your note." He glanced around. "This place is rather rough, but I suppose it will do for now."

I pushed my hair behind one ear. "I can't thank you enough for introducing me to your cousin."

"I'm glad to help." He twisted his straw hat round and round in his hands. "I...I wondered if we might have an outing Sunday afternoon. Perhaps a boat ride up the Mekong. If you're free, that is."

"I'd like that."

He released a long draft of air. "Shall I come by your house around one o'clock?"

"I could meet you by the river," I suggested. I wasn't certain if Catherine and Julian would be at home at that hour, but I preferred to tell them about a date with Bounmy after the fact.

"How about on the riverfront just past Pierre's?" he said, putting on his hat. "I look forward to it."

He walked to a waiting *pousse-pousse,* then turned and waved. I didn't know what to think of his attentions, but foolishly or not, I longed to spend time with him.

Arriving home from work that evening, I found two letters awaiting me. One was from Bridgette and the other from Luang Prabang. I ripped open the second envelope.

May 26, 1931
Société d'assistance aux Métis
Lambert Maison, Sakharine Road
Luang Prabang, Kingdom of Luang Prabang

Chère Mademoiselle Geneviève Dubois,
I received your letter of May 18 today requesting information about your parents who released you into the care of the Société d'assistance aux Métis in 1913. I am unable to provide you with any further background given the Society's longstanding policy of privacy regarding our charges' origins.
I wish you success in whatever you pursue in the future.
Regards,
Madame Gabrielle Lambert
Luang Prabang

I read the terse message twice then turned the page over, feeling sure there must be something more. It was blank. Unlike the kind and encouraging letter from the orphanage director in Pakse, this letter contained only five lines devoid of empathy or understanding. The answer was exactly as Director Bernard had predicted.

I'd been suspended midair for weeks, waiting for an answer, but now the gossamer thread of hope holding me up had been slashed, and I fell back to earth. I had my father's name, but nothing more than my mother's first name. How would I find her family in Luang Prabang? I folded the letter and replaced it in the envelope, setting it aside, too crestfallen to even muster any tears.

I opened Bridgette's letter, desperately needing her cheerful, innocent sentiments to lighten my disappointment.

Vivi, chère amie,

I keep rereading your letter that Catherine brought yesterday. I can't begin to describe how envious I am of your thrilling life—new clothes, a new job, and best of all a new beau! Or I should say a first beau! Hearing about Bounmy Savang (an actual prince!!) and your tea on Sunday made my heart race until I was quite short of breath. His effort to get you a job at River Transport is touching. He sounds like a dream: handsome, polite, kind.

You mentioned Catherine's brother Julian arriving on Monday. I know Catherine is over the moon to have him home again. Do you like him? Tell me more. And what about your job? More, more.

As usual there is little to report here. A shy little girl, only seven years old, arrived at the orphanage yesterday. I saw her weeping out in the backyard this morning, but one of the other girls sat down and put an arm around her, comforting her. It was so sweet and made me recall my first day, and how you befriended me. What would I have done without you all these years?

I'm enclosing a sketch I made of a red ginger plant. Maîtresse must be feeling sorry for me as she bought me some watercolors. It may take me a while to get the hang of them, but I did my best.

You haven't mentioned looking for Sylvie again after discovering she moved out of the boarding house, but I know you've been occupied with the job hunt. Once I'm a free woman, we shall search for her together.

Do come to Sunday Mass and wear one of your new outfits, so I can see it.

Miss you, miss you, miss you!! But I'm glad you are happy and doing well.

Love and kisses,
Bridgette
P.S. Hugs from Lucienne and Madeleine

Chapter 19

As I prepared to leave work at noon on Saturday, Kham emerged from his office and handed me my first pay. "You keep busy out here," he commented, before disappearing out the front door. It was not exactly a compliment, but I decided to take it as one.

I headed toward Wong's Mercantile near the covered market. Catherine had asked me to join her dinner party that evening to celebrate Marguerite's birthday, and I needed to purchase a gift.

"She's distraught over turning thirty, so don't mention her age," Catherine had said. "And she hasn't heard from Charles since he left for Luang Prabang, but it's only been ten days. He likely isn't there yet. For better or worse, she's desperately in love with him. I hope he doesn't turn out to be as unreliable as all the other men she's seen." A prolonged sigh had escaped her lips. "We've both had terrible luck in the romance department. Anyway, we must make her feel special. Julian invited André to come as well."

As I hurried along, I thought of Catherine and Marguerite and the complicated nature of love. Perhaps it was destiny that decided who could steal our hearts away rather than it being a conscious choice. How else to explain Catherine's affair with Monsieur Fontaine? Or my attraction to Bounmy? Thoughts of our date the next day preoccupied my mind.

Wong's was nearly empty when I arrived. Maîtresse Durand had brought me there several times to help her purchase table favors and small trinkets for our Christmas Eve dinners. Wondrous things were crammed onto the floor-to-ceiling shelves—everything from writing paper, books, porcelain figures, toys, and cooking pots to embroidered tablecloths, jewelry, and ammunition for guns. Men's and women's clothing hung from racks in the back next to shoes and hats. Ever since I'd left the orphanage, the store had beckoned to me, but I'd resisted, not wanting to be tempted to indulge in frivolous purchases.

I drifted up and down the narrow aisles, drawn to a china plate with a pattern of blue lilies, a vibrant green silk scarf, and a white blouse with a delicate lace collar, but none of these items were within my price range. Returning to the front of the store, I scanned the glass case holding jewelry and hair ornaments, hoping to find something more reasonable. A tortoiseshell comb looked perfect for Marguerite's luxurious tresses, which she often pulled back on one side. I would have loved one for myself, but I'd already dipped into my precious savings for new clothes.

As I paid for the comb, a deep voice said, "That must be for Marguerite."

I spun around to find Julian standing behind me. He was dressed in white pants and a pale blue shirt, open at the neck. His hair was mussed, and a few stray tresses hung down over his forehead. I thought him almost too beautiful for a man, like a movie star or a model in one of Catherine's fashion magazines.

"Yes. I hope she likes it," I answered, tucking my package in my purse—one of Catherine's old ones that she had given me.

"She'll love it, I'm sure," Julian said. "Would you mind helping me select something?" He gave me a rueful smile, undoubtedly think-ing it endearing and irresistible. "I'm helpless when it comes to buying gifts for women."

There was no polite way to refuse. "I saw some pretty scarves." I led him down the aisle to the green silk wrap I'd admired earlier. "This would go nicely with her red hair."

"Perfect." He carried the scarf to the cashier as I followed behind, hoping to slip out before he could finish paying.

He turned to me, all smiles and good humor. "If you're headed home, we could walk together."

Since his arrival, I'd felt uncomfortable at home, trying as best I could to avoid him. It wasn't hard given our vastly different schedules. Mali told me he and his friend André were out drinking late into the night, resulting in Julian sleeping in long past when I left for work in the mornings. Our paths had only crossed once, when I arrived home from my job as he was heading out for the evening. He'd greeted me warmly and asked about my new position. I'd wondered if he was gauging how long it would be before I earned enough money to move out.

Julian collected his package, and we strolled down the street in the afternoon heat. "It's wonderful to be back in Vientiane after so long," he said. "As I expected, nothing has changed."

"I suppose not," I said. "But I never saw much of the town growing up. We were only allowed to walk to school and church, with an occasional shopping trip with Maîtresse."

He cleared his throat. "Was your life at the orphanage that sheltered?"

I stared straight ahead. "Yes. It was an unhappy upbringing."

"Cat told me about your letter from Luang Prabang. I can't understand the reasoning in keeping you from learning about your parents or trying to hide your brother from you."

"I'll find them somehow."

"I've hardly seen you all week," he said. "But I've been keeping rather late hours." I offered no response, staring straight ahead. He chuckled. "André has led me astray once more."

A response to this silly excuse for drinking and staying out half the night escaped me, and a long silence followed. He stopped under the shade of a monkey pod tree, brushing a strand of hair from his forehead. "I've been wanting to speak to you...that is, I mean, I want to clear up any misunderstanding." He took a deep breath. "Cat thought you might have overheard us talking the other evening before dinner. She said you were on the stairs outside the salon."

I bit my lower lip, unsure if I should lie and pretend to know nothing or confront him with his callous words. "I didn't intend to eavesdrop, but I did hear some of your conversation."

He winced and stepped back, as if expecting me to slap him. "I said some incredibly stupid things that I deeply regret."

I stared at the ground. "I didn't realize Catherine hadn't told you I'd be living in the house. If my presence bothers you, I'll move somewhere else."

"No. Please, no. You may not believe me, but I'm truly happy to share our humble abode with you. I'm so sorry if I made you feel unwanted."

I met his eyes, uncertain of his intentions. All his arrogance had disappeared, and he seemed genuinely full of remorse.

"What I said was asinine and thoughtless. My only excuse is I hadn't been sleeping, and I felt a little overwhelmed." He glanced away, speaking almost in a whisper: "Life in Paris had become impossible."

"Since leaving the orphanage, I've discovered many people are uncomfortable around the *métis*. We don't easily fit in among the French or Lao." The emotions I tried to keep carefully hidden bubbled up, closer to the surface than I'd realized. Tears welled in my eyes. "I don't know who I am or w-where I belong." A sob caught in my throat.

"Oh God, I've made you cry." Julian handed me his handkerchief, then surprised me by taking hold of my shoulders and bending close to my face. "You're such a lovely girl, Vivi. I don't give a damn whether you're a *métisse* or not. And you're welcome to live with us for as long as you want." My heart wavered under his penetrating gaze. "I'd like us to start over. Please forgive me, and let's be friends."

I offered a weak smile, stepping back from his grasp, worried someone might see us and wonder about the relationship. His apology seemed sincere, but could I truly trust him? "We can try," I said at last.

He heaved a great sigh. "I won't disappoint you again."

Chapter 20

The birthday party started out full of friendly banter and laughter. Marguerite wore a traditional Annamese *áo dài*, a long emerald-green silk tunic with slits up the sides to her hips, over loose-fitting, white silk pants. The costume seemed incongruous draped over her tall, big-boned frame, unlike the delicate Annamese women I'd seen wearing them in town.

"I bought it in Saigon when I first arrived in Indochine," she said, after I told her how pretty she looked. She giggled. "Men find it very sexy, like silk pajamas they can't wait to peel away." I blanched at her suggestion, and she threw her head back laughing.

Marguerite began a long harangue about the new Resident Superior. "That man is impossible and demanding. He argues about every single detail, no matter how small." She ranted on, relating a story of how he had nearly torn to pieces a lowly civil servant from the customs department, not to mention the disagreement he'd had with Charles, which had ended in a shouting match. She crossed her legs and sighed. "The next thing we knew, Charles was sent packing to Luang Prabang!"

As Marguerite vented her frustrations, I studied Catherine's face across the room. She wore an unconvincing smile, and I could see her attention stray somewhere else several times, undoubtedly to Monsieur Fontaine. I had respected her wishes and not asked any further questions about him, but now it broke my heart to observe her sad, dull eyes.

After Julian refilled drinks, Catherine brought Marguerite's gifts from the side table. "Open your presents," she said.

"What about André?" Julian asked.

Catherine shrugged. "He's always late. We can't wait for him."

A smile lightened Marguerite's face. "I got a birthday wire from Charles this afternoon. He said the trip to Luang Prabang was quite exhausting as it rained incessantly, and they only arrived yesterday."

"As I thought," Catherine said. "After all that moaning about how he'd forgotten you."

Marguerite waved off the comment and pulled Julian's green scarf from its wrapping, oohing with delight. "It's such a beautiful color."

"I must give Vivi credit for choosing the scarf," Julian said. "She has an excellent eye."

Next came a bottle of Shalimar perfume from Catherine, which Marguerite sprayed on her wrists then mine. She unwrapped my tortoiseshell comb, ran to the mirror above the side table, and secured her hair back on the left side. "I love it," she exclaimed. "Thank you all. What would I do without my dear friends?"

Marguerite flipped through the pile of records resting on the table next to the Victrola that Julian had brought from Paris. "How thrilling to have new music!" She placed a disc on the turntable, and Maurice Chevalier sang "Toi et Moi." She begged Julian to dance with her, and soon they were circling the room in a foxtrot.

When the song ended, Julian restarted the record and bowed before me. "Mademoiselle, may I have this dance?" I protested that I didn't know the steps, as the only person I'd ever danced with was Bridgette, and we could never figure out who was leading and who was following. But he refused to take no for an answer and pulled me up from my chair into his arms. "I'll show you what to do." Stiff and blushing, I stumbled along, stepping on his foot several times, but he just smiled and explained the moves, counting out the beat. The song ended and he restarted the record for a second time. Before long, I relaxed into the song's rhythm under his confident lead—one hand holding mine, the other firmly planted on my back, guiding me across the floor. It felt like a dream, as if I were floating on air. When the music ended, my disappointment surprised me.

"Bravo, Vivi," Catherine said. "You're a natural."

"We'll go to the club one weekend and try out our moves on a proper dance floor," Julian said, waggling his eyebrows. Perhaps the invitation served as penitence for his past remarks, but I remained cautious nonetheless.

André joined us forty minutes late, reeking of gin. He apologized, saying he'd lost track of time while having a cocktail—obviously more than one—with a friend at Pierre's. He was not handsome and sophisticated like Julian as I'd expected, but short of stature, only a few inches taller than me, with big hazel eyes and the soft, pudgy body of a stuffed teddy bear. His constant laughter over the slightest amusement filled his fleshy face with fine lines. He wore dirty khaki pants and a shirt half-untucked with a dark blue stain on the front pocket. A habit of running his hand through his curly auburn hair gave him the air of having recently stepped out of bed.

As Julian introduced us, a silly grin spread across André's face. He took my hand into his clammy palms and stammered, "I...I'm delighted to, to meet you." He turned to Julian. "You're right, she's quite beautiful," he said, as if speaking of an inanimate object to be evaluated and rated.

Julian laughed and slapped his friend on the back. "Really, André, can't you monitor anything you say?" It soon became apparent that André rarely filtered his comments, less so as he continued to drink.

My first impression was of an overgrown puppy, madly wagging its tail for attention, full of enthusiasm for everything and everyone it encountered. Later, I understood that as he got more and more wound up, he issued tactless remarks without any awareness that he was inflicting pain on others. I didn't think he was intentionally mean, simply wildly self-absorbed and oblivious.

Julian poured a steady stream of cocktails and champagne. I tried to resist, but he kept insisting, "Just one more." I complied, not wanting to appear young and inexperienced. The alcohol deceived me at first with its warm glow, and the more I imbibed, the more at ease I felt, joining in the conversation and raucous laughter. It was almost as if I belonged among these privileged French friends with their comfortable lives. Almost. Until André blurted out another careless remark that drew me back to reality.

Mali had outdone herself, serving chicken cordon bleu and spinach soufflé for dinner. Marguerite continued to drink with abandon, complaining about growing old and how her life was empty and pathetic with Charles gone. At one point, she batted her eyes at Julian and made suggestive remarks. Her flirting seemed more a habit, an affectation, than a sign of any real interest in him. Julian brushed off her suggestions as a joke and changed the subject. Her outrageous behavior made me cringe.

The contrast between Julian—handsome, self-assured, and witty—and André, a bumbling fool, made them unlikely friends. Yet they recounted tales of their college days in Paris, interrupting each other and embellishing details, like a seasoned comedy routine. Incidents grew more hilarious as the night wore on and the alcohol kept flowing.

André launched into a tale about an evening in a Paris restaurant. "I heard these young oriental men speaking Lao and immediately introduced myself. They were students at the École Coloniale, sons of aristocratic families in Luang Prabang. The four of us shared a bottle of wine and waxed nostalgic for Laos. Nice chaps."

"And good sports," Julian added, "considering how Parisians treated them, pointing and staring. They recounted several appalling incidents that made me ashamed of my fellow countrymen."

André put a hand up to get our attention. "One day, shopping at a cheese shop, the vendor thought they were someone's servants and tried to cheat them out of their change." He chuckled, as if it were terribly amusing. "Another time at a reception at the French Ministry of Culture, several guests assumed the men were wait staff and asked them to refill their wine glasses. Too droll."

"None of that is funny, André," Julian said, his voice irritated.

A slow burn filled my middle as I thought of similar stories Bounmy had recounted of being ridiculed and mistreated. "So, anyone who isn't French is assumed to be a servant?" I snapped. "How ridiculous."

"Really," Marguerite said, draining her champagne glass. "French people are such pompous asses." I felt sure her statement included André.

"You have to admit, Julian, their French was absolutely abominable," André continued, as Mali emerged from the kitchen to clear dishes. He began imitating the men's accents in a small tinny voice, laughing so hard he never noticed that no one else shared his amusement.

"How well do you speak Lao, André?" I asked.

He glanced up, obviously irked by the question. "Can't speak a word. Impossible language. The Lao are much better off learning French, the only civilized language."

"André, you're an incorrigible snob," Catherine said, her voice dripping ice. "The Lao language is beautiful."

Mali never acknowledged the conversation, keeping her head down, her expression neutral as she carted off dishes to the kitchen.

Marguerite's head lolled to one side. "Tell us about your trip… from Singapore."

"Oh, a great adventure," André assured her. "I must say, we were surprised to find the train from Singapore to Bangkok as good as any in Europe. First class had sleeper cars and an excellent dining room."

Julian sipped his champagne. "From Bangkok we took the northern train line to a small town called Phitsanulok. A rougher ride, to be sure."

André joined in, "We met two Danish men who work for a logging company in the northern forests of Siam. They live in the middle of nowhere with half a dozen other Occidentals." He waved a hand through the air. "Of course, they all have their *phu sao,* like here in Laos. One of the men even submitted to a native wedding, paying the family a bride price and going through a hocus-pocus ceremony: praying to ancestors and mysterious spirits, lighting candles and incense on the Buddha altar. *Voilà*, wink-wink, he was married."

Catherine shook her head. "It's disgusting. I bet these men have wives and families in Denmark. One day they'll go home and abandon these poor women."

André shrugged. "Probably. And leave behind God only knows how many half-breed bastards."

"Really, André, must you be so crude and tactless?" Julian said. "Stop drinking!" He grabbed André's glass and set it aside.

I kept my voice even and stared at André. "You mean half-breed bastards like me?"

André shrank back in his chair, seemingly chastened. "Oh, I'm sorry, I didn't think—"

"You never do," Marguerite interrupted. "But you have it wrong, André. The men are the bastards, not their children."

Julian turned to me. "I apologize for my friend. He hasn't the slightest clue what he's saying." After a pause, he cleared his throat. "But at least the Danes saved us a great deal of trouble, telling us how to hire a car to drive to Nong Khai. We rode for four hours in a beat-up old Ford with a missing fender on bone-jarring, dirt roads."

"Twice we had to get out and push the damn thing up a hill," André said. "But we got through. A quick boat ride across the river, and here we are in Vientiane."

"How lucky for us," Marguerite said, smirking. Barely able to sit up any longer, she rested an elbow on the table. Her arm suddenly slipped off the edge, nearly landing her on the floor, but Catherine jumped up and caught her.

Catherine sighed, appearing remarkably sober. "I can see you'll be sleeping in the guest room tonight, dear." She called to Mali, who emerged from the kitchen with a cake and three lighted candles on top. We sang "Joyeux Anniversaire" in our slurred, discordant voices, and Marguerite made a wish and blew out the candles. Catherine cut slices of the banana cake topped with a tart mango sauce and passed them around.

By this time my head was spinning so fast that I had to support myself on the table to remain upright. I desperately wanted to go to sleep, but every time I closed my eyes, my stomach turned somersaults, and I was sure I'd be sick. I opened my eyes wide and blinked rapidly, trying to focus.

After the cake, Catherine stood up, making it clear the party was over. With considerable effort, André rose from his chair and bowed, nearly falling over. "Thank you, Catherine. You're a beaut… beautiful woman." He stumbled toward me. "And you're a lovely girl," he said, grabbing my hand and giggling like a young schoolboy. I pulled my hand from his sweaty grip, not bothering with a reply. He repulsed me.

Catherine shook her head. "Julian, walk him home, or Lord knows where he'll end up." Julian was swaying back and forth, but he managed to link arms with André and guide him out the front door.

Catherine and I led Marguerite to the downstairs guestroom, where she fell on the bed and immediately passed out. Catherine removed her shoes and closed the mosquito netting around her.

On wobbly legs, I staggered to the stairway, grabbing the railing for support. "Thank you for the evening. I'm terribly drunk."

"Everyone is. As usual." She turned away then stopped. "Are you going to Mass in the morning?"

"Yes, but first I'm going to Madame Ketthavong's to pick up my new clothes."

"Bridgette will be looking for you." She paused a moment. "I'm sorry André was such an ass tonight. He says such terrible things when he's drunk, and tomorrow he won't remember any of it."

"Maybe drinking reveals people's true feelings," I said. "I'm grateful you're not like that."

Catherine gave me a quick hug. "It's best to ignore stupid people. They don't deserve your attention."

Somehow I made it to my room and fell on the bed, not even bothering to take off my clothes.

Chapter 21

I woke at some point in the dark, needing to go to the bathroom. My head throbbed, and my limbs felt like blocks of iron pulling me down. I barely made it to the toilet before being sick over and over, my stomach going into spasms until nothing remained. When I finally climbed back into bed, clutching my middle, head pounding, uninvited memories of the evening filtered through—hours of drinking, Marguerite's inappropriate behavior, and André's hurtful remarks.

I feared that many Frenchmen, like André, felt perfectly comfortable demeaning the Lao and *métis*. We lived in a society where French and Lao existed side by side, yet in separate, unequal worlds. Naturally, the French considered themselves far superior to the lowly natives, while the *métis* straddled the chasm somewhere in between, like distant relatives that no one wanted to acknowledge. A few lucky *métis* garnered a favorable status if their French fathers legally married their Lao mothers and lived with the family. Aline Allard, who Prince Souvanna was courting, had been accepted in French and Lao society. But Bridgette and I were of a different ilk—lowly bastard orphans of uncertain origins.

Bridgette had always looked for the best in people and ignored unkind words, laughing off the taunts of French schoolmates, while I became furious and wounded. She didn't understand the pervasiveness of these attitudes that extended to French adults, with the constant reminders of our tainted background. Derogatory names issued from arrogant lips debased us, while other, more subtle gestures put us in our place—inquisitive stares, averted eyes trying to avoid someone too insignificant to acknowledge. A frown. A sneer. A small *tsk* of distaste.

I suppose it wasn't surprising that the French viewed the *métis* as below them. The government may have declared us French citizens, but we remained half Lao, lesser beings who were best suited as farmers, household servants, or compliant *phu sao*.

The Lao had their own qualms about those carrying "a touch of French blood." While some Lao families accepted their mixed offspring, sometimes even proud of them, many found it difficult to acknowledge the shame of children born out of wedlock from French fathers—foreigners who showed so little respect for the Lao and their way of life. They had names for the French, the strange pale-skinned people: *falang*, or foreigner; *kue ling*, like a monkey, given their hairy bodies; or *dang mo*, long noses. How could the Lao not resent these unwelcome masters, who fathered hundreds of half-French children? The *métis* were a reminder of the humiliations they endured every day.

It was exhausting to be trapped in the middle.

I woke again at seven thirty. My head still felt as if it might explode, my pulse thrummed loudly in my ears, and the sunlight pouring through the windows hurt my eyes. But I needed to hurry to Madame Ketthavong's shop to retrieve my clothes if I wanted to make it to Mass by ten. I would wear my new dress to show Bridgette and with Bounmy that afternoon. Perhaps Mali might make sense of what the old woman next door had to say and determine if she had actually known my mother.

Mali was in the kitchen putting away the previous evening's dishes. I sat at the wooden table, holding my head. "Oh, Mali, I drank too much."

She brought me two aspirin and a glass of water mixed with bicarbonate of soda. "Take these." Then she served me a boiled egg on a slice of toast. "Eat. You'll feel better."

I couldn't imagine keeping food down but forced myself to chew and swallow. After two strong cups of coffee, I felt almost human. "I'll never drink like that again." Mali only smiled, as if she had heard this promise before from others.

"I want to apologize for André last night. He said such awful things in front of you. And me. I wanted to slap him."

Mali laughed. "I don't listen to that man. Nothing but silliness come out of his mouth. In Lao we say people like him are *ngocha*, stupid." She patted my shoulder. "Ignore him."

The morning was still cool as we walked along the quiet streets toward the seamstress's shop. Vendors lined the river road, offering produce and different wares displayed on mats and colorful cloths. Several women called out to Mali, and she greeted them in Lao.

"Mali, I don't want to betray Catherine's trust, but I have to ask if you've heard anything from your friends about the…incident with Monsieur Fontaine? I hate seeing Catherine so sad still."

Mali nodded. "I know you are only concerned for her. From what I've been told, the young maid was not harmed. Monsieur Fontaine simply passed out on her porch, and one of his children found him there. But the wife chose to believe the worst."

"Have you shared this with Catherine?"

She sighed. "Yes, I told her. I think it helped her to know."

I nodded, relieved to hear this news as well. I would not bring it up again or say anything to Catherine.

Madame Ketthavong was waiting for me. She sent me behind the curtain hanging in the corner of the room to try on my new outfits, while she and Mali chatted in Lao. The linen skirt hugged my hips before flaring out into gentle folds and paired perfectly with both the blue and rose-colored blouses of soft, cool cotton. I stepped out to model them.

"Very professional, mademoiselle," Madame Ketthavong said. Mali nodded her approval.

I changed into the navy-blue polka-dot dress. The fitted bodice and full skirt emphasized my narrow waist. I thought perhaps it made me look taller. I drew aside the curtain and twirled around.

Mali smiled. "Lovely, Mademoiselle Vivi. Just lovely."

"I'll wear it, as I'm going to Mass from here," I said.

When I paid for the clothes, I asked Madame Ketthavong the name of the old woman next door.

"Madame Lansay," she replied. "But you must not take too much from what she says. Her mind lives in another place these days."

"I understand, but I'd like to talk with her for a moment. Just in case."

Madame Ketthavong walked us outside, calling into the entry of the home. A young woman emerged. The seamstress introduced me and Mali in French and explained about our last encounter with her grandmother.

The neighbor bowed then disappeared. She returned, leading the tiny lady to the door; her spindly legs threatened to collapse at any moment. The neighbor lifted her grandmother onto her back and carried her down the steps, then lowered her onto a stool. "This is my grandmother, Madame Lansay."

The ancient woman looked even more frail than I remembered, with paper-thin skin covered in brown spots. Her milky eyes sank into her skull, and I felt guilty bothering her. The old woman looked right past me, at first, into the morning sun, as if unaware of her surroundings or anyone's presence. I crouched down beside her and held a bony hand. "Madame Lansay, we met last week. Do you remember me?" Mali repeated my words in Lao.

The old woman glanced over, studying my face. Slowly, she lifted a hand to run her fingers along my cheek. Glancing down for a moment, she let out a small gasp. "Laya...Laya Thongsavat." My heart contracted until I could not breathe. Could Thongsavat be my mother's family name?

I waited impatiently as Mali asked the questions I'd suggested earlier. The granny concentrated before answering in halting bursts. "She remembers you from the big house in Luang Prabang where she cleaned for the French family. You tutored the young master," Mali repeated. "He was a sweet boy. You were both sad when he became ill and left with his mother for France. She says the mother was mean. You stopped the mistress from hitting Madame Lansay several times."

Stunned by these details, I turned to the granddaughter. "Did your grandmother ever live in Luang Prabang? Could she have worked for a French family?"

The woman nodded, her mouth agape. "Yes, it's true, but she hasn't talked of it for many years." She gently smoothed her grandmother's disheveled bun. "She was born in Luang Prabang and married my grandfather there. He died when only forty. My grandmother worked as a housekeeper for different French families to support her six children. When my father, her eldest son, took a job with the telegraph company in Vientiane, Granny moved here with us."

My pulse raced. "Does she know the name of the French family where she worked?" I asked. Mali repeated the question in Lao. The old woman became agitated and began rubbing her hands together over and over.

"Dubois," I murmured.

Her face lit up. "Dubois. Monsieur Henri Dubois."

A hitch seized my chest. I wanted to explain to her that I was Laya's daughter, but I was afraid it would confuse her too much, so I pretended to be my mother. "Is... is my family in Luang Prabang?"

She answered in French this time. "Yes. Your father is an important man."

The granddaughter shook her head in wonder. "Grandmother used to speak French, but we thought she'd forgotten. Usually she remembers nothing, only a little of her childhood."

Tears sprang into my eyes. The unlikely chance of meeting this ancient person with her treasure of information overwhelmed me. To learn my mother's family name, and to know my grandfather had been an important person, gave me a means of searching for my family. "Thank you. Thank you so much."

The old woman collapsed back, as if spent by the effort, and drifted to another place.

"I think she's tired," the granddaughter said. "You can come back another day and speak with her again if you wish."

I gave Madame Lansay a gentle hug and kissed her cool, dry cheek. "I will come to see you soon."

She patted my hand. "You must be careful. Don't trust the French." I wondered what prompted the warning. Had she known about the affair between my mother and father? I would think carefully about additional questions before returning.

I stood and thanked the granddaughter. It was difficult to pull myself away from the only link to my parents I'd ever found.

Mali held my elbow, quietly guiding us down the lane while I murmured my mother's name: "Laya Thongsavat." I turned to her with the wonder of it all, my eyes questioning hers.

"It was your destiny to meet this woman," she said simply.

"I've never believed in miracles…but now I do."

Mid-morning sun flooded our path and brought my thoughts back to the rest of my day. "We must hurry. You need to meet your husband, and it's almost time for Mass. I'm going to wait at the church and try to see Bridgette."

"Give me this," Mali said, taking the package of clothes from me. "Say thank you to God, then Buddha, for aiding you."

A half-hour early for Mass, I wandered in the Sacred Heart graveyard, hoping to catch sight of Bridgette before Director Bernard showed up. My mind raced with thoughts of Madame Lansay's revelations. I had a name, a path forward for finding my mother's family. Perhaps even my mother. Could there actually be a God watching out for me?

Reading the tombstones, it was shocking to see how many

children and young people had lost their lives to tropical diseases, which would never have touched them if their families had remained in France. Instead, they'd met a tragic end before truly experiencing life and were buried in the cemetery of a remote country. A place they'd never belonged.

As families began filing into the church, I spotted Maîtresse with her flock of orphans marching behind, like a mother duck with her ducklings. I waited until she led the girls aged eight and under to Sunday school in the adjoining building, then waved frantically to Bridgette and the others. Lucienne saw me first, rushing over with Bridgette and Madeleine trailing behind. I threw myself into the warm embraces of my friends.

"Look at you in your beautiful new dress," Lucienne exclaimed, stepping back.

"I'm jealous," Madeleine said wistfully. "Your life is terribly exciting." I grinned and nodded, unable to disappoint them with the full truth of my experiences over the past month.

Lucienne grabbed Madeleine's arm. "Come. We'll keep Maîtresse out of the way so Bridgette and Vivi can talk." I was grateful she understood our need to be alone.

Bridgette hugged me tight again. "I can't believe you're actually here. So, tell me everything."

"We don't have much time. My job is boring, and the men grumpy, but I got paid yesterday. That makes it worthwhile. Catherine and Mali are wonderful and take good care of me. I can't wait until you are free, and we can go everywhere together."

"What about Julian?"

"I haven't really...gotten to know him that well. He's handsome, almost beautiful."

She turned her head with a sly smile. "I can't wait to meet him. He sounds dreamy."

I studied my friend's face, thinking her eyes looked a little swollen. "Are you all right? You look pale."

"I'm fine. I've had a fever for a few days, but I think it's gone now."
She pushed her hair behind her ear.

"Do take care of yourself."

"Don't worry. And Monsieur Savang? What is he like?"

"He's very kind and—"

"Handsome," she interrupted, giggling.

"That too. I'm meeting him this afternoon for a boat ride on the river."

She hopped up and down, grabbing my hand. "It's too thrilling. Promise to write me every detail tomorrow."

"Of course." I paused a moment. "Being with him—just thinking about him—gives me this warm glow, a strange longing I've never felt before. I definitely have a crush."

Bridgette's face turned serious. "Promise me you won't run off with him before I get out of the orphanage."

"Today is only our second date. I'm not running off with anyone. I am waiting for you to be free."

I looked over and saw Maîtresse standing in front of the church, arms crossed, watching us with an amused expression. She waved for us to come. Sheepishly, we hurried arm in arm to where she stood.

"Director Bernard won't be here today. You can sit together if you like." And with that she disappeared into the chapel.

Bridgette made a face. "Can you believe it? She's turning into someone nice."

We sat in the pew behind Maîtresse and the other girls, holding hands, content to simply be together, speaking softly to each other when the choir sang, until Maîtresse scolded us. We made faces and giggled at Father Joseph's sermon about asking God's forgiveness for our sins, large and small. It was such a relief to feel so wonderfully at ease in the company of my dearest friend once again.

When we parted at the end of the service, it felt as if I were abandoning her once more. "I know it seems like forever until your birthday, but be strong."

She gave me a final hug. "I'll be fine, just keep sending letters—especially about Monsieur Savang."

Maîtresse gave a small nod and led the girls back toward their cloistered lives. Bridgette faded from view, leaving me with an acute sense of loss.

Chapter 22

Bounmy was already waiting for me when I arrived ten minutes early. The leaves of a kapok tree swayed above him in a gentle breeze, sending flutters of sunlight across his head and shoulders, as if sprinkling him with gold dust. He wore neatly pressed khaki pants and a white linen shirt with the sleeves rolled up. The sight of him, hands in pockets, gazing out over the great expanse of muddy water, left me yearning for something I couldn't quite define. I wanted to be by his side.

He turned toward me, a generous smile spreading across his face. My breath caught in my lungs as he bowed in a *nop*. "Mademoiselle Dubois, what a delight to see you."

I nodded, awkward and unsure, afraid of any movement I might make or word I might utter that would be wrong or embarrassing or ridiculous. "Monsieur Savang."

He eyed my new outfit. "You look very pretty."

"Thank you." I glanced down the riverbank where dozens of boats, large and small, had anchored. "It seems busy today."

"It's Visakha Bousa, bringing people from up and down the river to town."

"Mali told me. I'd never heard of the holiday before."

"How remarkable. Didn't the orphanage teach you about local beliefs and customs?"

"Maîtresse took us to the Lao New Year parade on Pi Mai a few times, but nothing else." I could hardly tell him that Maîtresse called Buddhism a superstitious, pagan religion and insisted it would be sacrilege to go near a Buddhist temple or learn about the beliefs.

"Visakha Bousa celebrates Buddha's life, from birth to enlightenment to death. It's one of the most important holidays of the year for Buddhists. Everyone goes to the temples to pray and make offerings. After dark, the monks have a candlelight procession through town. We could watch it this evening after we get back."

"I'd love that."

He nodded toward the riverbank. "I have a pirogue waiting. I thought we'd ride upriver and stop for a picnic." He indicated one of the longboats bobbing in the water below. The insubstantial-looking vessel of wooden planks was about twenty feet long and only wide enough for two passengers in the middle. The front and back ends narrowed and curved up, barely accommodating one person.

"I've never been on the river before."

"Truly? Mademoiselle, your life has been much too sheltered. We must change that."

I hesitated for a moment before taking the hand he offered. His grip felt warm and reassuring as he carefully helped me down the slippery steps carved into the muddy riverbank. Four Lao men, wearing sarongs, loose-fitting shirts, and wide-brimmed straw hats, manned the oars. They bowed and held the hull steady as we climbed in and sat on the wooden bench at the center under a rattan cover. Bounmy released my hand once we had settled, and I missed his fingers curled around my palm.

The men pushed off, rowing upstream with long, even strokes, laboring against the current. One stood at the back, using his oar to both propel us forward and steer our course, while the other three crouched in the front rowing with their oars off the sides. The boat hugged the shore ten feet out, navigating around occasional tree branches and swirling eddies. The distance to Siam on the opposite shore appeared vast from our vantage point low in the water. Outlying villages of wood-and-thatch houses perched on poles came into view through river reeds and stands of palm and mango trees. A larger longboat with an outboard motor passed nearby, creating a wake that rocked us from side to side. I held my breath, gripping the edge of the hull.

"I don't know how to swim," I admitted in a small voice.

"Don't worry. I spent my childhood swimming in rivers and ponds," Bounmy said. "If you fall in, I'll save you." His easy confidence helped allay my fear.

I sat back as we glided along in peaceful silence. Bounmy seemed content to listen to the sound of the oars slicing through the water and waves lapping against the hull, sometimes splashing us with a few drops. A cascade of gray-tinged clouds drifted above. There was a dream-like quality to the moment, and I thought how extraordinary it was that this man wanted to spend the afternoon with me. I studied his profile, drawn to every detail, from the small mole at the side of his left eyebrow to the way his thick hair curled around his ear.

Bounmy pointed out a fisherman in a cone-shaped hat crouched in a tiny skiff, casting his fishing net off one side. Four women knelt along a rocky stretch of shore, scrubbing clothes on the stones, while behind them shirts, pants, scarves, and *sins* hung over tree branches drying. The shoreline became steeper and the trees thicker.

"Tell me about your job," Bounmy said at last. "I hope Kham is treating you well."

"It's fine." I didn't want to complain about Kham's indifferent, curt answers and unsettling stares. Nor would I mention his volatile temper with the other employees. "I'm sorting through office records, but first I had to clean stains and layers of dust from the furniture and floors. It was filthy."

He started. "That wasn't necessary. I'm sure Kham would hire a cleaning woman if you asked."

"I don't mind." I explained how I was consulting with the other employees, asking questions and their opinions. "I want to develop a plan to improve the flow of paperwork and basic functions of the business." I paused. "There is a bit of resistance, of course. I know the men find it difficult to work with a woman."

He gave a small guffaw. "It's a shock for them, especially when the woman is so young and beautiful."

I stared at my feet, embarrassed yet pleased. "I want the men to think my proposals are their ideas, so they don't resent me."

"Very wise. I'm afraid most Lao men expect women to obey them without question, not examine their ways and try to change things."

I tilted my head to one side, smiling. "And you, Monsieur Savang, how do you feel about women in the workplace?"

He grinned. "The French women in our office have enlightened me. It is a more interesting place with them there, and they're full of excellent ideas." He paused. "Many of the women I met in Paris held strong opinions on the subject as well."

A wave of jealousy struck as I imagined him dining out with beautiful, sophisticated French women. "Did you meet a lot of women?" It was a stupid question that tumbled out before I could stop myself.

He shrugged. "Because of my father's position in the royal court, I was invited to social events hosted by French ministers or my father's acquaintances. It was my duty to attend. Some women seemed curious about meeting an oriental prince, making me feel like a novelty put on display for their amusement. It was uncomfortable."

"Are you sure I shouldn't address you as Prince Savang?"

He laughed. "Absolutely. My life is complicated enough with family obligations and court formalities. It's a relief to put that aside when I'm with you." I wondered what these obligations entailed.

He hesitated a moment. "If it's not too bold, may I address you as Geneviève? And please call me Bounmy."

I loved the way he pronounced my name, the gentle sound of each syllable in his nearly perfect French. "My friends call me Vivi."

"Geneviève is so lovely; I'd like to use that."

"In my file at the orphanage, I discovered my Lao name is Sakuna. But it sounds so strange to me."

"Sakuna is lovely as well." He smiled. "But I still prefer Geneviève." I could see he was not one to be easily dissuaded.

I glanced up shyly. "Do you mind if I ask you about growing up in Luang Prabang?"

"Whatever you want to know."

I considered the endless questions, big and small, that had floated through my mind as I walked to work each day or drifted off to sleep at night. "What was it like living in a palace?"

He chuckled. "I'm sorry to disappoint you, but only the king and his wives and children actually reside in the palace. Our family lives close by. I share a home with my mother and younger sister."

"And your father?"

"He lives in another house with his second wife and their children."

I thought I detected a trace of sadness in his voice. The idea of multiple wives still shocked me. "How…how old is your sister?"

"Dara turned seventeen last month. She'll be getting married in September. I also have two half-brothers, ten and twelve years old, and a half-sister who is seven."

"What are your parents like?"

"Very traditional and strict, especially my father, but they are good parents." He gazed into the distance for a moment, as if considering his next words. "When I was young, Father often took me hunting and fishing, using every opportunity to instruct me on my duties to the kingdom. It's essential for him that I fulfill my role as eldest son." He didn't define this role, but clearly it weighed on him.

"What else do you like to do in Vientiane, besides visiting temples and saving young women from drowning?" I teased.

"I started playing tennis in Paris." His mouth tensed. "But the Cercle has the only court in Vientiane, so I have to wait for invitations from French acquaintances to play."

As I struggled with how to respond, a huge fish flew out of the water and nearly landed in the boat. I jumped up from my seat with a gasp, rocking the boat and teetering toward the water. Bounmy grabbed my arm and pulled me down onto the seat. "Be careful. The fish is gone."

I took a deep breath to calm my racing heart. A chorus of birds chirped and squawked from the trees along the shore, as if reassuring me I was fine.

About an hour out, the pirogue rounded a small bend and the riverbank flattened out into a gentle incline, leading to a meadow.

"Let's stop here," Bounmy said, scanning the dark clouds congregating in the sky to the east. "It looks like rain soon."

I had not eaten since Mali's breakfast early that morning. As if on cue, my stomach let out a low rumble. "I seem to be hungry."

"Good. I brought lots of food."

We stepped onto the silty shore and traversed the meadow with its patchwork of wild grasses, stalks of yellow ginger, delicate wild orchids, and a scattering of palm and mango trees. One of the boatmen followed with a large picnic basket and quilt, leaving our provisions under a tree before returning to the boat. Bounmy spread the quilt out below branches covered in thick, glossy leaves, which formed a perfect umbrella, and tiny white flowers saturated the air with a sweet scent.

"What kind of tree is this?" I asked. "It smells like jasmine."

"It's a neem tree, or *phak kadao* in Lao. It has many medicinal uses, and new shoots are sometimes eaten in a Lao dish called *laab*. If you rub the oil from the leaves on your skin, it keeps mosquitoes away. Very handy."

He opened the picnic basket, pulling out a thermos of tea, a baguette, slices of chicken, sausages, a pot of creamy cheese, and a variety of fruits. A small rattan container had sticky rice and another had fresh spring rolls. There were plates, cups, silverware, and napkins. I wondered how he had managed to arrange such a wonderful meal. Perhaps he had a servant for such things.

"It's a feast." I piled food on my plate, savoring every bite. My hangover and lack of sleep had left me ravenous. I glanced up, my mouth stuffed with baguette and cheese, and found Bounmy watching with amusement.

"I should have brought more food," he said with a bemused smile.

I took a sip of tea. "Excuse me. It's so good, and I'm terribly hungry."

"I like a girl with a good appetite. Just leave me a few scraps."

My cheeks flushed. "I don't eat like this all the time."

"Ah, so you say." He put a spring roll on my plate. "It makes me happy to see you enjoy the meal."

I giggled. "I try to please."

"Have you heard anything from your inquiries about your parents and brother?" he asked.

His concern touched me. I explained about the letter from the orphanage director in Pakse who was trying to trace my brother's whereabouts.

"That's excellent news," he said.

"Yes. I hope to hear back soon on how I might reach Antoine. The waiting is hard." I sighed. "But on Friday, I received a response from the Assistance Society in Luang Prabang, stating their policy is not to reveal their charges' past. I was terribly upset." I paused a moment. "Then the strangest thing happened." I told him of my two encounters with the elderly Madame Lansay, and how she'd known my mother years ago. "She was confused and thought I was my mother. It's incredible I met her."

He considered my story for a moment then shrugged. "Perhaps it's your destiny to find this woman to lead you to your mother." His words echoed Mali's, with the acceptance of the most unlikely coincidence.

"Thanks to her I now know my mother's family name is Thongsavat, and that my grandfather was an important man. Do you think I might find them in Luang Prabang?"

He looked a bit startled by this news. "I know of a family with this name. Let me write to a friend in Luang Prabang and see what I can find out."

"I'd be very grateful." I pulled off a piece of baguette. "I plan to go back next week to see if Madame Lansay remembers anything more."

Bounmy stared at me. "Life gives us unexpected gifts sometimes." After a few moments, he picked up a wad of sticky rice. "I had many wonderful meals in Paris, but I craved Lao food. We found only one

Annamese restaurant with meals resembling anything close to those from home. But we had a tiny kitchen, so we learned to make simple dishes. A Chinese grocery sold most of the ingredients we needed."

"How was your cooking?"

He sat up, holding his head high. "It turns out I'm quite a talented chef."

"A prince who cooks. It's impressive."

"One day I'll make a meal for you." He glanced at my almost empty plate and smiled. "I have no doubt you'll be an appreciative guest."

"Now that Catherine's brother, Julian, is back from France, Mali serves more Lao dishes, and she's teaching me how to make some of them. I love Lao food, although some of it is too spicy. I don't know how you get used to the heat."

"Perhaps you must grow up with it." He paused. "By the way, Monsieur Courbet stopped by my office Friday afternoon. I remember him well from the *lycée* in Hanoi."

"He mentioned wanting to talk with you about the business he's starting."

"Yes, import/export. I fear the current world economic problems will make it a challenge, but our office will try to help." He kept his eyes focused on his plate. "You share the house with him as well now. It's not uncomfortable for you?"

His question surprised me. Would this arrangement be considered improper in a Lao home?

"I hardly see him. He's out late at night with friends, and I go to work early."

He nodded and started to say something but stopped, instead holding out a bunch of longans. "Do you like these?"

"I love them." I took four pieces of the small, round fruit. "As you can see, I like most everything." I concentrated on peeling the thin, fuzzy brown shell to reach the translucent white flesh that covered a large black seed. I popped the fruit in my mouth, closing my eyes and relishing the burst of sweetness, then discreetly removed the seed from my mouth into my napkin.

"When I was young, my cousins and I had contests to see who could spit their seeds the farthest," Bounmy said.

"My best friend Bridgette and I did that." I put the seed back in my mouth and shot it out with all the force I could muster. "Was that too rude?"

"No. It's a challenge."

Suddenly, we were ten years old, spitting longan seeds into the field, laughing with abandon, taunting each other about whose seed had sailed the greatest distance. Childish delight consumed his face, his reserved manner momentarily pushed aside.

Billowing clouds the color of charred wood eclipsed the blue sky, and a crack of thunder erupted nearby. Gusts of wind whipped the tree's branches into a frenzy.

"We'd better get back to the boat," Bounmy said, packing leftover food into the basket. But as we stood, the heavens unleashed a deluge, as powerful as a vast waterfall spilling over a rocky crag. He grabbed the quilt and draped it over our heads, pulling me back against the tree trunk.

We huddled together under our improvised tent and giggled uncertainly. Rain splattered my legs and soaked my shoes. A flash of lightning and an almost simultaneous roar of thunder sent goosebumps down my arms, and I let out a small cry. Bounmy stepped behind me, wrapping an arm around my waist. "We'll be fine," he said. "Don't worry."

His warm breath grazed my cheek, sweet with the scent of longan, and my heart thudded against my ribs until I thought it might explode. He rested his chin on top of my head and let out a long sigh. "Geneviève, I think of you constantly."

I longed to remain there, wrapped in his arms, our bodies spooling one into the other. I imagined turning my head and pressing my lips against his. Was this what he wanted? Was he waiting for a signal from me? But Catherine's warnings, always present in my mind, held me back. I didn't want to be misunderstood, to precipitate something I might regret.

Time became incalculable, seconds and minutes disappearing as we stood very still, breathing in unison. The quilt had soaked through, and water dripped down my face and back.

When the rain finally eased, as quickly as it had begun, Bounmy swallowed hard and stepped away, removing the wet quilt. Leaves dripped in a steady rhythm as light filtered through the clouds, now breaking apart and scattering to the west. It was like emerging from our own private cocoon. One I didn't want to leave.

"Let's make a run for it," he said, picking up the basket. I took the wet quilt from his arms as we hurried across the soggy meadow. The crew jumped from under the boat's cover to help us onto the boat. When Bounmy's fingers slipped from mine, I felt untethered. What was this overwhelming desire to touch him, to feel his warmth against my skin? Did he feel the same?

He pulled a gold watch from his pants pocket and opened the cover. "It's already four. We should head back if we want to see the monks' procession at dusk."

The pirogue slipped rapidly downstream on the swift current. We spoke a few times, remarking on a group of children splashing at the water's edge, shrieking with delight. Bounmy pointed out a pair of white-and-gray birds wading in a sandy shoal, graceful creatures who stood nearly two feet tall with long spindly legs and sharp black beaks, their heads bobbing in erratic movements. He said they were called Great Thick-Knees, which made me laugh. I had little knowledge of native species, but I felt an affinity for these unusual birds and their halting, cautious movements, wary of all things unfamiliar.

At one point he searched my eyes with an uncertain expression, as if seeking an answer to a question he couldn't quite ask, then he turned away. The words he'd whispered under the quilt swam in my head. I told myself to be grateful that he'd remained a gentleman, restraining himself from further advances, unlike Messieurs Simon and Toussaint. Yet, in truth, I desired more.

What could I expect from his friendship? Did he view me as an orphaned *métisse* floundering to find her future, simply someone he wanted to help? Or was I merely an amusement, a potential secret lover? Doubts crowded my mind as my emotions tumbled out of control toward a place where I feared disappointment and pain likely awaited.

Chapter 23

The boat pulled alongshore in town as the sun slowly faded, and we navigated the steep riverbank. "Let's find a spot along Avenue Lang Xang to view the procession," Bounmy said.

I thought again of Catherine cautioning me about being seen alone with him, but I hardly knew anyone in Vientiane. Who would notice?

The farmers who had sold their produce earlier in the day along the river road had packed up and gone home, leaving only a few disfigured long beans, broken stalks of lemongrass, and half-crushed papayas littering the ground. A group of elderly Lao men sat on their haunches under a tree, smoking and talking. They watched us pass, their regards inquisitive, perhaps disapproving. Or was that my imagination?

"What did you think of your first outing on the river?" Bounmy asked.

"It was wonderful. Thank you."

He smiled. "At least you didn't fall in the water, and I didn't have to rescue you."

I wondered if I needed him to rescue me, and what that might mean.

The sound of clanking metal came from behind us. We turned to find four members of the Garde Indigène, the local Lao law enforcement unit, with rifles slung over their shoulders, marching eight prisoners down the road. The captives' hands were shackled, and a rope tied them together. They appeared underfed in worn, tattered clothes. Bounmy pressed his lips together with distaste.

"What do you suppose they did?" I asked.

"Hard to know. There's been unrest on the Bolaven Plateau among workers at the coffee plantations. The Sûreté has stepped up efforts to uncover communist cells."

I recognized the name: Sûreté Générale, the French secret police. I looked into Bounmy's eyes with bewilderment. "Is there trouble in Laos? I read an article in the newspaper about rebellions at the rubber plantations in the Annamese colonies involving the Indochinese Communist Party, but I thought Laos was peaceful." I had seen the story by chance, which mentioned a man named Nguyen Ai Quoc who had formed a new communist organization and was in exile in Hong Kong. It warned that the group was creating an underground network throughout Indochine.

Bounmy nodded. "Trouble has started in a few Annamese villages in the south of Laos."

The chained men shuffled past, heads hanging down.

"But these men are Miao, from the mountains," Bounmy explained in a low voice. "If they're in the custody of the Garde Indigène, they must have tried to escape a *corvée* order."

"What is that?"

He sighed. "Because the colonies are always underfunded, native men are forced to work during part of each year on public work projects. The government uses the *corvée* labor to construct roads, telegraph lines, and public buildings."

"They don't pay them?"

He shrugged. "It's another form of taxation. Villages pay a head tax for each person who lives there, but the village chiefs are skilled at undercounting. The government developed *corvée* labor as another tax that helps fill the shortage of workers. In past years there were many abuses and unreasonable demands, as men were ordered to leave their fields in the middle of the planting or harvesting seasons. It's been better in recent years, but sometimes requests are still ill timed. As a result, there are always those who run away rather than serve."

"What will happen to them?"

"A judge will determine the punishment. I imagine they'll be in jail a few weeks, then they'll have to serve their *corvée* requirement anyway. The point is to discourage them from doing it again."

"Have you been called for *corvée* work?" I asked, unable to picture Bounmy on a crew, installing telegraph poles and stringing wires.

He shook his head. "Those who are well placed can simply pay a fee and be exempted. As a result, most *corvée* is performed by poor villagers, many from ethnic tribes in remote areas." He looked at me apologetically. "It's unfair. There are many practices like this one that I'd prefer to see changed."

"I feel sorry for these poor men."

"I agree."

We walked on in silence, reaching the busy Rue Maréchal Joffre. A tiny restaurant displayed a handwritten sign for Chinese food, and the smell of garlic and hot oil drifted from the open door.

"Mademoiselle Dubois," a voice called out of nowhere.

I turned with a start, feeling like I'd been caught doing something forbidden. André stood a few feet away, wearing the same rumpled khaki pants and shirt from the night before, as if he'd just tumbled out of bed. I could only imagine how hungover he must have felt after the vast quantity of alcohol he'd consumed the night before. He was the last person I wanted to see.

"Monsieur Robert," I said.

André held out his hand to Bounmy. "Prince Savang, André Robert. We went to *lycée* in Hanoi together. I understand you met with Julian Courbet recently."

Bounmy shook his hand and offered a tepid smile. "I remember you. Monsieur Courbet told me you had returned with him from France."

André inclined his head toward my damp dress. "Did you get caught in the rain? I'd forgotten how suddenly these storms come up."

"They can be surprising," Bounmy said evenly.

Julian emerged from a tobacco shop, walking toward us as he

studied the label on a pack of cigarettes. "André, they only—" He stopped midsentence on seeing us. "Vivi, Prince Savang, this is a surprise." Julian studied me for a moment. "Cat and I wondered where you had disappeared to all day."

"I was going to tell Catherine at Mass, but she didn't make it."

Julian smiled. "I'm afraid we were both done in by the party last night, but here you are, safe and sound."

"We're headed to Pierre's for a drink," André said. "Won't you join us?"

"Thank you, but we're going to watch the monks' procession. Another time," Bounmy said.

"Prince," Julian said, "I'll call you this week to schedule a tennis match."

"I'd like that." Bounmy gave a curt nod then took my elbow, leading me away.

His cool response surprised me. "You knew André at school as well?" I said at last.

"Unfortunately. Julian and I may have been academic rivals, but André was one of those boys who constantly caused trouble, taunting anyone who wasn't French. He and Kham got into fist fights almost weekly." A deep bitterness filled his words. "The French schoolmaster always took André's side, naturally."

I hadn't expected Bounmy's treatment in school to have mirrored my own. It seemed that being a royal prince had not protected him from the prejudices ingrained in French children at an early age.

"You've met André already?" Bounmy asked.

"He came for dinner last night." I explained about Marguerite's birthday party and how drunk André had been. "I can't understand how Julian can be friends with him. I found his behavior and the things he said disgusting. I hope to avoid him in the future."

"I feel the same."

We picked a spot along Avenue Lang Xang, blending into a crowd of Lao and Annamese followers waiting for the Visakha Bousa procession. As darkness descended, a steady line of monks filed past carrying candles. The flickering lights filled the night like stars that had descended from heaven to scatter their glow.

"It's magical," I whispered to Bounmy.

Once the procession ended, we strolled toward home. I already felt sad at the thought of parting, wondering when we might meet again. Or if we would.

"Mali has been teaching me Buddhist beliefs," I said. "I want to better understand how my mother was raised. I find the serene nature of Buddhism—striving for enlightenment and nirvana, freedom from human pain and torment on Earth, being kind and doing good deeds to earn merit in this life and the next—more appealing than the Catholic faith. I've always had trouble believing in a God that allows such terrible suffering around the world, and a church that threatens hell and damnation, punishing people for the slightest sins."

"I took a class on world religions in Paris and discovered all faiths, at their core, encourage good behavior with the promise of a better life beyond this one, yet balanced with the threat of severe punishment for any misbehavior. Buddhism takes a gentler approach in some ways, perhaps, but it's basically the same. Holidays like Visakha Bousa are an important reminder of the higher purpose in Buddha's teachings. Yet many people who call themselves Buddhists inflict cruelty and pain on others. Religious beliefs everywhere are easily misinterpreted and abused."

His philosophical, almost cynical, response surprised me. "Do you consider yourself a Buddhist?"

"I was raised Buddhist, and I try to follow its basic tenets, as it's so ingrained in our culture and daily activities here in Laos. But like you, there are aspects of my religion that I question." He looked down at me, his face unreadable in the dim light. "And you?"

"I'm still trying to figure it out. There is much I don't understand, and in school they never taught us anything about other beliefs."

"It's good you are curious and willing to consider other ideas. I like that about you."

I held on to these words of praise.

When we reached the house, I thanked him for the wonderful day.

Bounmy bowed slightly. "We'll meet again soon."

"I'd like that." Why didn't he suggest another date now? Had I disappointed him? Since we'd returned to town on the boat, he'd remained reserved and stiff, as if holding his emotions in check, not wanting to give away too much of himself.

Waiting to hear from him again would be agony.

I stepped through the gate and watched him leave. He turned, merely an outline in the dark, and waved one last time.

Chapter 24

The next evening Julian and I ambled along the garden path out back as the day faded into shadows and crickets tuned up for their nightly refrain. The scents of jasmine and frangipani filled the air, making me think of the neem tree where Bounmy and I had picnicked.

Julian had joined Catherine and me for dinner, saying he'd had enough of nights out drinking with André. He'd spent the meal detailing the steps for setting up his business, as if responding to questions at a job interview. I wondered if he hoped to convince Catherine that he was sincere about moving forward. She nodded encouragement and offered to help in any way, while I silently noted that after a week at home, the only thing he'd accomplished was a brief meeting with Bounmy. Nothing seemed urgent to him.

Now Julian held up a hand. "The breeze off the river feels wonderful. Walking out here with you is so much nicer than drinking at Pierre's with André." He gave a soft laugh. "He's always a bad influence, I'm afraid."

I kept quiet, still skeptical about a friendship with Julian, even though he'd vowed I was more than welcome in their home and asked for a second chance. His attentions early in the evening at Marguerite's birthday party had pleased me—being twirled around the room to the music—but André's inexcusable insults had ruined the night. The fact that Julian was close friends with such a person gave me pause.

He glanced over sheepishly. "I suppose I can't really blame André."

I couldn't let the moment pass. "André said a number of things I found very upsetting Saturday night. Doesn't his behavior disturb you?"

"I apologize. Catherine already gave me a dressing down. We drank so much, I don't even recall half the evening or what was said, and I'm sure André doesn't remember anything." He hung his head.

"Being drunk is not a good enough excuse."

"You're right, of course. I understand perfectly why you would feel insulted, but if you knew him as well as I do, you'd discover he's not a bad person at heart. He babbles on about things, trying to be clever and funny, wanting people to like him, but not realizing how offensive his comments can be."

"I think he wants to impress you as much as anyone," I said. "He doesn't know how to compete with your looks and charm."

Julian started, a tinge of pink creeping up his face. "Heavens. I never would have thought that."

We continued around the pathway, silence hanging between us like an unwelcome guest.

"I promise to talk with him—while he's sober—and make him realize how inappropriate his behavior was," he said at last. "He owes you an apology."

He brushed the hair back from his forehead. "By the way, I called Prince Savang today and we have a tennis match scheduled Thursday evening. Perhaps you'd like to watch."

"That would be fun." I jumped at the chance of seeing Bounmy again.

"Have you ever played?"

I shook my head. "The only sport we played at school was badminton."

Julian brightened. "Then I'll teach you."

I glanced over at him. "I'm not sure..."

"I have something tomorrow, but we can go Wednesday and make a start of it."

"On Wednesday Mali and I are visiting the elderly woman I met." I had explained about my unexpected meeting with Madame Lansay. "I want to talk with her again to see if she remembers anything else.

Bounmy—I mean, Prince Savang—is writing to a friend in Luang Prabang to see what he can find out about my mother's family."

"How considerate of him."

"Yes." I gave a little sigh. "I seem to be endlessly waiting for answers. Every day I come home from work hoping to find another letter from Pakse about my brother, and now I'm waiting again for news from Luang Prabang."

"I'm sure it's frustrating." He swatted at a mosquito buzzing near his ear. "Learning tennis will be perfect for keeping you busy, in the meantime. We can go to the club early on Thursday, and I'll show you some basic moves before the prince arrives."

I was about to protest when Mali called from the back door, "Mademoiselle Vivi, you have a phone call."

I hurried to the house, wondering who could possibly be calling me. When I reached Mali, she gave a conspiratorial shrug and whispered, "It's your prince."

My hand trembled as I picked up the receiver. "Hello?"

"Geneviève, it's Bounmy. I'm glad to catch you at home," he said, as if I must have a busy social calendar taking up all my free time. "I've been thinking about our nice day together and wondered if you'd be free next Sunday?"

"Yes. Yes, Sunday is fine." I cringed, knowing I sounded overeager.

"Shall we meet in front of Wat Sisaket at one o'clock? I'd like to visit a temple outside of town that is very old. We can take a picnic again."

I agreed, then said, "Julian told me you're playing tennis Thursday and invited me to come watch. I hope you don't mind."

He was silent a moment. "Of course not. I'll be delighted to see you then, as well. So, until then, goodnight." Abruptly he was gone, and the receiver issued a noise like a slow-moving bumble bee searching for pollen.

I turned around to find Julian standing in the doorway to the salon with his back to me. I wondered if he was eavesdropping.

I followed him into the room, where Catherine was sitting. "I hear you're going to learn to play tennis," she said. "I'll loan you one of my tennis outfits."

"Thank you, but I'm not sure if—"

"We can play doubles sometimes, as well," she interrupted. "That's a good way to start. It's great fun."

"Am I allowed to play without belonging to the Cercle?" The idea turned my stomach, as I could imagine the disgruntled, rude stares of French members on seeing my presence.

"You'll be our guest," Julian said. "No one will care."

It seemed pointless to try to convince Julian how many Frenchmen *did* care about the intrusion of an uninvited *métis* into their sacred world. But he and Catherine seemed determined to draw me into their plans, and I couldn't think of a polite way to refuse.

Chapter 25

On Wednesday evening after dinner, Mali and I crossed town to visit Madame Lansay again, but we found the house quiet.

Mali knocked on the closed door and called out, "Madame Lansay, are you at home?" No one responded. She tried once more, but still no answer.

Madame Ketthavong appeared in her doorway, bowing in a *nop*. "*Bonsoir*. Can I help you?" she asked. I explained that we'd hoped to talk with the grandmother once more about my mother, but no one seemed to be home.

Madame Ketthavong's face filled with sadness. "Madame Lansay died peacefully in her sleep on Monday night."

I grabbed onto Mali's arm. "I'm... I'm so sorry."

"Her funeral was this afternoon, and the family is still at the temple," Madame Ketthavong said. She pointed to the interior of her shop. "Would you like to come in and wait for them?"

"I don't want to intrude, but please tell them how sorry I am. She gave me a wonderful gift by remembering my mother."

As Mali and I retreated down the lane, my eyes welled with tears. "I'm afraid her death is my fault," I said. "Reliving those memories from the past must have been too much for her."

Mali shook her head. "No, no. She was very old and frail. It was simply her time."

"But it's a terrible loss for her family."

"They will be sad and miss her, but they know her soul is in heaven now and will pass on to the next life soon. This is the natural cycle of things."

I wanted to share her humble acceptance of this loss, but questions and doubts remained. All I knew for sure was that Madame Lansay was gone, and with her my hopes of learning anything more about my mother.

———

Julian and I arrived at the club at six fifteen on Thursday evening, heading directly out back to the two tennis courts and the patio with tables and chairs for spectators. Even though Julian wore white shorts and a short-sleeved knit shirt, I dragged behind him, unbearably self-conscious in Catherine's white, sleeveless shirt and tennis skirt, which barely reached two inches above my knees. I'd never publicly exposed so much of my body, and it left me desperate to wrap myself in towels and hide under a table. Four women in similar outfits sat under an umbrella at one table sipping iced teas and blotting their sweaty faces.

"Julian, how nice to see you," one of the younger women called out, tipping her head and batting her big gray eyes. She had long brunette hair tied back from her face with a deep purple scarf that matched her lipstick.

He waved and flashed a genial smile but concentrated on depositing equipment and towels onto the table next to them. "Try this one," he said, handing me a racket from his bag.

We moved to the far end of one court with our rackets and a bucket of balls. I could feel the women following us with curious eyes, their whispers drifting through the air. Julian showed me how to grip the racket, the proper position for my feet, and the basic movement of a forehand, stepping into the swing. I tried to imitate him, finding the racket heavy and awkward to control. Then he bounced a few balls into the air and gently lobbed them over the net.

"Now you try," he said. "Remember to keep your eyes on the ball."

I missed the first two balls completely, and the third one didn't reach high enough to get over the net. "I'm so uncoordinated," I moaned.

"Nonsense. You'll get the hang of it." He picked up the bucket of balls and headed to the other side. "Let's try hitting some balls back and forth. Just relax."

To my surprise, I slowly improved, and we were able to volley back and forth three or four times before I missed a ball or sent it careening off to the side. Julian, endlessly patient, issued constant encouragement—*well done, great hit, excellent.*

He checked his watch and returned to my side of the court. "The prince will be here soon, but I want to show you the basics of the backhand." He changed my grip and the position of my feet, showing me how to pull the racket back across my body then swing it forward. He smiled at me expectantly, so I gave it my best try, unsure if I was anywhere close to doing it right. He stepped behind me and took hold of my bare shoulders, turning me farther sideways, then with his head next to mine, reached around and grabbed my right wrist, swinging my arm and racket back and forth. "Like this," he said, repeating the movement several times.

The sudden touch of Julian's skin and his breath on my neck made my cheeks blaze, and memories of standing with Bounmy under the tree flashed through my mind. When he finally stepped away, I glanced over to discover Bounmy watching, his tennis bag hanging off his shoulder, a deep crevice between his eyebrows. My breathing turned shallow, and embarrassment consumed me. Whatever would he think?

"Prince Savang." Julian waved and loped across the court.

I trailed behind, unable to lift my eyes to Bounmy. He wore long white pants and a short-sleeved shirt, which made my bare limbs even more egregious. I grabbed a towel and sat down, draping it over my legs.

Bounmy and Julian chatted about the new electric lights that had recently been installed on the courts, allowing for night-time play when the temperatures cooled down. As they picked up their rackets and a fresh set of balls, I finally peeked up at Bounmy and raised my hand in a timid wave. He gave a curt nod before jogging to the far end of the court. Julian proceeded with a series of exercises—jumping up and down, swinging his racket over his head, stretching his arms and legs—as if he were competing in a gymnastics competition. Practice volleys sailed across the net.

The two older women at the next table said their goodbyes and left, but the brunette who had spoken to Julian earlier asked her remaining companion to stay. "This should be interesting. Let's order cocktails." She lifted a finger to signal the waiter standing by the back door.

"Who is Julian playing?" the other woman asked, removing her visor and running a hand through her wiry red curls.

"I've never seen him before, but he must be part of Prince Phetsarath's entourage. He reminds me of Prince Souvanna," the brunette said, then giggled, "but they all look alike to me."

Bounmy and Julian began the first game. Even to my untrained eye, it was clear Julian had far more experience and skill. He played with heavy, powerful strokes, rushing in to slam the ball over the net out of Bounmy's reach. He didn't exactly gloat, but every time he won a point, he shouted "*Allez!*" I had no knowledge of proper court etiquette, but his behavior struck me as annoying and arrogant.

Bounmy remained unruffled. Rather than trying to match Julian's hard-hitting, he carefully placed his returns to catch Julian off balance or to set up a pattern that allowed him to hit a winner in the next stroke or two, rather like a carefully orchestrated game of chess. I was fascinated by the effectiveness of his tactics, learning far more watching him than I ever would have from playing.

Julian won the first set six-three. "Shall we go another?" he asked, grinning at his victory. Bounmy nodded.

The redheaded woman inclined her head toward her friend. "Did you hear the latest? Marcel Fontaine is being transferred to Luang Prabang."

"Really! But why?" the brunette asked. "They cleared him of the accusation with the maid—the girl swore up and down he never touched her."

"Jeanette didn't care. She's had enough of his drinking and running around town. Everyone knows he's been seeing Julian's sister, Catherine." The redhead took a sip of her gin and tonic and gazed over at me, as if it had finally dawned on her that I might overhear them. "Anyway, she left for Saigon with the children on Monday and is booked on a ship home next month. She's filing for divorce. The Resident Superior ordered Marcel to stop drinking and warned that the assignment in Luang Prabang is his last chance."

I wondered if Marguerite had informed Catherine of the latest, and if so, how she felt. Perhaps it didn't matter, although it was a relief to have it confirmed that Monsieur Fontaine hadn't hurt the poor young maid. Did that ease Catherine's pain at all?

Bounmy and Julian played a second set filled with long rallies and lots of close points. Bounmy had agility over Julian's brute strength. In the end, Bounmy won seven to six, after a tiebreak. His expression was subdued, but I noticed a barely perceptible smile on his lips.

It was after nine when they quit and put their rackets back in their bags. Bounmy turned to me with a warm smile, and my heart fluttered with relief that he wasn't angry with me.

"Won't you stay for a drink, Prince Savang?" Julian asked.

"Thank you, but I have an early meeting tomorrow. And please call me Bounmy."

"Of course, and call me Julian." He ran a towel over his sweaty brow. "We'll schedule a rematch soon. You gave me quite a workout." His obvious surprise at Bounmy's tennis skills sounded condescending.

"I look forward to the next time," Bounmy agreed, his tone that of an indulgent parent with a small child.

"I was teaching Vivi a few basic strokes when you arrived. I thought we might play doubles with her and my sister sometime."

Bounmy nodded and lifted his bag to his shoulder. "Thank you for inviting me." Then he turned toward me. "I'll see you Sunday, Geneviève."

The muscles along Julian's jaw tightened as his eyes darted between Bounmy and me.

After Bounmy's departure, Julian gathered our things. "We can do tennis lessons every Tuesday," he said, as if it were a foregone conclusion. "You did so well tonight, you'll be a pro in no time."

I bit my bottom lip, wondering how to say no without disappointing him. "I'll have to see how tired I am. Sometimes work exhausts me."

"Exercise is just what you need to build your stamina and shake off the day's worries." He started to walk out, then spun around. "I promised you a night of dancing at the club. I can't this Saturday, but perhaps next week."

"It's not important." In truth, I'd hoped he would forget. "When I went with Catherine and Marguerite for dinner a few weeks ago, I felt terribly uncomfortable. I don't belong among these people."

"That's ridiculous." He grinned. "Besides, you'll be with me."

Chapter 26

June 15, 1931

Chère Bridgette,

Your last letter cheered me up considerably, when I am the one who should be brightening your days. I'm sorry to complain about my stupid job, which is nowhere near as terrible as your situation. At least today is Friday and I am getting paid tomorrow, so despite the way the men treat me, I hope Kham will keep me on.

I'm waiting, waiting, waiting, but still no news on my brother or my mother's family. Surely I will hear again soon from the orphanage in Pakse, but the mail is incredibly slow. Bounmy expects his friend in Luang Prabang to write back within a month. I feel so sad about Madame Lansay and worry I hastened her passing in bringing up memories of my mother. Life is full of unexpected losses.

After Mass yesterday—too bad Director Bernard showed up to keep us apart again—I met Bounmy for the afternoon. Our third date! He hired a horse-drawn carriage to take us to an ancient wat a few kilometers out of town where we had a delicious picnic in the shade of a huge tamarind tree. The temple was sacked by the Siamese over a hundred years ago—along with most of the temples in Vientiane—and it lies in ruins, overrun with grasses and vines curling around and through the mossy rocks. In the center is a giant stone Buddha (as tall as three people), sitting cross-legged with one hand resting in his lap and the other hand pointing to the ground. Bounmy says it is one of several common Buddha poses, which represent different episodes in his life. This one is called the earth witness pose, indicating the earth as witness to his achieving enlightenment. I love the way Buddha stares out at the world unperturbed by the drift of time, eternally content. If only I could be this accepting.

He is very intelligent and wise—Bounmy, that is—and I'm learning a great deal about Buddhism and Buddhist art. I might become a convert. Wouldn't Maîtresse be horrified!! I suppose you might be, as well. Bounmy is easy to talk with and a good listener, truly interested in what I have to say and how I feel. I am comfortable around him, both when we are sharing ideas and in silence. When his arm brushes against mine or he stares at me with those dark, searching eyes, my heart practically flies away.

As we wandered around the site, he took my hand and kissed it. Twice! But nothing more. He can be a bit reserved, even mysterious, so I'm not sure what to think. He said he enjoys my company and wants us to spend more time together, then invited me to have dinner next Friday. My heart melted. Why hasn't he kissed me properly on the lips? My impulse is to throw my arms around him—don't worry, I didn't. Oh Bridgette, I am totally infatuated with this man, maybe even in love, but having only read about such feelings in novels, how can I be sure?

Several weeks ago, when Bounmy first asked to see me, Catherine warned me to be careful about appearing in public with him too often, as people might gossip—some might assume we are lovers (what a delicious word, even if it makes my cheeks turn bright red). Sunday, she mentioned it again, asking if I found it wise to see him so regularly. I realize she cares about me and doesn't want me to be hurt or unfairly judged, but how can I follow her advice? All I want is to be close to Bounmy as often as possible. How could someone so lovely and kind end up hurting me?

Anyway, life at the house has changed dramatically since Julian arrived this month. At first I hardly saw him as he went out every evening with his friend André, but now he eats dinners at home, even when Catherine has other plans. We often end up walking in the back garden after our meal, speaking of anything and everything. Unlike Bounmy, Julian is never quiet or reserved! I enjoy his company, but I hardly have any time alone with Catherine or Mali these days (my Lao lessons have suffered).

You'll like Julian—handsome, spirited, and with blue eyes that take your breath away. Probably every French woman in Vientiane under the age of forty, single or married, has a crush on him. He's constantly making plans for us to do things together—tennis lessons, dancing at the club, and yesterday he announced we'll be playing belote (a card game popular in France these days) every Thursday evening with Catherine and Marguerite. Soon I won't have any free time left. Bounmy has made comments about Julian that make me think he's jealous of him. I've tried to assure him that he's only a friend, but I can hardly avoid Julian when we live under the same roof.

I have to sleep now so I can survive another day at work. Write whenever you have the urge, and I think your drawings are amazing. Who knew you had artistic talent?

Hugs and more hugs,

Vivi

I finished the letter and folded it into an envelope for Catherine to deliver the next day. The familiar guilt nagged at me as I hadn't written as often as I wanted, being preoccupied with work, Bounmy, and now Julian's demands on my time. While I was off living new adventures each day, poor Bridgette remained encased at the orphanage, trapped in time. Once she was free, I would make sure she discovered the world in all its wonders.

My days at River Transport grew more boring as the weeks passed and I continued probing the office's dysfunctional practices: too many invoices and payments not properly recorded or somehow misplaced (purposely destroyed?). Sometimes goods were logged into the warehouse, but the subsequent receipt of goods delivered to the client showed smaller quantities. Where did items go? The accountants refused to let me touch the ledger recording customs taxes owed to the government.

My campaign to win over my coworkers had floundered, and

suggestions for new record and filing systems had been repeatedly rejected. All they ever said was, "No, no, not necessary. Just file the papers we give you." Little changed. Business went on as usual. It was a test of wills, and I was losing.

I finally cornered Kham one afternoon to explain my proposals for improving his business, expecting his support. He barely listened, shuffling through papers on his desk as I tried to get his attention. "I'm having trouble getting the other employees to welcome my suggestions," I said. "Perhaps if you could encourage them—"

"Work it out yourself," he interrupted, waving impatiently. "I don't have time for this." It didn't make sense for him to be so indifferent when he was paying me to do a job.

I endured the obstinate, dismissive behavior of the others, even though it went against every fiber of my nature. What was it about my efforts that threatened them so? What were they hiding? I was determined to uncover the truth.

The only thing that kept me from falling into despair was my time with Bounmy—we now had regular dates on Friday nights and Sunday afternoons. He lifted my spirits and filled me with joy.

The last Friday in June, Julian showed up at the office for a meeting with Kham about shipping routes and rates for his proposed business. I'd never seen Kham act so obsequious with anyone—all smiles and friendliness. When they finished their discussion, Julian surprised me by insisting on taking me to lunch. We walked to Pierre's, where he ordered us both a croque monsieur and a glass of white wine. As always, he listened to my complaints about work with a sympathetic ear, then managed to make me laugh and forget my unhappiness. It turned out that consuming alcohol at lunch was a terrible mistake, leaving me completely useless the rest of the afternoon.

Near the end of the day, Kham stopped by my desk. "How do you know Monsieur Courbet?" When I explained that his sister had been my teacher and now rented me a room in their house, a smirk spread across his face. He leaned in close, his sour breath wafting across my face. "Do you have many friends like Monsieur Courbet?"

I blinked several times. "I don't understand what you mean." His proximity and the implication of something inappropriate made my cheeks burn. I'd done nothing wrong.

Kham simply laughed and returned to his office. When I looked up later, he was staring at me with a nasty smile that made me recoil.

Chapter 27

The next day brought banner news on two fronts. At work, Kham emerged from his office at noon and handed me my weekly pay as usual then cleared his throat. "Mademoiselle Dubois, I'd like you to continue working here. I find your efforts helpful."

"Thank you. I do my best." I bowed slightly. Helpful? What exactly did that mean? He seemed completely uninterested in my attempts to improve things, and I'd hardly made any progress. I didn't question him. Even though I detested the place and everyone who worked there, the money made it worthwhile, especially when the difficulty of finding another job was too frightening to fathom.

Kham gave a quick nod. "I'll be traveling to my office in Luang Prabang in September, and I'd like you to accompany me to continue your work there." He raised an eyebrow. "Bounmy suggested you would welcome the invitation."

His words fell like lucky charms dropped from the heavens, an answer to my dreams. I'd be able to visit my mother's family, with the outside chance that my mother might, just might, be there. Overwhelmed by my emotions, all I could do was bob my head in agreement. I couldn't wait to thank Bounmy. I had no idea how frequently they spoke or whether I was ever a topic of discussion between them.

I floated toward home filled with exuberant hopes, hardly noticing the dark clouds blotting out the sun. Without warning the skies opened up, drenching my hair and clothes, raising the scent of mud and wet leaves. I had forgotten my umbrella, but it didn't matter. Laughing and opening my arms wide, I spun in circles, celebrating my good fortune, not caring what anyone thought.

An older Frenchman stepped into my path. "Would you like to dance, mademoiselle? I can accommodate you." He put his arms out, as if to grab me.

I batted his arm and spun away, laughing. As time passed I'd become skilled at avoiding the advances of men like this, no longer frightened, only annoyed. The frequency of these encounters had dropped off substantially, perhaps because I carried myself with more assurance now. Or maybe the French men in town had come to recognize me, knowing I would not tolerate their mischief.

By the time I reached the house, the sun had reclaimed the sky and nearly dried my skirt and blouse. I breezed in the front door anxious to tell Mali and Catherine my news. On the silver tray, an envelope from the orphanage director in Pakse awaited me. I ripped it open, hardly able to breathe.

June 18, 1931
Société d'assistance aux Métis
19 Rue du Marché
Pakse, Laos

Chère Mademoiselle Dubois,
I hope this finds you well.
I finally received a response yesterday from the Lycée Chasseloup-Laubat in Saigon regarding your brother Antoine Dubois. They inform me he completed his baccalauréat (with honors) at the end of May and has taken an assistant manager position at a coffee plantation on the Bolaven Plateau, an hour and a half from Pakse. I wrote him immediately and forwarded your earlier letter to him at the address listed below. I'm sure he will write you directly.
I hope you and Antoine are able to meet soon and establish a familial bond that sustains you through life. Wishing you all the best in the future. I would love to hear from you both when you have the time.
With deepest regards,

Christophe Augustin, Director

New Address:
Antoine Dubois, Assistant Manager
Leblanc Caféière Postal Box
Pakse, Laos

Mali looked up, alarmed by my shrieks and tears of joy as I danced into the kitchen. My family was within reach, only a few steps away on the horizon.

Chapter 28

At last. The long circuitous route—to Pakse then Saigon and back again, across the Bolaven Plateau's rugged, sparsely populated mountains and forests to a remote coffee plantation—to find my brother had succeeded. After two anxious months of waiting, a thick tan envelope, slightly soiled and tattered, with my name and address written in hurried, messy letters, sat on the silver tray that Wednesday afternoon when I returned from work, like a brightly wrapped Christmas present. I rushed to my room and tore it open.

July 5, 1931

Chère Geneviève,

My sister. How strange and amazing to write these words. Monsieur Augustin forwarded your letter of May 18, which I received four days ago. This is the happiest news of my life. I have a sibling, a twin! I am truly shocked and extremely angry that the Assistance Society would try to keep us from each other, but grateful that Monsieur Augustin understood how wrong this was and made the effort to find me. I will visit him on my next trek to Pakse to thank him.

I want to meet you as soon as possible, but since I only began my job in late May, it will be several months before I can take time off to visit Vientiane. Be patient. I will come.

Meanwhile, we can correspond and come to know each other better. I have never had the opportunity to write to anyone in this manner, but I'll do my best. Where to begin?

My early years at the orphanage in Pakse were not unhappy. Monsieur Augustin is a good man who took an interest in me. Thanks to his efforts, my closest friend, Paul, and I moved to Saigon in 1924 to continue our education. We lived in a boarding house with French and other métis students from all parts of Indochine, while attending college and lycée at the Chasseloup-Laubat. While some of our French classmates were kind and accepting, others were less than friendly, calling us sale métis and half-bloods, making us feel inferior, nearly subhuman! I never understood why our mixed heritage threatened them so. I wonder if you experienced this as well. Annamese and Lao students, who attended separate classes from the French and métis, were more polite. A few became my friends.

Paul is in Saigon still but leaves for France next week to attend university. I decided it would be best to earn some money before going, but I hope to follow him next year. Even with a scholarship, it will be a struggle to get by in Paris.

After finishing my baccalauréat, I was offered this job at the coffee plantation, where I am the assistant manager, a title that sounds much grander than the reality. I oversee the daily tasks and needs of the laborers, which means the manager issues orders and I carry them out. Being fluent in both Lao and Annamese, as well as French, helped me acquire the position.

For the first time in my life, being métis proved an advantage as the French plantation owners viewed me as "almost French," almost equal. Presumably I'm more trustworthy than the indigène workers. I'm sure you understand this dichotomy in our lives.

There is much to share with you, but I will stop here, as I admit to being a little lazy and writing is an effort. I was much better at mathematics and science in school.

Please answer soon and tell me everything you are able to put in a letter. What do you look like? Can you send me a picture? The next time I go to Pakse, I'll have a photo taken to send you. I wonder if we look alike, or if I am better looking. Ha ha! What is your favorite pastime? What was your schooling like? Your orphanage? What are you doing in Vientiane?

I look forward to hearing from you. The company only sends a courier to Pakse once a week for the mail and to pick up supplies, so our letters will be slow to reach each other.

As you might expect, I have always questioned my origins and why our parents abandoned us. I want desperately to find answers. I hope that together, we can uncover their story.

My best regards,

Your brother,

Antoine

What joy! He wanted to meet me. To be a family. I reread his letter three times, impressed by his openness and the way our lives were different yet echoed each other's in many ways. He had shared the confusion and difficulty of being *métis* and having an unknown past.

His letter had taken ten days to reach me. I would have to be content for now to correspond with him, however slow the mail might be. I couldn't wait to tell everyone my news, most of all Bridgette and Bounmy.

———

The next evening, Marguerite arrived after dinner ready for another rowdy, fiercely competitive evening of belote. The four of us became wildly animated in the heat of battle, shouting out with glee in victory, bemoaning losses. Marguerite issued a stream of curses every time she lost, which always made me giggle. Drinks flowed, and we stayed up too late. Julian, the only one who didn't have to get up early and go to work, kept begging us to play one more hand.

As the first game got under way, Julian and I paired up against Catherine and Marguerite, and we each drew a card from the deck to see who would deal. Julian got the lowest card and began shuffling.

"Catherine told me you got a letter from your brother yesterday," Marguerite said, holding up her gin and tonic. "A toast to Antoine. I can't wait to meet him."

"It's so exciting," Catherine said. "I hope he can visit soon."

"Miraculously, I received a letter from Charles today," Marguerite said, picking up her cards as Julian dealt. "He's in Hanoi at the moment but headed back to Luang Prabang next week. He wants me to visit during my vacation in early October."

"This is getting serious," Julian said. "I have to meet this man."

Marguerite shrugged. "We'll see how it goes." She tried to sound indifferent, but a silly grin betrayed her.

Catherine sipped her sherry. "Vivi, I haven't had a chance to tell you that Bridgette passed her algebra exam today. She has officially completed her baccalauréat. I was concerned she wouldn't do well with that fever she's been fighting, but she scored eighty percent. You should have seen the look on her face when she saw the results!"

"I'm so happy for her," I said. "But why do you think the fever keeps coming back?"

Catherine frowned. "Perhaps it's a virus of some sort. I asked Maîtresse to take her to the doctor, but she said Director Bernard doesn't think it is necessary."

This sparked my anger. "What if she has an infection or something worse?" I picked up my cards, unable to focus on them. "She must get healthy. It's another three weeks until her birthday."

"If she's not better by Monday, I'll take her." Catherine patted my arm. "We'll have a grand celebration the night she arrives."

As the evening wore on, amidst all the jokes and teasing, I caught Julian studying me as he often did, in the way one might stare at a favorite photo, something that brings a happy memory, a smile to your lips. Whatever was he thinking?

At midnight, Marguerite threw her cards on the table after another defeat. "I absolutely have to go home." She took her leave.

As Mali had gone to bed long before, we carried dirty glasses, bowls of nuts and fruit, and overflowing ashtrays to the kitchen. Catherine yawned and said goodnight, heading upstairs. Julian folded the card table. I rearranged chairs and turned out lights.

In the semidarkness, he stepped in front of me at the bottom of the stairs. "I...I wondered if we couldn't finally go to the club this

Saturday…with Catherine and Marguerite, of course. They're going to have a live band."

I stared down at the complicated pattern of the hallway's Persian rug, searching for yet another way to politely say no. But I'd long ago run out of reasonable excuses. Bounmy had mentioned that he spent Saturdays with his cousin Prince Phetsarath and other family members, often dining at the Cercle, where Prince Phetsarath was an honorary member due to his royal rank and high position in the government. I couldn't risk him seeing me there with Julian.

It would be dishonest to pretend I didn't feel a certain attraction to Julian's handsome face and buoyant personality, or that I didn't enjoy our flirting, joking, and unrestrained laughter. His attentions made me feel special and slightly smug, knowing that half the French women in Vientiane would give anything to be in my place. I could see the envy and resentment in other women's eyes when Julian and I played tennis at the club or lunched at Pierre's. Spending time with him pleased me, rather like the warm feeling I got after reading a novel with a happy ending. I considered him a friend, a pleasant diversion; after all, it was important that we get along, for Catherine's sake. But my feelings for him were subdued; nothing like the tingling thrill that ran through my body when I saw Bounmy.

"You can't possibly turn me down again," he said, with a short, harsh laugh. "It's only dinner and dancing, Vivi."

"Thank you, but no. You're all so good to me. I don't want you to feel obligated to invite me."

Julian took both my hands in his. "I don't feel obligated in the least. I want to spend time with you." He flashed one of his easy smiles. "We have fun together."

I should have pulled away, but his warm grip felt comfortable. My cheeks filled with heat. "Yes, but…"

"You're worried about Bounmy." His voice became impatient.

I looked down once more. "In part."

"Would he really begrudge you an evening out with friends? What does he do on the Saturday nights that you're not together?"

I resented that he expected me to justify my relationship with Bounmy.

"Vivi, I treasure our friendship." His eyes searched mine, seeking something in return. "I'd like us to be…better friends." And then his lips touched mine, soft and light, and his arms encircled me, pulling me close, our hearts pounding one against the other. My first thought was how lovely it felt, and I didn't want to stop. But an image of Bounmy flashed in my mind and guilt overcame me. What was I doing? How could I kiss Julian when it was Bounmy who held my heart?

I stepped back. "I can't do this."

I fled to my room, closing the door and sinking onto the floor, a storm of pleasure and guilt roiling my chest. How extraordinary that my first real kiss had come from Julian and not Bounmy—and more so that I had enjoyed it.

What *did* Bounmy expect of me? He'd never made any promises or talked of the future, and yet he clearly disliked, perhaps feared, my relationship with Julian. Why had he never offered more than a few chaste kisses, never on my lips? His affection and warmth remained a whisper, never a shout. I had no idea why he was holding back.

Chapter 29

All the next day I nervously awaited Bounmy's arrival. My mind cycled back again and again to Julian's kiss, and the unexpected pleasure I'd felt in the moment, then remorse for having strayed. I felt unworthy of Bounmy's attentions and affection. Would he know something had happened? Would he read the guilt in my face or voice?

It was after six already and still no sign of Bounmy. We'd agreed it was better for him to come for me after Kham and the others had left work, not wanting to fuel further speculation about our relationship.

We had our regular dates on Fridays and Sundays, although Wednesday he'd come by saying he wanted to be with me even if it was only to walk me home from work. On our dates, we'd spend contented hours strolling leisurely along the river, exploring temples and new neighborhoods, wandering through the Friday night market, riding a carriage into the countryside, or drifting on a boat down the Mekong. Mostly, we avoided places where French *colons* gathered. The destination mattered little to me, as long as he was by my side. In the shadows where no one could see, we held hands, and occasionally he kissed my forehead or cheek, tenderly gazing into my eyes. Desires I'd never felt before blossomed and deepened, as my heart rejoiced over every detail and nuance of his being: his beautiful smile and dimples; his calm, reassuring voice; the warmth of his hand encircling mine; his subtle jokes and sweet laughter. Thoughts of him crowded my waking hours, and I counted the moments until we would be together again. So why had I responded to Julian's kiss?

At six thirty, Bounmy burst into the office. "*Désolé*. I was stuck in a meeting and couldn't get away."

Overwrought and ashamed, I didn't know what to say. "A letter came from my brother Wednesday," I blurted out.

His face lit up, and he pulled me into a quick hug, which only made me feel worse about what I'd done. "What wonderful news. What did he say?"

"That he's surprised and happy to find he has a sister. He promises to visit as soon as he can get time off from his new job."

"I look forward to meeting him...that is, if you want to introduce us."

"Of course. He wants to know everything about me, so I mailed him a five-page letter yesterday describing my life."

Bounmy took my hand and squeezed it. "I would have liked to read it, so I could know more about you as well."

I averted my eyes, thinking of my betrayal. "I've probably told you most things already. My life is simple and unexciting."

He put a hand over his heart. "I'm wounded."

"Oh, I didn't mean...not my time with you, of course."

He chuckled. "I hope not."

"I have good news for you, as well." He pulled a paper from his pocket. "My friend from Luang Prabang found your mother's family and where they live. When you go there with Kham in September, you'll be able to visit them."

"How can I thank you enough?" I gazed down at the name and directions in Bounmy's careful script: *Family Thongsavat compound, two kilometers southeast of Luang Prabang center on the road to Xieng Khouang.*

His fingers touched the side of my face. "Let's have dinner at the chicken curry stand we like and celebrate. I missed lunch, and I'm starving."

"That sounds perfect." I gave him my first genuine smile. His calm, easy presence settled my nerves, and I buried my guilt, not wanting to spoil our precious time together. I'd made a mistake with Julian, but everyone makes occasional mistakes. I wouldn't do it again.

Going out for a meal together had proved challenging, as the division between the *indigène* and French communities in Vientiane left us without easy choices. The Cercle was out of the question, since we weren't members and it was the center of French life. Pierre's and the Café Français were equally unsuited. The few Lao, Annamese, and Chinese restaurants that catered to *indigènes* only drew attention to my mixed background. Bounmy had reluctantly agreed that a Lao prince in the company of a young *métisse* attracted gossip and disapproval. We never specified what that gossip might imply, but Catherine's numerous cautions constantly niggled at me. Bounmy sometimes brought extravagant picnics that we ate in sheltered spots along the Mekong, or we stopped at out-of-the-way stands serving basic Lao fare. Bounmy complained bitterly that our circumstances didn't allow him to take me somewhere nice. I didn't care in the least.

We walked down the river road and passed Pierre's, which was packed with Frenchmen enjoying drinks after work. I kept my head down, focusing straight ahead, hoping no one at the bar would notice me with Bounmy. Catherine or Marguerite might be there—or Julian.

"I saw you here with Julian on Tuesday," Bounmy said casually, as if it were nothing more than a passing observation. "Do you eat lunch out with him often?"

I stared at my feet, feeling like a small child who'd been caught sneaking a forbidden sweet. "He invites me sometimes when he has business nearby." I looked over at Bounmy. "He's only a friend."

"Of course." Small lines formed around his eyes and mouth. "However, people might assume there is something more between you. Perhaps it's best not to invite gossip."

"Yes, I know." We walked along in silence, a slight mist of tension swirling around us. How ironic that Bounmy would warn me about Julian in the same way Catherine had alerted me about him. His obvious jealousy made me smile inside.

We reached the food stand and settled under a palm tree, ordering two bowls of chicken curry.

"Tell me about your brother."

I explained the history of Antoine's time in the orphanage and then Saigon, including the prejudice and difficulties he'd faced. "He's the assistant manager at the coffee plantation, but says he simply follows orders."

"I understand the subtle ways in which the French put the Lao and *métis* in their place," he said, a bitter tone to his voice. "My position in the royal family has not shielded me from these humiliations." He scraped the last of the sauce from his bowl. "But let's talk of other things." He smiled. "I'm playing tennis with a French acquaintance tomorrow morning. I'd like to establish some regular matches, but it's not easy."

"What about Julian?"

"He hasn't invited me again." He pushed the bowl aside. "Have you had more lessons?" The edge returned to his voice, prompting another quiver of guilt.

"A few times. I'm not sure I'm getting any better, but the exercise is nice after a long day at work."

His lips became a fraught line. "I wish I could take you there to play, but it's impossible...on many levels."

"It's not important," I said.

After dinner, we wandered through a Lao section of town with simple wood houses where families were eating their evening meal, the scents of lemongrass and fish sauce wafting through the air. We stopped in a Buddhist temple we'd visited once before and found charming with its brilliantly colored murals, painted with the exuberance of a child, recounting one of the many stories of Buddha's life. Kneeling down next to Bounmy before the altar and giant Buddha to pray, I stole a glance at him, observing his face visibly relax and his earlier contrary words dissolve in the smoke of incense.

The sky shimmered with stars as we strolled down a quiet lane toward my home. "I love being with you, Geneviève," he said then pulled me behind a plumeria tree heavy with sweet smelling blooms.

His hands trembled as he held my shoulders and bent down to kiss me as softly as a feather grazing my lips. Immediately an image of Julian's kiss reared up. I wanted to erase that picture, to think only of Bounmy at this moment.

"Geneviève, so beautiful and innocent," he whispered. He leaned me against the trunk, kissing me again, only this time our lips met with force, and his tongue probed my mouth. He pressed his body against mine with an urgency both frightening and exhilarating. "I desperately want you," he said, his voice barely audible.

My lips tingled and my breath came short and fast. "I care for you very much." This was the man who possessed my heart, the man I wanted to be with. Not Julian.

Abruptly, he stepped away and took a deep shuddering breath. "I'm sorry." He stroked my hair. "There are things I must resolve. My life is not my own." He sighed. "Please know that I would never do anything to hurt you."

What did that mean? I stood on tiptoes and wrapped my arms around his neck, kissing him softly once more. We held each other for a long time.

"I must take you home," he said at last.

When we reached the gate at Catherine's, Bounmy kissed my hand. "We'll meet Sunday, as usual. I need to be with you." He had a sheepish grin. "I promise to behave."

I laughed. "Not too much, I hope."

Once again, Bounmy slipped into the darkness. I stood for a moment reliving our evening, the thrill of his kisses. He was my first love, and my feelings for Julian could never compare.

There was no turning back.

Chapter 30

Mali and Julian were waiting for me in the hallway as I came through the door.

"Mademoiselle Vivi, your friend Bridgette…" Mali began, her voice cracking.

"The orphanage called Catherine a few hours ago," Julian said. "They've taken Bridgette to Mahosot Hospital."

I searched their troubled expressions, trying to comprehend why Bridgette would be at the French hospital. "But why? Her fever isn't serious." A hard lump formed in my chest.

"Her illness took a turn. She's very sick," Julian said. "I'll take you there."

My mind finally registered the gravity of his words, the sympathy in his voice. We ran all the way from the house over two streets to the hospital, the world passing by in a blur.

The main building, a two-story concrete structure with white walls and a red-tiled roof, was designated for French and European patients, while separate buildings treated locals. The moment we entered, smells of disinfectant, rubbing alcohol, and medicines washed over us. Two ceiling fans circulated the odors around the room in the hot, humid air. My stomach lurched.

The woman at the reception desk directed us to the first room on the right upstairs. We found Catherine and Maîtresse standing beside Bridgette. An Annamese nurse, a tiny woman with dark hair piled on top of her head, held Bridgette's wrist, measuring her pulse.

Catherine turned to me, tears streaming down her cheeks. I stopped short. My dear friend was a diminished figure swamped by a sea of white sheets and pillows. Her mottled skin had turned a pale yellow, the color of a plucked chicken. Sweat pasted her hair to her forehead, and her chest rose and fell with gasps as she strained to take in enough oxygen. Her eyes remained closed.

The nurse glanced up, startled by our arrival. "I'll get the doctor," she said. "We can't allow this many people. Two of you must leave." I read despair in her expression, letting me know that we were gathered to say goodbye to Bridgette. "You should have brought her sooner," the nurse murmured as she hurried off.

"I thought it was a virus," Maîtresse said, her voice barely audible. "Not malaria." She looked up, as if surprised she had spoken these words out loud. "I must bring Father Jérôme." She placed a hand on my shoulder. "Pray for her soul, Geneviève. Pray for her eternal soul." She disappeared with Julian trailing behind her.

What good would it do to pray to a God who allowed Bridgette to suffer to this point, who might let her die, when she had hardly begun her life? Father Jérôme promised this unseen God had a greater plan for our lives, but this was the same God who had brought Bridgette and me to the orphanage, abandoned by our parents, only to be persecuted and harassed by Director Bernard. I wanted no part of this God.

Catherine put an arm around my shoulders. "I don't know if Bridgette is conscious, but talk to her. I believe she can hear and understand us. She needs to know she is loved and not alone."

"Why didn't...they bring...her before?" I asked, as great sobs garbled my words. "How could they be so...so cruel?"

"Director Bernard thought Bridgette was being overly dramatic, playing on his sympathy to get away from the orphanage," Catherine said. "It's despicable."

Of course the director would be indifferent to her illness, thinking only of his power to control and punish. This time he'd gone too far. Now, he would be a murderer.

I forced myself to control my crying and sat at the side of her bed. I took Bridgette's hot, damp hand and began to speak in a calm, quiet voice. "It's Vivi, *chérie*. I'm here. You know how much I love you, how much I need you in my life. You must get better right away." I talked and talked, describing what our lives would be like in a few weeks after she left the orphanage—all the fun things we would do, the places we would visit, how we would go to school in Paris the following year. "We'll find our perfect husbands and live near each other, raise our children together." I described the latest temple Bounmy had taken me to, the meal we had shared along the riverfront, until my voice broke, and tears flooded from my eyes, raining down on our hands. If only it were possible to send my strength to heal her. But I had no special powers, only my love.

"Don't leave me, Bridgette," I begged. "Fight for your life." At one point, she turned her head my way and opened her eyes halfway, and for a few fleeting seconds, she seemed to recognize me. Then she slipped away to another place.

Time had no meaning, no framework. It may have been minutes or hours before a man in a white coat stood beside me, his name tag reading *Dr. Vogel*. He was short and middle-aged with a substantial stomach, pudgy cheeks, and a kind smile. He observed the world from behind thick lenses, which made his pale gray eyes enormous.

He patted my shoulder and spoke softly. "I see Bridgette is very special to you." He gently felt Bridgette's forehead, then listened to her heart with his stethoscope. His gaze went to Catherine and back to me. "You must prepare yourselves. There is nothing more we can do at this point but try to keep her comfortable. She will leave us soon for a better place."

I wanted to scream at him that there was no better place! How could he utter such an absurd lie, a fairy tale meant only to placate the living? She would be gone forever, lying alone in a wooden box beneath the ground. My closest, dearest friend, the only family I had ever known, would vanish. The reality of the loss began to sink in, and I struggled to catch my breath.

"It's always terribly sad with one so young," Dr. Vogel said, issuing a deep sigh before disappearing from the room.

The nurse gave Bridgette a shot of morphine, which she said would ease her distress.

Maîtresse returned with Father Jérôme. His expression bore the gravity of administering the last rites. Sunday after Sunday, Bridgette and I had attended Mass at his church and witnessed his unwavering faith in a higher being, the complicated promise of heaven and the threats of purgatory and hell. He believed in his powers to absolve Bridgette of her sins and guide her to this mythical place called heaven. In that moment, I wished more than anything I shared his faith.

Catherine and I retreated across the room to the window. I could not bear to watch Father Jérôme issue prayers, repeatedly making the sign of the cross over Bridgette's body. I held on to Catherine's hand, staring through the wooden shutters to the town below, now dark and quiet. The night would pass, time ebbing and flowing into another dawn and another day without regard for the loss of my cherished friend.

The priest finished his ministrations, offered his condolences, and left. Maîtresse stood next to Bridgette, dabbing her face with a handkerchief. "Please forgive me for failing you," she whispered. I stepped beside her and placed a hand on her arm. She turned to me, her eyes filled with such pain and regret, I had to look away. "I'm so sorry, Geneviève." She gave me a quick hug before rushing from the hall.

Catherine and I sat on either side of the bed once more, holding Bridgette's hands, speaking occasionally in soothing voices, trying to ease her passage. At twenty-two minutes after three in the morning, she let out one last defeated breath.

Chapter 31

Someone was shaking my shoulder. I tried to rise from the deep fog of sleep pulling me under, wondering why I needed to wake. Hadn't I just gone to bed? Catherine stood over me in her blue silk robe, her face drawn and pale, eyes ringed in red. The hospital. Bridgette. My body contracted with pain, as if someone had kicked me in the abdomen. "No," I moaned.

"It's nine o'clock. Maîtresse called to say Bridgette's funeral will be in an hour, before the heat gets worse. We must hurry. Julian went to your work to tell them what happened, and that you won't be back for several days."

Still half asleep, the string of events slowly played in my mind: clinging to Bridgette's cold, clammy hand after the life had drained from her body; the hazy memory of Julian lifting me from the hospital chair and leading me and Catherine home; Mali bringing me to my room and easing me into bed. Then the escape of sleep.

In the bathroom I splashed cold water over my tear-stained face, shocked by the grotesque ghost staring back from the mirror, my eyes tiny slits surrounded by puffy red skin. I didn't own anything black so I pulled my new green dress from the armoire to wear to the funeral, sure Bridgette would love it.

Mali brought me a cup of strong coffee then picked up my brush and slowly ran it through my hair, soothing me. Bridgette's lovely face stared out from the framed photograph on the dresser. Her prescient words the day I'd left the orphanage echoed in my ears: *Be sure to take this, so you don't forget what I look like.*

I retrieved my silver bracelet that Bridgette had always loved and slipped it into my purse. Somehow Catherine and I arrived at Sacred

Heart Church in a haze of disbelief, slipping into the pew behind Maîtresse Durand and four girls from the orphanage. Madeleine and Lucienne turned to me with tear-stained faces, reaching out to squeeze my hands.

A simple wooden casket rested near the altar, the cover open. Pulling the silver bracelet from my bag, I walked to the front. Bridgette lay in a crudely made box of light-colored planks, but it wasn't really her, only the empty shell of her body. Maîtresse had dressed her in her one good dress, a pale pink linen, trimmed in navy, as if she were going to a tea party. Frangipani blooms had been scattered over her in an attempt to mask the odor of decay already setting in. I gently placed the bracelet under her folded hands and softly kissed her icy cheek. "Dear sweet Bridgette, I'll never forget you," I whispered. "You will always be in my heart." My shoulders heaved with sobs, tears rolling down my face, as I made my way back to the pew. Catherine handed me a handkerchief and put her arm around my shoulders.

Julian and Marguerite arrived at the last minute, sliding into the pew on the other side of us as Father Jérôme stepped to the front. He recited the funeral Mass, a jumble of unintelligible Latin words spilling over the room. When he finished, his eyes scanned the small group of mourners. "It's hard to understand God's will, when one is taken from us so young," he said, switching to French. "Do not despair. God has called this innocent, pure soul to heaven for a special purpose."

I stopped listening to the rest of Father Jérôme's meaningless words, envisioning the coffin lid being nailed down, the box lowered into the ground, Bridgette trapped in darkness for eternity. Alone. Waves of panic rippled through me, and I gasped for air, my head spinning as if I'd been hanging upside down and suddenly sat upright.

Julian placed a hand on my back. "Put your head between your knees," he whispered, "and breathe slowly in and out." I did as he suggested, and my breathing gradually calmed.

When the service ended, the small group of mourners filed out to the cemetery and gathered around the freshly dug pit. Time and motion and senses became distorted: the creak of ropes lowering the casket into the ground, the scent of the lotus flowers dropped by each person into the open grave, the thud of each shovelful of dirt thrown on top of the casket. My knees buckled, and Julian caught me as I wailed and sobbed. Lucienne, Madeleine, and the other girls stopped to hug me and whisper their sympathies. Maîtresse simply held me close for a moment, wearing an expression that required no words. I knew she felt culpable for not saving Bridgette, but I didn't blame her. Only Director Bernard.

Maîtresse pulled an envelope from her pocketbook. "I found this letter addressed to you on Bridgette's dresser this morning." I stared at the envelope with my name written in her familiar handwriting and dropped it into my pocket.

Julian took my arm, murmuring that we should head home. Then, somehow, Director Bernard was standing before me, his face as pale as the new moon, distress etched into the lines of his face. His eyes remained on the ground, as if he were mesmerized by the scraggly grass and yellow-flowering vines climbing across gravestones. At first I thought he must be a hallucination. How could he dare to show his face on this day? If there truly was a God, he would punish this man for his callous indifference, for being the instrument of Bridgette's death.

"I'm so terribly sorry for your…unimaginable loss, Geneviève," the director said, his voice cracking midway.

I wanted to rail against him and expose his guilt to the world, to tear at his hair, to slap his face the way he had slapped mine so many times. But I couldn't find the energy to respond. It wouldn't bring Bridgette back. So, I simply stood there.

His eyes finally met mine. "I truly regret what happened. I never imagined she could be so ill." He sounded near to tears. "Please forgive me."

I shook my head slowly. "You'll have to live with what you did." And I turned and walked up the path to where my friends were waiting.

———

We returned home and had a light lunch before Catherine insisted we retire for naps. It was after five when I woke from a dark, terrifying dream, my heart racing. I had fallen into the Mekong River, where the swift current had swallowed me and pulled me down into the depths. Bounmy was swimming toward me with his hand stretched out, but he remained just beyond my reach. It took me several moments to clear my head, to remember why I was sleeping in the late afternoon. Bridgette. The crushing ache of loss returned.

The house was quiet. I dressed and took Bridgette's letter, slipping down the back stairway, needing to breathe fresh air, hear the pond's swirling waters, and smell the sweet scent of jasmine. Sitting on the bench in the back corner under the banyan tree, I slowly opened the envelope and pulled out Bridgette's last words to me, written on Thursday, a day and a half before she died.

Chère Vivi,

I keep reading your latest letter, and every time it brings me to tears. You've heard from Antoine. What greater joy can there be than finding your brother?

Can you believe I actually passed that impossible algebra exam? I am capable of great things if I apply myself. Of course, it would never have happened without Catherine.

Only three weeks to freedom!! I thought it would never arrive, but it's so close now I can almost grab it from the air and wrap it around me. I'll leave Director Bernard behind.

My valise is already half-packed, and I've made a list of all the things I want to do—touring the covered market and the prettiest Buddhist temples (with you as my guide). Maybe a boat ride down the Mekong River. I plan to eat all the almond croissants and chocolate tortes that I can stuff in my mouth at Estelle's! Then I'll visit your office and give the evil eye to those mean men you work with. I'm so excited to meet Bounmy and

Julian, and of course Antoine, whenever he comes. Who knows, in another year, perhaps we'll go to Paris!! Oh, we'll have such fun.

This annoying fever keeps coming and going, getting worse at night, so I wake up soaking wet. It makes me very tired. Maîtresse says we'll go to the doctor on Monday if it persists.

I await a full report on your next date with Bounmy. Will he finally give you a proper kiss? Don't keep me in suspense!! I hope I'll meet someone as wonderful soon.

Love and hugs,
Bridgette

I had the oddest sensation that Bridgette was sitting above me on a branch in the banyan tree, telling me her thoughts, smiling and laughing. But the only companion I spotted was a dove cooing in the dense leaves. My mind fought to grasp reality. It was a mistake. Tomorrow I would wake to find Bridgette was fine. She'd want to know more about Bounmy, and I'd write her a letter for Catherine to deliver. As quickly as these thoughts brought a smile to my lips, the vision of Bridgette lying in the casket washed them away.

I leaned over with elbows on my knees, holding my head in my hands. How could Bridgette be dead? Vanished. It wasn't possible that someone so young, so full of humor and love and grace, could be gone.

A hand touched my shoulder, making me jump, and Julian sat down beside me. "Did you sleep at all?" he asked.

"I woke up from a nightmare."

"It takes time, Vivi. A lot of time." He paused. "I know how much you're hurting and how hard it is to believe it's real. But I'm sure Bridgette would not want you to suffer."

"Yes. I can hear her scolding me." A new rush of anguish spilled down my cheeks. I handed him Bridgette's letter. "She wrote this just…" I couldn't finish.

He passed me a handkerchief and took the letter, reading it

through. He closed his eyes for a moment, his expression pained, as if fighting back tears of his own, then patted my back. I placed my head on his shoulder, needing the comfort of his touch, a shelter from the pain. He ran his hand down the back of my hair. "Oh, Vivi." After a moment, he cleared his throat and pulled away.

His tenderness touched me and left me oddly disquieted. Silence wrapped around us as I dabbed my tears and blew my nose.

"I lost someone very dear to me last year in Paris," he said at last, his voice shaky and strained. "A woman I planned to marry."

"I'm so sorry." Suddenly the world did not revolve around me and my loss. How little I knew of this man, beyond his good looks and lighthearted humor. He, too, was in pain. "Do you mind telling me what happened?" I asked.

"Her name was Lily. She was only twenty-one, but that didn't stop the cancer that took her life. It's something you can't imagine happening to one so young and beautiful." He gave a sad little smile. "We met in the Louvre one afternoon. I immediately fell in love, a true *coup de foudre*."

I placed my hand over his. "I had no idea."

"I don't mean to take away from your grief, but I want to assure you that it does get easier with time. You think you can't possibly go on at first, yet you do. It forces you to rethink life and map out a different future. I hadn't planned on returning to Laos until I lost Lily."

His words were meant to ease my suffering, but I couldn't imagine how this pain would ever diminish.

I looked up as Mali crossed the bridge over the pond. She stopped not far from us. "Mademoiselle Vivi, Prince Savang is here to see you." I quickly withdrew my hand from Julian's and followed her back to the house.

Bounmy stood in the salon dressed in a suit, as if he'd come from his office. He turned to me, his face a pattern of sadness and worry, then enveloped me in his arms, holding me close. "Geneviève, I'm so sorry. There is nothing I can say to ease your loss, but I am here for you."

Sinking into the shelter of his arms, I was grateful he didn't offer the same useless platitudes I'd been told repeatedly. *Bridgette is in a better place now with God. It's good she went quickly and didn't suffer.* Empty words that filled me with anger. I closed my eyes and breathed in his comforting scent. "How did you know?"

"I tried calling you at your office this morning to ask if you wanted to have lunch. Kham told me." He continued holding me, rocking me gently back and forth, as if I were a small child.

Julian came around the doorway and started on seeing our embrace. "Prince Savang."

Bounmy stepped back. "Monsieur Courbet." He nodded ever so slightly. "I came to offer my condolences."

Julian crossed his arms. "How thoughtful of you. Would you like a drink? We're all a bit raw right now."

"No, thank you. I only want to be with Geneviève for a bit," Bounmy answered, his tone icy.

Julian shrugged. "Of course." But instead of leaving us alone, he poured himself a drink and sat down in one of the chairs. How could he be so obtuse? Or was it on purpose?

I turned to Bounmy. "We could go out back."

"Why don't we take a short walk, if you feel up to it?" Bounmy said.

We left the house and wandered down the lane to the river. He stopped for a moment, folding his hands around mine. "I understand how much Bridgette meant to you, and that no one can ever replace her."

I could hardly speak, fighting back tears once more. "It isn't possible she's gone." I rested my head on his shoulder until I got hold of myself.

"It takes time. Allow your tears to heal your heart," Bounmy said softly, handing me his handkerchief. "When I was twelve, my older brother died of typhus. He was two years older, my best friend."

Hearing of Julian's and Bounmy's losses, I understood I was not unique. Everyone faced tragedies at some point in their life. "I'm so sorry for your family."

"Be kind to yourself, Geneviève."

We continued down the lane, and I tucked my hand under his arm, needing to tether myself to his strength.

"Will you go to work Monday?" he asked as we reached the river.

"I'm not sure. Perhaps it would be best to keep busy."

"Take as much time as you need. I'll talk to Kham. Whenever you return to work, I'll take you to dinner. Or, if you don't feel up to it, I'll simply walk you home."

"Thank you." I squeezed his arm with appreciation, and the thought of dining with him lifted my spirits. Then a twist of guilt struck my gut. How could I think with pleasure about a date with Bounmy at a time like this?

"Bridgette and I had so many plans: we were going to live together once she left the orphanage; she was going to help me find my family; we planned to go to Paris to university." My voice wavered, and my throat tightened. "What will I do now?"

"I'll help however I can," he offered. "If you need to talk to someone…" His words trailed off.

We idled our way along the river path as daylight faded from the sky, listening to the waves lapping on the shore and birds crying out as they circled overhead. The ache in my heart momentarily eased.

After half an hour, we returned home in the dark. "I'm grateful you came."

"I wish I could ease your pain." He sighed. "Call me if you need anything." He kissed my forehead and left.

How caring and kind Bounmy had been in my darkest moment. It broke my heart anew that Bridgette would never meet him.

Chapter 32

Days disappeared and suddenly two weeks had slipped past. I struggled to comprehend that Bridgette existed only in my heart. Images of my dear friend lying in the hospital bed and the coffin haunted my waking hours. I collapsed into the bliss of sleep each night, only to wake from nightmares, frantically searching for Bridgette in a forest as a tiger roared in the distance. Each morning brought the fresh realization of her death, like a knife being plunged into my middle over and over again. I dragged myself back and forth to work, my mind shrouded in a hazy fog. She was never coming back.

I turned to Catherine for support. She urged me to allow myself time, insisting there was no rush to make plans or worry about the future. Sometimes she simply sat with me in the back garden, holding my hand as I cried.

Mali nourished me with concern through her cooking, entreating me to eat when my appetite failed, as if I were a small child she had adopted. She insisted we resume our Lao lessons and attempt to carry on conversations. I tried, even though it was difficult to find the right words, and she laughed at my abominable pronunciation. The lessons were only a temporary diversion, and the moment my thoughts returned to Bridgette, I nearly suffocated from my sense of loss.

I was filled with questions for Mali. Urgent questions. As a Buddhist, what did she think happened to people when they died? How did reincarnation work? Having been raised a Catholic, would Bridgette be accepted in the Buddhist world? I went with Mali to her temple each morning before I left for work, and we lit candles and incense and prayed for Bridgette's *khuan,* her soul. I wanted desperately to believe, to cling to anything that might bring comfort.

While Catherine and Mali showered me with understanding, Julian took it upon himself to distract me. He couldn't bear to see me cry, so he tried to keep my attention elsewhere. Silence was banned from the dinner table along with any mention of Bridgette, and he told endless stories of his childhood and time in Paris, or talked of world events—anything he could think of. He mentioned Lily occasionally, how she had kept him dangling when he'd offered her his heart, as if this too were part of an amusing story. He complained of the ludicrous government bureaucracy in Vientiane impeding his efforts to set up his business. Even I laughed when he imitated the officious French administrator blocking his path.

Julian held his head in the air, looked down his nose, and sniffed. *"Monsieur Courbet, you must understand, this is simply the way things are done. Be prepared to wait."* Julian chuckled. "He treated me like a half-wit."

As much as Julian implored me to continue with tennis, I simply couldn't face being at the Cercle among those impervious people. But our Thursday evening belote games resumed, and Marguerite entertained us with the latest gossip in town. The world kept turning.

At work I kept as busy as possible, arranging and rearranging office correspondence and invoices. No task was too small to engage me, as long as I avoided the despair threatening to consume me. The accountants, the warehouse manager, and even Kham were kinder. They tiptoed around me, as if I were a delicate piece of china that might break, obviously terrified I would dissolve into tears.

But no one relieved my sorrow like Bounmy. He was a balm for my aching soul. I refused to feel guilty for allowing myself these brief interludes of pleasure. Bridgette would understand. We continued to spend Friday evenings and Sunday afternoons together, but often he turned up at the end of the workday to walk me home. When we settled in a quiet spot along the river for a picnic, he encouraged me to talk about Bridgette, to cherish the memories and express my grief. Inevitably, when I began to cry, he held me in his arms, saying it was good to let the tears release my pain. Sometimes he kissed me tenderly, but he refrained from any passionate embraces. Perhaps he thought me too fragile, or that it was simply inappropriate.

———

In early August I received a second letter from Antoine. His cheerful words reminded me how suddenly life could turn around—happiness lost, then restored.

July 26, 1931
Chère Vivi,
I shall call you Vivi, as your friends do. I received your wonderful long letter of July 16 (only seven days in transit—a miracle). I'm relieved to hear mine reached you, as the mail is so uncertain.

The story of your unhappy upbringing at the orphanage made me very sad, but at least you had your good friend Bridgette to get you through. I look forward to meeting her when I come. My childhood was happier, but I don't know what I would have done without my best friend Paul. The director of your orphanage sounds like many of my teachers in Saigon, more interested in their power and ability to intimidate than in helping students. They should all be fired and sent back to France!

I am delighted to hear you want to attend university in France in the next year or so, depending, of course, on the search for our parents. Perhaps we can carry out this plan together, and if we find our mother, we will take her with us. We'll see how it unfolds.

You asked what the coffee plantation is like and what we do, so I'll try to describe the operations. The owners are two middle-aged Frenchmen, who are gambling on growing coffee beans despite several other failed plantations over the years. This time they have planted a different variety called Arabica, which seems to be thriving in the altitude and cool weather of the Bolaven Plateau. While only three hundred trees are producing beans right now, each season more reach maturity (it takes five years). We continue to plant seedlings every day.

I am struggling with my conscience, trapped in a difficult situation. The owners have little regard for the laborers, and the conditions and pay here are appalling. My job is to oversee a hundred and fifty men and women, toiling from sunup to sundown, six days a week, with little time to rest. It is exhausting work, stooping and crouching down to plant seedlings, water, and remove insects and weeds (which pop up again within a week). When the harvest starts in November, they will spend three months passing through the trees over and over, carefully picking only the very ripe red beans, or "cherries," as they're called. My job is less demanding, as I simply ride around on my horse, supervising and solving problems. Yet I earn five times as much pay as these poor people.

Most workers live on the plantation in barracks with thirty bunkbeds jammed together—men and women are separated, of course. They are fed meager meals of rice and soup, which hardly sustain them. There is no care for the sick or injured, and taking a day off due to illness is met with anger and no pay. Some are even dismissed.

My direct boss is the French plantation manager. He is a cold person who treats me as far below his level and expects me to do whatever he demands without question. We both have one-room shacks to ourselves and a separate outhouse. While a cook prepares us decent meals, it is hardly a luxurious life.

I'm making myself unpopular by speaking out about the workers' conditions and the need to improve them. If I'm not careful, I might lose my job. The owners and manager are on alert for outside agitators, like those who have incited rebellions at the rubber plantations in Cochinchina.

This is probably more than you wanted to know. I'm sorry to be so negative, but I have no one else to complain to. I'll write again in a few days when I'm not so tired and can be more positive! I hope to receive another letter from you soon as well.

With affection,
Antoine

I felt badly that I had not written to him again, but I'd been unable to find the will after Bridgette's death. With a heavy heart I took up pen and paper to explain my silence.

August 6, 1931
Cher Antoine,
You probably wonder why you haven't heard from me recently. Two days after I wrote you last, my best friend Bridgette died. She was the only family I've ever known until now, and the loss feels unbearable. It's as if half my soul has flown off to another place where Bridgette now resides. She contracted malaria, which worsened over many weeks until it took a sudden turn and extinguished her brief life. How could someone so young and good die like this? She never got to leave the confines of the orphanage, never had a chance to be free and find happiness.

Today would have been Bridgette's eighteenth birthday, when she would have come to live at Catherine's house with me. I ate a piece of her favorite chocolate torte at the French bakery to honor her and cried a great deal. We had so many dreams and plans that will never come to be. In my memory, she will remain a beautiful young woman, about to embark on her life, the loyal friend who helped me survive life in the orphanage.

People assured me my grief will slowly ease, which I found difficult to believe. Yet, the sharp debilitating pain I felt on waking each morning is now more of a dull ache. I go to work and keep busy, spend time with people I care about, and think about good things to come, like meeting you. More and more I keep my mourning for private moments.

I'm sorry for this dark letter, but I do have happy news. I am to travel to Luang Prabang at the end of September with my boss to help organize the company's office there. A friend was able to find the location of our mother's family home, and I plan to visit as soon as possible. I'm excited and nervous and full of hope. Soon we will have answers to our past.

Please take good care of yourself as I couldn't bear to lose you, when I've only just found you. I promise to write again next week.
With love,
Vivi

Chapter 33

The following evening, Bounmy and I strolled along the river and ate noodle soup at one of the food stands. I could hardly believe that three weeks had passed since Bridgette's death. Life went on. Bounmy's presence brought comfort and happiness; but given how fragile our existence seemed to me now, I was impatient for him to declare his feelings, to make clear where he saw me fitting into his life. I'm not sure what I expected or wanted. Being only eighteen, I wasn't ready to marry, and I still hoped to go to a university in France with Antoine. Yet it made me uneasy that we never talked of the future. Why was Bounmy holding back? I lacked the courage to ask him, afraid of the answer I might hear.

As we said goodnight outside the gate, he took my hand. "I won't be here Sunday. Prince Phetsarath and I are traveling to Bangkok for a meeting with the Siamese trade minister on Tuesday."

"How exciting." I squeezed his hand. "When will you be back?"

"By next Friday. I'll come for you at work as usual, or send a note if anything changes." He kissed my lips gently. "Be well."

On entering the house, I heard Catherine and Marguerite talking in the salon and peeked in through the door. Julian was sprawled across a chair, one leg dangling over the arm. His eyelids drooped, and he seemed to have difficulty focusing. I hesitated, debating if I should speak to them or continue upstairs.

Catherine glanced over. "There you are," she said. "Did you have a nice evening?"

"Ah…Cinderellaandtheprince," Julian said, slurring the words together. He waved his cocktail glass in the air, and the contents sloshed onto the floor.

"Julian, go to bed," Catherine said, her voice sharp. She got up and removed the glass from his hand. "You've had more than enough to drink."

He gazed at Catherine for a moment, then pulled himself up from the chair with difficulty. He wove his way toward me and bowed deeply, sweeping his arm in a flourish, like a cavalier doffing a grand, plumed hat. "Mademoiselle, the woman I love." He straightened up, swaying from side to side. "But you continue to break my heart."

I stood very still, unsure how to react to such an unexpected declaration. He was drunk and not thinking clearly. Simply showing off.

"Oh, Julian, really," Catherine said, grabbing his arm and leading him toward the hall.

"*Bonne nuit, mes chéries*," Julian called over his shoulder.

Mali appeared from out of nowhere and helped Catherine get him up the stairs.

"What happened to him?" I asked, sitting down next to Marguerite.

"Catherine and I went to dinner at Café Français, and you were out. With André off looking for gold, he's like a child who doesn't know how to entertain himself, so he drinks too much. Don't take him seriously." She paused a moment. "To be fair, it's a difficult day, the anniversary of when he met Lily."

"I haven't seen him this drunk in ages, but I know how much he loved Lily." I sighed. "Why would he say such a crazy thing to me?"

She finished off her gin and tonic, placing the glass on the side table and nearly dropping it on the floor. She was clearly intoxicated as well. "You've been lost in your grief, but Julian believes he's in love with you, Vivi. At least madly infatuated. It drives him wild every time you go out with Prince Savang." She lit a cigarette and took a long drag.

"He's been so good to me since Bridgette died, but…" I knew Julian's interest in me was complicated, most likely a mix of competition with Bounmy and sympathy for my grief over Bridgette. I thought of it as a simple flirtation, a habit of his personality and the proximity of living in the same house. There had been the kiss we'd shared weeks before and his constant entreaties to go with him to the Cercle dancing, but these were not serious. He cared about me and wanted to be closer, yet it was simply his way of forgetting Lily.

Marguerite sighed. "Catherine's furious with him. They had a big row this afternoon. She told him to leave you alone and not interfere."

I winced. "The last thing I want is to cause trouble after all they've done for me."

"Be careful around him. He's as fragile as you at the moment. It could spell disaster."

"He's talked to me many times of Lily." I glanced at Marguerite. "He's confusing his grief and loneliness with caring for me."

"You're probably right, but try telling that to him."

Catherine reappeared and sank onto her chair. "He's passed out, thankfully. I apologize for his behavior."

"It's nothing," I assured her.

Catherine sighed. "I do worry about his drinking…and his emotional state."

I wondered if she might be thinking of Monsieur Fontaine and their unhappy ending. She had not mentioned his name for some time, but I felt sure he still preoccupied her thoughts. Did she still love him? It mattered little at this point since his wife and children had left for France and he had been transferred to Luang Prabang.

In my room, I heard Julian snoring loudly through the adjoining wall. I didn't want to cause him any more unhappiness after all he had suffered losing Lily. He was so vulnerable.

After breakfast on Saturday morning, I retreated to the back garden to start another letter to Antoine, determined to sound more cheerful this time.

Julian appeared at my side a short time later looking contrite. "May I sit with you?"

I nodded, unsure how to react after his behavior the previous night and his drunken declaration of love. Did he even remember?

He sat on the bench, clasping his hands in his lap. Dark circles colored the skin under his eyes. He took a deep breath. "My apologies for last night. I was terribly drunk, but, of course, you already know that. I don't remember what I said, but Catherine assures me I was a total ass." He looked down. "I've made a habit of drinking too much and behaving badly in front of you."

He stared off into the yard for a moment, his expression one of sorrow. "I don't have a good explanation. Sometimes life simply becomes too much with memories of Lily, and..." He turned to me. "I'm so sorry."

I was right: he didn't love me, but Lily. "You're still grieving, but perhaps drinking only makes it worse," I offered.

He chuckled. "So wise for your young age. Can you forgive me?"

"Yes. No one has ever bowed before me, as if I were royalty. I rather liked it."

He winced, letting several seconds of awkward silence tick by. "Let me make it up to you. Come to the club tonight for dinner and dancing."

"I've told you before how out of place I feel there."

"Who gives a damn about those stuffy old people?" He took my hand. "We'll dance and laugh. It will lift both our spirits." He scrunched his mouth to one side. "And don't tell me you can't because of Bounmy. Has he asked you out for tonight?" I shook my head. "It would be wrong if he didn't allow you an evening with friends when you are going through such a hard period."

My heart softened, understanding how desperately Julian needed to put aside his sadness over Lily. Since Bounmy was leaving for Bangkok, I didn't need to worry about seeing him at the club. A pang of guilt nipped at my middle, but I ignored it.

"We'll go with Catherine and Marguerite. I'll have to fight off the other men to dance with you." A dazzling smile lit up his face. "Say you'll come."

I nodded, giving in to his excitement and anticipation. It was only dinner and dancing with friends. Surely Bounmy would understand.

Chapter 34

Catherine seemed startled, then disconcerted, when Julian announced we would be going to the club with her, but she recovered quickly. I hoped she could keep Julian from drinking too much.

She insisted on loaning me one of her dresses, a lovely creation of sky-blue chiffon, and Mali basted the hem to accommodate for my shorter height. I giggled with excitement as Catherine added a sweep of gray eyeshadow, a dusting of pink rouge, and magenta lipstick to my face. She pulled my hair back on one side and attached a sparkly blue butterfly barrette. We stood next to each other in front of the mirror, she in her lavender silk, me in the blue chiffon, grinning and admiring ourselves.

As we started downstairs, Catherine took my hand. "Julian is very susceptible right now. Be careful. Hearts can be broken on all sides."

"I only want to be friends."

Julian was waiting at the bottom of the stairs, looking stunning in his black tie and dinner jacket, hair slicked back. "Magnificent! How can one man be so lucky to escort two such gorgeous ladies?"

We found Marguerite at the Cercle sitting at the bar, and we all continued on to the dining room. The maître d' led us to a table near the dance floor. Catherine and Marguerite seemed to know everyone, greeting friends as we walked past. Several women nodded and smiled at Julian with an unspoken invitation. Once again I felt the unwelcoming eyes of other guests raking over me.

"Shall we have champagne, ladies?" Julian asked in high spirits.

Catherine shot him a look. "Let's take it easy tonight. A bottle of wine with dinner will be enough."

"Don't I even get a cocktail?" Marguerite complained.

"Catherine's right," Julian said. "We must set a better example for Vivi." He grinned at me. I hated to be blamed for curtailing their fun, but it was a relief.

"It's the usual boring crowd," Marguerite said, sighing. "The same couples come every Saturday night."

"Oh well, the food is always good, and the music is nice," Catherine said, lighting a cigarette. "Who are those men sitting with the Resident Superior? I've never seen them before."

"They met with him yesterday at his office," Marguerite said. "The big fat one is German and the other two are Dutch. They claim to be looking for investment opportunities in Laos."

"What exactly would those be?" Julian scoffed. "They're probably planning to hunt tigers and elephants illegally under the guise of business. Look on the bright side, ladies. There are more single men to dance with." He laughed. "Although I'd watch my toes with that German fellow."

I spotted a table on the far side of the room, and my heart skipped a beat. A French couple were seated with Prince Phetsarath, Prince Souvanna and his companion Aline Allard. There was a second woman with them who looked a great deal like Aline. I was thankful that Bounmy was not among them, for they had not yet left for Bangkok, it seemed.

Slow jazz tunes drifted over the room as we ate our meal. "I'm afraid it's records on the gramophone tonight," Catherine said. "Sometimes there is a small band."

Marguerite tossed her head back and laughed. "Believe me, the records are much better than that sorry excuse for a band."

As we finished our entrees, a livelier foxtrot started up, and two couples immediately stepped onto the dance floor. Julian jumped up and extended his hand. "Mademoiselle, may I have the honor of this dance?"

Flustered and uncertain, I followed him out. "You'll have to remind me of what to do."

Julian smiled reassuringly and took my right hand, placing his other arm lightly around my back, maintaining a proper distance. "It's a foxtrot, like we did at the house. You'll be fine."

Julian counted softly in my ear for the first few turns until I found my footing. All the while I blushed crimson, sure everyone would notice my clumsiness. We danced a second song, circling about the room, lost in the rhythm. Julian smiled and squeezed my hand.

As the music ended, I glanced up and froze. Bounmy stood in the doorway to the dining room, staring directly at me with wide eyes. His expression darkened. He gave a curt nod and proceeded to Prince Phetsarath's table, taking a chair next to the other young woman in the party.

I sat down, my legs shaking. Julian led Marguerite to the dance floor, and a shy young lieutenant asked Catherine to dance. My stomach churned. Why had I come? I looked over surreptitiously and spied Bounmy sitting up very straight, his face devoid of expression. The woman next to him chatted away, smiling, tilting her head coyly to one side. A dinner plate was placed in front of Bounmy, but he didn't touch the food. An intense jealousy overcame me until I could hardly breathe. Did he not invite me out on Saturday nights because he was sharing them with this woman?

Julian and Marguerite returned when the song ended. Julian looked at me, his expression defiant, and I knew he had spotted Bounmy. He grabbed my arm roughly as a waltz started to play. "Come." He pulled me close, twirling me around the room until everything was a blur. I closed my eyes, wanting to disappear.

"Your prince is here," Julian whispered in my ear. "You know he won't speak to you in front of his family and all these people." His voice was angry. "But we're having fun, aren't we?"

Julian was right. Bounmy would never acknowledge me, a lowly *métisse*, in this public place with his royal family. He needed to keep me hidden.

By the time the dance ended, Bounmy's chair was empty.

Julian asked Catherine to dance, and I sat down next to Marguerite. She whispered in my ear: "You're here with Julian. Enjoy the evening." She filled my wine glass. "Drink."

I took a large gulp of wine, telling myself I had no reason to feel bad, nor any need to explain myself to Bounmy. Julian was only a friend. But my heart ached.

Bounmy never returned. For the rest of the evening, Julian and I danced to almost every song. Spinning around the room in his arms took my mind off Bounmy, as did another glass of wine. In between foxtrots, waltzes, and tangos, we gyrated to the Charleston and the Black Bottom Stomp, laughing with abandon.

The evening wound down, and the music turned slow and melancholy. Lucienne Boyer sang "Parlez-Moi D'Amour." Julian pulled me close with trembling arms and nestled his face in my hair. He smelled of sweat and a woodsy-scented soap. My cheek resting against his shoulder, I listened to the calming, steady beat of his heart.

The night ended at midnight. Exhausted, we dragged ourselves home, Julian holding on to Catherine's and my arms. We had finished two bottles of wine over the course of the evening, leaving us slightly tipsy, but far from drunk. Instead, I was intoxicated by the thrill of the music and dancing. And if truth be told, I'd thoroughly enjoyed being in Julian's arms, even as questions about Bounmy continued to haunt me. Why hadn't he said hello to me? Why had he left so abruptly?

Catherine went upstairs, leaving us in the entry hall.

"Thank you for the evening," Julian said with a silly grin on his face. He bent down and gave me a quick, light kiss.

I felt my cheeks grow warm. "I had a wonderful time."

He hesitated a moment. "I care for you deeply, Vivi. I don't want to see you hurt. At some point, Bounmy will break your heart."

I glanced away, not wanting to hear his prediction, even if it might be true. "I'm very tired."

He pulled me into his arms and kissed me with a longing I understood, the longing I felt for Bounmy. For a moment, I succumbed to his embrace, melting into his arms and lips. I felt safe, at home. If Bounmy were not in my life, how different might things be with Julian?

I stepped back, my heart beating madly. "Goodnight." I ran upstairs and closed my door, turning the lock, not sure if I was frightened of Julian or myself. I flopped on the bed, drowning in a sea of bewilderment and guilt. Thoughts of Bounmy left me with nothing but questions, doubts, and an immense ache. Had he been angry, or—worse—hurt, to see me with Julian? But what did he expect of me? What was his relationship to the woman next to him? Most of all, how could I explain my feelings for Julian when I adored Bounmy? Perhaps it was possible to care for two people at the same time. Love, infatuation, desire, friendship—these tangled emotions made life more complicated than I'd ever imagined. And Bridgette was no longer there to give me counsel.

Chapter 35

Filled with fear and guilt, I waited in agony for Friday night and Bounmy's return from Siam. I kept picturing the expression on his face when he saw me dancing with Julian. Why had I tempted fate and gone to the club? A few glasses of wine, an evening of dancing, and I'd easily given in to Julian's attentions. I felt more confused than ever.

I expected a note from Bounmy canceling our date, ending our relationship. When that didn't come, I felt sure he would simply not show up, and I would never hear from him again. How could I possibly survive losing him, on top of Bridgette? I ached to see his sweet face, to know the grace of his smile upon me once more.

Everyone left the office by five. I waited, jumping every time I heard a sound, watching the clock and endlessly smoothing my hair and skirt. To my relief, Bounmy suddenly appeared, standing in the doorway, twirling his straw hat. His eyes and the lines around his mouth were drawn with hesitation, but not anger.

"You're here," I said, jumping up.

"Where else would I be?" He put his arms around me and hugged me tight. "I've missed you so much."

I closed my eyes. "I've missed you."

"Come. There's a *pousse-pousse* waiting." He took my hand. "I have a surprise for you."

The porter carried us down the river road southwest of town. We pressed our arms and legs against each other, holding hands. The warmth of his body sent an electrifying ripple through me.

His face drew close to mine with a puzzled expression. "I didn't expect to see you at the club Saturday night." There was no trace of reproach in his voice, only uncertainty.

"Catherine and Marguerite insisted I go with them." I let the lie slip as easily as if describing the weather.

"And Julian had to come, of course," Bounmy said.

I paused a moment, staring down at my lap. "I thought you might be upset with me for joining my friends."

"Not really, except you know I dislike you spending time with Julian." He touched my cheek. "I'm jealous of him." His honesty was touching.

"I was startled you were there. I thought you'd gone to Siam." I placed my hand on his arm. "Then you left so suddenly."

"I had a wire from my father that afternoon, saying my sister had a high fever. I didn't feel right staying at the club knowing she was ill. I only stopped by to say hello." He shook his head slowly. "I'm never comfortable there, but Prince Phetsarath enjoys it greatly."

I remained quiet a moment, wondering if Julian had been right that Bounmy would never speak to me in front of his family. "Are you embarrassed to acknowledge me in front of your family?"

Bounmy bit his lip. "Not embarrassed, not at all, but there are circumstances that make it awkward at the moment. I'm working to resolve them." He sighed. "I'm sorry if that hurt your feelings. Be patient with me."

His mysterious explanation only raised more questions, but I would honor his request and try to be patient. "I recognized your cousins, but who were the women at your table?" I asked, trying to sound nonchalant.

His eyebrows shot up. "Ah, Aline Allard, who Prince Souvanna is courting, and her sister. I've only met the sister once before." He squeezed my hand. "No more questions. Let's forget last Saturday and enjoy tonight."

I nodded, relieved to know he wasn't unhappy with me. "How is your sister feeling?"

"They think it's dengue fever, but she's recovering."

Five minutes out of town, Bounmy directed the porter down a narrow lane partially hidden behind a stand of bamboo. The road ended in a lovely, unkempt garden. Orange hibiscus, climbing jasmine, red ginger, and wild grasses filled flower beds with vibrant colors and fragrant scents; bees droned lazily from bloom to bloom gathering pollen. Beyond the garden, a tiny wooden house sat along the edge of the Mekong River.

"How did you find this place?" I asked, filled with wonder.

"It belongs to a friend who comes here for a quiet place to write," Bounmy said, helping me down from the *pousse-pousse*. "Close your eyes, and I'll lead you to the surprise." I squeezed my eyes shut, and he guided me along the pathway as stray fronds and blooms tickled my arms and legs. "You can look," he whispered.

I opened my eyes and gasped. Behind the house, a table and two chairs had been set up under a giant flame tree overlooking the water. It was set with a white linen cloth, fine china, silverware, and crystal glasses. On a small side table an ice bucket cradled a bottle of champagne.

"How did you ever manage this?"

He grinned. "I decided if I couldn't take you to the Café Français, I'd bring the café to you."

A young Lao boy stepped forward, bending in a *nop*. Bounmy held out a chair for me. "Mademoiselle." The boy removed the cork from the champagne bottle with a loud pop and poured the bubbly liquid into crystal flutes then placed a plate of toasts points and pâté de foie gras before us.

I couldn't believe he'd gone to this much trouble for me. It was terribly romantic and touching. My heart overflowed, and my eyes grew misty.

Bounmy held up his glass. "*Santé*. To special times together." He paused for a moment, gazing into my eyes. "To one day being in Paris together."

I clinked my glass against his. "That would be a dream come true.

Perhaps when my brother and I go to university in France, you could visit." The idea of leaving Bounmy and going off to France was impossible to imagine at the moment.

We sipped champagne and nibbled foie gras, gazing over the river as it slowly swirled past, content to be together and at peace once more. Everything else in life slipped into the background, rendered unimportant. Two longboats and a fishing skiff glided by as the sun dipped toward the hills in Siam. A gray heron landed at the water's edge and extended its long white neck, pecking at the mud with its sharp orange beak. The bird cast a wary eye in our direction.

The boy ran into the house and reemerged with two covered dishes, removing the lids with great fanfare. "*Voilà!*"

I stared in wonder at strips of beef and mushrooms in a dark wine sauce, potatoes dauphinoise, and sautéed haricots vert. On rare occasions we'd eaten meals like this at the orphanage. "It smells delicious."

Bounmy smiled. "It's not exactly Paris, but it's the best I could do."

We ate in silence, suddenly shy with each other, occasionally swatting at pesky bees and flies. The boy remained unobtrusively in the background, ready to refill our glasses with champagne, then pouring red wine. Everything was perfect. Like Bounmy.

"How was your trip to Bangkok?" I asked at last.

He shrugged. "Truthfully, rather tedious—a long drive on terrible roads, then a three-hour train ride—all for a two-hour meeting with the Siamese trade minister. It achieved little, but for Prince Phetsarath it's all about appearances and establishing relationships." He shook his head. "I'm not well suited for the politics of this job."

"Do you enjoy your work?"

"Yes, but I often have to create tasks to occupy myself. I write reports about opportunities for trade and detail ways we could promote selling goods from Laos. Currently we export mostly natural resources, such as wood and tin, or agricultural goods, like cardamom, coffee, and opium, although much of the latter is smuggled out illegally. Laos desperately needs to develop manufacturing capabilities, but first we have to identify markets and create a trained workforce." He pushed his potatoes around on the plate. "All my initiatives are bogged down right now given the dismal state of the world economy and our reduced budgets. There is no funding." He laughed. "You must find this very boring. I often do."

"Not at all. I want to understand your work."

"Well, today we had a meeting at work with a Chinese trade emissary," Bounmy began. "I was shocked by his arrogant and rude manner, offering an agreement that would clearly benefit China and do nothing for Laos. But Prince Phetsarath is adept at putting people like this in their place without ever seeming the least offended or perturbed. I always learn a great deal from him."

"Did you say anything?"

"I restrained myself, not wanting to embarrass Prince Phetsarath. Laos's past is filled with episodes of neighbors—China, Burma, Annam, Cambodge, and Siam—invading and plundering our land, then demanding heavy tributes for their so-called protection. Even now with the French in control, the Chinese feel superior and want to exploit our homeland." He sighed. "I'd like to help establish a stronger, more prosperous Laos that will garner more respect from other countries."

I touched his arm. "I'm sure you can accomplish it."

The Lao boy cleared our dinner plates and disappeared in the house.

"I did have some good news today. King Sisavang Vong has named me to the Indigenous Consultative Assembly. I'm sure it's a favor to my father, but I'm excited about the new role."

I took a sip of wine. "I don't know what that is."

"It's a council consisting of one Lao representative from each of the eleven provinces under French administration along with two members from the kingdom of Luang Prabang. The group confers with French officials and advises on economic and commercial matters."

"It sounds important."

"In some ways, but the Lao members don't actually make decisions, only offer recommendations." He wiped his mouth with his napkin. "In the end, the French control everything. I'd like to see the assembly given a greater role, some decision-making power."

"Isn't the king in charge of Luang Prabang?"

Bounmy let out a big huff of air. "Luang Prabang has more autonomy than the Lao provinces"—his voice grew bitter—"but the king and his advisors are limited to decisions over education and justice, while the Governor General of Indochine in Hanoi has authority over everything else. Ultimately the French must agree with the king's policies. The Indigenous Consultative Assembly was created to appease the Lao aristocracy's feelings of helplessness. A bone thrown to the dogs."

"I've never understood why Indochine is important to France. Is it purely about making money?" I asked. "My teacher at school last year became irate when I raised this question. He said the French want to help the colonies of Indochine develop to provide a better life for the people. I find that hard to believe."

Bounmy's face tensed. "That's the official explanation. The other Indochine colonies provide an important source of income for France. However, Laos is a disappointment, a backwater where little of value has been produced. The main advantage for France of being here is that Laos acts as a buffer against Siam's power."

The frustration and anger in his words surprised me. "Do you think the French will leave one day and give us independence?"

"It seems highly unlikely. How ironic that the French Republic proclaims all men have a right to liberty, equality, and freedom. Except, of course, when it comes to French colonies like Laos. We may not be ready for independence quite yet, but...one day."

He tore a piece of bread from the baguette. "I ask your discretion. What I've said could be considered treason by some. The king of Luang Prabang seems content to rule under French tutelage for now, because he remembers when Siam held the Lao kingdoms hostage, stealing our lands and people and burdening us with heavy taxes. The king and many of his advisors, my father included, fear that could happen again if the French leave. Perhaps they're right for the moment."

"Why shouldn't the Lao people determine their own future?"

He looked surprised. "Aren't you a French citizen?"

"I'm half Lao. This is my country, too, the place where I was born. I hate how the French treat the Lao." The wine had loosened my tongue. "I see how they look down their noses at my mixed blood. What gave them the right to decide my fate?"

Bounmy jerked his head back, startled by my outburst. "I'm glad you share my sentiments, but be careful. Those words could get you into trouble." He leaned back in his chair and took a sip of wine. "And how is everything at River Transport?"

"I admit I'm a bit bored at times. I don't understand why Kham isn't more interested in my suggestions for improving the business." It was the first time I'd felt comfortable enough to be honest about my job. "I don't mean to complain, but it is frustrating."

"Kham has many responsibilities right now. His wife gave birth to twins last month and his mother is not well. Perhaps he can't focus clearly on the business."

"He told me we'll be leaving for Luang Prabang at the end of September."

"Excellent, although I don't know what I'll do with myself while you're gone."

The boy reemerged from the house and bowed before leaving.

"He'll come back tomorrow morning to clean up," Bounmy explained as he stood. "I thought we might walk along the river."

He took my hand, and we strolled down the weedy path that edged the steep riverbank. The last rays of sunlight cast shadows across the swirling waters, turning the river from muddy brown to a deeper taupe, then dark gray. A million noisy insects filled the air with the sounds of dusk. My body felt loose and relaxed.

When the path ended abruptly, we retraced our steps. "I have a chocolate torte for dessert," Bounmy announced. He grabbed our champagne glasses and led me into the house.

The building consisted of a single room filled with a desk, typewriter, two chairs, a small bookshelf, and a divan covered with a Lao cloth in hues of red and orange. In the back was a door to a tiny water closet, and on the left side of the room a makeshift kitchen had been created with wooden planks balanced on cement blocks. Bounmy placed the glasses on the counter and lit two kerosene lamps. He lifted another bottle of champagne from a pail of cool water, popping the cork.

"Thank you for the elegant dinner," I said.

"We can finally be alone." He turned to me with a smile that carried the warmth of a hundred sunny days. "The hours I spend with you are the happiest moments in my life."

"And mine," I said, searching his eyes for answers to all the questions that remained unspoken. "I don't know how I would have survived these past weeks without you." I put my arms around his neck, inhaling his essence.

"May I kiss you?" he asked. "I don't want to make you uncomfortable."

I stood on tiptoe and met his lips, as he wrapped his arms around me and pulled me close. We kissed slowly, deeply. The air drained from my lungs, leaving me dizzy and giddy, my legs weak.

He whispered in my ear, "I love you, Geneviève. I've loved you from the first moment I saw you at the temple. All I truly want is to be with you..." His voice trailed off with a hollow sadness.

"I love you, too."

We clung to each other, kissing until the heat of our passion overpowered all sense of time and reason. The outside world didn't exist any longer, and there was only Bounmy and me. The touch of his lips, the feel of his body pressed against mine, quieted any doubts. Although inexperienced in matters of the heart, all I needed to know was that he loved me. I felt the truth of his words deep in my soul. With that realization, I wanted nothing more than to give myself to him totally, to be his—the only gift I had to offer. Then he would never leave me, not as my father and mother and Bridgette had done.

"I want to be yours," I whispered. "Now. Here."

"You're very young. I don't want to take advantage of you."

I put a finger over his lips. "It's my decision."

He hesitated for only a moment, then lifted me effortlessly and carried me to the divan. He slowly removed my skirt, blouse, chemise, and bloomers, piece by piece, caressing and kissing each curve of my body. I lay naked before him, only mildly embarrassed as his eyes devoured me in the shadows of the lamp's flame. He quickly undressed. I brushed my fingertips across the taut muscles of his arms and chest, amazed by the silkiness of his skin. Little by little, with restrained urgency, he introduced me to the meaning of pleasure, the miracle of two bodies melding together as one. The definition of joy.

After, I nestled in his arms, in awe of our physical and emotional connection. I had crossed from the world of a young girl to that of a woman. Now I understood the true measure of love.

He buried his face in my hair. "Are you all right? Did I hurt you?"

"Only for a moment. Then it was wonderful."

"I treasure you, Geneviève. Don't ever forget that." Sorrow infused his words, almost as if he were saying farewell, leaving me unsure what to think.

We sat on the divan naked and ate giant slices of chocolate torte, laughing at nothing but our happiness as we fed each other bites. He poured more champagne, and we toasted to the days and nights ahead that we planned to spend together wrapped in each other's arms.

"You have no idea how much I love you, how I've desired you from the beginning," he said. "It's been so hard to hold back, but this feels right, removing the last barrier between us." He lifted my hair and gently placed it over my shoulder.

"Why did you wait so long?" I asked.

"It had to be your decision. The first time is a big moment in your life. I wanted it to be perfect." He kissed me gently on my neck.

"It was." I stared down at my plate. "You are."

"I'm honored you chose me." He ran his hand down my breasts and belly to my lower parts, making me gasp with pleasure. "From now on we must say whatever we feel. No more pretenses or secrets."

"I want to be with you as much as possible."

"I do also." He placed our plates and champagne glasses out of the way. His hands slowly explored every inch of my body, as if he were memorizing each bone and muscle, every crevice, the smallest marks on my skin. We made love slowly, passionately. I had never experienced such bliss in my young life.

We remained at the house until nearly midnight, sharing childhood stories, making love once more and reveling in the intensity of our feelings, our newfound intimacy. I belonged to this man, protected and warmed by his love.

Reluctantly we dressed and left our retreat beneath a crescent moon and twinkling stars playing hide and seek under scattered clouds. Bounmy had arranged for the *pousse-pousse* to wait on the main road, and the porter ferried us back to my street. We walked the last half-block to Catherine's, Bounmy holding my arm in the dim glow of the moonlight. I didn't want to leave him, to go back to my ordinary life. Nothing would ever be the same.

A lamp burned in the salon. I hoped no one was up to witness my late return, most of all Julian. After a last kiss, I left Bounmy at the gate and slipped into the house, running upstairs to the refuge of my room.

Chapter 36

September 5, 1931
Cher Antoine,

I received your letter of August 24, which arrived yesterday. Thank you for your sympathy and thoughts for Bridgette. I still grieve deeply, but life continues on. I am extremely fortunate to be in this beautiful house with Catherine, Julian, and Mali, who care for me so well. Mali and I are still working on my Lao, which is slowly getting better.

Your descriptions of the beautiful forests and waterfalls in the mountains of the Bolaven Plateau are so vivid, I feel as if I were with you. How lovely to wander about on your free days, exploring the area and meeting rural villagers, who sound warm and welcoming. One day I hope to visit you there.

I didn't mention this before, but I am seeing someone. His name is Bounmy Savang. He is one of the many princes from the kingdom of Luang Prabang. It sounds very grand, but he is not at all like that. He is sweet, thoughtful, and modest. He went to school in Paris for four years, and I love hearing stories about his experiences. We crossed paths by chance one day at a Buddhist temple and found ourselves attracted. When you come to Vientiane, I hope to introduce you to him.

I will leave with my boss for Luang Prabang in two and a half weeks. I am to stay with Kham's wife's sister and family. The husband is the manager of the Luang Prabang operations, and I am tasked with better organizing the office.

We are traveling overland by horse, as it's difficult by boat at this time of year given the high water and swift currents of the river, although that will be an advantage for my return trip by boat. I've never ridden a horse and have no idea what to expect. The rains have been much lighter the last few weeks, so hopefully it won't be too muddy and wet in the forests. Depending on weather and unexpected delays, it will take us anywhere from ten to fourteen days to get there.

Catherine was concerned about me traveling alone with a group of men. Luckily her friend Marguerite was able to move up her departure to Luang Prabang and will accompany me. Catherine joked that Marguerite isn't exactly the best chaperone—she has an outspoken personality and is known for flaunting society's rules—but I enjoy her enormously and will feel much safer being at her side.

It will be a great adventure as I've never been farther than a few kilometers outside Vientiane. Of course, we came from Luang Prabang as children, but I remember nothing of that trip. Do you have any memories of this?

I can't wait to search for Mother's family. I have goosebumps thinking about it, dreaming that perhaps our mother is still living. If only you could come with me... but I will write immediately with news.

I hope things are going better on the plantation. I know it is difficult. Watch out for tigers and other wild beasts when hiking in the jungles. Maybe I worry too much, but I want you safe.

With love,

Vivi

The evening before my departure for Luang Prabang, Bounmy and I decided to walk the twenty minutes from my office to our secret house. Heavy rains had fallen during most of the afternoon, only to clear, leaving the sky a glorious lapis blue.

Since our first night at the tiny house, we had spent every Sunday and as many evenings as possible there. We cherished our private world, delighting in being wrapped around each other, our hearts beating in sync. Our desire seemed insatiable, and a powerful emotional bond, as essential as breathing, enveloped us body and soul. I longed to stay there all night, gazing at his lovely face and naked body in the pale moonlight, but propriety demanded we drag ourselves back in the darkness to our separate homes, our separate lives. We burned with desperation for our next moments together.

Bounmy arranged for dinners to be delivered, and we often sat out back, overlooking the river, gazing at passing boats and the sunset. Sometimes he read me poignant poems of love and loss. He said his friend had written them, but I began to wonder if they might be his creations, and the house, his house.

It hadn't slipped Catherine's attention how many nights I spent out with Bounmy, or the late hours we were keeping. A week earlier she'd tried once more to caution me about the risks of the relationship—what people might think, and the possibility that Bounmy might disappoint me.

"Two friends mentioned rumors about you and Bounmy that are spreading in the French community," she'd said, her face etched with concern. "You know I only say this because I care about you. It's good you'll be apart from him while you're in Luang Prabang—perhaps it will give you a clearer perspective."

"But we love each other," I said with great confidence. "I trust him completely." And I did, even if unanswered questions about his family and the future wormed their way into my thoughts in the middle of the night. I pushed them aside.

"I understand how wonderful the bloom of new love can be, but circumstances change. And then what? You don't want people to view you as another Sylvie, swayed by a false romance and ending up in desperate straits."

I started, appalled at this comparison. "I'd never fall so low."

"Of course not, and I'll never let you, but you have to see what a slippery slope you're walking. You're so young still." Catherine sighed and shook her head, perhaps knowing she would never convince me to give him up. "I know you love him, and I hope it works out the way you envision. I'm here if you need to talk."

Now as Bounmy and I walked toward our little retreat, thoughts of Catherine's warnings left me anxious. I had to believe our love was true and our future together bright. With Bridgette gone, I needed him by my side more than ever.

Bounmy turned to me suddenly. "You'll find the scenery on the way to Luang Prabang beautiful and wild. The guides who lead the overland trips are experienced and will keep you as comfortable as possible, but it's probably rougher than you expect." He smiled down at me. "Are you excited?"

"A little nervous. I'm relieved Marguerite will be with me."

"I wouldn't have let you travel alone with a group of men like that. I don't trust Kham to watch out for you."

I looked up, startled by the authority in his voice, commanding and possessive. His concern touched me. "I've never ridden a horse. Is it difficult?"

"It's going to be a long, rough trip, and after a whole day in the saddle, your backside will cry out. It's good to get down and walk sometimes to keep the blood flowing." He frowned. "I should have taken you out riding the past few Sundays to show you the basics. Why didn't I think of that?"

"I'll be fine. Catherine is loaning me her riding pants and boots. And I bought some men's khaki pants and several shirts."

We came to a tiny café along the riverbank, where groups of men were gathered, drinking beer or the rice liquor *Lao Lao*. A young French officer and a woman sat at one of the tables. The woman turned, and our eyes met. Sylvie. She looked Bounmy up and down then stared at me, her expression changing from one of surprise to a smug, knowing regard. She thought I was no better than her, but she didn't understand. Bounmy and I loved each other completely.

The Frenchman looked up. "Prince Savang," he called out, lifting his glass of beer. "Come and join us."

Bounmy smiled without warmth. "Another time." He put his hand under my elbow, hurrying me along.

"You know him?" I asked.

"We played tennis a few times. He's a pompous ass."

I'd never heard Bounmy swear before. The only other time he'd expressed such disdain was when we'd run into André. Was he embarrassed to be seen with me, or worried for my reputation? As we continued on, I told him about Sylvie, how I'd discovered her situation and that I wanted to help her escape her rude existence.

He held my arm tighter. "Stay away from her. There is nothing you can do."

"Perhaps, but this is why I want to study law, so I can help other *métis* and women like Sylvie."

"That's an admirable ambition, and I encourage you to pursue your dream, but associating with someone like Sylvie will only taint your reputation."

The severity of his voice startled me, and I wondered what it was that worried him so.

As soon as we reached the house, Bounmy pulled me onto the divan. Without speaking he removed my clothes and made love to me with a force that startled me. It was as if he needed to possess me, to claim me as his alone.

After, he wrapped me in his arms, our legs entwined. He kissed my forehead. "I love you more than anything, Geneviève. What will I do while you're gone?"

"Six weeks will feel like an eternity, but I can't pass up this opportunity to find my mother." I could barely contain the desperate hopes consuming my thoughts. Everything depended on visiting my mother's family. I had no other path to follow.

"Of course. I will pray at the temple every day for you to find answers to your past." He kissed me gently and became aroused again. This time we made love slowly, tenderly.

The sun had already disappeared, so we ate our cheese, bread, and fruit, sitting on the bed. Bounmy wore his undershorts, while I had wrapped myself in the flowered kimono he'd given me the week before. I loved the feel of the silk fabric floating over my skin.

He caressed my cheek with his fingertips. "Do be careful. I won't be there to keep you safe."

I laughed. "Luang Prabang can't be that dangerous."

"No, but don't be too trusting of people, especially Kham."

I wondered where this sudden protectiveness had come from. What did he fear might happen? His warning about Kham gave me pause. "I haven't mentioned this before, but I've found some irregularities in the River Transport accounts, and they won't even let me look at the ledger for customs taxes. I feel they must be hiding something, but when I talk to Kham, he waves me away. Why doesn't he care?"

Bounmy scrunched up his face in an expression of distaste. "I wouldn't be surprised if he is doing something...questionable. But don't confront him or mention it to anyone else."

"I wouldn't, but you should know."

"It's best if you simply go along with the status quo."

He lifted his pants off the floor where he had thrown them and removed a packet of papers and a small box from the pockets. "If you have some free evenings in Luang Prabang, there are many beautiful temples to see. I've written down the names of the most famous ones with information on their art and a map of the locations. My favorite is Wat Xieng Thong, which was built in the 1500s and recently restored with help from the French. The Luang Prabang kings are crowned there. *Xieng* means city and *Thong* means bodhi tree—after the ancient bodhi tree in India where Buddha attained enlightenment."

I took the papers, covered with his neat, even script, and kissed his cheek. "I can't wait to see them."

He handed me the small box. "And this is for you."

Inside I found a silver chain with a small flower hanging from it. "It's beautiful."

"Do you recognize the flower?"

I studied it a moment, unsure. "An orchid?"

"It's the bloom of the tamarind tree. I had it specially made to bring you luck in searching for your mother." He took the necklace from the box and draped it around me, closing the clasp. "A story about Buddha says the tamarind seed is the symbol of faithfulness and forbearance. It seems appropriate, given all the years you've waited to find your family."

I fingered the delicate bloom as tears filled my eyes. "I can't believe you remembered."

"Of course I remembered." He wrapped his arms around my shoulders and pulled my head onto his shoulder. "I picture you sitting in that tree, watching for your mother year after year, and it breaks my heart. If only I could protect you from everything bad."

"It's the most wonderful gift I've ever received." I loved him more than I'd ever imagined possible.

Bounmy lifted my head, looking into my eyes. "Promise me something. If anything should come between us, swear to me you won't turn to Julian. I couldn't bear the thought of you being with him. He's not worthy of you."

I sat back, shocked by this strange request. "I don't know what could come between us, but I love you, not Julian. He's only a friend."

He pulled me into his arms again. "I don't want to lose you."

It was after eleven when I returned home. It felt physically painful to tear myself from Bounmy's embrace knowing we would be separated for so many weeks. We'd made love twice more and shared a thousand kisses. I was emotionally spent, already missing him, when I stepped inside the house.

Julian appeared in the doorway to the salon. "You're back, finally."

My body tensed. Our friendship had continued, but on a more tenuous note since Bounmy and I had become so deeply involved. I tried to maintain a clear distance between us. We still spent evenings with Catherine and Marguerite playing belote, laughing as if everything were the same as before. He seemed to accept my boundaries and, at least, didn't cross them. He'd stopped coming to take me to lunch and never asked questions about Bounmy.

"I'm surprised you're up so late," I said.

"I wanted to say goodbye, since you're leaving early tomorrow." His eyes locked on mine, as if searching for a clue to my feelings. "Where were you and the prince at this late hour? Do you have a secret love nest somewhere?"

The sarcasm in his voice filled me with dread. He didn't appear drunk, but I could smell alcohol on his breath. "I have to be up early. I must get to bed."

"Your last night with Bounmy. 'Parting is such sweet sorrow.' Have you read *Romeo and Juliet*? You two are as ill-fated as those famous lovers. A tragedy in progress. Surely you see that?"

"My relationship with Bounmy is none of your business." I was too tired to cope with his jealousy.

He ran his hand through his hair. "I worry for you."

"Bounmy wouldn't hurt me." I stood very still, defying the power of Julian's words to instill doubt. "He loves me."

"How can you be so naïve, Vivi? Do you actually think Bounmy's family will let him marry you, an orphaned *métisse*? After he's had his fun, he'll abandon you." He grabbed my arm. "You know I'm right."

"Stop. Please stop." I wrenched my arm from his grip. "Leave me alone." I turned and ran up the stairs. His words struck like knives piercing my heart. Perhaps he was right. Perhaps Bounmy would leave me one day. But I would cherish the time we had together. I loved him too much to do anything else.

Chapter 37

Marguerite arrived at seven on Wednesday morning in the Resident Superior's black Renault motorcar, driven by his chauffeur. I'd never ridden in an automobile before and thought it quite thrilling. Marguerite wore voluminous white cotton pants and a long flowing robe with black riding boots. All she needed was a turban wrapped around her head to match an Arabian prince in an illustration from *One Thousand and One Nights*. Even wearing Catherine's jodhpurs and coffee-colored riding boots, I looked unremarkable in comparison.

"What an ungodly hour. I barely had time for coffee," Marguerite grumbled, as I sank into the pleated leather folds of the back seat. "Charles had better appreciate the sacrifices I'm making to travel to Luang Prabang. I'm either crazy or in love. I'm not sure which, yet."

We continued to the French guesthouse near the Cercle to collect the overweight German and his Danish companions, who we'd seen at the club the previous month. Marguerite said they'd recently returned from Champasak in southern Laos. The three men staggered out of the inn with their valises, reeking of gin. Dark circles surrounded their sleepy eyes. They nodded a curt greeting and crowded into the car. One Danish man was sweating profusely, and his face was white. I feared he might be sick on the way to our destination.

The chauffeur drove us north on the still-under-construction autoroute to Luang Prabang. "The road is only a hundred kilometers long at the moment," Marguerite said. "They've been working on it for nearly a decade, but budgetary constraints keep getting in the way. The recent economic collapse has brought construction to a halt again."

The route was nothing more than an eight-foot-wide stretch of packed dirt, which Bounmy had told me had been hand-excavated by *corvée* labor crews. Once out of town, we passed through rice paddies and small villages until the landscape turned into a seemingly impenetrable jungle, like the pending darkness of nightfall, threatening to reclaim the colonial government's efforts to create a link to the north. Rain the day before had made the dirt slick, causing the car to repeatedly slide and swerve. In some spots downpours had washed away chunks of the road and created enormous potholes, which the driver had to veer around or slowly traverse. I began to think I might be better off on a horse, as frightened as I was at the prospect.

Two hours out of Vientiane, the route ended abruptly. Ten Lao guides, eight small horses, and two elephants awaited us. The men were busy saddling horses and attaching square platforms atop the elephants' backs, before loading on supplies and luggage. The guides were small of stature and spare, barely taller than me, but their wiry arms and legs proved remarkably strong. They went barefoot and wore loose cotton shirts over sarongs tied about their waists.

Kham showed up in a battered old Ford convertible ten minutes later with two Chinese merchants.

"Prince Savang, may I introduce Mademoiselle Vanier, secretary to the Resident Superior of Laos," I said.

Kham smiled and made a *nop* in a deferential manner that was out of character. "Mademoiselle, what a great pleasure." He introduced his companions as Messieurs Wong and Lee. All the men disappeared briefly into the trees before reemerging.

Marguerite whispered in my ear, "We should probably use the facilities before we start."

Startled, I looked around. "There's an outhouse?"

Marguerite laughed. "No such luck. Get used to nature's water closet. And watch where you squat. God only knows what might be crawling on the ground or in the plants. The jungle is full of lethal snakes."

I wrinkled my nose. "If you're trying to reassure me, it's not working." I followed her into the trees and found a private spot, examining the earth below me as I gingerly crouched down. It would be a very long trip.

The horses stood only four to five feet tall, sporting harnesses with silver adornments and saddle blankets woven with bright colors. The animals appeared unbothered by the people and commotion around them, perhaps resigned to the long trek ahead. One of the older guides led me to the smallest horse, presumably because I was the smallest person in the group. The horse's ears shot back, and it retreated several steps as I approached.

The guide laughed as I recoiled in fear. "Like this," he said, showing me how to stroke the animal's neck and speak in soothing tones. The horse relaxed and allowed me to climb onto its back. The saddle felt more like a hard plank of wood than leather. How would I manage for the next twelve days?

Marguerite mounted her horse, squirming in the seat as the guide adjusted her stirrups. She turned to me with a guffaw. "Get used to your derrière being numb, Vivi."

After a great deal of heated discussion, the guides relegated the German to riding on one of the elephants. The diminutive horses could not possibly support his corpulent frame. He huffed and mumbled what must have been German curses as they hoisted him up on the palanquin seat.

We struck out at last, plodding along a narrow dirt path that led into a tangled mass of trees and vines. Two guides rode horses at the head of the procession, while another guide took Marguerite's and my reins as we followed. The other riders followed in pairs, while the elephants trailed behind. The early hour and Marguerite's grim expression discouraged conversation, but it didn't matter. I was exhausted and consumed by thoughts of Bounmy and Julian's comments the previous night. The swaying gait of my horse rocked me back and forth, and my thigh muscles soon felt stretched to their limit. My backside ached.

We trekked over rolling hills where giant mahogany and teak trees towered over stands of bamboo and purple flowering vines. Suddenly forest gave way to verdant valleys with vast stretches of flooded rice paddies and small villages. Farmers, harvesting bananas and mangos from their orchards, stopped to wave to our party. Houses were built on six-foot poles above the ground, and small children peeked at us from under the verandas. The familiar scent of wood smoke from cookfires drifted through the air. Almost every village had a simple brick-and-plaster Buddhist temple, where monks and young novices went about their daily chores.

We passed a burly young Frenchman and his *corvée* crew repairing the ubiquitous network of telegraph lines, which had been knocked down by monsoon storms. The Frenchman called out a greeting and waved his hat.

Cultivated lands soon disappeared into untamed jungle, a wonderous place of colors and shapes and smells. Marguerite pointed out a peacock, spreading its glorious tail feathers as if trying to get our attention. Soon we spotted a troop of white-faced gibbons, swinging between tree branches and squawking at one another, making us laugh as they peered out through the leaves with curious eyes. The sound of the elephants stomping down the trail startled a flock of blue and green parrots, sending them into careening through the canopy. We crossed a series of shallow streams that meandered downhill, destined for the Mekong River, where we paused for the animals to drink.

A few hours out, we stopped to rest. My legs nearly collapsed beneath me when I slid off my saddle, and I thought of Bounmy's predictions of the rigors of riding. Marguerite and I found a log to sit on apart from the rest of the group. My throat was parched, and I gulped down coconut water from fruit that the guides had cut open with machetes.

"You seem far away," Marguerite said. "You were out with Prince Savang last night. Did you have a nice time?"

I smiled. "We always enjoy being together. It was hard to say goodbye."

"I'm sure." She lit a cigarette, taking a deep drag and exhaling the smoke, which swirled around us and melted away. "How are you and Julian getting along? It's difficult for him right now."

I bit my lower lip. "I appreciate his friendship, but—"

"You're in love with the prince." She finished my sentence. I nodded. "Be careful, Vivi. You're so young." She chuckled. "Trust me, you'll have plenty of time to fall in love and make foolish choices later on. Look at me. I have no idea why I'm going all this way to visit Charles."

"Why does being young disqualify me from falling in love and making rational decisions?"

"You're right." She sighed. "But don't let it go too far. Men are men. They'll say they love you in the heat of the moment, then do exactly what suits them." She crushed her cigarette with the heel of her boot. "It seems unlikely that his future is his to choose."

I swallowed hard and kept my eyes focused on the damp earth below, watching a line of industrious army ants carry fragments of leaves and small sticks four times their size. Everyone kept cautioning me. It was true that I had no idea what Bounmy thought about the future or what his options might be. But how could I not be with the man I loved?

Marguerite inclined her head to one side. "I can see I'm a little late for warnings. You're already lovers."

I blushed to the tip of my scalp. "Yes." I met her gaze, relieved to confess to someone. Marguerite was the one person I thought would understand my surrender. "We love each other."

She sighed and offered a wan smile. "That's how it should be. If you have any questions, feel free to ask me. I hope he's using protection."

I nodded. Bounmy had used condoms most of the time, but sometimes in the rush of passion, it was forgotten.

"Don't say anything to Catherine," Marguerite said. "She's too close to the situation with Julian."

I smiled. "I hadn't planned on telling you."

She patted my arm. "I won't say a word to anyone." She started to speak again but stopped, instead standing up and stretching her arms over her head. "Shall we walk a bit and get some feeling back in our derrières?"

———

We stayed in communities of twenty to forty homes perched on hillsides among the trees. Each village had *salas*, small huts built of wood and bamboo with woven rattan floors, meant to accommodate passing travelers. Marguerite and I were given a separate *sala* from the men, where we would collapse, weary to the bone, on cots under mosquito nets. I was thankful for Marguerite's presence, as I couldn't imagine feeling secure if I had been the only woman in the group. Sleep would come to me within minutes, lulled into oblivion by the incessant drone of insects and mysterious calls of unknown creatures.

The days fell into an exhausting pattern. We marched five to six hours up and down mountains, through deep river ravines, and across narrow green valleys, stopping occasionally to rest along the way. The guides seemed in no rush to reach our destination. Twice we were forced to take shelter under giant palm fronds from torrential rains that made it impossible to proceed.

On Marguerite's advice, I had bought an inexpensive pair of men's khaki pants and two long-sleeved cotton shirts to have a change of clothes. We washed our things in streams and hung them to dry on tree branches overnight. But the fabrics remained damp the entire trip, smelling of sweat and mud and horses.

The sixth night out, village elders joined our party for a dinner of chicken, vegetables, and sticky rice. Except for the rice, which the guides had brought, we purchased fresh foods from the farmers and paid local women to prepare our meals. We were often entertained by a villager playing a *khene*, a bamboo reed flute, dipping and twirling to its haunting notes that echoed into the night.

"Monsieur Borck, are you all right?" Marguerite said suddenly, addressing the thin, blond Danish man, who had looked unwell since the day we embarked on the trip.

His head lolled to one side, and his face flushed. Sweat beaded his forehead. He looked up bleary-eyed, as if trying to focus on Marguerite, then keeled over on the mat.

"Malaria," the German offered, seeming remarkably unconcerned for his colleague.

After several rounds of interpreting in multiple languages between the German, the other Dane, Kham, and the village chief, the guides carried poor Monsieur Borck to the *sala*. Marguerite and I trailed behind to see if we could help. He was soon delirious, rolling around and crying.

"He's very sick," I murmured to Marguerite, holding on to her arm.

"Sleep will help. We had a long day." She tried to sound reassuring, but worry filled her voice.

"I know malaria doesn't have to be fatal, but what can they do for him out here?" Despite the warm night, my body shivered as I thought of Bridgette and the uncertainty of life. Everything could change in an instant.

Three village women appeared and began wiping his face and arms down with cloths dipped in cool water. They managed to get him to drink a foul-smelling herbal tincture, then fed him several spoons of a brown paste.

"Opium," Marguerite said. "That will calm him down so he can sleep."

Monsieur Borck fell into a deep sleep, and an hour later his fever broke. While I tossed and turned on my cot, worrying about him, he slept soundly.

The next morning Monsieur Borck arrived for breakfast, looking relatively normal. "I'm a little weak, but I'm able to continue."

"Quinine," the German proclaimed. "He'll be fine with quinine."

Marguerite rolled her eyes at me. "I guess that settles the problem."

The sun beat down on mountaintops where Miao hilltribes had cleared trees to plant vegetables and dry rice. Marguerite said that after four or five years the crops leached the nutrients from the thin topsoil, forcing the entire village to move to a new location.

One morning we passed a hillside bursting with cup-shaped, purple flowers on tall stalks. "How beautiful. What are they?" I asked.

"Opium poppies," Marguerite said. "They extract a white sticky substance from the bulb at the center of the flowers. Very profitable, as you might imagine. The colonial government requires that all opium be sold to the French-run monopoly Régie d'Opium, so they can collect taxes, but most of the drug gets smuggled out through Chinese traders."

"Goodness." I'd had no idea where opium came from, only that it was abused by many and could ruin lives.

Marguerite and I liked to walk for short stretches to give our horses a rest, and to ease the constant ache from sitting in our saddles. In some places the steep climbs made it too difficult for the animals to support us. Sore calves and painful blisters plagued me, but the worst was the leeches, which latched onto my legs, even inside my riding boots, causing me to bleed on my pants and socks. Everything in my body hurt.

On the eighth night, we stayed with a hilltribe high in the mountains. The lead guide announced, "The chief says not to wander far. A tiger has been stalking the village and has already killed a water buffalo."

Marguerite looked at me with true fear in her eyes. "We must stick together every minute."

That night before bed, we only stepped a few feet into the forest, nervously scanning the shadows and staying close to each other. "I don't care who sees me," Marguerite snapped.

I squatted down, ready to spring up if necessary. Could I outrun a tiger? I had no idea. "I can hardly do my business," I whispered.

She laughed. "Let's hope we don't have intestinal problems tonight. I'm not leaving the *sala*."

I woke repeatedly throughout the night, my body tightly coiled as I listened for the tiger. We woke early in the morning to a not-so-distant roar that seemed to grow louder as the sun rose. Marguerite reached out and took hold of my hand.

I clung to her. "Are you scared?"

"Damn right. Being mauled by a tiger is hardly the way I plan to exit this world. Especially before I get to spend another night in bed with Charles."

I giggled, thinking how I longed to be back in Bounmy's arms.

Everyone was jumpy that morning as we prepared to set out. Kham looked over at Marguerite and me and winked. "Don't worry, mademoiselles. You'll be safe." But his insincere smile didn't instill confidence.

"I don't trust that man anywhere near me," Marguerite whispered. "Be wary, Vivi."

Three of the guides shouldered shotguns almost as large as they were. A half-hour on, my horse jerked his head up and his ears shot back as the horse behind us whinnied. On my right a streak of orange and black dashed through the trees. "Over there!" I cried. My heart thudded, and my breath came hard and fast. I considered jumping off my horse and running, but a strange heaviness paralyzed my limbs. Where could I go? What could I do?

The lead guide brought the group to a halt as two others lifted their shotguns, pulling back the locks, ready to fire. The elephant carrying the German stepped back and forth nervously and trumpeted loudly, the sound reverberating through the trees. The tiger peered out from behind a giant mahogany tree, its pale-yellow eyes riveted on one of the guides. It took two tentative steps forward, growled, and bared its teeth, crouching down on its front legs, back muscles taut, as if ready to pounce.

A shot rang out. The bullet hit the tree above the tiger's head, gouging the bark. A second shot hit the ground just short of the beast. The tiger jerked back, turned, and bolted into the dense foliage. We waited ten minutes without any sign of the beast before starting down the narrow trail once more. A few distant roars slowly faded away.

As our trip neared its conclusion, we stayed in a Kha village. I tried not be embarrassed by the bare-breasted women wearing only sarongs, and the men with nothing but tiny loincloths. As in other settlements we had passed, many of the inhabitants' teeth and mouths were stained red from chewing betel nuts. Marguerite said it gave them a boost of energy, similar to caffeine. Although these people lived in the most basic, dirty shelters, they welcomed us warmly and shared their food.

On Sunday, eleven days after our departure, we reached the autoroute to Luang Prabang. It seemed highly improbable that this remote road would ever connect to its counterpart near Vientiane, given the vast stretches of impenetrable terrain in between. Like the other road, this one was packed dirt, full of potholes and muddy ruts, running sixty kilometers into town.

French officials and Kham's family had been notified of our pending arrival via telegrams sent from the last village. The only two cars in Luang Prabang, belonging to the French commissioner and the king, waited to ferry us on the final stretch of the trip.

Kham indicated I should ride with him, while Marguerite would go in the government car with the German and two Danes to the French guesthouse. Monsieur Borck had held up remarkably well for the remainder of the trip, although he was still running a mild fever and had noticeably lost weight. Marguerite said they would drop him at the French hospital for treatment.

"I'd invite you to stay with me, Vivi," Marguerite whispered, "but Charles lives in the officer quarters, so he'll be sleeping in my lodgings—very discreetly, of course." She winked at me. "But come for dinner tomorrow night at seven at the French Cercle. Be safe." She kissed me on both cheeks and climbed into her car.

I took a deep breath and joined Kham and the two Chinese men in the king's car, missing Marguerite already.

Chapter 38

When we finally reached the home of Kham's sister-in-law, located in a compound near the royal palace, it was late afternoon. Like other traditional homes I'd seen, the teak structure was built on posts, only this one was decorated with elaborately carved elephants, tigers, and monkeys dancing across the eaves of the high-peaked roof. The simply furnished front room held two low tables and an altar covered with offerings of food, candles, and incense. Two beautiful silk weavings in shades of lime green and pale yellow were draped over carved rosewood holders and hung on the back wall.

I was embarrassed to meet his relatives looking like a street urchin. Anticipating our arrival, Marguerite and I had washed as best we could in a cold stream the previous evening, but my hair was stringy and coated with dust. My stained and wrinkled khaki pants and slightly yellowed white blouse undoubtedly smelled of sweat.

Kham introduced me to his wife's sister and her husband, both much older than him. The wife was petite and delicate in appearance, but her face had been marred by deep pockmarks. She wore a lavender silk *sinh* and *pha biang*. Her unusually tall husband had a swarthy complexion, a wispy beard, and graying temples. He stared down at me with an expression of distaste. After all, I was merely Kham's employee, worse yet a *métisse*.

Kham instructed me to meet him downstairs the next morning at eight o'clock to leave for the office. He turned his back, making it clear that I was dismissed. A servant appeared at my side and led me to a small room attached to the back of the house. Four mats and quilts covered the floor, and clothes hung from nails in the wall. The servant spoke to me in Lao, repeating her words several times until I finally understood that I would sleep there with her and two others. I tried not to show my surprise. But it didn't matter how they treated me, so long as I had the opportunity to search for my mother's family.

The servant offered me a bath in a large copper tub of cold water next to the outhouse behind the home, shielded from view by a bamboo screen. I gladly accepted the coarse bar of soap, grateful to wash away the accumulated dirt of the long trek from my hair and body. What luxury to be clean again and dress in fresh clothes!

The other two servants were pretty, young sisters, fifteen and sixteen years old, nieces of the older woman. They smiled patiently as I attempted to speak Lao, using hand gestures and repeating the words over and over. They strained to understand, wearing puzzled expressions until an inkling of recognition spread across their faces, and one of them would utter a long "Ahh," and correct my pronunciation. The conversation progressed full of misunderstandings, followed by vigorous nodding and lots of laughter. On the whole, I thought Mali would be proud of me.

The older servant presented a meal to me on the back veranda. She shook her head when I suggested I eat with her and the girls. It seemed my status in the home fell somewhere between: not good enough to join the family, but slightly above the servants. I sat on a rattan mat at the low table, ravenously devouring a delicious pork and noodle dish and fresh mangoes.

I decided to take a walk after dinner and explore Luang Prabang, finding it a small, sleepy town. There were few people about, except for a Lao family in an oxcart and a French soldier in his white uniform and helmet trotting by on a horse. Colonial offices and homes lined the road I was on, before giving way to a row of Chinese shophouses. I passed two lovely Buddhist temples not far apart, with multiple sloping roofs and extravagant gold decorations that glittered in the fading light of day. The familiar, comforting sounds of the monks chanting, and the scent of sandalwood incense, greeted me. I smiled, thinking of the list of temples Bounmy had prepared for me.

I turned down a narrow, dusty lane and reached the swirling waters of the Mekong. A dozen or more longboats, fishing skiffs, and barges bobbed at their moorings as owners lounged on the prows, chatting with one another, prompting thoughts of Bounmy and our afternoons along the river. I missed him desperately.

I headed back to the house and collapsed on my appointed quilt, sinking into a deep, dreamless sleep.

One of the young girls woke me a little after seven the next morning. I dressed quickly and ate a small bowl of rice congee before rushing down the back stairs and around the front to meet Kham.

Fifteen minutes later he appeared, not bothering with a greeting or an apology for being late, but simply marching off down the road to the River Transport office. The rundown building looked much like the one in Vientiane, only half the size. Kham introduced the lone Chinese accountant, who occupied the tiny front office, and an older Lao man, plump and disheveled, who managed the dusty warehouse. He instructed them to assist me with my work. They nodded, failing to conceal their consternation at the disruption to their routines. I sighed, weighed down by the task of once again trying to convince my coworkers to cooperate.

Kham retired to the tiny office at the back and was soon joined by his brother-in-law, who surreptitiously glanced up at me from time to time. Was it possible Kham had told his family of my connection to Bounmy?

I perched on the only other chair in the office, near the Chinese accountant, using the top of a file cabinet as my desk. Loose invoices and receipts were scattered haphazardly on the bookshelves and floor. Clearly patience and persistence would be called for.

As the afternoon wore on, my eyes grew weary from deciphering illegible notes on bills of lading and lists of warehouse inventories. At six o'clock, long after the others had left, I straightened the growing piles of paper surrounding me and returned to my lodgings. After changing into my blue dress, I set off for dinner with Marguerite and Charles.

The French Cercle was a five-minute walk from my lodgings. It was a much smaller club than the one in Vientiane, given that only two dozen French *colons* resided in the Luang Prabang area. Colorful tiles decorated the floor of the large airy front room, cooled by punkah fans swaying back and forth from the high ceiling. A few men and women were lounging in chairs, sipping cocktails. The men were dressed for dinner in uniforms or black tie, while the women wore tea dresses. Several people glanced up, registering surprise at a lone stranger, a young *métisse*, entering their sanctuary.

Marguerite and Charles jumped up and waved from their spot at the bar. Inquisitive eyes and low murmurs followed me as I traversed the room. Marguerite kissed my cheeks. "Sit down, dear. Have a drink." She signaled the bartender.

"*Bienvenue*, Mademoiselle Dubois." Charles bowed and kissed the back of my hand.

We made small talk about the weather, the sleepy nature of Luang Prabang, and the beautiful temples to be explored.

"How was your first day at work?" Marguerite asked. "Are you comfortable with Kham's family?"

"I'm fine," I insisted. "The work is the same as in Vientiane." There was no point in mentioning my sleeping quarters with the servants, or the hostility of my coworkers. I wouldn't tell her of Kham's cold indifference, as if he were punishing me for doing something wrong. I didn't want Marguerite to feel she must rescue me. What would Bounmy say about his family's treatment of me? Would he be indignant, or consider it unfortunate but expected?

Marguerite was glowing, constantly laughing at Charles's jokes, foregoing her usual sarcastic remarks. "Even though it's small, the club here is quite nice, don't you think? And the chef is incredible."

Charles smiled and took Marguerite's hand, gazing adoringly into her eyes. "I think it's the company that makes the food so outstanding."

Marguerite giggled and blushed.

We finished our cocktails and moved to the dining room, located between the club and the guesthouse. French *colons* filled the half dozen tables, along with our German and Danish traveling companions.

As we began our meal, a figure appeared, looming over us. I glanced up, startled to see Monsieur Fontaine. He was perfectly groomed, wearing a black dinner jacket, with his pomaded hair combed neatly in place, but his jacket hung loose on his tall frame, and his handsome face was lined with fatigue.

He smiled and nodded. "Mademoiselle Dubois, what a pleasant surprise to see you." He glanced at Marguerite. "You didn't mention that your young friend accompanied you here."

"Why would I?" Marguerite said, her voice icy.

He turned back to me and bowed. "I hope your visit is enjoyable." He walked off, joining a young officer at a table across the room.

"It's impossible to avoid anyone in this tiny town," Marguerite grumbled. "Keep your distance, Vivi."

"He's on his best behavior, these days. Hasn't touched a drop of alcohol since he's been here," Charles offered. "You must give him credit for that."

"I should think not, if he doesn't want to be sent back to France," Marguerite scoffed.

"I heard he was cleared of any wrongdoing with the maid," I said in a low voice.

"Yes, at least he's not a pervert or rapist," Marguerite said. "I suppose we can be happy of that, for Catherine's sake. But he's still a despicable person."

There was no point in my defending him. I knew little about the man, only that Catherine had loved him, which made me believe there was something good about him. And I was grateful for the time he'd saved me from Monsieur Toussaint.

The dinner was delicious and the company kind, but I felt like an intruder at a private party. Marguerite and Charles were lost in their own world, constantly brushing arms and holding hands, as if needing to reassure themselves of the other's presence. I understood. I ached for Bounmy.

After coffee and brandy, we said our goodbyes. I agreed to meet Marguerite at the French guesthouse on Sunday morning to visit my family's home. She had offered to accompany me.

Slightly tipsy, I ambled down the street under the pale light of a nearly full moon. Lamps flickered in the windows of a large house, and strains of a piano étude drifted into the night. Footsteps pounded behind me, and my body tensed, ready to flee.

Monsieur Fontaine came to a stop beside me. "Mademoiselle Dubois, I didn't mean to frighten you, but can we speak?"

Whatever did he want? "What is it?"

"I only want to know how Catherine is doing."

I studied his haggard face, reading pain and regret. "She's well. Her brother Julian has returned, and that makes her happy."

"I heard." He ran his fingers over his carefully arranged hair. "I've sent several letters to apologize, but she never writes back." He paused. "I know my behavior was inexcusable."

"She needs to get on with her life," I said. "She suffered a great deal."

"I understand her distress over the false accusations and the scene I made at Pierre's." He took a step back. "Alcohol destroyed my life."

"Can you really blame it all on the drinking?"

"No, of course not. I have many regrets, but not about my relationship with Catherine. Please tell her how sorry I am and that I'll always love her. She's a wonderful woman and deserves someone… better."

"Yes, she does," I said, perhaps being too harsh. It was evident she'd been much more to him than an insignificant fling. "I'll give her your message."

"I appreciate it. May I accompany you to your lodgings, since it's late? Although you couldn't find a safer place than this small town."

I hesitated. "Thank you."

"What brings you to Luang Prabang?" he asked as we walked.

I explained about my job with River Transport. "I'm not sure how long I'll be here. Several weeks, at least." After a pause, I told him of the search for my mother's family. "I have the name and location of the family home. I'm going to visit on Sunday."

"And your father?"

"All I know is he worked here from 1910 until he returned to France in 1915."

"I could check the personnel records, if you like. They're in the office next to mine."

"I would greatly appreciate it. His name was Henri Dubois."

"I'll send you a note at River Transport if I find something."

We arrived at the house. "Thank you for offering to help."

He bowed slightly. "My pleasure."

Chapter 39

The days of the week dragged on endlessly as I waited for Sunday to arrive. Between the dismissive treatment of Kham and his family and the hostile environment at the office, I'd lost any remaining shred of enthusiasm for work. I longed to be back in Vientiane with Bounmy, living in my lovely room at Catherine's house. Safe and cared for.

I found a disturbing level of disarray and mismanagement. My instincts told me that the misdeeds in this office ran even deeper than those in Vientiane. Kham's brother-in-law unnerved me the most. His eyes tracked me, like a bird of prey preparing to swoop in and grab its helpless victim. I could only guess that he feared I might reveal his malfeasance to Kham.

In the evenings, I returned to the house to dine alone on the back veranda. After eating, I chose one of the Buddhist temples in Bounmy's guide to visit, taking pleasure in reading his descriptions of the *wats* and beautiful art, which he had lovingly prepared. Wearing the silver necklace he'd given me, I felt him there in spirit.

Although still uncertain of Buddhist beliefs, the serene temples eased my anxious thoughts and buoyed my hopes, as I lit incense and prayed before the altars, that I might find my mother. The day before I left for Luang Prabang, Mali had given me an amulet half the size of my palm, a red stone carved with an image of Buddha. She'd had the monk at her temple bless it to bring me luck in finding answers to my past. I cherished the aura of love and good wishes in Bounmy's necklace and Mali's amulet.

On Saturday morning a note arrived at work from Monsieur Fontaine, suggesting we meet at three that afternoon at La Patisserie

Française for coffee. My pulse quickened as I read that he had information regarding my father. Surely his desire to help me was an act of love for Catherine, a means of reaching out to her.

He was already seated at a table when I arrived. A middle-aged French woman ran the small establishment, which sold dark roasted coffee and an array of French pastries, biscuits, and cakes. I'd been too nervous to eat lunch, and now my stomach rumbled with hunger.

Monsieur Fontaine greeted me with polite reserve and ordered us coffee and a plate of golden madeleines. "How is your work progressing?"

"Slow and tedious."

"My current position is much the same," he said with a rueful smile. He pulled a paper from his jacket pocket and unfolded it. His sad expression foretold unhappy news before he even spoke. "I found the personnel file on your father. As you thought, he worked in Luang Prabang from 1910 to 1915, arriving here when he was twenty-nine years old. He worked as an assistant to the Luang Prabang French Commissioner, coordinating issues with the royal palace." He took a sip of coffee and focused on the paper, avoiding my gaze. "He was married with one child. His wife and seven-year-old son joined him here in early 1911, but they returned home five months later. Your father left in 1915."

All the air left my lungs as my worst doubts and fears were confirmed. My father had another family, a French family. Questions swirled in my head. Had he seduced my mother and taken her as his mistress to fill the void when his wife and son went back to France? Was it loneliness and desperation, or had he loved my mother? I couldn't fathom how he was capable of starting a second family, a Lao family, only to abandon us.

"Does it say why he returned to France?" I asked at last.

"Like many of the men here, he went to fight in the Great War." He cleared his throat. "I regret to tell you, he was killed in action in March 1916 at the Battle of Verdun. He received the Croix de Guerre for his bravery."

I blinked several times taking in the news, trying to absorb the loss of this person called my father, but emotions failed me. I had no memory of him. Perhaps he was a good person who had loved me. Or he could have been a selfish, immoral man who took what he wanted without any regard for my mother and the children she bore him. I had no way of knowing. Regret washed over me for what might have been, the relationship we could have shared.

Monsieur Fontaine folded the paper and slid it across the table. "It's terribly sad. I'm so sorry."

"I'm grateful to you." I took a sip of coffee. "Why did you help me?"

"You've had a difficult time. I don't understand the Assistance Society's policy of hiding your past." He glanced out the window for a moment. "I suppose Catherine's passionate beliefs in righting the wrongs of this world influenced me."

"Do you hope this will somehow bring her back?"

He shook his head slowly. "I realized much too late how much I love her. Only with her did my soul feel at ease." His voice grew tight, and his eyes glistened. "I have no illusions about winning her back. I simply want her to understand the depth of my love for her."

"And what about your wife and children?"

"My wife filed for divorce and is seeking sole custody of the children. I can't blame her. I was a total failure as a husband and father." He sounded contrite, not bitter. "My wife and I married too young and were not a happy match, but I miss my children terribly. I hope someday they'll forgive me."

This was a very different person from the one I'd met in Vientiane. His despair was etched in the wrinkles that marred his handsome face. He pulled an envelope from his pocket. "Would you please give this letter to Catherine for me?" I nodded and took it.

"Are you still going to your mother's family home tomorrow?" he asked. I nodded. "I wish you luck…and peace of mind. If there is anything else I can do for you, mademoiselle, please don't hesitate to contact me." He stood and strode quickly out the door.

I remained at the table, slowly eating the rest of the madeleines, feeding the emptiness within. I wavered between disgust with Monsieur Fontaine's drinking problems and infidelity, the pain he had caused Catherine, and empathy for his dark unhappiness. Even if he had only himself to blame for his circumstances, he was drowning in sorrow. Finally tears welled in my eyes for the father I would never meet.

Chapter 40

barely slept on Saturday night, dozing in and out of consciousness, listening to the soft breathing of the women around me and the rolling thunder of passing showers outside. My mind became a spinning wheel of hopes and dreams as I imagined meeting my mother, as I had imagined it a thousand times, seeing the shock on her face at finally finding her lost child. Would she recognize me right away? Had she been searching all these years? I felt sure the Assistance Society had hidden the location of her children from her. I tried not to think about my father, dead now fifteen years, a phantom from my past whom I would never know. I fervently prayed to any possible higher power to return my mother to me. Once I found her, we would join Antoine, restoring our small family, which had been torn apart many years before. We could live together in Luang Prabang or Vientiane, or even Paris. It didn't matter where.

The servants rose before dawn to start a fire and prepare breakfast for Kham's family. I slipped quietly down the back steps to the outhouse, washing my face and brushing my teeth in the makeshift basin by the water barrel, then dressed in my polka-dot dress and set out. I wandered up and down the dusty lanes of town, needing to fill the hours until ten o'clock, when I would meet Marguerite. At times the anticipation of what lay ahead brought a cascade of panic surging through my body, my heart racing in leaps and bounds. I fingered the red stone amulet in my pocket and the silver tamarind flower hanging around my neck.

It seemed an entire day had passed before I finally made my way to the French guesthouse where Marguerite was waiting. Charles had arranged for a carriage to take us to my family's home, two kilometers from the center of town.

The horse carried us out of town on a dirt road full of ruts and puddles, the wheels flinging clumps of mud into the air. A farmer hoed weeds in his vegetable patch while his wife hung washing on a line between two trees near the house. Three young children gathered around their mother to gape at the passing carriage. One little boy grinned and waved. I envied the farmers' simple lives, tending fields and following centuries-old traditions. Despite their modest home and constant hard work, they had each other, a family, a place where they belonged.

Twenty minutes on, the driver turned down a grassy lane between rows of tamarind trees. Their May flowers had long since transformed into reddish-brown pods of fruit, which hung from the branches like misshapen fingers. Could these have been the trees my mother talked of when she gave me to the orphanage?

We passed through an open gate leading into a fenced compound. Three large traditional homes, similar to that of Kham's family, overlooked the Nam Khan River. At the far end of the expansive enclosure, a collection of sheds, livestock corrals, and smaller wooden huts lined the bamboo fence. Was this where my mother's life had begun, where she had grown up?

An older woman with silver-streaked hair knotted at the nape of her neck, wearing a simple cotton *sinh* and blouse, shook out quilts on the veranda of the first home. In the open space underneath a second building, two men sanded the sides of a longboat. A bevy of children of varying ages squealed and chased one another around an enormous banyan tree in the open courtyard, sending chickens and ducks scurrying in all directions. All heads turned our way as the carriage rolled to a stop.

I touched my necklace. "I'm terrified." Marguerite patted my arm, for once seeming at a loss for words.

The woman left her quilts hanging over the railing and ran down the stairs to meet us. She gave a *nop*. "*Sabaidee*, mademoiselles."

I searched her ordinary features—a broad, flat nose and forehead, a narrow chin. Could she be my mother? Yet nothing in her face struck me as familiar. My mouth turned dry, and I could barely utter the Lao words Mali had helped me practice. "I…I'm searching for Laya Thongsavat." I could not quite manage to say *my mother*, the word being too extraordinary to speak out loud.

The woman's eyes opened wide. After a moment, she said, "Please come." She held her hand out, indicating we should follow her up the stairs.

As we reached the wide veranda, another woman emerged from the open doorway. She wore a silk *sinh* woven in shades of orange and burgundy and a white blouse edged with lace. Her dark hair was wrapped on top of her head, secured with silver combs. High cheekbones, a delicate mouth, and wide dark eyes formed a strikingly beautiful face. I couldn't gauge her age, as her skin was smooth and free of wrinkles, neither young nor old. A faint memory from long ago caused my heart to flutter wildly. Could this be my mother?

The older woman repeated my request for Laya Thongsavat.

"You're looking for my older sister, Laya?" the younger woman asked in French in a hushed, disbelieving voice.

I took a deep breath. "I believe she's my mother."

The woman gasped, and a hand flew up to her chest. "Sakuna?"

No one had ever addressed me by my Lao name. I nodded, too overcome to speak.

She took my hand. "I'm your aunt Chanida." Tears flooded her eyes. "You look so much like your mother, but I didn't dare to imagine it could be you."

She turned to Marguerite with a *nop*. "I'm Chanida Thongsavat. Welcome."

"Mademoiselle Marguerite Vanier. I'm a friend of your niece."

"Please come," my aunt said, ushering us to the far end of the veranda with its view over the Nam Kham River, where sunlight glanced off the water's surface. Marguerite sat in one of the rattan chairs while my aunt invited me to sit on a teak bench next to her.

She turned to the older woman. "Khantalay, please bring us coffee." An expression of wonder filled my aunt's face. "I've spent fourteen years searching for you and your brother, Vinya, without finding a trace." She took a deep breath, wiping a stray teardrop from her cheek. "I wrote to all the orphanages in Laos and the Resident Superior. They claimed there were no children with your names. I thought perhaps you'd been sent to France." She took a deep breath. "Wherever did they hide you?"

"I was raised in an orphanage in Vientiane until I turned eighteen in May. They called me Geneviève Dubois. The director at the home kept my past secret from me, but I managed to view my file and found my parents' names. I also discovered my twin brother, whom I didn't know existed. They took him to an orphanage in Pakse and called him Antoine Dubois."

My aunt covered her mouth as she sobbed softly. "I'm...I'm so thrilled to...to find you. I'd given up all hope." She shook her head slowly. "However did you find us?" she asked.

I gave a brief account of my time since leaving the orphanage, the kindness of Catherine and Marguerite, and my work with River Transport, which had brought me to Luang Prabang. I explained about the old granny who had known my mother and remembered her family name. "A friend inquired about the Thongsavat family and found where you lived."

"It's a miracle." My aunt wiped her cheeks with a handkerchief and took my hand again, as if needing to touch me to believe I was not an illusion.

"I contacted Antoine, and we've been writing. He went to school in Saigon for many years and is working on a coffee plantation near Pakse now."

I looked out at the river as a giant white crane swooped low and dove into the water, emerging with a small glistening fish squirming in its beak. Why had my aunt been the one looking for my brother and me? Why not our mother? I didn't want to hear the response to this question, which sat in my middle like a jagged strip of metal destined to shred me into tiny pieces.

"Can you tell me about my mother?" I whispered at last.

My aunt squeezed her eyes shut and let out a faltering breath. After some moments, she met my gaze. "You and your brother came from a deep and profound love, despite the circumstances and the disapproval of many. Your father returned to France to fight in the war when you and your brother were two years old."

"An acquaintance recently retrieved his government personnel file for me. I know he died in battle the next year."

Marguerite tipped her head. "Who was that?"

"Monsieur Fontaine," I answered.

"It was a difficult decision for your father to leave Laos, as you and Vinya were only two years old," my aunt said, "but he felt obligated to defend his country. When your mother learned of his death, it shattered her fragile heart." My aunt sighed. "She was alone and unmarried with two babies, shunned by the Lao and French communities alike. Your grandfather Thongsavat refused to allow her back home. No matter how much my brothers and I begged him to reconsider, he wouldn't relent. It tore our family apart, and I never forgave him.

"No one would hire your mother any longer. She was tainted, scorned as a lowly *phu sao*, a Frenchman's mistress. When the money your father left her ran out, she took in sewing and laundry, barely making enough to feed you and your brother. She often didn't eat to make sure you had enough."

My aunt's soft voice and her lightly accented, almost lyrical French soothed and lulled me into thinking this tale might still reach a happy conclusion.

"Your grandfather forbade anyone in the family from seeing her. But I visited her whenever I could without your grandfather finding out, bringing small stores of food and what money I could pilfer from home. Your mother grew so thin, I could hardly bear it." My aunt's eyes grew damp again.

"A close friend of your mother's felt sorry for her situation and offered to take you children into her home temporarily, until she could reassemble her life. After many tears and self-recriminations, your mother agreed to place Antoine with the friend, so he would be fed and cared for properly. But she couldn't bear to part with both of you." This explained why I had no recollection of my brother.

Khantalay arrived with a tray of coffee and a plate of biscuits and mangosteen. It appeared oddly festive and inviting, as if we were merely old friends stopping by for a chat. I grasped the cup of hot liquid placed before me, needing to warm my icy, trembling hands.

My aunt sipped her coffee, trying to compose herself. "As your mother grew weaker, she couldn't care for you any longer. It destroyed her to see you hungry. French officials from the Assistance Society hounded her for months, insisting she give you and your brother up to an orphanage, promising that you would be well fed and given a good education. Since she had your father's acknowledgement that you were his children, you would be French citizens. When she continued to resist, they threatened to get a court order. It wore her spirit down until, hopeless and desperate, she acquiesced, insisting it was only for a short time until she found a good job and regained her life. She talked of nothing but getting you back."

My aunt paused again, staring down at her hands. Her lips quivered and her voice caught in her throat. "But your mother contracted yellow fever and left this world. I was at her side the last few days and promised to find you children. You must understand how deeply she loved you." Tears coursed down her face. "I should have done more. I should have found a way to save her, but I was only sixteen."

A searing pain spiraled through me, like a stream of hot oil poured down the middle of my body. Fourteen years of hoping to find my mother ended here in this tragic tale. All along, both my parents had been dead. Antoine and I were truly orphans. A piercing wail escaped my lips, and I buried my head in my hands.

My aunt pulled me into her arms as I surrendered to my grief, my body convulsing in sobs. I don't know how much time passed before my crying finally eased. I pulled back to wipe my face with the handkerchief Marguerite had placed in my lap, and my ragged breathing slowly evened out. Marguerite stood at the railing, staring out over the river, wiping her cheeks with the back of her hand.

"I'm sorry to cause you such sadness," my aunt said at last, "but you've found your family now. Your grandfather passed from this world shortly after your mother. I think the trauma quickened his death." She shook her head. "I am haunted by how differently things might have been if he'd died first, and my brothers and I could have saved your mother and kept you children with us. But please know, our family will welcome you and Vinya as part of our own."

Overwhelmed, I struggled to speak. "All these years…I dreamed of finding my mother. I am…grateful to finally know what happened." I pushed my hair behind my ear, wiped my tears. "Antoine has promised to visit me when I return to Vientiane. He will be grateful to know the truth."

My aunt patted my back. "Shall I call you Geneviève and Antoine for now? It might be less confusing than using your Lao names."

"Perhaps for now. My friends call me Vivi."

A little girl appeared out of nowhere. My aunt pulled her close. "This is my youngest child, my only daughter, Phitsamay." Aunt Chanida turned to her child. "Say hello to your cousin Vivi."

The little girl gave a *nop*. "*Sabaidee.*"

My aunt smiled. "You must stay for lunch and meet the rest of the family. We have so much to talk about. Unfortunately, my husband is visiting our forests and won't be back until later in the week, but your uncles are here."

Marguerite cleared her throat. "I must get back to town as a friend is waiting for me. Vivi, you stay, and I'll have the carriage return for you later this afternoon."

After Marguerite left, Aunt Chanida sent Khantalay to inform the other households of my arrival and invite them to lunch. She showed me around her home, explaining her parents had built it when they married. "My husband and I stayed here after our marriage as my parents were both gone. The other two houses were constructed when your uncles wed and started their families."

The lovely old structure was made of teak and rosewood, the wood slightly worn in places but polished to a beautiful sheen. The simple furnishing in the front room included several low tables with mats and cushions and two glass-fronted cabinets displaying carved Buddhas, large silver bowls, and decorative silk fabrics. My aunt led me to a teak table at the back of the room, which held a bronze seated Buddha, candles, and incense sticks in bronze dishes. Fresh flowers and food had been arranged next to two small paintings and two photographs.

"This is the family altar where we pray to our ancestors to honor them and wish for happiness and peace for their souls." She picked up a photograph of a young couple. "This is your parents in 1912, shortly after your mother discovered she was with child. A friend of your father's was a photographer and took it for them. I want you and Antoine to have it."

I stared with amazement at the faded, black-and-white photo. "I have a vague memory of Mother, but nothing of Father."

My father was standing very straight, a head taller than my mother, wearing a white suit. He was slight of build, his face serious. It was hard to identify any distinctive features other than a large mustache and a strong chin. One arm was wrapped around Mother's waist in a protective manner. She leaned against him, staring directly into the camera with only the slightest hint of a smile, eyes opened wide, as if the photographer had told her an astonishing story. She seemed so tiny, dressed in her *sinh* and *pha biang*, her hair pulled into a plentiful knot atop her head. She looked like Aunt Chanida, delicate and pretty, and I thought perhaps I resembled her a tiny bit.

"This photograph of your grandfather was taken at court when he was honored by the king." I saw an elderly man wearing formal court attire, unsmiling and stiff. "And these paintings are of my parents and grandparents on their wedding days." My mother's ancestors had posed in their wedding attire with dour expressions, the wives sitting and the husbands standing beside them. It was hard to imagine I was related to these people from a distant time and place.

Aunt Chanida showed me the large bedroom where her four children slept, then a slightly smaller room, which she shared with her husband. She opened a wooden chest in the far corner and retrieved a thick bundle wrapped in silk and tied with a ribbon. "I saved these letters for you and your brother with the hope of one day finding you. Most are from your father after he left to fight in the war in France, but one is from your mother to you children. She wanted you to know about her life and what happened. I think she knew she wouldn't live to see you again."

Tears threatened once more as I held the packet next to my heart. These thin sheets of paper covered in ink, some having traveled halfway around the world, held answers to my questions, the story of my parents' love for each other and their children. I stared at my aunt, unable to find my voice to thank her for such treasures.

"You'll want to read them when you get home," she said. "We can put them in the front room with the photograph until you leave." Reluctantly I let her take them.

"I hope you can visit often while you're in town." She placed the items on a low table. "Come back outside and tell me about your brother."

We settled on the veranda, and I recounted Antoine's news from the few letters I'd received.

"You must both come to Luang Prabang as soon as possible," she said. "You'll always be welcome."

Aunt Chanida then began to recount our family's history. "Your uncle Khamphet, your grandfather, and several generations of men before them were appointed to the royal kingdom's tax administration, managing revenues from the *muangs* in surrounding districts.

The position became largely ceremonial after the French assumed responsibility over taxes, but don't bring that up with Khamphet, as he gets very indignant about the way the French have slowly usurped the king's powers. He complains constantly, at least in private." She pulled her scarf up higher over her shoulder. "But we are fortunate to have been granted farm lands and forests, which support our family."

As she spoke, I studied her features, the gentle smile that caused her eyes to nearly close, the way her graceful hands fluttered through the air emphasizing certain words. Her warmth and honesty eased my grief and disappointment. She was the link to my mother that would sustain me now.

My uncles' families arrived mid-day. Aunt Chanida introduced Uncle Khamphet and Aunt Dara, then Uncle Chanta and Aunt Noi. We greeted each other with repeated *nops*. My cousins, a total of thirteen children, ranged from toddlers to a fourteen-year-old girl, who shyly glanced at me.

Uncle Chanta broke into a broad smile. "It is like having your mother among us again. We are happy to know you, Vivi."

When it was time to eat lunch, we sat on mats around a string of low tables on the veranda, with me placed in the middle of the adults. The servants brought dozens of hot and cold dishes, scurrying back and forth to the kitchen off the back side of the house to keep the platters full.

Aunt Chanida led the conversation in French, in which they were all fluent. Uncle Chanta and both aunts had strong Lao accents, and I had to strain to understand them. They asked about my upbringing at the orphanage in Vientiane. I offered a simple account, trying to focus on the positive rather than complaining about the many injustices I had suffered.

"What are you doing in Vientiane?" Uncle Khamphet asked. I

explained about my living situation with Catherine and my work at River Transport. He nodded. "I know Prince Savang. We sometimes ship goods with his company."

This startled me, and a twinge of unease settled in my middle. Did he also know Bounmy, and if so, how would he feel about my relationship with him? There were few secrets in this land. Like the vines entangling and connecting trees and bushes in the vast jungles, the links among royal family members and aristocrats ran deep in the kingdom of Luang Prabang and throughout Laos.

The afternoon slipped by with easy banter and lots of laughter. It was a family comfortable with one another. Toddlers drifted over to sit in their mothers' laps, while older children examined me, the mysterious stranger in their midst, not quite Lao, not quite French.

Uncle Chanta talked of the forest and farm lands that the family managed in the area. My aunts Dara and Noi explained how they had formed a cooperative for women weavers in surrounding villages to help market their silk fabrics. The beautiful scarves and wall hangings had become popular with the French and other Europeans.

Uncle Khamphet remained mostly quiet, appearing a bit more circumspect about my presence than the others. Did he harbor reservations about accepting someone of mixed blood into the family, given his position in the royal government? Maybe attitudes had not changed as much as Aunt Chanida had assured me.

As the sun fell lower in the sky, a pottery jug was placed on the table and bowls of sticky rice and boiled eggs were passed around. A silver bowl filled with banana leaves, chrysanthemums, and what looked like a tree of white strings was placed on the center table.

"Before you go, we will perform a *baci* to mark this remarkable occasion and welcome you into the family," Uncle Chanta said. "We are grateful to have you returned to us."

"Have you seen this before?" Aunt Chanida asked. I shook my head. "Khamphet, as head of the family, will offer a blessing to keep your *khuan*, your soul or spirit, whole and safe with your body. We do this blessing ceremony on holidays and special occasions, or when family members are sick."

Uncle Chanta poured small glasses of clear liquid from the jug and gave one to each adult. We held the drinks in our right hands and placed our left hands on the table's edge.

Uncle Khamphet began chanting in a low sing-song voice that reminded me of the incantations of the monks at Buddhist temples. When he finished, we held up our glasses in a toast and swallowed our drinks. I choked and coughed as the fiery alcohol burned all the way down my throat and into my stomach. Everyone laughed.

"I see you have not had our *Lao Lao* before," Aunt Chanida said, patting my back. "We should have warned you. It's fermented sticky rice."

One by one, family members tied a white string around my wrist, murmuring a welcome and wishing me happiness and health.

I made a *nop* over and over, in awe that my newly discovered family considered my visit a special occasion, a reason to celebrate. My heart filled with joy that I belonged among them, as my mother had before me. I felt her spirit watching over us.

Chapter 41

Riding back to town, I studied the photograph of my parents—my father's brows, the curve of my mother's lips, the shapes of their noses, chins, and eyes—trying to find myself in their faces. Did I look like Mother, or were there traces of Father, as well? I couldn't wait to sit quietly and read the letters, to better understand these strangers who had brought me into the world.

The driver dropped me in front of the French guesthouse. Marguerite had invited me to the club for dinner, but the tumultuous emotions of the day had drained me. I left a note at the desk, saying I would join them another night. Strolling aimlessly down the leafy sidewalks of the main street, I reached the gate to Wat Xieng Thong. Bounmy had put a star next to the temple's name and written a long description about its architecture and art. When I entered the courtyard, I understood why it was his favorite *wat*. The main building, the *sim*, had nine tiered roofs, which swept low, ending in graceful curves that nearly touched the ground. Intricate designs carved into the gilded wood danced across the outside walls and portals.

I found a bench next to a small golden pagoda. The perfect retreat. Sheltered by the shade of an ancient bodhi fig tree, I closed my eyes, slowly breathing in and out, listening to birdsong until I felt ready. Untying the ribbon around the packet, I counted ten letters penned by my father, arranged by the date received. The first one was a slightly yellowed, single sheaf of rice paper covered on both sides in faded blue ink. I recognized the uneven scrawl from the tag attached to my doll Giselle. The letter appeared to have been folded and unfolded countless times, causing a small tear on one side. Two round stains near the bottom blurred the ink. Perhaps my mother's tears?

Monday, April 19, 1915

My precious Laya,

I hope this finds you and the little ones well and not lacking in any material way. Tomorrow I shall wire more money. Words can hardly express how my heart aches for you, to feel your warmth and comfort next to me and the children's sweet kisses on my cheeks. Please forgive me for answering my country's call to duty. Leaving you was the hardest decision I've ever made.

I write from my house in Aix-en-Provence, having arrived in Marseille early yesterday morning. Passage on the Paul Lescat *was uneventful despite the captain's concern over the possibility of encountering German U-boats in the Mediterranean. I hope you received the two letters I posted in Port Said and Colombo. Mail service from these ports of call is notoriously unreliable.*

I stopped to look through the letters again but found nothing from these towns.

The house is in good repair, thanks to the efforts of my sister Helene and her husband Bertrand. But the empty rooms echo with loss and loneliness and unbearably sad memories. Sometimes I think I hear little Mathis racing down the hallway, clutching his teddy bear and calling out for his papa. Why did God take him from us so soon?

I dined with Helene and her family at their home last night. She told me of her visit to Paulette in Marseille last month. I'm saddened to hear my former wife is still consumed by grief for Mathis and a bitter hatred of me. She has finally agreed to file a divorce petition, blaming my infidelity for the failure of our marriage, even if this has nothing to do with the truth. No judge will care that Paulette deserted me emotionally and physically almost from the beginning of our marriage. I will gladly assume culpability to be free. By the time the war is over, and I return to you, we will be able to marry.

I reread the last paragraph several times, trying to understand my father's unhappy marriage and what had brought it to an end. He appeared to feel no remorse for his affair with my mother, only relief to be free of his earlier commitment, and I could not help but feel sympathy for this woman Paulette, who must have suffered as well. How much I had to learn of the complicated machinations of love.

Spring is unfolding with cherry and almond trees in full bloom and fields full of wildflowers. This season of renewal makes me think of our days together, when your love restored my soul. Despite the beauty, the dark clouds of war cast a long shadow across the countryside. Provence is removed from the major fighting in the north, but many young men have left to join the army's ranks, and as I walked the streets in town today, I crossed several people wearing black arm bands of mourning. Neighbors and shopkeepers talk of nothing but the terrible battles and loss of life that consume newspaper headlines each day. Surely it cannot last much longer.

I registered at Military Command today and expect them to send orders by the end of next week. I will write as soon as I receive an assignment so you can write back and tell me how you and the twins are doing. I promise to return to you safe and healthy as soon as possible.

With all my love and kisses for you, Sakuna, and Vinya,
Your devoted Henri

My eyes welled up. The intimacy of my father's words gave me the impression of knowing him in some small way, as if a curtain had been pulled aside to reveal a rough sketch of the man I had only imagined. His testament of devotion to my mother and his children consoled me. Here was the truth I had been seeking.

I staggered back to my lodgings, feeling close to fainting, as fatigue and heat overtook me. One of the young servants was at home and offered me a bowl of vegetables and noodles, which I gratefully accepted. A little after six, I collapsed on my quilt and slept for the next twelve hours.

Over the next few days I would wait impatiently for work to end so I might return to my quiet sanctuary at Wat Xieng Thong. I stayed until the light faded, reading Father's letters, devouring each word and turn of phrase like a person starved of sustenance, examining the details of his thoughts and feelings, searching to comprehend the man I could not remember.

Father's correspondence had been written over eleven months, the first notes beginning with great optimism—the war would soon be over, France would prevail. He found it extraordinary when the military made him a first lieutenant in the Second Army in charge of a platoon. His rank was based on his education and government position in Laos, since he had no military experience other than a two-month stint in a reserve unit in Provence at the age of nineteen. He barely knew how to fire a rifle. He was sent to training camp for a month, then on to a city (the name was blacked out by censors) at the heart of the fighting, which endured constant attacks from nearby German encampments.

His tone grew more somber as the reality of war crushed his spirit, yet he continued to promise to return safely to Laos. Only once did he let down his guard to describe the fighting on the front lines, parts of which had been blacked out by censors. It was as if he could no longer contain his overwhelming despair.

*Here on the front line, **XXX** miles from Paris, we live with the constant noise and smoke of shells exploding around us and the relentless rat-a-tat-tat of German machine guns spraying bullets at **XXX** per minute. Our unit has been reduced from **XXX** to **XXX** men. My soldiers and I hunker down in the muddy trenches, reeking of sweat and fear, until we become too numb to care. Many suffer from dysentery and fevers. I find the quiet moments the most unnerving, when I have time to reflect on the situation. My men look to me for reassurance, but I have none to give* *them. This morning a young man was laughing and telling me about his fiancée when, without a sound, he slumped over dead, a bullet in his head, his surprised eyes still open. I grieve for every loss.*

I have no right to burden you with these grim scenes. But I am beyond exhaustion and cannot think clearly. Do not fear for me. Know your love is always close, protecting me.

The scenes he painted horrified me. I could not bear to know his life had ended in this hell. The last few envelopes contained short cryptic sentences, hurriedly scratched with parsed words meant to convince Mother he would be one of the lucky few to survive when so many others did not. I longed for more, to hear his life story, rather than these brief accounts of war. A million what-ifs sprang to mind, as I pictured a different outcome, a father who had survived the war and returned to his family.

His last communication arrived in late March 1916, written over a month before. Father had already been dead for several weeks by the time Mother received it. These last words tore me apart.

Sunday, February 20, 1916
Laya, my heart and soul,
How blessed I have been to share our deep and perfect love, the joy of our beautiful children. Such sublime happiness is all one can ask for in this mortal world. Tomorrow we begin a major offensive, one I hope will turn this dreadful war in our favor. If I should not make it through, remember my devotion to my petite family in Luang Prabang. We shall meet again in a better place.
All my love forever,
Henri

Chapter 42

On Wednesday evening I finally read my mother's letter, anxious to hear her story, but at the same time frightened of what it might reveal. It had been written almost two years after Father's death, as her life slowly slipped away. My heartbeat slowed and my breathing grew shallow as I unfolded the faded sheets of rough-textured paper made from mulberry bark, like the paper I'd seen at a stand in the covered market in Vientiane. This was all I had left of my mother, the sum of her life contained in six pages covered front and back with her even, compact script. It seemed unlikely it could ever begin to answer the hundreds of questions that filled my thoughts, the longing to understand the choices she had made.

Wednesday, September 22, 1917
Mes chéries Sakuna and Vinya,
I write this letter for you to read when you are older and seek answers about the parents who lovingly brought you into this world...just in case. I am fighting to regain my health, but I fear my soul may soon disappear into the heavens. As a Buddhist, I believe my destiny was determined long before I was born, shaped by the karma of former lives and actions in this life on my journey toward enlightenment and nirvana. I strive to transcend suffering and attain a higher place in the cycle of life, but I still struggle with my grief over losing your father, my beloved Henri. My only reason for living now is to bring you children back from the orphanage and into my arms. I pray to Buddha every day to guide me, however everything in life is transitory.
Your father and I shared a deep love for each other beyond the bounds

of this earthly existence. In the small, insular world of Luang Prabang, the French and Lao communities alike judged us harshly, condemning our devotion as something shameful and wrong. We did not, could not, obey the narrow confines of other people's misplaced morality.

Your grandfather, my father, was among those who denounced our love, banishing me from my family. He was unable to appreciate the joy and happiness your father's love brought me and refused to recognize his own grandchildren born of this union. It was a cruel blow from a father I had been devoted to all my life. But please know I have no regrets.

After your father's death, my efforts to keep you nourished and safe failed. Your Aunt Chanida was the only person in my family to help but, being only a young girl living under the control of our father, she was incapable of resolving my problems. It saddens me that no one else was willing to assist me. With a broken heart and terrible guilt, I entrusted you to the care of the French Assistance Society. This sacrifice reflects my fierce love for you. I will reclaim you as soon as I am able.

I reread these paragraphs several times, trying to imagine her despair and resignation as her world fell apart. She had lost everyone she loved, save Aunt Chanida. Tears prickled at my eyes. My suffering growing up in the orphanage and losing my dear friend Bridgette felt insignificant in comparison.

I believe your father and I were destined to meet. We both lost our mothers at an early age and grew up seeking a love that could fill the empty spaces in our hearts. In time, we found that love and comfort in each other.

She went on to describe her gentle mother, the center and soul of her family, who had taught her children Buddhist values of respect for elders and compassion for all living things. But the unthinkable had happened when my grandmother had died giving birth to Uncle Chanta when Mother was only ten. My grandfather had retreated into work to escape his grief, leaving Mother to care for her three younger siblings.

Your grandfather holds an important position in the royal court. He did not embrace the arrival of the French as readily as some, resenting the way these foreigners declared our kingdom a French protectorate, as if the Lao people were helpless orphans in need of guardians to oversee their lives. Despite his dislike of the French, your grandfather understood the need to adapt and hired a young tutor from Hanoi, Tran, to teach him the French language. He struggled to master this foreign tongue and endured humiliation by French officials, who smirked at his limited vocabulary and Lao accent. Some even dared to correct him in front of others. Not wanting his children to be treated this way, he insisted we become fluent in French. Tran stayed on to tutor us in the language as well as mathematics, history, and science. I was fortunate to have been given a proper education when few Lao girls received one.

When I was seventeen, a widowed aunt, who had no children of her own, came to live with our family, and I was freed from the responsibility of running the household. On Tran's recommendation, a French family offered me a position tutoring their three children. When they returned to France six months later, another family employed me, then another. This work led me to your father.

I longed to know about the French families whose children she had taught. What had she felt in these situations? But there was nothing more beyond these few spare lines. A breeze brushed my face and ruffled the pages in my hands. Perhaps it was Mother's spirit come to comfort me, saying there was nothing more of importance that I needed to know.

The letter continued with a brief description of my father's upbringing. His mother had died when he was only six years old, and he and his little sister, Helene, had been left to the care of nannies, rarely seeing their father or receiving any affection. After Father finished university, my grandfather pressured him to marry seven-teen-year-old Paulette, the only child of a wealthy business associate. Father complied, but he soon found himself disillusioned with his young wife and trapped in an unhappy, loveless marriage. But they had Mathis, whom he adored, and so he stayed with Paulette.

I glanced over at the stoic expression of the golden Buddha sheltered in the pagoda next to me as I tried to accept these facts, but I desired more details to understand his unhappiness in the marriage and the reasons he turned to my mother.

A friend from university visited your father after returning from Saigon and urged him to consider a new beginning in a faraway place. Your father applied for a position with the French Indochine colonial government, hoping this might improve his marriage.

On July 14, 1911, I attended a Bastille Day party. The mother of the French children I was tutoring at the time introduced me to Monsieur Henri Dubois, assistant to the French Commissioner of Luang Prabang. He had come from France three months before. Henri mentioned his wife and son, who would arrive in a few months, and wanted to know if I would be available to tutor his son.

Our meeting seemed inconsequential at the time. It is funny, remembering how unremarkable he appeared to me. With his light-brown eyes and big mustache, he looked like so many of the Frenchmen I'd met. When we crossed paths in town several weeks later, he had to remind me of his name and our previous encounter.

I forgot about your father until he contacted me in September, asking if I could meet his wife and six-year-old son Mathis. Paulette was a beautiful woman with pale, clear skin and fine features. But she was an unhappy soul. She treated me like a servant, shrugging off my credentials as unworthy, saying I would have to do. No Lao person of good upbringing would ever be so rude. I wanted to decline her offer, but Mathis, your dear half-brother, raced into the room with his father chasing after him, the two of them out of breath and giggling. On seeing his mother, the boy stopped cold, and his sweet face quivered as his eyes darted toward his father, seeking protection. I could not turn away from this child with his big, sad eyes.

Paulette relinquished the care of her son to me, expecting me to serve as nanny and tutor, watching over him all day and most evenings. I didn't mind. Mathis was a gentle, sweet child, whom I quickly came to love. We made forays through town, pretending to be explorers, and studied insects in the yard outside the house and along the banks of the Nam Khan River. I taught him to read and how to add and subtract. In the evenings we read books aloud as he snuggled in my arms. Your father started joining us and, in these intimate moments, our friendship first flourished. It pained me that Paulette remained locked away in her dark room, seemingly indifferent to her family, incapable of displaying warmth or true affection for her husband or son.

Your father realized there was no hope for his marriage, but he endured Paulette's constant complaints and disgraceful behavior in order to keep his beloved son with him.

You might think I am overly critical of Paulette, biased by my love for your father. It was a difficult situation, and perhaps there were reasons I didn't understand causing her to behave in this manner.

I put the letter down to reflect on my mother's account of the woman who had become her rival. Was she being unfair, or had Paulette truly been an unforgivably difficult and selfish person? I strolled around the temple grounds to loosen the stiffness in my legs and backside from sitting on the hard bench. As twilight descended, the peaceful beauty of the *wat* tempered my sadness for what my father and mother had borne. Had my parents ever come here, like me, seeking solace?

Mathis was diagnosed with tuberculosis in early February. He had been frail and unwell ever since I'd met him. Given how far the disease had progressed, the doctor thought he must have contracted it long before leaving France, but he warned that the humid climate in Luang Prabang might result in a more rapid decline in the boy's health. Paulette blamed Henri, and three weeks later, she and Mathis left for France. My heart broke when Mathis said goodbye, clinging to me and sobbing. He told me he loved me and promised to return when he was healthy. I knew we would never meet again.

It was strange to think of the half-brother I would never meet, except through this account. How terribly sad that his life had been so fleeting. What might our relationship have been? Mathis had been lucky to enjoy the love and affection of my mother and father, even though brief—a love Antoine and I could not remember.

When Paulette and Mathis returned to France, your father and I finally surrendered to our love for each other. My dear children, it is true your father was still married when we formed a bond, something I never could have imagined, but do not think too badly of us. We were meant to meet and love as we did, and you are the welcome fruits of that union.

A wire in April brought the devastating news that Mathis had passed away. Your father was drowning in sorrow and guilt that he had not returned to France with the boy, so I encouraged him to go back to find peace with himself. He returned to Provence to make sense of his life, but found he no longer belonged in that world. In August, he returned to Laos, to me and his true home, and we learned soon after that we would have a family of our own.

The few short years we spent together were the happiest of my life, and, I believe, your father's as well. He doted on his "darling twins," spending all his free time playing with you, taking turns carrying you on his shoulders, singing silly songs. He constantly brought you small gifts and treats. On Sundays, we often went to a stream outside of town and sat in the shallows, splashing and laughing until your little eyes grew heavy. At night, with one of you on each of our laps, we read stories and rocked you to sleep. These magical moments sustain me.

When I lost your papa, everything became small and insignificant. I'd been cut off from family and friends and all vestiges of respectability. But how could I regret one moment of our happiness, dear treasures?

Your roots come from two distant parts of the world, two cultures intertwined in a strong and loving bond. Be proud of your mixed heritage, even if others do not always appreciate your unique beauty. If we are not able to meet again in this life, I pray you find the happiness and love your father and I knew.

With all my love and blessings,
Your Maman

I could not stop crying. The doomed love story of my parents had left my brother and me orphaned and abandoned to the misguided mercy of our French wardens. Should I feel angry with my parents for bringing us into the world, one that held so much contempt for the *métis* born out of wedlock? But they never imagined their lives would end so soon, leaving us without their love and protection. The gift of their letters would allow me to finally come to terms with my past. I hoped Antoine would find the same sense of relief and peace from this knowledge.

My parents' love had endured despite the obstacles. I could only hope the love Bounmy and I shared would prove as resilient and true.

Chapter 43

Marguerite sent me notes on Monday and Wednesday, asking me to join her for dinner, which I declined, saying I needed solitude to reflect on my parents' letters. On Thursday, I found her waiting for me outside River Transport at the end of the day. She kissed my cheeks and placed her arm through mine, drawing me down the road.

"I'm sorry to come unannounced, but I was worried about you. You need a friend to talk with." She pointed to herself. "And that would be me."

I laughed. "I'm glad to see you. It's been an emotional week."

She stopped. "More importantly, I have something for you. It arrived at the guesthouse yesterday." She pulled a letter out of her handbag, and my heart did a somersault at the sight of the white linen envelope with *Mademoiselle Geneviève Dubois* written across the front. "I wonder why Bounmy sent it to me," she said.

"Maybe he didn't trust Kham to deliver it." I didn't add that Bounmy might not want Kham or the people at work to see his correspondence.

"I know you're dying to rip it open right now, but can you wait? There's a nice place run by a couple from Hanoi where we can eat a quick dinner."

"Of course." I placed the envelope in my purse.

She led me to the road along the Nam Khan River and a small café serving a selection of Annamese and French dishes. We sat outside under an arbor overgrown by Rangoon creeper, its pink and red blooms filling the air with an intoxicating sweetness. Marguerite ordered beers and a plate of spring rolls. I relaxed, grateful for her company, for someone who cared about me. She was right; I needed to talk.

"What have you and Charles been doing?" I asked.

"Enjoying each other's company." She gave me a wicked smile. "Especially at night."

I giggled. "What do you do while he's at work?"

"The French wives invite me to luncheons and card parties. It's all very dull. They do nothing but gossip and complain about their servants and the lack of decent teachers for their children. Their most pressing problem in life is finding the ingredients for a good French meal." She lit a cigarette and took a deep drag. "Really, can you picture me as a dutiful spouse, staying home with a pack of little imps?"

"Not really."

"Tell me about the rest of your visit last Sunday," Marguerite said.

"After you left, Aunt Chanida gave me a photo of my parents and a packet of letters they wrote." I tucked a stray wisp of hair behind my ear. "It's the first picture I've ever seen of them. I have no recollection of my father and only vague memories of my mother."

Her face softened. "How special. And was the lunch with the rest of the family nice?'

"I met my two uncles and their families. Everyone was friendly and curious about me. Although my uncle Khamphet seemed a little less welcoming, or at least unsure about me."

She touched the cotton strings tied around my wrist. "They did a *baci* for you."

"Yes. They made me feel like I was truly part of their family."

Marguerite flicked her ashes into a battered tin ashtray. "And you've read all the letters?"

I nodded. "Most are from my father, sent from France after he left to fight in the war. It's hard to read them." I looked down at my plate as my chin trembled. "He knew he'd never survive."

She reached over and patted my hand. "I understand. My father died at Verdun in 1916. I was fifteen. My mother, brother, and I had to move in with my grandmother in Nantes."

I started. "My father died at Verdun, as well. I'm so sorry. I had no idea." A twinge of guilt came over me that I had never thought to ask where she was from or about her childhood.

"Do you know much about the war?" she asked.

I shook my head. "All they taught us in school was that it was long and difficult, but that France and its allies were victorious. My father didn't write many details."

"The censors would have blacked out most things, anyway." She took a long swallow of beer. "I read accounts in the papers every day at the time. It was a living hell. Soldiers fought from miles of muddy trenches that stretched across the countryside, filled with rats and disease. The damned Germans, with their machine guns trained on our soldiers, could fire six hundred rounds a minute. Imagine how terrified those young soldiers had to be, knowing they were sitting ducks about to be shot. Poor bastards. Hundreds of thousands of young men were sent to their slaughter, their sheer numbers the only thing holding the Germans back. Battles always ended in a stalemate, with one side or the other gaining maybe half a mile of territory at the cost of thousands of lives." Her voice was filled with bitterness. "By the end of the war, twenty million soldiers and civilians had been killed. That was our so-called victory."

We sat in silence. I toyed with the spring rolls on my plate, unable to eat, thinking of the terror my father had lived through before finally being struck down.

"And the letters from your mother?" Marguerite asked gently.

"Only one. She wrote it shortly before she died, after everyone had abandoned her except Aunt Chanida and she'd given my brother and me to the orphanage. She told of her childhood and how she met and fell in love with my father. She recounted a few memories of when my brother and I were little, before my father left for France. It's terribly sad." I slowly turned my beer glass round and round, my eyes swimming once more. "I'm grateful to know my parents' story and how much they loved each other. It helps me accept the loss."

Marguerite dabbed at her cheeks with a handkerchief. "Look at me. You've turned me into a sentimental fool." She pointed a finger at me. "Don't you dare tell a soul. It will ruin my reputation."

I smiled. "Would you like to walk up to Mount Phou Si this evening? Bounmy says the view is beautiful. It might cheer me up."

"I've been meaning to go. We'll be a sweaty mess by the time we get there in this heat, but I don't care."

We walked the short distance to the sacred hill located in the heart of Luang Prabang and climbed the windy, steep pathway to the top. We had to stop to catch our breath twice. At the crest of the hill, the stupa and golden spires of That Chomsi angled for the heavens. Spectacular vistas stretched before us of the town, rivers, and surrounding mountains. I wondered if my parents had ever climbed to this serene spot, content in their happiness together. How perfect it would be to have Bounmy at my side.

Marguerite patted her forehead with a handkerchief. "I'm dripping, but it's worth the view." She turned to me, grinning. "I can't stand it anymore. I have monumental news to tell you."

"Oh good! I need to hear something happy."

"Charles is being transferred back to Vientiane soon." She hesitated. "And, amazingly enough, he's asked me to marry him."

I gasped and threw my arms around her, squeezing her tight. "I'm so thrilled. And you said yes, right?"

She laughed. "Only after he promised I can keep working. And no children. I suppose it's selfish, but I'm not cut out to be a mother."

"He doesn't mind?"

"He's relieved. He has four children in France from his first wife that he's still supporting."

"Have you told Catherine?"

"I want to tell her in person when I return."

"How I wish I could go back to Vientiane right now. I miss Bounmy so much." My shoulders drooped. "I can't stand being in this office with these awful men. I'm sure they're hiding something illegal in the account books."

"How much longer are you supposed to stay here?"

"I'm not sure, but probably a month." I sighed. "Kham doesn't bother telling me about his plans."

"Now I know Charles is going back to Vientiane soon, I've decided to leave for home a week early. I want to start planning the wedding." She glanced over, her face lighting up. "Come with me! You can find a better job. I've heard some unsavory stories about Kham's business dealings recently. He's a snake, and I don't trust him."

The thought of quitting my boring, unhappy job and returning to Vientiane lifted my spirits. I would spend as much time as possible with my family in the remaining weeks and then leave this job behind and return to Vientiane. Hopefully Bounmy missed me as desperately as I missed him.

Chapter 44

After work on Friday, I wandered through town as the evening eased its way toward night. I tried to shake off another suffocating day in the dusty, dimly lit office, surrounded by my coworkers' hostility and silence. I felt sure that large amounts of goods and revenues were being diverted, based on missing and questionable records, ledger numbers that didn't add up. Time and again, the accountant and warehouse manager refused to provide the information I requested. "No, no," they repeated. "The boss says it's not necessary. Don't worry. Not a problem."

Late in the afternoon, I had followed Kham out of the building. "I need to speak to you in private," I said. "I'm concerned about the accounts. There are too many irregularities."

A strange expression crossed his face, and a small smile played at the edges of his overgenerous mouth. "Later," he'd said. "I'm meeting a client right now."

Hopefully he would be receptive to what I had to tell him, and not feel I was crossing a line by reporting on his brother-in-law and the other employees.

I strolled down the main street as a welcome breeze stirred the leaves and ruffled my skirt. All I could think about was Marguerite's suggestion that I quit this miserable job and go home with her. Back to Bounmy.

Instinctively, my path took me to the tranquil bench at Wat Xieng Thong. I pulled out Bounmy's letter and unfolded the single page. I'd read it over and over the night before and half a dozen times at work.

September 28, 1931
Chère Geneviève,

I hope your time in Luang Prabang will prove fruitful. I look for a letter from you every day, anxious to hear how your visit with your family passes. May this connection bring you peace.

Are you enjoying the temples? I picture you visiting with my guide in hand, as if we are sharing the time together in a small way. If only I could show you in person. One day.

I have little to report on this end, except how much I miss you. You have only been gone five days, but it feels like an eternity. I spend hours at work distracted by thoughts of your beautiful face and sweet voice. Prince Phetsarath must think a wandering spirit has kidnapped his assistant's soul.

Evenings I stroll along the river and stop in places where we have spent time, dreaming of you beside me. I ache to hold you in my arms, to cover you with kisses. My body burns for yours.

Please trust in me and hurry back. My heart beats only for you, and each day apart is agony.

I love you a thousand times,
Bounmy

His words sent joy catapulting through my body, his love wrapping around me to protect me from all the losses and pain of my past.

As dusk neared, I left the temple to walk home along the Mekong River, imagining Bounmy strolling by the riverbank in Vientiane. The gentle view and sounds of boats bobbing in the water, waves lapping against the muddy banks, were a balm for the longing in my heart. Forested hills across the wide expanse of water slowly turned from dark green to shades of purple and indigo as the sun disappeared behind the trees. Bounmy's words of love floated through my head. Farther down shore, several groups of men sat on stools around small tables drinking and eating, their voices and laughter echoing through the darkness.

My empty stomach rumbled, anticipating the meal that awaited me. Aunt Chanida had sent a note on Wednesday, inviting me to visit the family again on Sunday, saying a cart would come to fetch me at ten in the morning. I looked forward to seeing her and discussing my parents' letters, hoping she could answer my questions and add more to my parents' story.

I passed a boisterous group, and a familiar voice called out my name. Squinting into the dim light, I recognized Kham's squat shape as he navigated his way toward me, stumbling over a tree root, then laughing as if it were a trick he'd performed to entertain me.

"What are you doing out?" he asked. He smelled of liquor and cigarettes.

"I visited Wat Xieng Thong. I'm on my way to the house." I stepped back, uncomfortable with his overly familiar tone.

He grabbed my arm. "You wanted to talk to me. Let's go to the office."

"Now?" I asked, my voice filled with alarm. The last thing I wanted was to be with this unpleasant man after he'd been drinking. "It can wait until tomorrow."

"It won't take long. Show me these problem accounts." He began weaving his way down the road, dragging me by the arm.

An uneasy feeling gripped me, like heavy stones settling on my chest. I tried to free my arm, but Kham only tightened his grasp. We passed a string of small stores lit with oil lamps. Shopkeepers and their families could be seen eating dinner in the back rooms. I thought of calling out for help but foolishly kept quiet.

Kham turned to me with a strange smile. "Do you like Luang Prabang?" The alcohol had made his Lao accent even more pronounced, and I strained to understand his French.

"It's beautiful. Bounmy wrote me a guide for the temples."

"Ah, my cousin, the great patron of the temples." His voice turned angry and bitter. "While he went off to Paris for his fine education, I had to care for my dying father and run our family business. He was always the lucky one."

"I met my mother's family last Sunday," I said, wanting to change the subject and let him know of my family's presence. "They live here in Luang Prabang. I believe you are acquainted with my uncle, Khamphet Thongsavat."

Kham appeared startled by the news. "Of course. They must have been surprised to discover their lost relative with a touch of French blood. But all families have their secrets."

I stiffened at the insult and tried again unsuccessfully to free my arm from him.

We reached the deserted office, and Kham unlocked the door and lit a lamp, which cast an eerie shadow across the crowded space. I retrieved the file containing the questionable invoices and inventory sheets, which I'd been collecting, hoping to get our meeting over with quickly. Kham motioned for me to follow him to his desk, where he collapsed heavily into his chair.

"What's so important?" His eyelids drooped as if he might nod off at any moment.

I reached across the desk and placed the open file before him, leafing through several pages, which I'd underlined with question marks. His glassy eyes focused on the front of my blouse, and my hand flew up involuntarily, pulling the sides tighter together. "These figures don't add up," I said. "There are large amounts of goods and money disappearing. I wanted to alert you."

His head lolled back, then he burst out laughing. "You must think you're very smart," he said, trying to catch his breath. "I already know this. My brother-in-law likes to augment his income."

"You're not concerned?" I stepped back, wondering if the liquor had muddled his brain.

He shrugged. "They're family."

His indifference surprised me. Yet why should I care? It was his money, his family. "I'm sorry. I shouldn't have bothered you."

He struggled to stand up, an ugly leering smile spreading across his thick lips. "You just wanted to get me alone." He reached across and grabbed at my arm, pulling me around the desk, banging my hip on the corner in the process. "Let's be better friends."

I struggled, trying to break free. "You're hurting me." Fear coiled down my middle, taking the air from my lungs.

He threw his arms around me. "Be nice to your boss."

The more I fought, the tighter he held me. "I'll tell Bounmy," I cried.

"He won't mind sharing." Kham's foul breath turned my stomach upside down until I thought I'd be sick. "I hired you as a favor to him. He's paying your salary—a way to buy your favors. And I only brought you to Luang Prabang because he asked me to. All the things I've done for him because of you, and does he appreciate it? Does he do anything for me in return? Never."

"He loves me." My limbs were nearly numb, and my ears rang as if damaged by a loud noise.

"It's a certain kind of love, mademoiselle. Did he mention his wedding in December when his bride returns home from school in Saigon? I guess not." Kham rubbed his lower body against mine, groaning. Panic consumed me. I remembered the suffocating fear I'd felt when Director Bernard would lock me in the storage closet overnight. I had to get away.

It happened so quickly. I fought with all my strength, to no avail. He shoved a hand down the front of my blouse, grabbing at my breasts. I began to scream over and over, "Stop! Help!" I garnered all my strength and kicked his shin, but I couldn't break free.

Kham slapped me hard across the face, knocking my head back. "Shut up." He threw me onto the desk, his weight pushing me down. Notebooks and pens dug into my back. With one hand over my mouth, he lifted my skirt and ripped open my bloomers. I squeezed my eyes shut, willing my mind to be somewhere else besides this unimaginable nightmare. There was terrible pain as Kham forced himself inside me, pounding against me over and over. Finally he let out a loud moan and collapsed in a heap on top of me. After a moment, he stood and pulled up his trousers.

"Don't say a word to anyone, especially Bounmy, or I'll tell everyone what a little whore you are." He slapped me hard across the face again, then strode out of the building, slamming the door behind him.

I tried to stand up, but my legs couldn't support my weight, and I collapsed on the ground. My torn bloomers hung off my legs, the cotton stained with blood and semen. It felt as if he had ripped my insides apart. Unknown minutes passed before my body began convulsing with sobs. Then it struck me that Kham might come back, and I needed to escape. Standing up, I removed the ruined bloomers and wiped myself off. The smell of his body nauseated me, and a stream of bile rose up my throat, splashing onto the desktop. My horror turned to anger. I stuck the bloomers in the top desk drawer with a note: *You will pay for this.*

I grabbed my purse and staggered out into the dark of night, unaware of anything around me. My only thought was to reach Marguerite. I ran as fast as I could manage.

Chapter 45

When I finally reached the French guesthouse, I noticed two missing buttons on my blouse and the front gaping open, revealing my torn chemise. My hair, which had been tied back with a ribbon, hung down in a tangled jumble. Several ragged boys, no more than eight or nine years old, sat out front begging for money or food from passing guests. Fear and distrust filled their eyes as I approached. I handed one of the urchins a coin. "Go to the restaurant and ask for Marguerite Vernier," I said in my imperfect Lao, then repeated it in French. The boy scurried off. I sank onto a step and waited, barely able to breathe. My body felt inexplicably cold and numb despite the warm night air, and my teeth began to chatter. I wiped my nose with the hem of my skirt and discovered stains of blood. Instinctively, I reached for my necklace, seeking solace from the only thing I had to link me to Bounmy and his love. It was gone. Kham must have torn it from my neck in the struggle to overpower me. The loss was crushing, as if he had ripped my heart from my body.

Marguerite arrived in a lapis blue dinner gown and silver heels, her appearance grossly incongruous with our surroundings and the terror that had befallen me. She wobbled over, a bit woozy from cocktails and wine. Taking in my disheveled state, she crouched down beside me. "Oh, dear God, Vivi. Whatever happened?"

A knot formed in my throat and a fresh stream of tears erupted. It took a minute to find a way to speak the unspeakable. "He for... forced himself on me."

She took my hands. "Who? Who did this? Was it Marcel Fontaine?"

"No," I replied with surprise. "He wouldn't." I hesitated, afraid of the repercussions of naming my aggressor, but I knew Marguerite would never allow me to remain silent. I focused on the missing buttons of my blouse. "Kham. Kham Savang," I whispered.

"That rotten bastard." She helped me stand. "Come." We stumbled into the guesthouse and down the hall to her room. I sat on the bed as she wrapped a quilt around me. I couldn't stop shivering.

"Tell me what happened. Where were you?" She spoke in a quiet soothing voice, her arm about my shoulders.

I recounted how I'd run into Kham sitting with his friends drinking, how he'd dragged me to the office on the pretext of talking about work. "He was drunk." Doubt seeped in. Had it been my fault? Could I have done something different to prevent this outcome? "He said... said such terrible things. I tried to get away, but he was too strong." I buried my head in my hands. "I'm so ashamed."

"*You* have nothing to be ashamed of," Marguerite whispered hoarsely. "How could you have possibly known? It wasn't your fault."

I wanted to believe her. If only I hadn't asked to speak to him in private. If only I'd gone straight home from the temple. If only I'd run away or called out for help. These thoughts would torment me forever.

She began to pace up and down the room. "That son of a bitch. We should report him to the local guard."

I blinked slowly. "What would they do?"

She shook her head. "Probably nothing. That pervert would be protected as part of the royal family. It's your word against his."

"And no one will believe me, a *métisse*, who followed him into the building alone."

She sat on the bed again and took me in her arms. "We'll make sure this son of a bitch pays, one way or another. I promise you."

"I want to go home. To Vientiane."

"We'll leave as soon as I can arrange a boat. Let's get you into the shower. Sleep with me tonight, and tomorrow I'll get you a room of your own."

She led me into the bathroom and turned the water on. "I'll tell Charles what's happened."

I shrank back. "Do you have to?"

"We need his help to—" Marguerite stopped midsentence. "Vivi, your skirt is covered in blood." A gush of warm liquid ran down my legs.

She turned off the water and sat me on a small wooden chair in the bedroom wrapped in the quilt. "I'll be right back." She ran out. I waited, too numb and dull of mind to move. My head began to spin, and I braced myself on my knees.

Marguerite and Charles burst into the room. Charles, smelling of brandy and cigars, swept me into his sturdy arms and carried me through the dark streets to the French hospital. There were words back and forth as an attendant asked if I was Lao.

"For God's sake, she's French," Charles exploded. "She needs immediate attention."

I was placed on a bed in the ward for French patients. Smells of disinfectant and the stale air of illness assaulted my senses. Memories of the night Bridgette had died flooded back, and I wondered if I was dying. Then everything went black.

Rays of sunlight seeped through the window shutters on the other side of the room and fell across my face like warm ribbons. My whole body felt unbearably heavy, and I could barely move my arm to shield my eyes. Marguerite, still dressed in her blue gown with Charles's dinner jacket over her shoulders, sat in a chair next to me, sleeping with her head on my bed. My brain finally recognized the hospital. I was wearing a faded green gown, and a cotton pad was secured between my legs. My abdomen ached. Memories of the night before came rushing back, and acid churned in my stomach.

I touched Marguerite's hand, and she sat up with a start. "Vivi, you're awake." She hurried to the end of the room, calling for help.

A young Annamese nurse took my pulse and temperature, asking questions in a quiet, soothing voice. What was my name and birth date? How did I feel? Was there pain? She replaced the pad between my legs, which had blotches of dried blood. She would bring me some breakfast and call the doctor.

At Marguerite's insistence, I took a few sips of hot broth, even though I couldn't imagine ever wanting food again. From the blur of the night before, Kham's ugly face, sweaty and distorted, loomed before me. I tried to block the image of him slamming me down on the desk, crashing on top of me. Confusion and panic overcame me until I couldn't catch my breath.

Marguerite took my hands. "Vivi, you're safe. Nothing is going to happen."

A young French doctor entered the ward and picked up my chart, shaking his head. He turned to Marguerite. "I understand you're a friend, but I must talk to mademoiselle in private. Could you step out for a moment?"

"No, I want her to stay," I said, clinging to Marguerite's hand.

He nodded. "This is a very sensitive situation. Do you want to tell me what happened last night? I know someone assaulted you." I shook my head, unable to meet his eyes. "I understand your hesitation," he continued, "but we should report it to the authorities so this man can be punished. You don't want him to do this to another woman." My throat choked. I had no response that would begin to explain my terror and shattered emotions.

"We believe it would be futile, given this person's position," Marguerite said in a hushed tone. "There were no witnesses. He would deny it, and she would only be further harmed."

"I see." The doctor shook his head with a pained expression. "There is something else. I'm afraid you had a miscarriage last night. We had to cauterize the bleeding. Did you know you were six or seven weeks' pregnant?"

I gasped, staring into his eyes to be sure of what he'd said. I shook my head, trying to remember how long it had been since my last monthly cycle. I'd lost a baby. Bounmy's baby.

"You can go home this afternoon, but stay in bed and take it easy for the rest of the week. Your body needs to recover from the shock."

How could I make him understand? My body might heal, but I would never recover.

Chapter 46

I moved into a room at the guesthouse across from Marguerite's. She and Charles watched over me, bringing meals that I hardly touched. A young woman was sent to collect my things from Kham's family with instructions not to tell anyone of my whereabouts.

Alone with me, Marguerite swore and raged, pacing up and down in my tiny room, talking of ways Kham might be punished. "When we return to Vientiane, I'll seek advice from an attorney," she said.

Charles had threatened to beat Kham to a pulp, at first. Only after he promised not to become violent did Marguerite allow him to confront Kham. I learned later how my former employer's eyes had filled with fear when Charles burst into his office late on Saturday morning. Kham had quickly become defiant, claiming I'd been drinking with him and offered myself for money. He called me a whore and a manipulative little bitch. Barely able to contain himself, Charles brandished his pistol and threatened to kill Kham if he ever repeated these lies to anyone, demanding I receive a year's pay for my suffering. Kham balked at the suggestion, but when Charles grabbed him by the neck and slammed him against the wall, he took out a cash box. I was grateful to Charles, but the thought of touching Kham's filthy money made me sick. Yet my financial situation didn't allow the luxury of refusing it. I pictured Kham's embarrassment on seeing that I'd thrown up on his desk and left my torn, bloody bloomers with the note in the desk drawer. I hoped his brother-in-law had found them first.

In the light of day, sober, did Kham regret his actions? He'd not been so drunk that he wouldn't remember his monstrous crime. I couldn't fathom why he wanted to harm me, to be so cruel. Whatever had I done to him to deserve this?

In shock, disbelieving, my brain struggled to comprehend the ways in which my existence had unraveled into nothingness. The world was no longer round but flat, and I had fallen off the edge into an abyss. I cried and slept and cried again, my hands resting on my emptied womb. Surely Kham had lied about Bounmy; all the things he'd said to humiliate me couldn't be true. I reread Bounmy's letter—he loved me. As days passed into nights, reality slowly seeped in. I mourned my loss of innocence. The loss of Bounmy. The loss of our baby.

Aunt Chanida appeared at the guesthouse early on Monday morning, having received a note from Marguerite Saturday evening informing her of the attack. On seeing the dark-blue bruises on my cheeks, a small cut above my lip, and my red swollen eye, she rushed over to fold her arms around me. "Vivi, my poor darling."

After several minutes, she sat back, eyes filled with tears. "Marguerite said you saw a doctor." I nodded. "This kind of crime is so rare in Luang Prabang. Are you comfortable telling me what happened? Were they after money...or something else?"

I stared at the intricate pattern of her green silk scarf, unable to meet her eyes. "It was a man...drunk. He overpowered me."

Her face crumpled. "You were violated." She paused for a moment. "Do you know this person?"

"Yes."

"Have you gone to the police?"

"They'd never believe me. We were alone in his office." I continued looking down. "He promised to say terrible things about me if I told anyone what he did."

"You poor child." She lifted my chin. "Was it Prince Kham Savang?"

I bit my lower lip for a moment. "How did you know?"

"He contacted Khamphet yesterday. They met last night."

I gasped. "What did he want?" Had Kham repeated the same ugly lies he'd said to Charles?

"He didn't say anything about this." She paused. "But he talked about your relationship with his cousin, Prince Bounmy Savang. He said he thought the family should know."

I felt sick, barely able to breathe. "Kham is a horrible person. He trapped me, and when I tried to fight him off, he hit me and threatened to tell everyone I was a whore." I sobbed with despair.

"I know it wasn't your fault, but he painted a very unkind picture of you. Even though we don't believe him, your uncles worry for your reputation…and the family's honor if Kham continues to spread such unpleasant stories. Will you tell me about it?"

Once again I felt trapped. "Bounmy and I became friends shortly after I left the orphanage. He has been nothing but kind and gentle." I considered how much to reveal, taking a deep breath. "We're in love." I could not possibly tell her about the lost pregnancy.

Aunt Chanida's brow furrowed. "I see." We sat in silence as the fan stirred warm, stale air about the room. "I'm sure he loves you, Vivi," she said at last. "You're young and beautiful. But you must understand that Bounmy's father is one of the most important people at the royal court, and the family's position dictates Bounmy's future. A match has been arranged for him with a young Lao woman of equal rank. They will marry this year."

The things Kham had said were true. I wanted to beg her not to go on, to scream at Kham and Uncle Khamphet, at everyone standing in the way of our love. "Bounmy never told me," I said at last. I stared into my aunt's eyes, searching for a different outcome. "I can't believe he'd marry someone else."

"I know it's hard to accept, but unless he abandons his family and royal life, he'll not have a choice. The court wouldn't even accept you as a second or third wife. You'd never be anything but his mistress."

"Because I'm a *métisse* and a bastard? Because my father was French?" I spat out the words.

"The king insists on preserving the Lao heritage of the royal family. They marry only royals and highly placed aristocrats, never anyone French."

Anger consumed me, like a phantom swirling through my body until my blood pulsed fast and hot. Everyone had warned me, but I'd chosen to ignore and deny the truth. Bounmy had never promised me anything, beyond our brief moments together and idle talk of going to Paris one day. How naïve and ridiculous my dreams seemed now. I couldn't decide if I was more upset with Bounmy or myself.

My aunt let out a long sigh. "I know it's painful, but you must break off the relationship immediately to save your reputation. We want you to be part of our family."

Her demand was issued, leaving no room for discussion. I must choose my future. I squeezed my eyes shut. "I understand."

She took my hand. "Mademoiselle Vanier told me you'll be leaving Friday on a boat for Vientiane. Focus on meeting Antoine and planning a new life with him. You both have a family here who will always welcome you, but you must resolve this problem."

In the midst of my misery, I had hardly thought of Antoine, the only person bringing hope to my future. First, I had to make the impossible choice of giving up Bounmy.

For the next four days, I stayed in my room at the guesthouse. Sleep only brought nightmares where I woke screaming and crying. Always the same thing: Kham in one setting or another—on Phou Si Mountain, in the courtyard of Wat Xieng Thong, trapped in the River Transport office—chasing me, overpowering me. In one dream, Bounmy stood by, silently watching with his arms crossed.

October 21, 1931

Cher Antoine,

I don't know how to ease the pain of what I must tell you. Both our parents are gone, having died many years ago when we were small. A week ago Sunday, I visited Mother's family—a sister, two brothers, their spouses, and many children. They were greatly surprised by my appearance but welcoming. Our aunt Chanida had searched for us without success ever since Mother passed. The Assistance Society once again blocked the way, denying our existence.

Aunt Chanida shared our parents' story with me, giving me a photograph and a packet of letters from Father and Mother. There is so much to tell you, but I feel it must be in person.

I am leaving for Vientiane tomorrow and will arrive there within the week. I know you said it would be hard to get away before January, but I desperately need to meet you. My life has been turned upside down by events since I wrote you last. I am unemployed for the moment, so perhaps I could come to you in Pakse.

Hopefully, this note will reach you in a timely manner. Write me back to the address in Vientiane with your plans.

With love,

Vivi

P.S. Did you know that your Lao name is Vinya? Mine is Sakuna!

Aunt Chanida returned on Thursday, comforting my shattered soul in her quiet, gentle way. My aunts Dara and Noi had sent a gift, a beautiful silk *sinh* and *pha biang* in shades of emerald green and peacock blue. Aunt Chanida showed me how to fold the *sinh* around my middle and wrap the *pha biang* around my shoulders. I couldn't wait to wear them.

She buoyed my spirits by recounting stories of her childhood with my mother. "We spent endless hours playing hide and seek or sometimes tag with the boys, who would get so wound up and start pushing and pinching me. Your mother was fierce, boxing them on the ears to protect me. They were afraid of her. One time Laya and I snuck up on Khamphet and Chanta while they were fishing in the river. She set off three firecrackers—I'm not sure where she got them—sending the boys flying into the water, screaming for help. We laughed until our sides ached.

"Your mother was a terrible seamstress. Never mastered a needle." Aunt Chanida laughed. "Once she made me a new blouse. I was so excited. The first day I wore it to school, a seam came undone and the left sleeve fell off. The children laughed and pointed. I was so embarrassed."

"That must be why I'm terrible at sewing," I said, thrilled to find a common link.

"And oh, how she hated to cook—couldn't be bothered. Thank heavens we had Khantalay." She waved a hand in the air. "Laya was too smart, our tutor Tran's best student. She always had her nose in a book. He couldn't have been prouder of her if she'd been his own child." She paused a moment. "I'm sure he was in love with her. He was twelve years older, but too shy and insecure to declare his feelings. I don't think she would have accepted him.

"Lots of young men came courting, hoping to win your mother's heart, but no one caught her eye. She loved her work teaching and didn't want to get married only to be tied down with children and a household to run." She shifted in her chair. "At least, not until she met your father. She fell madly in love with him."

I closed my eyes for a moment, trying to match the picture of the women in the photo to my aunt's descriptions. "Was Mother angry with her brothers for not supporting her? Why didn't they help?"

Aunt Chanida considered the question for a moment. "Disappointed, not really angry. Chanta was too young at the time to be of any help, while Khamphet was nineteen and could have done more to persuade our father, but he wanted to preserve the family's honor, as he would inherit father's position in the court." She shrugged. "I had less to lose. I was likely to marry and move in with my husband's family, although, as it turned out, we stayed in Father's home." She paused. "I was furious with Khamphet at the time. He refused to even come to see your mother when she was dying. He regrets it now." She blinked several times. "It took me a long time to forgive him."

"I want to know more about my father. His letters are brief, and Mother explained little about his past."

"I can tell you what your mother shared with me. Your father had a sad life."

"Did you know him well?"

"I spent some time with him. He was a quiet, thoughtful man. Very kind. I liked that he made your mother so happy and adored you and Antoine."

"Why did Father marry Paulette, if they weren't in love?"

"Henri's father, your grandfather, wanted him to marry Paulette for her family's money, as he needed an investor to open a bank in Aix-en-Provence. Paulette was young and pretty. I believe Henri thought love would follow. But circumstances worked against them."

"What happened?"

"Henri helped his father found the bank, but he was unable to stop your grandfather's disastrous management. Within three years, the business failed, and rumors and accusations of fraud and embezzlement followed. Henri's family became social outcasts. Sadly, your grandfather began drinking and died six months later."

"Father must have been devastated."

"Paulette, being young and spoiled, was more concerned about her place in society," Aunt Chanida continued. "That fell apart with the scandal, and the marriage collapsed. She took three-year-old Mathis and moved back to her parents' home in Marseille. Your father was left alone to face creditors and accusations. He had to sell his family's lands and go to work for three years in an accounting firm to pay off the remaining debts. All he cared about was Mathis. Every Sunday, he rode his horse over twenty miles each way to spend the day with the boy."

"And Paulette abandoned him for all that time?" I asked. My aunt nodded. "How unfair." Now I understood why Father didn't express guilt over his affair with Mother. Paulette had not deserved his loyalty.

"Your father moved to Indochine with the hope of starting over where no one would know his past, but he couldn't leave without Mathis. He forced Paulette to come by threatening to file for divorce on the basis of spousal abandonment. I think he tried to make her happy in Laos, but she was miserable from the start, unable to tolerate the heat and humidity. She rarely left the house and refused to mix with other French wives, saying they weren't her social equal. She was rude and demanding with Laya. What upset your mother most was how she bullied the servants, yelling and slapping them for the slightest mistake."

I thought of Madame Lansay, now passed away, who had told me how my mother saved her from the anger of the mistress.

"Then Mathis got sick, and Paulette took him back to France. It was a terribly difficult year. After Mathis died, your father left for Aix-en-Provence, and your mother was terrified he would never return. But he was so in love with Laya, she didn't need to worry. After he came back, they had you and Antoine and spent three happy years together."

"And then they died," I murmured.

"Your mother never regretted her decision. Even if their time together was short, she said it was worth it to have experienced such a perfect love. Her greatest sadness was leaving you and Antoine."

I was grateful to learn the complicated truth surrounding my parents' story, to forgive them for leaving Antoine and me to grow up in an orphanage. But the loss and emptiness would never go away.

Chapter 47

The boat ride down the Mekong River was quick and mostly restful in contrast to our overland trek on horseback. The "boat" was a large raft, close to twenty feet long and eight feet wide, with a platform of bamboo poles lashed together and secured atop two pirogues. Rattan-covered seats and two tiny huts provided protection from the relentless afternoon sun and occasional downpours. We'd been fortunate to get passage on a mail boat with an outboard motor, greatly reducing our travel time to six days. The rainy season was nearly over, but water levels were still high enough to reduce the number of protruding rocks and other hazards.

Five Lao men steered the cumbersome vessel through the swift-moving waters. When we reached cascades and swirling pools, they pulled up the motor and plied their oars to navigate around exposed hazards—tree snags and floating debris. Several times I held my breath and gripped the platform, convinced we would be upended, sure that I would drown. Miraculously the raft bounced and bobbed its way to safety. On three occasions, we were required to get out and walk onshore, while the men lifted the boat up and over boulders and rapids, boarding again on the other side. Each day as the sun faded over the mountains, we docked along the shore for the night and slept in tents. The Lao men cooked us simple meals of rice, fish, vegetables, and fresh fruit purchased from villages along the way.

An older French couple, who had traveled from Hanoi to Luang Prabang, accompanied us to Vientiane. Marguerite visited with them on and off, but I lacked the strength for polite conversation with strangers.

The tangle of dread and terror in my middle slowly eased the farther we traveled from Luang Prabang and Kham. Even though he would soon return to Vientiane, I would feel safer at Catherine's. On the boat in the fresh air, I breathed more freely.

The sun played hide and seek behind layers of white and silver clouds scuttering past. The river was alive with familiar activities—men fished in tiny skiffs, and pirogues carried children to school and farmers to markets with their produce. Women washed laundry on rocks and hung it to dry along the shore. We floated past green fields and forested mountains, removed from the threat of tigers, leopards, and other animals of prey.

I used the quiet time to prepare myself for what lay ahead, to craft words to tell Bounmy our time together was over. He'd loved me in his own way, as best as he was able in the time we spent together, just as Monsieur Fontaine had loved Catherine in his own way. Now I understood that love, to love someone, was an interpretation of each person's needs. Bounmy had never promised me forever. Our love had limits defined by his birth and upbringing. By his desires. It was like plunging into a pond, expecting to be submerged in the cool blue depths, to discover the water reached only to my knees. It would never be enough.

We arrived in Vientiane mid-afternoon on Thursday. Marguerite had wired ahead to announce our early return, saying only that I had experienced a terrible trauma. The Resident Superior's car met us and took us to Catherine's house, where she and Mali were waiting. I fell into Catherine's open arms spilling tears of overwhelming relief, like a baby bird fallen from its nest then returned home, battered and bruised, nestling into the shelter of its mother's wings.

Catherine held me tightly and cooed words of comfort until I could catch my breath. "Mali is going to run you a nice bath. Relax. Take a nap. We'll have an early dinner."

"Where is Julian?" Marguerite asked.

"He went off into the wilds with André two days ago. I don't expect them back for several weeks. Possibly a month."

Marguerite rummaged in her purse and pulled out her cigarettes. "It's probably for the best."

I dried my tears on the handkerchief Catherine handed me. "I don't want him to know what happened."

Catherine nodded. "Of course not."

Mali took my arm and led me upstairs. Marguerite would inform Catherine and Mali about the attack, as I couldn't bear to talk about it. But we'd agreed that no one would learn about the miscarriage, not even Catherine.

In my room the organdy curtains flapped around the open window, as if welcoming me back. Mali had placed pink orchids in a vase on my dresser, and they filled the room with their sweet scent. Home. Over the last five months, this room, this house, had become more of a home for me than the orphanage had been during fourteen years. How fortunate I was to have this haven and my good friends to support me.

"There are fresh towels in the bathroom. I'll fill the tub," Mali said, giving me a gentle hug.

I turned to undress and noticed the envelope propped against the lamp on the nightstand. My heart contracted.

My darling Geneviève,

If you are reading this note, it means you are home. What happy news! It's unbearable not knowing when you will return. Hopefully I'll receive word in advance, but if for any reason you were unable to forewarn me, call me at work. Tell me the earliest time we can meet.

I am lost without you and long to hold you in my arms once more.

All my love,

Bounmy

I could not face him yet. Physically and emotionally spent, I allowed myself quiet hours in the house and garden, recovering from my wounds, wavering and struggling to muster the courage to meet with him. To face the inevitable. After a week, bolstered by Catherine and Marguerite's advice and support, I wrote Bounmy and suggested we meet that Saturday in our usual place.

I left the *pousse-pousse* driver on the main road, asking him to wait for my return within the hour. With each step I took down the lane, my heart split apart a little more, like glass crashing to the floor, scattering in a thousand tiny pieces.

When I reached the garden, Bounmy was opening the house shutters, softly humming. He lifted a slat that had fallen halfway off, trying to reattach it. A lock of hair had slid over his brow, which he swept aside, but it stubbornly fell back. He wore his usual white shirt and khaki pants that fell gracefully over his long, slender limbs. My body and soul ached for him.

He hadn't heard me approach. I stood very still, memorizing this image of him waiting for me. Innocent and carefree. Anticipating an afternoon of pleasure.

As if feeling my eyes upon him, he turned. His beautiful face, the face that had been my constant joy, transformed with a wide grin. He dropped the errant slat and raced to my side, throwing his arms around me and swinging me in a circle. I felt my resolve teetering toward failure in his embrace.

"I didn't think you'd come home this soon." He pulled back, beaming. "I only received your letter from Luang Prabang yesterday describing the meeting with your family. I'm so sorry about your parents, but at least you've found your aunts and uncles."

Ah yes—the letter I'd written a few days before my world had collapsed, when everything good still seemed possible. My chin trembled, and tears swelled in my eyes. I studied his features, searching for traces of betrayal and hidden secrets.

"What's wrong?"

I rested my head against his chest, listening to his racing heart, savoring the scent of sandalwood and the soft cotton of his shirt on my cheek. One last time, I would relish the comfort of his warmth, the strength of his arms, to carry me into a future without him. He stroked my hair as I sobbed. I hadn't been sure of my reaction to his touch, if the memories of Kham's assault would make me recoil from Bounmy with fear and loathing. But this was where I belonged. I was thankful to have experienced the beauty of making love with this man I adored, discovering what physical love is meant to be, before Kham could ruin it.

"Come. Talk to me." He sounded uncertain, but he led me to a wooden bench under a flame tree. "You're frightening me."

Tears choked my voice. I searched for the words I'd carefully rehearsed over the past weeks. "Everything has changed."

Bounmy took my hands. "How?"

"Something happened."

"Tell me."

"Kham...did something."

"What?" His voice became a growl.

Words spilled out. Not the ones I'd carefully planned, but those I'd intended to keep from him. Anger suddenly overwhelmed me—anger with Kham, with Bounmy and the secrets he'd kept from me, with my own stupidity for falling into this hopeless affair. I hadn't intended to reveal Kham's brutal attack, the horrible names he'd called me, the threats he'd made. But it erupted, and I spared no details. My body shook uncontrollably as I relived each terrifying moment.

Bounmy sat next to me, confused at first, shaking his head as if I were speaking a foreign language he couldn't comprehend. His body grew taut, and he gripped my hands tighter and tighter. When I stopped speaking, he let out a howl and slammed a fist onto the bench. "I'll make him pay. I swear, I'll make him pay."

I touched his arm. "It will only complicate matters. He threatened to say terrible things about me if I tell anyone. I'm a *métisse*, already an outcast in the eyes of many Lao and French."

"Did you go to the police?"

"No. Marguerite agreed they wouldn't do anything. Why would anyone believe me over a prince? I'd only be further humiliated."

He hung his head, unable to assure me otherwise. "I should never have trusted him and let you go to Luang Prabang. But I wanted you to find your family. I thought Marguerite could keep you safe."

"Kham called me your whore."

"That's a lie! I love you more than anything."

"He told me you paid my salary in order to buy my favors."

"That's ridiculous. I only wanted to help you. I never expected anything in return." He took hold of my shoulders with trembling hands. "I should have protected you. Kham's always been jealous that I've had more privileges in life. Growing up, he constantly found ways to undermine me and make trouble. He only hurt you to harm me."

I swallowed hard, knowing I would never be whole again until he understood the consequences of his actions. "I was pregnant with your child but lost it after the attack."

He withdrew, as if I'd slapped him violently across the face. Tears flooded his eyes. "Our baby." His head fell onto my shoulder, and he cried like a small child.

I let him grieve. "It's for the best," I whispered at last.

"Don't say that." He sat up, wiping his face on his sleeve. "Forgive me. Please, forgive me. I can't imagine your pain."

We sat for a long time in silence as he stroked my hair and face and kissed my forehead. Birds called out from the branches above us, and bees droned among the flowers. For just a moment, I allowed myself to think everything would be fine. Bounmy would make it right again.

I stared at his shattered face. "You're getting married in December."

There was not the slightest note of emotion in my voice. It was a simple statement of fact. He took in a quick breath.

"When did you plan to tell me?"

"I…I've been trying to convince my father to end the betrothal." Explanations poured out—a marriage arranged when they were small children, a single meeting when ten and thirteen years old. A duty, an obligation. Nothing more. "I managed to postpone the wedding until after my return from France. But now…our families insist we marry." He sounded like a spoiled child who had been issued an unjust punishment. "I'm the oldest son and must produce an heir to carry on the family name and honor our ancestors." There was no need to add that having a son with me would never fulfill this duty.

"How could you have not told me this at the beginning? How could you lead me on with false hopes, letting me think you wanted a future with me?" I pushed my hair from my face. "I feel stupid, a naïve child who trusted you without question."

"I'm so sorry. I fell in love with you from the start and couldn't bear to think of losing you if I told you about my situation. I needed to work out a solution first."

I didn't hesitate. "So, you will marry her."

He licked his lips. "Give me time. I begged Father to break it off and let me return to France." He took my hand again. "We'll go together."

"Your family will never accept a *métisse*."

He ducked his head. "Probably not."

"And if your father insists on the marriage?"

His eyes stayed focused on the ground. "I'll obey. But once there's a son, we can leave for France. She means nothing to me. You needn't worry."

"How could you be so cruel? To allow this poor girl to marry you when you don't love her. To make her bear you a son, knowing you will abandon her and the child?" I shook my head in disbelief. "I could never be with someone who could consider such a hideous thing."

He didn't answer.

"And what would I do while you're busy producing an heir with your wife?" I asked.

He looked up, hopeful. "I'd get a house for you and be with you as much as possible."

"I'd be your whore, your *phu sao*. No better than Sylvie."

"Geneviève." He sounded indignant. "How could you say that? Don't you love me?"

"How else would people view me?" I thought of my mother's lonely existence once Father had left for France. She'd been shamed and rejected by everyone, left to fade away from neglect. "When you grow tired of me, I'll be alone and ruined."

He shook his head. "I'd never leave you. Once we go to France, we'll marry." He spoke as if it were perfectly logical. How could I possibly have any objections? "Many Lao men have multiple wives."

I gazed up at the leaves dancing in the breeze, trying to collect my thoughts. "In the past few weeks, I've lost everything that matters—my innocence, my faith in you...our baby. My reputation. Kham took everything from me then met with my uncle and told him of our affair, warning him about my stained character. If I want to be part of my newfound family, I can't remain with you."

Bounmy's shoulders slumped. He seemed incapable of a response.

"I loved you with all my heart, believed in you completely, but you betrayed me by not being truthful. Your idea of loving me is limited to what is convenient for you."

He took a shuddering breath and wrapped his arms around me, whispering in my ear as his tears dripped down my neck. "I've made a mess of things, but give me a chance. I want to be with you for the rest of my life." He sat back. "I'll defy my father and refuse to marry. We'll go to France. Next week. I have money."

"I don't want you to renounce your family, and I don't want to give up mine when I've only just found them. We could never be happy." I bit my bottom lip to stem the quiver in my voice. "You're bound to your heritage and position in life, promised to another. If you truly love me, let me go."

I stood and put my hand on his cheek, looking into his eyes, dark pools of pain and guilt. It took every ounce of strength in my body to walk away, down the road to the waiting *pousse-pousse*. Memories of the day we'd first met, our boat rides down the Mekong, the first night we made love swam in my mind. Giddy, happy hours filled with promise and hope, now dashed. My first love.

I turned once to look back. He remained where I had left him, his head in his hands.

The affair was over.

Chapter 48

Three days after our meeting, Bounmy sent a letter. I was afraid to read his words, afraid of my weakness. If he begged me to return to him, to reconsider living a half-life as his mistress, would I agree? Part of me longed to be convinced, to embrace his love at any cost, as my mother had done for my father. If only the overwhelming agony would cease. He professed his deep and enduring love for me, but in the end, it was merely an apology for an impossible situation. A final goodbye.

Days and weeks folded one into the other, and October drifted into November. I mourned for Bounmy and our baby, for everything Kham had stolen from me, the death of my parents, and the end of a childhood spent waiting for a reunion that would never come. Once more the loss of Bridgette assaulted me, reopening the wound that had never healed. The depth of my losses seemed unbearable.

When Bridgette had died, work had filled my days, providing a brief reprieve from my grief, while the attentions of Julian and Bounmy had distracted me from the pain. Now the hours passed without shape or purpose. Each morning brought the heavy burden of remembering anew. Secluded in my room, or sitting in the garden, my thoughts wandered, trying to make sense of it all, creating scenarios where things would somehow end differently. What if I had heeded Catherine's warnings and parted from Bounmy before it truly began? But I would have always wondered what might have been. I'd had an inexplicable attraction from the start, which grew with each meeting. The truth remained that given a second chance, I would make the same choices, even if they brought me to this dismal conclusion.

A jumble of irrational thoughts and rants filled my journal. I had been born under an unlucky star, damned by a Catholic God for my parents' sins. Perhaps it was my Buddhist karma reflecting unforgiveable errors in a former life. How had I merited this terrible destiny?

Dreams invaded the night, so lifelike they could hardly be distinguished from waking hours. My heart thrashed against my ribs as Kham tried to overpower me again and again. One night, my anger sought revenge with images of Kham being dragged away in chains while I stood by laughing. Another time my imagination invented a happier outcome—Bounmy's family wanted him to marry me rather than his fiancée—my love and I would leave for France, where my parents waited for us.

In more lucid moments, I understood that somehow I must put the past behind me and find a fresh start. But it felt like I was rowing a boat upstream, trying to make it to safety, only to be pushed back by swift and unrelenting currents.

Catherine left me to my solitude, offering a shoulder to cry on and an ear to listen when needed. Mali fed me bowls of rice porridge and teas laced with turmeric and lemongrass to restore my spirits, lighting incense and praying for me at the Buddhist temple every evening. Thankfully, Julian had not returned home yet to witness my misery. I couldn't bear to be reminded of his predictions that Bounmy would break my heart, to acknowledge he had been right.

I received a short note from Antoine, thanking me for my letter about our parents and saying he regretted he couldn't visit until the end of January and hoped I would be able to cope until then. I still had the promise of reuniting with him, but in darker moments, I feared that he, too, might disappoint. How could I trust anyone again?

The monsoon season had ended, bringing mild and pleasant days, which helped clear the fog from my brain. The injuries to my body had healed, even if the emotional scars remained deeply etched in my heart. My love for Bounmy became something intangible, a painful memory no longer part of this world.

I gradually emerged from my isolation, chatting with Mali in the kitchen and sharing dinners with Catherine and Marguerite. Marguerite provided the latest gossip and amusing stories to divert my attention, keeping the mood light, while asking Catherine and me for advice on her wedding plans. She and Charles would wed on New Year's Day—a new départ in the new year. Her excitement was contagious.

On returning to Vientiane, Marguerite had met with an attorney, who affirmed that trying to bring legal charges against Kham would be pointless. She'd been stewing over how to harm Kham's business. Then one night she arrived for dinner, bursting with excitement.

"I have the most astonishing news." She raised her gin and tonic in the air, as if making a toast. "The Customs Bureau director met with the Resident Superior on Monday to deliver an audit of River Transport's financial accounts, showing tax evasion and other irregularities. It seems Kham has been pocketing more than half the import taxes he's collected on goods from out of the country rather than submitting them to the colonial government."

I bit my lower lip, feeling a deep sense of satisfaction over the news. "I knew they were hiding something."

"And that's only the half of it," Marguerite went on. "When the auditors discovered his misdeeds, Kham tried to bribe them to keep quiet."

"The man is a complete fool," Catherine said.

"And much worse!" Marguerite said. "Since Kham is part of the royal family, the colonial government doesn't want to embarrass the king by sending him to jail. They asked Prince Phetsarath to negotiate a deal. A steady stream of wires back and forth with the king and his chief advisors finally produced an acceptable settlement. All of Kham's assets have been seized and the back taxes paid, and the king has transferred River Transport's charter to another family member in the royal court. Kham will be moving to a remote district in the kingdom of Luang Prabang as a lowly administrator."

"He deserves much worse, but it's better than nothing," Catherine said, before giving Marguerite a sly smile. "Did you give the bureau the tip?"

Marguerite shook her head. "I wish I'd thought of it." She turned to me. "Vivi?"

"If only I'd been that clever." I puzzled over the possibilities. "It must have been Bounmy. I told him about my concerns over the company's accounts, and he promised to make Kham pay for what he did to me."

Marguerite shrugged. "All I could get out of the Customs Bureau director was that it came from someone Lao."

Bounmy had taken his revenge. His last gift to me.

Marguerite took my hand. "Kham is leaving Vientiane immediately, and you'll never have to see him again."

Suddenly it was the first week of December, and I had no idea where the time had gone. It would be Christmas in three weeks, a holiday that had been particularly special for Bridgette and me, a rare moment of celebration at the orphanage. Each year a spindly pine tree had been cut in the mountains and hauled to the home. We tied red ribbons around the boughs and hung decorations fashioned from paper, scraps of fabric, flowers, and bamboo.

Catherine and Marguerite announced on Tuesday evening that we were going shopping the next day for new dinner dresses. "We're taking you to the Cercle Saturday evening," Catherine said. "Besides, you need something special to wear to Marguerite's wedding, so why not get it now and enjoy it?"

I started to protest, but Marguerite held up a hand. "We refuse to let you mope around any longer. You must get on with your life, Vivi."

"Think of it as a coming-out party," Catherine added.

"How will I face the people who knew about my affair with Bounmy?"

"Who gives a damn?" Marguerite said impatiently. "Hold your head high, and dare them to say anything. Every French person in the colony has secrets."

Catherine laughed with derision. "At least half the men keep a *phu sao* on the side. And many of the women are having affairs, as well."

Her argument rang hollow given the numerous warnings she had issued about being seen with Bounmy and the harm it might cause to my reputation. But I didn't argue, as she meant well.

Marguerite grinned. "We're allowed a few mistakes when we're young, Vivi. Heaven knows, I've had more than my fair share."

"Look at my situation with Marcel. It couldn't have been more public," Catherine said. "But people forget. They're too busy with their own problems."

I had delivered Marcel Fontaine's letter to Catherine on returning home from Luang Prabang. She hadn't mentioned him since, but I'd glimpsed her reading it a number of times on the front veranda. I wondered if she wished he might convince her to picture a different outcome as well, to give their love another chance. It wasn't my place to ask.

"The trick is to learn from our failures and not repeat them," Marguerite said. "That's the challenge."

—

We were drinking tea after returning home from our successful shopping expedition on Wednesday when Julian sailed through the front door, sunburned and bedraggled. Catherine's shoulders visibly relaxed. She had worried excessively the entire time he was gone.

"Good God, you look like hell," Marguerite said.

"Thank you. It's lovely to see you, too, Marguerite." Julian grinned. "I'm just happy to be alive. There were moments when I doubted I'd make it."

Catherine stepped close to him, then backed away. "I can't even hug you. You smell like a pigsty."

"A bath is definitely in order." He stared at his own filthy, torn clothes. "I have scratches and bites all over my body." His hair had grown long, and his face had sprouted a pale blond beard and mustache, too scraggly to be taken seriously.

Marguerite eyed him. "You've lost weight."

"A slight bout of dysentery, but it could be worse; André picked up malaria." Hearing the word sent chills down my back.

Julian gave me an uncertain glance. "Vivi, I'm happy to see you."

I gave a tentative smile, feeling ill at ease given the strain between us before I'd left for Luang Prabang. "I'm glad you're back safely. You must have many stories to tell."

"I'll bore you with them over dinner," he said, heading upstairs.

"There's a letter from Father on your bed," Catherine called after him.

When I came downstairs at six, Julian and Catherine were sipping gin and tonics in the salon, deep in conversation. He looked like a different person after a bath and shave, his hair combed back. A white linen shirt set off his reddish tan and bright blue eyes, rendering him more handsome than ever. My feelings for him had been complicated from the start. At times I'd thought him spoiled and self-centered, and his jealousy of Bounmy and drunken outbursts had been inexcusable. Always I'd compared him to Bounmy, who I'd believed perfect, but neither one was what they'd appeared. Bounmy had failed me, while Julian had proven to be a caring friend, there for me when I needed him. I couldn't help wondering what might have developed between us without Bounmy's presence. There would always be "what ifs."

Julian jumped up. "Vivi, let me get you a drink."

I assumed Catherine had told him about my break with Bounmy, and what I'd learned about my parents' deaths. We'd agreed she would tell him I'd quit my job because of the scandal over Kham's tax evasion. Nothing more.

Julian handed me a cocktail. "Catherine says you met your mother's family in Luang Prabang, and that your brother will be visiting after the holidays. That's wonderful news."

I nodded. "I can hardly wait. I only wish he could come before Christmas."

Mali came into the room to collect us, beaming at Julian. "Dinner is ready."

To my relief, the table was set for three, as Marguerite had left to dine with friends at the club and André was not feeling well enough. Wonderful aromas rose from steaming bowls of beef curry, *laab moo*, fried tofu, green papaya salad, rice, and hot sauce—all of Julian's favorites, now some of my favorites as well. After weeks of little interest in food, my stomach growled with a ravenous hunger.

"Mali, I can't begin to tell you how delicious this looks," Julian said. "If you could have seen the food we ate in the mountains. Absolutely horrendous!"

Mali patted his shoulder. "You must gain some weight. What girl will want you so skinny and weak?" She hurried off to the kitchen as Julian sputtered a protest.

I chuckled. "She's been forcing food on me ever since I returned from Luang Prabang. She says I'm too thin for any boy to look my way." I paused. "How lucky we are to have someone who cares for us so well."

"Indeed," said Catherine.

Without warning, my throat grew tight and tears threatened. They'd all been so kind, adopting me, a misplaced soul who belonged nowhere, offering a safe harbor. How desperate my life might be without them.

"How sick is André?" I asked.

"Not too bad. He's been taking quinine and went to the doctor as soon as we got back." Julian shook his head. "It might sound heartless, but after spending day and night with André for over five weeks, I need a break."

Catherine sighed. "I suppose he was drinking, as always."

"Of course. We ran out of gin after two weeks. All we could get was the villagers' rice liquor. Deadly stuff." Julian held out his wine glass. "I'm not swearing off alcohol, mind you, but I *am* a reformed man. Moderation is my new motto."

"You're finally growing up, little brother," Catherine said.

I dished rice and beef curry onto my plate. "Tell us about the trip."

"Quite an adventure. Or ordeal, depending on how you look at it. I might have given up weeks ago, but André was determined to keep going until we'd found gold."

"Did you?" Catherine asked.

Julian shrugged. "It's not clear. We brought back a handful of rocks with traces of gold running through them. Or it could be fool's gold. We won't know until André does the tests."

"Where did you go?" I asked.

Julian rested his elbows on the table. "We rode horses to Vang Vieng and spent a night in a guesthouse, our last taste of civilization. The next morning we met our four Muang guides, and the trek began in earnest. We paddled up the Nam Song River in two flimsy pirogues that looked like they might fall apart any minute, especially when we ran aground on a sand bar mid-morning. A half-day out, we turned east, floating into smaller and smaller tributaries heading into the mountains." His eyes sparkled with mischief as he squeezed his shoulders together and described how tightly packed they were in the narrow boats. He gave a hearty laugh. "You should have seen André squirm at having to sit next to one of the half-naked Muang men." Arms flailing, Julian described the dangerous eddies in the streams and the roar of water plummeting over rocky outcrops. "One day a panther stalked us for hours along the stream banks, as if waiting patiently to make one of us his next meal."

Julian ran his fingers through his hair. "I lost all sense of direction. If anything had happened to our guides, I'm not sure how we would have made it home."

"How far did you go in the pirogues?" Catherine asked.

"Quite a long way. Sometimes we had to carry them around rocks and other debris. I got dumped in the water twice. The second time I almost drowned, but one of the guides dragged me onto shore with his oar. For small people, the Muang are amazingly strong and capable. I have nothing but respect. When it was no longer possible to navigate the streams, our guides led us along the banks, clearing a trail with their machetes."

His enthusiastic, animated stories, weaving together threads of adventure and daring, were quite endearing. It struck me how much I'd missed his cheerful company, how comfortable I felt in his presence.

"How did you know where to look for gold?" I asked.

"According to André's mining books, the most favorable conditions are found where rushing water has removed silt from the stream bed and broken the rocks into gravel. Gold nuggets are often found in protected nooks where the water's course has taken a sharp turn."

"But there must be hundreds and hundreds of places like that in the mountains," Catherine said.

"Exactly," Julian said with a guffaw. "Like searching for a needle in a haystack. But André was undeterred. He completely ignores the fact that dozens of miners and fortune hunters have combed the forests and streams of Laos for years, each one sure they'd strike it rich. Even Prince Souvanna led an expedition last year. All that came of it were two tin mines." He waved his hand in the air with disgust. "And now the price of tin has collapsed, along with much of the world economy."

"What happens next?" I asked.

Julian took a sip of his wine. "André's optimistic it's truly gold. If so, he'll return and search for more deposits." He relaxed in his chair. "But I'm not going out there again anytime soon."

"Good," Catherine said. "You must get back to organizing your import/export business."

"Hah. To be feasible, there must actually be a market for trading goods. With the depression in the United States spreading all over Europe, no one is buying anything. My grand business plan is a failure before I even get it underway."

"Surely you can find something else," Catherine said cautiously.

Julian stared at his food, fingering the edge of his plate. "I'm thinking about returning to France."

"What?" Catherine's face paled. "But you've only just arrived. Whatever would you do at home?"

"Father has a friend willing to hire me in his wine distribution business." He looked up. "No matter how bad the economy, the French never give up their wine. In fact, they drink even more!"

"I know it's selfish, but I'll be desolate if you leave." Catherine's voice trembled, as if she was going to cry.

"I hate to leave you, as well," Julian said, reaching across the table to pat Catherine's hand. "I'll investigate what other options are available."

Disappointment settled over me at the thought of one more person dear to me disappearing from my life. I cherished Julian's friendship, someone I could count on. He had been my confidant, always there to lend support. There remained a deeper emotion, a spark that one day might flourish. Not now, but possibly in the future when he was truly over Lily and I recovered from the loss of Bounmy. If Julian returned to France, whatever possibilities might exist between us would vanish. Did he still believe he loved me or had that faded away?

The mood turned somber as we finished our meal. Mali came to clear the dishes. "I have coconut cream cake for dessert."

"Wonderful. I'd love some coffee, please," Julian said. He turned to Catherine and me. "Shall we go out on the veranda?"

Catherine stood up, sighing with defeat. "I'm rather tired and need to write a letter. I'll see you in the morning." She stopped to give Julian a kiss on his forehead. "Thank heavens you're safely home."

Julian and I settled on the veranda with Mali's cake and steaming cups of coffee. He lit lemongrass candles on the table and near our legs to fend off voracious mosquitoes. The sky had turned velvety black, and we quietly contemplated the first stars flickering to life, serenaded by crickets and katydids and the occasional croaking frog.

"It's lovely to be with you again." His deep voice drifted across the space between us. "Vivi, I"—he hesitated, taking a deep breath—"I must apologize for my behavior before you left for Luang Prabang. Once again, I drank too much and said some inexcusable things."

"You might want to work on changing that pattern." I looked over at his profile and smiled. "But I forgive you. I know it was only because you care about me."

"My pride was wounded. I was jealous and angry that you chose Bounmy over me." He gave a chortle. "I sound like a spoiled brat fighting over a toy."

I sipped my coffee. "You wanted someone to fill the void that Lily left."

"In part. I had a lot of time to think, these past weeks out in the jungle. I know now that coming back to Laos to escape my grief over Lily was misguided. You can't run away from pain." We ate our cake in the flickering candlelight. "Although I care deeply for you, it's different than my love for Lily."

I had been a passing infatuation for Julian, a pleasant diversion in his time of grief and loneliness. But then, he had never captured my heart the way Bounmy had. It was a relief to discuss our situation without any more misunderstandings or false hopes.

Julian cleared his throat. "My motives in pursuing you were not all selfish. I wanted to protect you from Bounmy taking advantage of your inexperience. I knew you'd end up hurt."

"Catherine must have told you it's over. Bounmy knew from the beginning that he would marry someone his family selected. He offered only what suited his needs, without considering the consequences for me." I stopped, debating if I should say more. "He broke my heart—as you predicted. And yet, I still love him."

"Our emotions can't be turned off like a water spigot. I'll always love and miss Lily."

"And I will always love Bounmy. But I have to accept that I'm not Cinderella." I let out a harsh laugh. "There will be no fairytale ending with my prince."

"You'll find someone else, someone better who will love you completely." Julian sat forward and took my hand. "We aren't right for each other at this moment. You're young and have much to learn and experience, and I need to find my footing back in France. But I am grateful for this time we've had together, the ways in which you've helped me see myself in a new light. I am a better person for knowing you."

"Thank you," I said, squeezing his hand. "Your friendship has been an important gift that I will always treasure."

He laughed. "Don't write me off completely, mademoiselle. If you and Antoine come to France next year to attend university, I hope to renew our friendship."

"I'll write once we make plans," I said.

Julian put his face close to mine, grinning. "It is possible that one day my charms will overwhelm you, and you'll fall madly in love with me."

I giggled, my heart feeling lighter than it had in months. "We'll just see then."

Chapter 49

Julian and I spent happy hours together over the next few days, comfortable now that we understood the boundaries of our relationship. He accompanied me to shop for new shoes on Friday then we ate a leisurely lunch at Café Français, where I shared details about my family in Luang Prabang and what I had learned about my parents. His compassion helped ease the sadness I felt. He nearly fell off his chair laughing as I recounted stories of riding horseback to Luang Prabang—my aching backside, the hazards of finding a safe spot in our "outdoor" water closet, the scourge of insects and leeches, and our encounter with the tiger. We talked of sleepy Luang Prabang and its beautiful temples, which he had visited once as a young teen. Hopefully he couldn't sense the dark cloud lurking in the background, the horror I struggled to erase from my mind.

"What will you do once your brother comes?" he asked, sipping an espresso after the meal.

"I'm not sure. It depends on how much time he has off from his job."

"Do you think he might move to Vientiane?"

"I want us to be together somewhere. Perhaps I should go to Pakse. If I stay in Vientiane, I'll always be afraid of running into Bounmy, especially after he brings his new wife here. I can't bear to think of it." I took a deep breath to quell the tremor in my voice. "Wherever Antoine and I settle, I hope we'll be as close as you and Catherine."

He put his hand over mine and squeezed it. "I have no doubt you will be."

"When exactly will you leave for France?" I asked. That morning over breakfast, he had announced his decision to leave for home. Poor

Catherine had put on a brave face, but it was clear she was heartbroken.

"I have to check the ship departures from Saigon for Marseille, but as soon after Marguerite's wedding as possible." He smiled. "She threatened bodily harm if I don't attend."

"Will you live in Paris?"

"I'll be in Burgundy with my parents. My father's friend has offered me a job at his vineyards and winery to start, so I become familiar with the business. But I hope to transfer to their offices in Paris within the year to work in sales and distribution. They're a large organization with an international market. Given the economy, I'm lucky to have such a generous offer."

"I'll miss you."

"We'll write."

"Of course." I smiled, suppressing my deep disappointment at losing Julian. "Then I shall see you next in France. I'm determined to get an education and future of my choice. I can't depend on anyone else to take care of me, not even Antoine."

He smiled with satisfaction, like a proud parent. "You're an independent woman! I can see no one will stand in your way."

Charles arrived in Vientiane on Friday afternoon, and we all celebrated at the Cercle Saturday night for a raucous prelude to his and Marguerite's upcoming marriage.

I was reveling over the news Catherine had delivered that afternoon. She had sat me down on the front veranda. "Maîtresse Durand called me a little while ago," she'd begun. "You'll be relieved to hear the board of directors for the Assistance Society in Paris has recalled Director Bernard to France. He's being replaced by a very nice woman who my mother knows. Things should improve dramatically for the girls."

A heavy lump deep inside my middle, like an undigested bite of food, slowly dissolved. Finally, Director Bernard was being held accountable. "That's wonderful. Was it your mother's letter to the Society that convinced them?" I asked.

"In part, but it seems Maîtresse also wrote a scathing report to the board after Bridgette's passing," Catherine answered. "She simply couldn't let Bernard continue to get away with his abuse and neglect. She is a woman who often surprises me." I was almost ready to forgive Maîtresse for her part in Bridgette's death.

Now, sitting at our table at the Cercle, Julian lifted two champagne glasses from the tray of a passing waiter, handing me one and raising his in a toast. "Good riddance to Director Bernard," Julian said. "His karma has caught up with him."

"I'm happy for the sake of the other girls. At least Bridgette's death has fostered some good."

The first dance began, and Julian whispered in my ear, "The next one is mine."

A half-hour later, Prince Souvanna and Aline Allard arrived, joining a young French couple at their table. A moment of panic swept over me that Bounmy might show up, but there was no sign of him. Most likely he was avoiding the club and the possibility of seeing me. A vengeful part of me hoped someone would inform him that I was having a grand time with Julian. Perhaps he would feel a pain equal to my own.

As the evening wore on, the music and gaiety filled me with a joy that had eluded me since the trauma of Luang Prabang and my breakup with Bounmy. I decided I didn't care in the least what any of the other patrons at the club thought of me. Let them gossip and spread rumors all they wanted, if they didn't have anything better to do. I refused to be intimidated and made to feel ashamed of being a *métisse*, cowering and hiding away like a criminal. Newly emboldened, I greeted several couples Catherine had previously introduced me to, daring them to snub me. To my surprise, they responded with genuine smiles and asked me how my life was going. Perhaps if I was friendly and confident, some of these people would be kinder.

Julian and I happily twirled around the room all evening, as comfortable in each other's arms as an old married couple. At one point Prince Souvanna and Mademoiselle Allard glided past us, her arm brushing my shoulder as they gazed into each other's eyes, oblivious to everyone around them. How had Prince Souvanna found the courage to pursue his love, despite the disapproval of the king and royal court and the gossip that circulated throughout Laos? Why couldn't Bounmy have been as brave?

Late in the evening, I found Catherine in the lady's room, sitting on a bench in the corner of the lounge. Tears coursed down her pale cheeks.

"Catherine, what's wrong?" I knelt down and took her hand.

She dabbed her tears with a handkerchief. "I'm feeling sorry for myself. Julian is leaving for France. Marguerite is getting married. I'm afraid you'll leave once your brother comes." Her shoulders shook with a sob. "It's terribly self...selfish of me. I really do want...others to be happy."

"I'm sorry. I've been so wrapped up in my troubles, I haven't even asked how you're doing."

She stared into my eyes, her face filled with sorrow. "Tell me. When you saw Marcel, how was he? Marguerite said you had coffee with him, and he brought you information about your father."

This was the first time she had asked me anything about him. "He seemed very different from the man I met here. He's stopped drinking and is living a quiet life. He was kind enough to offer to look up my father's employment file." I took a deep breath. "His face seemed worn and tired, his eyes full of pain, and he's lost quite a bit of weight." I stopped, unsure what more I should say. "He told me how much he loves you, that he realized too late what a remarkable woman you are. I believe he was sincere."

She bit her lower lip for a moment. "Do you think people can change?"

"I'm not sure."

"What a silly question. You're eighteen and hardly know anything about the world."

I chuckled. "True. And yet, I've managed to make a complete mess of my life." I paused. "Do you think of him often?"

"All the time. The letter you brought me broke my heart." She took in a deep breath. "I finally wrote back, and we've exchanged letters. He's begging me to come to Luang Prabang. I have eight weeks' leave starting in January. I know it sounds insane, but I still love him."

"You want to go?"

"Desperately." She looked into my eyes, as if begging for approval. "If he has truly stopped drinking, and he's no longer with his wife…"

"I'm not the least bit qualified to give advice, but I think you should follow your heart."

"You are the dearest girl." She gave me a hug. "Marguerite will kill me when she finds out."

I chuckled. "Remind her that she gave Charles a second chance and look where that led."

She sat back. "I'm a terrible hypocrite, after telling you to break it off with Bounmy."

"Monsieur Fontaine is getting divorced, while Bounmy's about to get married. It's an important distinction. I don't regret loving Bounmy, as he brought me great happiness. But now I must stand on my own and figure out who I am and what I want in life."

Catherine smiled. "You're such a sensible girl!"

Chapter 50

I slept until almost nine the next morning, awakened finally by a pounding headache brought on by too many glasses of champagne. I pattered down to the kitchen in search of aspirin and something to settle my roiling stomach. Mali had left for her village, while Julian and Catherine were still asleep. I was making coffee when a soft knock sounded at the front door.

A slender young man, a head taller than me, stood on the porch, a large rucksack by his side. I knew immediately, even though his hair was the rich tawny shade of tamarind fruit, not black like mine. His nose, eyes, and the curve of his chin looked remarkably familiar, like a masculine reflection of myself in the mirror. Happiness burst from the depths of my soul, as if I had opened a hidden treasure chest to discover a cache of sparkling jewels.

My hand flew to my mouth. "Antoine."

He stood very still and searched my eyes uncertainly. We had shared a lifetime of longing and wondering where we had come from, who our parents were, and if we were alone in the world. All of this was answered in an instant. Brother and sister. Twins. Family.

"Geneviève, I've found you."

I threw my arms around his neck and held him close, a sob rising up from my chest. He drew in a deep breath, his arms hanging stiffly at his sides. Slowly he exhaled and put his arms around me, patting my back. We remained this way, time standing still. I was afraid to let go, afraid he might be a dream that could disappear in a puff of smoke.

At last I pulled back and wiped tears from my cheeks as words spilled out. "I can't believe you're here. Why didn't you write? You said it would be January. How did you arrive? How long are you staying?"

He grinned. "All good questions with long answers."

"There is so much to talk about." My hands trembled, and my heart felt like it might gallop right out of my chest. My twin brother was truly standing before me.

"I don't know where to begin. But at the moment, I'm very hungry. Could we go somewhere for breakfast and talk?"

"I was fixing coffee, and there are rolls and other things. You drink coffee? You must, you work on a coffee plantation." He nodded, and I pointed to a chair. "Sit down. Don't move. I'll be right back."

I fixed a light meal, grateful to Mali for all the good things she had prepared for us to eat in her absence. Antoine devoured her sweet rolls, a generous piece of quiche, and slices of mango and banana. We glanced at each other in silence, floating in a surreal dream, the awkwardness of this initial meeting stretching between us like a vast bridge across a canyon. Slowly questions and answers flowed back and forth, and we began to relax, to feel our way to a connection.

"I took the ferry from Pakse five days ago. We arrived late last night, so I stayed on the boat. I wasn't sure how early I should come."

"Why didn't you write and let me know of your arrival?"

He scrunched up his mouth on one side. "It was a last-minute decision. I could have sent a wire, but I decided to surprise you and be here for Christmas."

"This is the best Christmas gift ever. How long can you stay?"

"As long as you'd like, since I've resigned from my post. I simply couldn't continue working in those conditions. And being with you seemed more important."

I bit my lower lip, thrilled by this announcement. "So, you're truly here. For good." He nodded.

Catherine and Julian emerged from the house, looking sleepy and slightly hungover. They started on finding a stranger next to me, and we jumped up.

"This is my brother, Antoine," I said, the words strange and astonishing to my ears.

Julian grinned. "I could have guessed that. You look a great deal alike."

Antoine stood and gave a *nop*, then shook hands with them both. "It is an honor to meet you. How can I ever thank you enough for taking care of Geneviève? You've been very generous and kind."

Catherine put her arm around my shoulders. "She is very dear to us—part of our family now, and I hope you will be as well."

"Please make yourself at home in the guest room for as long as you want," Julian added.

Antoine and I retreated to the back garden, leaving Julian and Catherine to their coffee and breakfast. I dashed up to my room and retrieved the photograph of our parents and their letters.

Antoine studied the picture. "I see you in Mother. She's familiar to me, but...it was so long ago. We were so young." We compared sketchy memories of our early years in Luang Prabang, hazy, unformed images, subject to doubt and contradictions. It felt like trying to piece together a song from small snippets of a tune, the words long forgotten.

He remembered living with a family not his own. "Mother would visit. She always promised that the next time, she would take me with her." He gazed at me, his eyes filled with sadness. "I'd often sit out on the front steps, waiting for her. Then one day two French women arrived. They said they were taking me to live in a nice place with people who would care for me. I thought they meant Mother, but they delivered me to the orphanage in Pakse."

"I have a vivid memory of Mother promising to return when the tamarind tree bloomed. Did she say that to you?" He shook his head. "I always believed she'd brought me to the orphanage here in Vientiane, and that she meant the tamarind tree in the home's courtyard. Then I discovered the Assistance Society had taken me from her in Luang Prabang. It wasn't that tree at all. I keep wondering, where is it? Did I make it up?"

"Perhaps she was simply describing the time of year in a way you would understand, rather than a specific tree."

"Of course. I took her words too literally." I told him of my vigils each year, watching from the boughs of the tamarind tree at the orphanage, seeking our mother's face in the streets below, always hopeful.

An expression of pain flickered across Antoine's face, then he put his hand over mine. "It's a miracle we've found each other. I'm grateful you broke the rules and searched your file. It makes me furious every time I think of how the Assistance Society tried to keep us apart, when we had nothing else of our own in this world."

"But now we have the rest of our lives ahead of us."

He smiled. "We won't let anyone separate us again."

I touched Antoine's arm. "Why don't you get settled in your room, and I'll leave you to read the letters and reflect on what happened. Call me when you're ready to talk again."

Antoine found me later on the front veranda writing a list of places in town I wanted to show him—mostly where Bounmy had taken me at one time or another. His expression was somber, and traces of tears stained his cheeks.

"Catherine and Julian are out shopping for dinner, and they've invited Marguerite and Charles to join us."

He managed a smile. "It will be fun to meet Marguerite after the things you've written about her in your letters."

"Are you all right?" I asked.

"I will be. I'm content at least to know what happened and that our parents loved each other...and us. How tragic their lives ended so young, and that our mother had to suffer so at the end. The world can be very cruel to those who don't deserve it."

I took his hand. "We have each other and a family in Luang Prabang. They told me we're welcome to live with them if we want."

"Please tell me about your visit and what each person is like," he said. "I shall write them soon."

And so we spent the afternoon discussing our aunt and uncles, their families, and everything I could remember about their lives. I repeated the stories Aunt Chanida had shared about our mother growing up, small gems that linked us to a common beginning. We were no longer alone in the world.

Later, Catherine and Julian cooked a giant pot of cassoulet to welcome Antoine. Marguerite and Charles, floating in their happy bubble, arrived with great fanfare. Marguerite gushed over Antoine and grabbed his arm to sit next to her on the settee.

"Charles, you'd better be on your best behavior," she threatened, "or I might run off with this handsome young man."

I worried my twin would find my boisterous friends overwhelming, but he seemed unfazed by their attentions and a barrage of questions, listening intently and formulating thoughtful responses. I sat by quietly observing, feeling shy in the presence of this new being, my brother. I learned Antoine didn't like to drink—he nursed one glass of wine the whole evening—and that his laughter erupted quickly, a hearty chuckle of unrestrained mirth. His strict training at the French *lycée* and boarding house in Saigon had polished his manners. If the conversation led to difficult experiences in his past—the way French classmates had taunted him, or the harsh treatment of *indigène* students by French teachers—he seemed philosophical about them, proclaiming they had helped build his character. Even when discussing the dreary conditions of the workers on the coffee plantation, he ended on a positive note with his hope that changes might soon come. I wondered if he was truly so easygoing and congenial, or was he simply trying to win over my friends...and me?

Throughout the evening, Catherine eyed Antoine and me with a contented smile. "Do you have any idea what you will do now you've found each other?" she asked once we finished our meal.

Antoine spoke up immediately. "Our first task is to apply for scholarships to French universities. I hope we'll be able to go next fall." He smiled over at me. "I'm so happy Vivi has the same ambitions."

Julian nodded. "Excellent! And I'll be in France to welcome you and help however I can."

"You'll need references for starters," Marguerite said. "I'll introduce you to the Resident Superior and enlist him to write glowing recommendations."

"Of course I'll write one for you, Vivi," Catherine said. "And Maîtresse will as well."

Antoine pushed his plate back. "I have two letters of recommendation from my teachers in Saigon."

"You can stay here at the house, of course," Catherine said. "Julian is leaving for France after the wedding, and I'll be going to Luang Prabang through February. Mali will be happy to have you here, although she'll be spending a few weeks with her family."

"We need to find jobs and save money," I said.

Catherine pushed her hair from her cheek. "You should both apply for teaching positions. They're desperate for qualified instructors at the French/Lao schools, and the pay is decent. Now that Director Bernard is leaving in disgrace, he won't be an obstacle. Maîtresse Durand will help arrange things for you."

"Antoine speaks Lao and Annamese, which should help," I said with pride. My fluency in Lao was still floundering, but I would redouble my efforts with Mali and Antoine to help.

Charles sat back in his chair and crossed his legs. "What do you plan to study at university, Antoine?"

"Medicine. Eventually, I'll return here and care for *indigène* patients."

"You'll make a fine physician," Marguerite said. "And the need is overwhelming."

"And you, Vivi, what is your dream?" Charles asked.

"I want to study law and defend those who have no power to fight for their rights."

"She'll be a force to be reckoned with," Julian said, grinning. "I feel sorry for anyone who has to face off against her. They won't stand a chance."

Catherine held up her wine glass. "A toast to your successful futures. I have every confidence in both of you."

Chapter 51

Such bliss. Antoine and I spent the following days getting to know each other as we wandered through Vientiane and along the Mekong River, enjoying the cool season's temperate days, free from unexpected downpours and crushing humidity. I showed him the covered market, my favorite Buddhist temples, and little out-of-the-way neighborhoods with interesting houses and shops—all places I'd planned to show Bridgette, places filled with memories of Bounmy. In the evenings we shared dinners with Catherine and Julian over lively conversations that covered everything from the growing world depression and French politics to the local temple fair that we'd attended with Mali on Monday night.

It amazed me how effortlessly my brother slipped into my world, as if he'd always been part of it. He was far more at ease with new people and situations than I was. Mali was smitten with him, treating him with the same reverence she reserved for Julian. I'd find him early mornings in the kitchen chatting away with her in Lao, sometimes drying dishes and putting them away in spots that were hard for her to reach. She would beam at me, patting my arm and saying what a nice boy he was. I kept waiting to find flaws—an annoying personality trait or a selfish lack of consideration. Perhaps we were both simply on our best behavior for the moment.

Life began anew with Antoine, the stars and earth realigning to replace our painful past and set us on a happy path forward. We talked for hours without artifice, laughing, occasionally becoming teary-eyed over the loss of our parents and a normal childhood. We had fourteen years to catch up on. It broke my heart when he told me I was the first person to hug him since he'd been a small boy at the orphanage. Our souls shared an unspoken connection, originating from our French and Lao roots, uniquely intertwined and bound together. Neither the Assistance Society nor the Lao or French communities, with their disdain for our mixed heritage, could destroy the link between us.

Antoine insisted we make going to France the following year our first priority. Marguerite helped us assemble the numerous documents needed for university and scholarship applications, while Antoine kept me on task filling out forms and writing essays, which I could have happily put off to another day.

On Friday I took Antoine to meet Maîtresse Durand, my first time returning to the orphanage. As we entered the courtyard, my body became nearly paralyzed with a thousand memories of Bridgette, Director Bernard, and my long afternoons gazing out the branches of my old friend the tamarind tree. Lucienne and Madeleine met us in the entry hall and nearly swooned when I introduced my brother. I laughed as Antoine's cheeks turned pink.

Maîtresse welcomed Antoine with uncharacteristic warmth. "It does my heart good to meet you, Monsieur Dubois, and to see you and Vivi together." She sat us down and proceeded straight to business in her usual efficient manner. "I contacted the headteachers at a number of schools and scheduled interviews for both of you on Monday afternoon," she announced, handing over a paper with names, times, and phone numbers. "Really the meetings are more of a formality. Monsieur Rochefort at the Collège Auguste Pavie is intrigued by your training at the *lycée* in Saigon, Monsieur Dubois. He feels you'd be an excellent addition to their staff. And, Vivi, now Monsieur Bernard is gone, several of the schools would be happy to hire you, but I think the best fit is the French/Lao elementary school for girls. Madame Gagnon is a lovely person who you'll find a delight to work with. And the children are adorable."

There seemed little need for further discussion. How could we ask for more? I knew her intervention was penance for all the ways she'd failed me and Bridgette over the years.

I thanked Maîtresse repeatedly. She took my hand as her eyes became watery. "Bridgette would be so happy for you."

The following week, Antoine and I mailed our applications to two universities in Paris and one in Lyon. I insisted we ask a monk at Mali's temple to bless them first, then Antoine suggested a stop at Sacred Heart to light candles and say a prayer. I conceded, willing to try anything that might help.

"Do you think we'll be accepted?" I asked for the third time that morning.

"Of course. We both excelled in school, and the French education system is one of the few benefits available to the *métis*."

I nodded. "How ironic that they're willing to send us to study in France when our existence is such a source of embarrassment."

A wry smile crossed his lips. "They want us to become productive and loyal supporters of France and the colonial government."

"Whatever the reasons, I'm grateful. I'll treat us to lunch to celebrate our new teaching positions and mailing our applications." On Monday we had been enthusiastically received at our interviews and hired on the spot. Everything was falling into place.

On our way to lunch, we turned down a quiet lane toward the river. Antoine glanced back briefly, then a second time. He furled his brow. I turned to find two men in dark suits walking a short distance behind us.

"Is something wrong?" I asked.

"I think those men are following us," he whispered.

"But why? Do you know who they are?"

"I'll explain when we sit down to lunch. Don't look back again."

We picked up our pace, marching to the Quai Francis Garnier. I led Antoine to a little outdoor food stand along the river where I had eaten many times with Bounmy. We sat down at a table and ordered bowls of noodle soup.

I couldn't help searching for the two men, but they were nowhere in sight. "Who do you think was following us?" I whispered.

He blinked a few times, as if uncertain how to respond. "They might be with the Sûreté Générale."

"The secret police? Whatever would they want with you?"

"I had to leave the coffee plantation so suddenly because my complaints about the working conditions and pay for the laborers had raised suspicions. The owners and French authorities labeled me a troublemaker, and I believe they notified the Sûreté Générale that I might be a communist agitator."

My throat caught. "But…but are you?" I sputtered.

"No, no. I became friends with a communist group of students in Saigon last year, and after I started working on the plantation, a local cell contacted me, soliciting my help. While I sympathize with their grievances and desire for a more equal society, I don't agree with their methods or larger vision."

Bounmy had spoken to me of unrest on the Bolaven Plateau and the Sûreté's investigations. I'd never imagined Antoine might be involved. "Could they arrest you?" I asked, suddenly frightened.

"I've done nothing wrong; however, I'm sure they're keeping an eye on me. They probably followed us today simply to intimidate me. I wouldn't be surprised if I'm taken in for an interrogation at some point to try to extract the names of communists I've met."

"You're terrifying me." What other secrets could he be hiding? "Do be careful."

"Don't worry. I'll be a model citizen from now on. This will pass."

"I hope so." I gazed out over the sparkling water, busy with boats and people coming and going. Memories of my first boat trip with Bounmy flashed through my mind unexpectedly, and a stab of pain caught me off guard. Despite my efforts to bury him in the past, he remained with me more than I wished. As I traversed the streets of town, I constantly searched for him, hoping for, yet dreading, a glimpse of his face.

"You look sad," Antoine said.

"I was thinking of Bounmy." I had shared the basic history of our relationship and the reason for our unhappy ending without including intimate details or dark secrets. I could never reveal Kham's attack, my lost pregnancy, or the yawning hole in my heart that would never heal.

"You must miss him a great deal," Antoine said.

"At times."

"I'm sorry he hurt you. If you tell me where to find him, I'll beat him black and blue."

I gasped. "Oh no. Don't do that." It was unthinkable that my brother could harm someone, especially Bounmy.

Antoine laughed. "I'm only kidding. I'm not a violent person, but I'd like to give this bastard a piece of my mind." He took a sip of beer and softened his tone. "I imagine he loves you a great deal but is trapped by his family and royal status."

"He didn't love me enough to find a solution," I said sadly. "And what about you? Given Lucienne and Madeleine's reaction to meeting you the other day, there must have been a lot of girls interested in you at school."

A shadow passed over Antoine's face. "Not really. There was one girl, but…" His voice trailed off.

"Tell me."

"Her name is Dông. We used to walk along the river after school and talk—always in a group, of course. She's beautiful and sweet, but her family is wealthy, and they would never allow her to be with an orphaned *métis*. After school ended in May, they married her to a boy in another aristocratic Annamese family."

Antoine looked up. "We can thank the French for taking over Indochine and fathering thousands of *métis* without assuming any responsibility for the consequences."

The animosity in his voice surprised me. "How do they justify their actions?" I said. "They have nothing but scorn for their *métis* children." I paused. "I don't believe our father was like that. At least, I hope not."

He sighed. "I realized early on that there were things I couldn't surmount on my own, situations out of my control. The best way to fight injustice is to get a good education. The situation at the coffee plantation made me lose my way momentarily. But how could I keep quiet?"

I patted Antoine's arm. "I understand. I was never one to hold back on what I thought, and all it did was get me into lots of trouble. For now, we must concentrate on our new jobs and saving money. I hope once we complete our university degrees and have a clearer understanding of how the world works, we can come back and try to improve things."

"Let's hope so."

Chapter 52

Two days before Christmas, I headed for Wong's Mercantile to purchase my last gifts: a leather briefcase for Antoine and a silk embroidered jewelry pouch for Catherine, which would be perfect for her trip to Luang Prabang. I'd been stewing over spending so much, but I couldn't resist. What better way to use my secret cache of money from Kham than on the people I loved?

It was a bright sunny day, and the town had a festive air. Carriages, horses, and bicycles wove their way in and among a stream of pedestrians on Rue Maréchal Joffre. I glanced across the street and there was Bounmy, walking in the same direction as me. My whole body quaked, and I could barely breathe. It was remarkable our paths had not crossed before in this small town. I ducked behind a stand selling dried mango and coconut, peeking around the startled vendor as I watched him. He trudged along as if in a trance, his expression haunted, never lifting his gaze from the ground. His shoulders were stooped, and he appeared thinner than before. Or perhaps I was only imagining these things, reflecting my own pain.

I took a few steps forward, trying to keep pace with him, and stumbled over a palm frond that had fallen from above. I longed to call out, to run to him and throw my arms about his neck, to feel his body pressed against mine. A flush of desire ran through me. There would be nothing sweeter than feeling his fingers caress my cheek, to gaze into his eyes. I could hardly bear to watch him turn down Avenue Lang Xang, slowly disappearing from sight. How was he coping? Did he feel as desolate as I did? It struck me that he should be in Luang Prabang getting married. Why was he still here? Then he was gone. I forced myself to walk the other way. He was no longer part of my life, and I couldn't allow myself to fall down this well of misery.

———

I spent a joyous Christmas Day with the people I loved. Marguerite and Charles joined us mid-afternoon to exchange gifts and feast on the wonderful treats that Mali and Catherine had been preparing all week. Carols played on the Victrola, and we never stopped laughing. I pushed thoughts of Bounmy aside. What more could I ask for when I had Antoine and my dear friends who cared for me?

After dinner we sat in the salon in a stupor, stuffed with roast duck, *bûche de Noël*, and champagne.

"What about a game of belote?" Julian suggested. "Or charades?" No one moved.

"I'm too tired," Catherine groaned.

Marguerite came to my side. "Vivi, I want to talk to you in the library for a moment." I followed her out of the room, puzzled.

Once she'd closed the door, she turned to me, her expression oddly worried. "I have something to tell you, or rather a message to deliver. My friend Annabelle came to see me yesterday. She and her husband are good friends with Prince Phetsarath, who told her some news she thought you should hear." She paused a moment, as if still uncertain about relaying the information. "It seems Bounmy has told his family he won't marry the girl they arranged for him and that he wants to be with you."

I stared at Marguerite, dazed. "I… I don't understand."

"His wedding was cancelled. Needless to say, his family and the king are furious. They blame Prince Souvanna for encouraging Bounmy to defy the royal court the same way he did. A new generation is rebelling against their ancient traditions, and it's causing quite a ruckus."

"What will happen to Bounmy?"

"They'll find a way to punish him, I'm sure. Maybe cut off his allowance, but it seems unlikely they'll banish him from court. His father is too high placed." She put a hand on my shoulder. "He did it for you. That has to please you."

"It doesn't change anything between us. His family will never accept me."

"Perhaps. Yet Prince Souvanna and Mademoiselle Allard have announced plans to marry next year, in spite of the consequences for Prince Souvanna at the royal court."

It was too much to take in. What did it all mean?

"One more thing. I told you I invited Bounmy to the wedding, given his position in the royal family. I received his response today saying he is unable to attend, but he sent a beautiful silver bowl. I didn't want you to worry about him showing up at the reception."

I wasn't sure if I felt relieved or disappointed.

It took me several days to sort through my reaction. I had no doubt that if I contacted Bounmy, he would come to me in an instant, yet where would that leave us? I confided in Antoine, but he seemed uncomfortable offering advice, saying he had no experience in matters of the heart. He only wanted me to be happy. I already knew what Julian's reaction would be, and I didn't feel up to hearing it. Everyone else was busy with last-moment preparations for Marguerite's wedding, and I couldn't disturb them. And so I settled in the back garden with pen and paper to write a letter, needing to organize my thoughts and clear my head.

Cher Bounmy,

Marguerite informed me of your canceled wedding. My thoughts and emotions are a hopeless tangle. I pray you took this momentous decision for yourself and not for me. After your time in Paris, you must have felt trapped by an arranged marriage to someone you do not know, a tradition of the royal court that is no longer appropriate in these modern times. I encourage you to stand strong against the pressure of your family to fulfill their wishes rather than allow you to follow your heart.

First, know that I still love you as before, despite the history of our affair, your deceit, and the pain I suffered. Being only eighteen—as everyone constantly reminds me—my inexperience led to unwise decisions. I blame myself, as much as you, for what unfolded. You were my first love and, in the blush of our astonishing happiness, I ignored the warnings of others. Instead of asking questions to understand your intentions and what my role in your life might be, I kept quiet. Allowing myself to get pregnant was unpardonable, as was disregarding the harm to my reputation in the French community and with my family in Luang Prabang. The lessons learned have helped me mature. In the future I must focus on taking care of myself and fulfilling my dreams. I won't let anyone else lead me astray.

My brother Antoine is now living here with me, a true blessing. We are alike in many ways, as you might expect of twins, and very compatible. I feel so fortunate to have found him. Next year we will go to France to university, and nothing will deter me from this.

I do not trust myself to see you at present, fearing it would be inevitable that we fall back into our previous relationship as lovers. How could I be near you without succumbing to the temptation? At this point, your family would never accept me, and I must honor the demand of my mother's family to break off contact with you. There remain too many barriers as yet to be resolved.

Perhaps one day the king and your father will allow you to choose the person you love. Perhaps that person will be me. In the meantime, try to be happy and know I think of you constantly.

With all my love,
Geneviève

I folded the letter and held it against my heart. Perhaps I would mail it to him one day—next week, next month, next year. Not now. My emotions were too raw and unsettled.

Chapter 53

On January 1, 1932, Marguerite and Charles, standing on the bridge over the pond in Catherine's garden, exchanged wedding vows as the sun faded behind the trees, surrounded by forty of their closest friends. Since Marguerite had proclaimed herself an atheist, and Charles was divorced, a Catholic wedding at Sacred Heart had been out of the question. Instead, the Resident Superior of Laos officiated.

As Catherine had said with a laugh, we couldn't expect anything involving Marguerite to follow conventional traditions. The bride wore red chiffon that flowed around her curvy frame, mirroring the red and orange koi fish that darted back and forth in the water below. Catherine, maid of honor, stood beside her in a simple blue tea dress, while Julian, Antoine, Mali, and I gathered at the back of the crowd, beaming and dabbing at stray tears. Mali, dressed in a beautiful silk *sinh* and *pha biang* in shades of orange and sienna, quietly murmured Buddhist blessings. Like Mali, I wore the beautiful green-and-turquoise *sinh* and *pha biang* my aunts Dara and Noi in Luang Prabang had given me.

A reception followed at the Cercle, attended by the entire French *colon* community from the Vientiane area, a number of officers from Luang Prabang, and a select group of Lao aristocrats, including Prince Phetsarath and Prince Souvanna.

The wedding party roared on through the evening with champagne, extravagant food, and dancing to a live band. The air pulsed with joy. Julian and several young officers took turns twirling me and Catherine around the dance floor, but Antoine refused to budge, saying he'd never learned to dance. I vowed to teach him, but he laughed and said we'd see. He preferred sitting with Mali, speaking Lao over the din of the revelers, easing her discomfort at being in the French club. It had taken Marguerite days to convince her to attend.

The bride and groom cut the four-tiered chocolate wedding cake then bid their friends *adieu* a little after midnight. They were driving to the private home of a friend half an hour downriver for a short honeymoon. The evening wound down, and guests departed.

Our small group set out for home, slightly tipsy and a bit deflated after the high spirits of the day. Catherine put her arm through Julian's and rested her head on his shoulder, while Antoine and I followed with Mali. The dry, crisp night and a refreshing breeze held the promise of new beginnings. Our lives were shifting in positive ways—Marguerite was a married woman, Julian was leaving for France, and Catherine would board a mail boat in two days for Luang Prabang full of love and hope for a future with Marcel. Mali would be spending an entire month in her village helping to organize her son's wedding, while Antoine and I would begin teaching after the end of the New Year break.

I counted my blessings—Antoine, our mother's family in Luang Prabang, and my wonderful friends who had given me shelter and adopted me as family. As much as I missed Bridgette, I was grateful for the years we had spent together when we so desperately needed each other's love and support. No one could take that away. The future held endless possibilities for Antoine and me. Who could say where things might lead with Bounmy? Or Julian? Or a new life in Paris? But whatever path my future followed, I was determined to make peace with my past—half French, half Lao, at ease with who I was and who I might become.

Acknowledgements

I want to thank Edward Willis at the History Quill for his excellent suggestions for developing my story and the team's editing. And to Craig Hillsley for his careful work. I also want to thank my dear friends in my writing group—Susanne Sommer, Mary Euretig, and Sharon Frederick—for reading countless drafts and offering excellent advice and comments. You kept me going! And, as always, I am thankful for my wonderful husband, Roy McDonald, and his loving support and encouragement.

About the Author

Elaine Russell is the award-winning author of two adult novels, *Across the Mekong River* (French edition *De l'autre côté du Mékong*) and *In the Company of Like-Minded Women*, as well as six children's books. She has been writing for over twenty-five years, drawing upon her love of history and traveling to other countries to learn about their cultures and past. She lives in Sacramento, California, with her husband.

Laos is a country dear to Elaine's heart, and she has visited many times. She served for six years on the board of the U.S.-based non-profit Legacies of War, which advocates for increased funding for the clearance of unexploded bombs. Illegal U.S. bombing in Laos during the Vietnam War left over 80 million unexploded cluster bombs that continue to kill and maim civilians fifty years later. She authored two essays on the history of this aftermath published in anthologies: *Southeast Asia, The United States, and Historical Memory* (Haymarket Books, June 2019) and *Interactions with a Violent Past: Reading Post-Conflict Landscapes in Cambodia, Laos, and Vietnam* (Singapore: NUS Press, 2013).

Made in the USA
Middletown, DE
08 June 2024